~*The Duke's Daughter*~

Part 1 : Assumptions and Consequences

Shana Granderson, A Lady

Cover Art Design by: Veronica Martinez Medellin
ISBN 13 - 979-85-9036-4619

This Book Is Dedicated To The Love Of Life, The Holder Of My Heart. You Are My One An Only And You Complete Me.

CONTENTS

INTRODUCTION

Lady Elizbeth Bennet is the Daughter of Lord Thomas and Lady Sarah Bennet, the Duke and Duchess of Hertfordshire. She is quick to judge and anger and very slow to forgive. Fitzwilliam Darcy has learnt to rely on his own judgement above all others. Once he believes that something is a certain way, he does not allow anyone to change his mind. He ignored his mother and the result was the Ramsgate debacle, but he had not learnt his lesson yet. He mistakes information that her heard from his Aunt about her parson's relatives and with assumptions and his failure to listen to his friends the Bingleys, he makes a huge mistake and faces a very angry Lady Elizabeth Bennet.

ACKNOWLEDGEMENT & THANK YOU

First and foremost, thank your E.C.S. for standing by me while I dedicate many hours to my craft. You are my shining light and my one and only. I want to thank my Alpha and my Betas, Will Jamison, Caroline Piediscalzi Lippert, Kimbelle Pease and Leah Pruett. Your assistance is most appreciated.

Thank you to my professional editor Tameka Harmon. My undying love and appreciation to Jane Austen for her incredible literary masterpieces is more than can be expressed adequately here. I also thank all of the JAFF readers who make writing these stories a pleasure.

PROLOGUE

Four and twenty years ago...

Miss Francine Gardiner, Fanny to her friends and family, had a plan. The rich, very handsome owner of Longbourn and Netherfield, Mr Thomas Bennet, an untitled gentleman, or so she believed, had taken up residence at the home at last. At seventeen, Fanny only had one aim in life: to marry a landed gentleman, preferably a very rich one. Her victim, who was yet ignorant of her designs, met both of her criteria in spades.

Fanny was the youngest of three Gardiner children. She had a brother, Edward, not quite two years her senior, who was studying at Oxford. The oldest was Hattie, five years older than Edward, who had recently married her father's clerk at his legal practice in Meryton, a Mr. Frank Phillips. Fanny had decided to flirt with her sister's betrothed one day and was surprised that he had no interest in her. She had always got what she wanted! She, with her golden locks and her cerulean eyes, was acknowledged as Meryton's beauty. What those around her also knew was that she was mean of understanding, vain, selfish, and vindictive. Phillips' rejection of her had angered her greatly, and she swore that she would get even with him one day. She did not care for Phillips in her heart; she wanted something that her sister had, and she did not.

Fanny, although lacking in intelligence, was devious. She hated anyone else having something, be that person or material possession that she wanted. Fanny broke the commandment, *'Thou shalt not covet...'* daily. The monthly assembly would be held in a sennight and Thomas Bennet's housekeeper, told Sarah Lucas, that her master would be attending the upcoming event. Fanny was somewhat friendly with Sarah, or as friendly as she could be with someone who had married a man in the trade, some five years previously. As Fanny was only twelve at the time, she had made no attempt to interfere with Sarah's courtship, and subsequent marriage to William Lucas. Mr Lucas was merely a tradesman after all, and Fanny would never accept a man with the stink of trade on him.

Armed with the knowledge that Mr. Bennet would be at the assembly, she used what little intelligence she had to plan a compromise of the unsuspecting gentleman. She would have her gown pre-weakened and then would fall into his arms, making sure that her gown 'tore' and her reputation ruined by the 'careless' man. Fanny Gardiner thought of nothing but her plan; she did not even spend time and money buying fripperies like bonnets as she normally did. She had a plan and she meant to see it succeed!

~~~~~~~/~~~~~~~

As was usual for Miss Francine Gardiner, she only knew a ridiculously small part of the story. Yes, Thomas Bennet was a rich landowner, much richer than Fanny with her small mind could conceive of, and it was true that he owned Netherfield, a large and prosperous estate, while his father, for now, owned the much larger estate of Longbourn.

The man that she was planning to entrap was in fact Lord Thomas Hayward Bennet, Marquess of Netherfield. His father was Lord Hayward Sedgewick Bennet, His Grace, Duke of Bedford and Hertfordshire. He had two sons, Lord Sedgewick Hayward Bennet, called 'Sed' by his family and friends, Marquess of Birchington, who was ten years older than Thomas Bennet. Their mother had a few miscarriages before she was blessed with Lord Thomas Bennet. After the future Duke of Hertfordshire was born, sadly, the late duchess never managed to become *enceinte* again. The brothers had been as close as brothers could be their whole life. They were not just brothers; they were best friends.

The current Duke held both titles as his father had been an only son and the titles were coparcenary. Until Thomas had been born, his older brother had held both secondary titles, giving him the second, or lesser title. Most second sons did not receive such a blessing and he was deeply grateful to have been granted it.

Both titles had massive fortunes and multiple estates attached to them, the Bedford title having more as one would expect to go to the eldest. Lord Thomas Bennet had nothing to repine; he had more money than he could ever use in twenty lifetimes, Netherfield, and a second estate. When the sad day came and his father went home to God to be with his beloved wife, he would inherit four more estates that came with the Dukedom of which Longbourn was the largest, as well as all of the wealth attached to the Hertfordshire title.

There were only a few select people in the area who knew Lord Netherfield's true lineage and wealth. Thomas Bennet was not an outgoing man; he preferred to live a quiet life in the country. He had enjoyed Cambridge where he had met and made friends with some of his colleagues. One was Lord Cyril De Melville, Viscount Westmore and heir to the Earl of Jersey. He had also become close to Lord Reginald Fitzwilliam, Viscount Hilldale, and heir to the Earl of Matlock. Lord Fitzwilliam was ahead of him by three years, but the age difference did not influence their connection. He had visited Fitzwilliam's family estate, Snowhaven, once or twice while at university, had met the Viscount's sisters, and was fascinated by the history of the castle that the first Earl of Matlock was presented for playing a key role in the Wars of the Roses. His older sister was Lady Catherine Fitzwilliam who loved to dispense unwanted advice but was otherwise harmless, and the younger sister, who was not yet out, was Lady Anne Fitzwilliam. She was beautiful and was favoured with the blonde hair and blue eyes of the Fitzwilliam's, as was her older brother. Lady Catherine had her mother's colouring, with auburn hair with light brown eyes. He did not consider her as pretty as her younger sister, but she was not homely by any stretch of the imagination. His friend had fallen for Miss Elaine Woodhouse who he was planning to court as soon as he finished Cambridge that year.

Thomas had also visited the Jersey estate, Ravenswood, in Warwickshire. There he met Cyril's family, which included his younger sister Sarah. She had been fifteen at the time and not out, but Thomas Bennet knew when he saw the raven-haired beauty and her hazel eyes with flecks of gold and green that he had met his wife. Over the next year, Lord Jersey had taken note of Lord Netherfield's interest in his only daughter and informed him that he would welcome a courtship, but not before Lady Sarah was nineteen and had completed her first season. Until then, he forbade Bennet from declaring himself in any way, but he was not blind. He saw that Lord Thomas was not alone in his feeling; his daughter returned them fully and was looking forward to leaving the nest well before her father was ready to let her go.

~~~~~~~/~~~~~~~

Longbourn's butler, a Mr. Hill who had only been in his current position for a few months, brought his master a glass of port as he sat in his study. Thomas' mind was on his lady-love, wishing time away so that he could finally claim her heart as his. '*Only a month until the end of the season and then I will be able to declare myself to Sarah. I can finally start to live my life fully. I know that I prefer to be in the background, unknown and away from people, but Sarah with her vivacious personality always draws me out.*' He sighed as he thought about the woman that he loved beyond any in the known world, '*Soon, my love, soon. Once we are together, my days of books and port will be behind me and I will walk life's path with the only woman that I could and will ever love.*'

Lord Thomas Bennet, Marquess of Netherfield had but one 'flaw'; he was one of the most honourable men that one could find. His family placed being an honourable man above almost all else, and Thomas Bennet, the scion of Dukes, epitomised the ideals of honour and honesty. Unbeknownst to him, in a few short days, he would meet a woman who could never be called a lady, who could not spell honesty or honour, never mind live the ideals behind the words, and who would make him question his constancy to both honour and honesty.

~~~~~~~/~~~~~~~

On the night of the assembly, as Lord Netherfield was dressing, Miss Gardiner was putting the finishing touches on her dastardly plan to entrap the 'wealthy gentleman' who owned the two primary estates in Hertfordshire. She had her pre-torn dress held together with pins that would give way as soon as she pulled on the gown. Fanny was waiting like a spider in her web as the unsuspecting man walked in. Not one to let the grass grow under her feet when she wanted something, she waited only until the man entered the assembly hall where all could see him. She 'tripped' in front of him and he, being a gentleman, instinctively tried to stop the unknown beauty from falling. As she was falling toward his arms, Fanny gave a hard pull of her gown and the pins flew free. By the time she was in her victim's arms, one breast was free of its restraints!

"What have you done?" the woman shrieked, her performance worthy of Drury Lane.

"I-I did nothing, madam, besides try and stop you from falling." The Viscount was starting to become concerned. He was a highly intelligent man and had no doubt that the damage to the dress that he was seeing had not been caused by the woman's fall.

"You did nothing? Oh, my nerves, where is my papa? You have ruined me! What am I to do?" Fanny Gardiner started crying; one of her so-called talents was her ability to cry on demand.

"**What have you done to my daughter**?" Elias Gardiner yelled when he saw the man standing in front of his clearly distraught daughter, crying, and exposed for all to see. Every person at the assembly was watching the performance. Few doubted the truth of what happened, even if her indulgent father was too blind to see what his daughter was. Or, pretended well enough people wondered if he realised it.

"As I was telling the young lady, Sir, I saw her start to fall and I tried to be of assistance..." Thomas stated as calmly as his frustration allowed.

"Be of assistance?" Fanny sobbed, acting the height of desperate and wronged. "You compromised me! You ripped my dress and exposed me before all of Meryton!" She wailed loudly as she looked at her father with big tear-filled eyes. "I am ruined, Papa. What will happen to me now?"

"This man will marry you, darling, or I will call him out!" Her irate father announced, even though he had no knowledge of either fencing or pistol shooting.

"Papa," Hattie Phillips said quietly, "I saw it all. The gentleman did nothing other than try and save my sister who tripped over her own feet. He never touched her gown so I cannot imagine," she said with an accusatory look at her sister, "how the dress was rent as it is now."

"Oh, hush Hattie." Fanny hissed.

"Go to your husband and keep out of men's business." Gardiner knew then that his older daughter spoke the truth, but if he could make this man take his unruly and unkind daughter off his hands, his life would be much more pleasant. He had struggled to deal with his youngest since his wife had passed four years previously, so this was ideal for him. Hattie Phillips was used to being dismissed by her father, so she turned and went to her husband.

"I am a gentleman of honour, Mr.?" Bennet did not know the father or the daughter's name beyond the 'Fanny' that he had heard called across the room.

"Gardiner, Mr. Elias Gardiner, solicitor." Gardiner said, puffing up with self-importance.

"I am staying at Longbourn. Can I expect you and Miss Gardiner at ten on the morrow?" Bennet asked as the reality of his fate sunk in. He had been trapped by what he was sure was a fortune hunter.

As soon as Mr. Gardiner nodded, Lord Thomas Bennet turned on his heel and made for his carriage. By the time his conveyance started to move, his thoughts started to circle around in his mind. *'How many times has Sed told me to never go into a place like this without my guards, and what do I always do? '* Bennet berated himself. *'I tell him he worries too much. Look at where I am now! Oh God, what have I done for You to punish me so? And my Sarah! This will break not only my heart but hers as well.'* As the full realisation of the love that he was about to lose hit him, Thomas Bennet started to cry, his tension releasing with deep wracking sobs of despair.

As soon as he was relieved of his outerwear by a butler, surprised that his Lordship had returned so soon, Bennet ensconced himself in the study with a bottle of his best port. His first task was to send an express to Sed and Rose at Birchington House on Russel Square in London. Lord Sedgwick Bennet had recently married the delectable and very pleasant Miss Rosamond Davies. It was a love match, and he liked his sister-in-law very well, her wit and thoughtfulness were well beyond her twenty years of age. Unlike many in the Ton, Lord Thomas did not question Sed's choice of an untitled daughter of an insignificant baronet with only ten thousand as a dowry for an instant. He liked the unassuming, strong woman, the instant his brother introduced her when they were courting. When they married and she became the Marchioness of Birchington she did not change who she was and never took on the airs and graces of many in the Ton.

5 August 1786
Longbourn, Herefordshire

My Dear Brother and Sister,
Sed, the worst has happened. You have warned me so many times that I should protect myself, and tonight at the assembly in Meryton, I was compromised by the worst kind of woman. She is pretty, but that is all she is. Her character, from the few minutes I

was forced to be in proximity with her, was spiteful and dismissive of her sister while whinging to her father. To call her silly and stupid would be an insult to all silly and stupid people! Should have, would have, could have will not change the fact that as a gentleman of honour, I must marry this...harridan!

My heart is broken, not only for myself but for Sarah, and yet I must deliver the news to her. The doxy and her father, a solicitor with not much more character than the daughter, will be here at ten in the morning. Once the unpleasant business is settled, I will be for town. I will have to see Sir Randolph to draft an airtight settlement. I will not settle more than five thousand pounds on this woman that entrapped me.

I do not say this lightly, but I hate the woman and I have never hated anyone in my life before. Please do not say anything to Father. Once I have been to see Lord Jersey and spoken to him and Sarah, I will come to you and we can go to Father at Bedford House together.

I love you both and will see you on the morrow.

Thomas

As soon as he sealed the missive, he had his personal courier hie to Birchington House in Town directly.

The following day, a few minutes before ten the knocker was heard on Longbourn's door. Miss Gardiner, looking like the cat that caught the canary, was eyeing the estate and the house with avarice. '*What pin money, what jewels I will have, and oh the carriages that I will have. I will be the envy of all of Hertfordshire,*' she told herself as her father and she were shown into Mr. Bennet's study.

"Good morning Mr. Bennet, how are you on this fine day?" Gardiner offered with exaggerated pleasantness. Bennet was already disgusted with the Gardiners, and he had no intention of revealing his true title and connections to these swine.

"Mr. Gardiner, please let us dispense with the pleasantries. I believe that you know your daughter entrapped me." Both father and daughter made to refute the claim, but he did not allow them to talk. "I should leave her ruined at her own hand and take the duel, which I believe will be preferable to being married to one such as she." Both father and daughter blanched at this statement, each one for different reasons. "Unfortunately, however, unlike some in this room, I am a gentleman, and one of honour. As such, I will return from town five days hence with a special licence and the settlement. As soon as you sign the settlement we will marry. If you refuse to sign it, then we will part and go our separate ways." Lord Thomas saw that Gardiner was about to interject but concluded the meeting. "This is not a negotiation, this is a take or leave it situation. Either you sign and I marry that," Bennet spat out with disgust, "or not, and our business is concluded."

Gardiner was a fairly shrewd solicitor, so he knew when not to speak. '*I will sign no matter what, as I will get Fanny out of my house.*' he thought.

"Will you not propose to me?" The child batted her eyelashes at him.

"No, I will not! Now leave!" Bennet pulled the bell and Mr. Hill appeared with two large footmen to show the Gardiners out. As Fanny Bennet left, she passively considered that she may have miscalculated. The man had called her '*that*' and seemed to hate her. How could he hate one so beautiful as her? Surely, she was not so pretty without the expectation of marrying a wealthy man such as he. With the reminder that he was rich, she again thought about the pin money and jewels and was instantly happy again. Bennet was on the road to London within the hour after the objectionable people departed.

~~~~~~~/~~~~~~~

A very dejected Bennet knocked on the door at Birchington House and was welcomed in with a bow by the long-time butler, Mr. Sam Hodges. He was directed to his brother and sister's private sitting room. When he walked in expecting censure, he saw only sympathy and for the second time in four and twenty hours, Thomas Bennet, Marquess of Netherfield, wept like a baby. Once he had calmed himself and taken a sip of port, he related his heart-breaking visit to Jersey House on Portman Square.

He had told Lord Jersey everything that had transpired about the entrapment, all of it. The Earl had recommended that he pay them off, but as much as he had wanted to, his honour was engaged. After they had spoken, Lord Jersey had summoned Lady Sarah to his study. She had entered and was instantly full of joy when she saw Lord Thomas was with her father, thinking he was there to declare himself.

Her joy was soon turned to anguish, and her anguish to tears. It took a long time for her to calm, but when she did, the look of resolve on her countenance was one neither man in the study had ever seen before. Thomas then related her words, the only words he had heard in the last four and twenty hours that had offered him the thinnest sliver of hope.

"I cannot believe that God Almighty is such a cruel being, Lord Thomas. You are the only man that I love, the only one that I will love, and I know, as surely as I am sitting here now, that one day, be it sooner or later, we WILL be together. I just know it!"

Before he left, Lord Jersey pulled Lord Thomas Bennet aside and apologised to him. When asked what he was apologising for, the Earl had said that he regretted the imposition of the full season. He blamed himself for his daughter's heartbreak that would have been alleviated without his demand to wait. Bennet had absolved the Earl of any fault; none of them could see the future and the fault lay with the conniving, social climbing, dishonourable woman that had entrapped him, no one else.

He also related the details of the meeting he had with Sir Randolph, the head of the firm of barrister and solicitors Norman and James. He went to them because they had a reputation of being the most feared and powerful firm at the Inn of Courts, indeed in the realm. He had settled only five thousand on the fortune hunter. She would only receive five pounds per month in pin money, get no jewels, and would not be allowed to use a carriage without permission from her husband.

If there was any infidelity proved against her, the marriage would be immediately annulled. Sir Randolph would have the final draft and the special licence ready for him before he departed four days hence.

The Bennet brothers made their way two doors down to Bedford House. Bennet looked longingly at Netherfield House, knowing that he would never bring *her* here, as they passed it on the way to their father's house. The Duke of Bedford and Hertfordshire was not well; he was ailing and was not expected to live more than a year further. The brothers went up and when they learned he was not resting, went to talk with him in his bedchamber. The Duke was physically weak, it was true, but he had all his mental faculties about him.

He sympathised with his younger son's plight, did not admonish him for not better protecting himself, and agreed that his Thomas was doing the only honourable thing that he could. Once their father started to wane, the brothers returned to Birchington House. Before Bennet returned to face his fate, one he saw as worse than death, he went to visit Reggie and Elaine Fitzwilliam, Viscount and Viscountess Hilldale, who had married a few years before. They had two sons; Andrew was a little over four and Richard was now just three. Reggie's younger sister, Lady Anne, had married a Mr. George Darcy of Pemberley in Derbyshire and had an almost two-year-old son, Fitzwilliam, or William as they called him, and his older sister, Lady Catherine, had married a baronet, Louis de Bourgh, who owned an estate in Kent called Rosings Park. Lady Catherine was with child and the family was overjoyed at the blessings they had been granted with their children. His friend sympathised with Bennet but agreed that there was little that could be done.

Early Friday morning, armed with his iron-clad settlement papers, Bennet returned to Hertfordshire to face his punishment. The only thing that gave him purpose was his beloved Sarah's statement that replayed in his head over and repeatedly.

Gardiner and his daughter were shown into Longbourn just after luncheon. His soon to be wife was seated in a drawing room while her father joined the reluctant groom in his study. Elias Gardiner may not have been the most upright man, but he knew the firm of Norman and James, and he knew that there would be no way to change the terms, as outlined in the settlement. He became more and more apprehensive about the situation that his daughter had gotten herself into. He questioned the settlement amount, the five pounds a month pin money, and anything else he could think of, but his soon to be son-in-law was implacable. He was faced with the same choice that Mr. Bennet had offered him prior to his trip to London, sign or take himself and his daughter home and never darken Longbourn's doorstep again.

In the end, Gardiner's desire to rid himself of the silly, indulged, and selfish problem that was Fanny won out over his fatherly protective instincts and he signed. As soon as he signed, he was informed that he would never be welcome on *any* Bennet lands again, however, his daughter was free to *walk* to Meryton to see him if she desired to do so, and then Bennet rang for Mr. Hill.

On entering the master's study, the butler bowed and then asked, "You rang your L..." He stopped when he saw the look that the master gave him. "Mr. Bennet." The butler cleared his throat with exaggeration after a cough to cover his almost mistake.

"Hill, please summon Longbourn's vicar to perform the wedding ceremony that I discussed with him prior to my trip." The butler bowed again and went to do as he was bid.

While they waited for the clergyman, Mr. Nigel Lipton, Elias Gardiner went to see his daughter to break the news of the contents of the marriage settlement to her. It was not above a minute in that Miss Francine Gardiner was crying real tears for the first time in memory; driven by anger and fear of what she had done to herself, blaming all except the one responsible for her situation...herself.

"How could you sign such a thing, Papa? This man is obviously rich! I would not have trap...er wanted to marry him if he were not. What am I to do with a measly five pounds a month? No carriage! No jewels, and a pittance of a settlement! This is not to be borne!" She shrieked, stamping her foot like the spoilt and petulant child that she truly was.

No matter how much she protested and lamented her new situation, Mr. Lipton was shown in, and ten minutes later after she had pledged to obey the man that was clearly punishing her for her actions, Miss Gardiner was Mrs. Fanny Bennet. Had she known that she was, actually, a marchioness, she would have felt that it had all been worth it, but until her dying day, that was information to which she would never be privy. She was shown to her room by Mrs. Hill, the housekeeper, a small chamber and certainly not the mistress's chambers. She would not have her own lady's maid like she had dreamed that she would. If and when one of the upstairs maids was available to help her, they would do so.

She was not mistress of the estate. The servants understood that unless an order came from the Hills or from the master, that they were to ignore the woman who had entrapped their master. It was explained on pain of dismissal with no character that not a word about the master's title or his family was to be breathed to his new 'wife'. The Bennet's paid much more than the expected wages by position so no servant would risk his or her position by doing anything that would cause them to be discharged.

As distasteful as it was to him, Bennet did his duty and consummated the marriage. Each time he lay with her she cried, and it did not move him. He did nothing overt to hurt her, but he could not care less about the woman. He did not take meals with her and spent no time with her other than when he did his duty. As each day passed, it started to creep into Fanny Bennet's consciousness that she may have made the biggest mistake of her life.

A sennight into his hellish marriage, Lord Thomas opened

a letter that he had let sit on his desk for three days as it was from one Mr. Edward Gardiner, who he remembered was the woman's older brother. He almost consigned it to the fire suspecting it was some sort of demand or the like, as he believed that the son must be like the father. When he remembered that the oldest, the one married to the solicitor's clerk had tried to tell her father the truth the night that the abominable compromise was affected, he relented and broke the seal and started to read.

8 August 1786
Oxford University

Lord Netherfield,

Before you think that I will reveal what I know to my sister who, in her avarice and selfishness entrapped you, you have my word of honour that I will never do so. Nor have I shared what I know with my older sister, Mrs. Hattie Phillips, who informed me of the despicable behaviour of my sister Fanny and then my father.

My Lord, there is nothing that I can say or do that will make their actions any better, but I want you to know that neither Hattie nor I condone or support the actions of either my youngest sister or my father. I know that we are commanded by God to 'honour thy mother and father', but I believe that honour is the important word.

If there is anything that either my older sister, her husband, or myself can ever do for you, please do not hesitate to ask.

Again, on behalf of the Phillips and myself, I send you my most profound and deepest apology for the actions taken by members of my family. Unless I hear from you my Lord, I will not impose upon you again.

Your humble and mortified servant,
Edward Gardiner

Bennet appreciated the sincerity, especially as there was no attempt to make excuses for the father and sister. He wrote back to Mr. Edward Gardiner and so started a friendship that would last a lifetime.

Luckily for Bennet, his wife fell with child in the first month of their marriage, so he was able to stop the distasteful and infrequent visits to the woman. Once her state was confirmed by Mr. Jones, the young new physician and apothecary that had recently started practicing in the area, Bennet had his trunks packed and left to be with his brother and sister at Birchington. He left her in the charge of the Hills and Longbourn's servants with instructions to make sure that she stayed in the house or walked no farther than the park and to summon him when she was ready to enter her confinement. As the dust settled from his conveyances and the attendant outriders, a furious virtual prisoner was left behind.

~~~~~~~/~~~~~~~

Eight months later...

As their father had succumbed to his illness two months prior, the newly minted Duke of Hertfordshire started the dreaded trip back to Longbourn, which was now his, along with the other estates and massive fortune that he had inherited. He had a month of full mourning left, but there was no getting around having to return to *her* as the Hills had informed the Duke that she was inordinately large and had entered her confinement period. In addition to his honoured father, the solicitor with no honour, the one that had supported his daughter when she entrapped him, had shuffled off the mortal coil a few months after his exodus from Longbourn.

His Grace the Duke of Hertfordshire was welcomed back to Longbourn with all the reverence due to his exalted rank. Not only was he a duke, but they were cousins to the royals through his late, beloved mother. When he entered his house, he heard caterwauling that he had never imagined ever hearing. He was informed by his butler that Mr. Jones and the local midwife were attending the woman. After he changed and washed the road dust off, Bennet repaired to his study to read Plato and have some port. He was not sure when, but after a while, he noticed that the house was blissfully silent. It was not long after that Mr. Jones knocked on his study door, and after his Grace bid him enter, he took a deep breath, bracing himself to say what needed to be said

"I have good and bad news sir." Mr. Jones met the Duke's eyes.

"Well, out with it man!" Bennet demanded, not in the mood for a protracted conversation, his annoyance obvious.

"I-I am pleased to inform you that you are the father of two of the most beautiful identical twin girls that I have ever seen," the man paused and took a deep breath, "I am however loath to inform you that your wife did not survive. There was too much bleeding..." Before Jones could go on, Bennet interrupted him.

"Mr. Jones, this may sound callous, but both pieces of news are good news!" Bennet looked at him with the most animation Mr. Jones had seen since he had learned his wife was pregnant. He was again hearing Sarah's prophetic statement and was for the first time in over a year feeling happiness as they could soon be together. Jones could not understand the look of unadulterated joy that spread across the man's face. "I know that you are new to the area, but did you know that the woman entrapped me? If I were not a man of honour, I would have run the other way. I was, and still am in love with another woman. I was but days of asking for her hand, and *she* stopped our betrothal with her despicable actions. *That* is why I look happy, Mr. Jones. I do not wish death on *anyone,* regardless of what they have done, but I will not reject this gift from God." As an afterthought, he added, "My name is not *Mr.* Bennet."

"Are you not Thomas Bennet, master of this estate, and is not the lady that passed away upstairs not your wife?" asked a very confused apothecary.

"Yes, all of that is true. But as I said I am not *Mr. anything*, I am his Grace, the Duke of Hertfordshire!"

"Your Grace, please forgive me. I did not know." A mortified Jones said as he genuflected to the Duke.

"There is nothing to forgive, Mr. Jones. Neither you nor anyone else in the area knew, which was by my design. I never wanted her to know the truth about my family or my title. Hill!" he called through the open door knowing that the butler was waiting just outside the study.

"Yes, your Grace?" Hill could not help but smile when he said it.

"Did Mrs. Hill, your ever-capable wife, retain a wet nurse and a nursemaid?" Bennet grinned.

"Yes, your Grace, she did." Hill grinned with him, the relief of being free of that millstone was felt by all in the house.

"Please inform her that she will need to retain one more of each as I have twin daughters." Bennet's grin widened, not that anyone would know it was possible. The butler bowed and exited the study to comply with the Duke's command. Bennet stood and followed Jones up to the nursery to see his daughters. He did not hear as much noise as would be expected for two babes. When he entered, he saw that the physician had not exaggerated; before him were two of the most gorgeous babes he had ever beheld. Like their dead mother, they had blond hair and the deepest blue eyes. One seemed very serene and the other was more vocal. The serene one had a light blue ribbon on her wrist. When he asked why she had the ribbon, the midwife, just packing up the last tools of her trade, informed him that the ribbon denoted the firstborn and a way to tell them apart as they were identical.

He sat in a chair and requested that his first born be passed to him. Once he held her, he knew that he was forever lost. She had stolen his heart with a look. He named her Lady Jane Ingrid Bennet for his beloved late mother. Jane was returned to her cradle and he was passed his second daughter who he could swear was looking at him with inquisitiveness. She was not crying, but she was making baby noises where Jane had been almost silent. He named her Lady Marie Janet Bennet using a combination of his maternal and paternal grandmother's names.

He would not allow the Gardiner woman to be buried on any Bennet land. He sent an express to Gardiner, and he and his sister moved the body to the undertaker in Meryton where she was interred next to her father and mother. In death, she was with the tradespeople who raised her. Her name was never mentioned again by the Bennet's, or their family and friends.

Within a week, his brother Sed and sister Rose, now their Graces the Duke and Duchess of Bedford, arrived at Longbourn to be with Bennet and meet their nieces. They were followed within days by Lord and Lady Jersey, and with them came Lady Sarah and her brother Lord Cyril. As soon as Hertford-shire saw her, he knew that the feelings on both sides were as strong as ever. He invited Hattie and Frank Phillips and Edward Gardiner to come see their nieces. Given that he had forged a friendship with both honourable men, he would not stand in the way of them being uncles and aunts to the girls. To say that the Phillips' were shocked that Bennet was part of *those* Bennet's and a duke, was an understatement.

The girls thrived surrounded by a loving father and family. As soon as the deep mourning for his late father passed, Thomas Bennet proposed to the love of his life, Lady Sarah De Melville. It was no true surprise that her father quickly approved with true affability. When they were married but a month later, the prophesy that Sarah had made on that terrible day Bennet had to tell her about his entrapment came true. Their nuptials had been delayed, but their love never waned. If anything, the trial, and separation had seen it strengthened. His girls had a mother, the only one that they would ever know, and they were never treated differently by either the Duke or his Duchess. No one in their circle would hold the actions of a fortune hunter they would never call mother against them. The Duke of Hertfordshire was happy, indescribably, and incandescently happy, and his love for his beloved duchess and all their children grew daily.

The King and Queen showed their support for their

cousin's wedding very publicly. If there were any in the Ton that dared to criticise the Duke for marrying while he was in half-mourning, they would have been severely dealt with in society, so much that those who had thoughts of censure were wise enough to keep them very private.

CHAPTER 1

A little more than three and twenty years later...

Darcy had been working hard to make the changes he had sworn to make. And he had made real changes, as he had promised *her,* he would four months earlier in the Duke's study in Hertfordshire. He had made amends, taken his lumps, and continued to make choices to prove to himself and others that he had changed. Even though he was not fully restored with all his friends, at least most of the hurdles that had been placed between him and society had been removed.

The very lady that he had insulted in Hertfordshire now occupied his heart. How he loved her, even if she did not like him much yet. She was magnificent, especially when those fine eyes of hers showed her emotions so clearly. He would do anything for her, even die for her if need be! Some weeks before, she had finally acknowledged that he had made meaningful changes, not just paid lip service to the idea of bettering himself which had led to the restoration of his position in society. A benefit from the whole affair was that his dear mother and sister had been accepted into the Bennet's circle of friends, and Georgie was included almost like another sister; she was awfully close to the twins, Ladies Mary and Catherine, and looked up with adoration and respect to the vivacious and gorgeous Lady Elizabeth.

His sister, Georgiana, his mother, Lady Anne Darcy, and her brother, the Earl of Matlock, his wife the Countess, and his mother's older sister, Lady Catherine de Bourgh, had all told him how proud they were of the man that he had become, one that was worthy to be called a gentleman. '*What a shock to me when Aunt Catherine said that she recognised her former behaviour in the way that I used to be. We have that in common, that we were both pointed down a better path and took the second chance that we were given. Praise the Lord,' he thought.* As happy as he was that Lady Elizabeth had recognised that he had made such real and meaningful changes, the approbation of his family was deeply felt.

The friendship with the Bennet's had an added benefit for Georgie; they knew all the details about her near elopement and accepted her, without judgement or censure. Their friendship, and especially the guidance from Lady Elizabeth, had restored her self-confidence, and his sister was now better, happier, and more confident than she had ever been. As she saw her daughter flourish with Lady Elizabeth's help, guidance, and friendship, an especially strong bond had been built between his mother and the middle Bennet daughter.

Two months previously his cousins Andrew and Richard had married the eldest of the Bennet siblings, the classically beautiful Ladies Marie and Jane, respectively. He had been invited, but not yet fully forgiven by Lady Elizabeth, he did not want to detract from the festivities, and politely declined. His mother, sister, Lady Catherine, and Anne de Bourgh had all attended, and from their reports, a good time was had by all at a wedding attended by more peers of the realm than one could imagine. Prince Edward and Princess Elizabeth had represented the royal family and been gracious, keeping the focus on the brides and the wedding party.

Even though he would not attend the nuptials, he had offered to help both cousins with their wedding trips. The Viscount and Viscountess Hilldale had used his house near Brighton, Seaview Cottage, while Richard and Lady Jane Fitzwilliam had stayed at the house that he owned in the lake district. It overlooked Lake Windermere, the largest of the lakes, and had a good view of both the small Esthwaite Water and the larger Coniston Water. He had done none of this to impress the lady that unknowingly owned his heart, he had done it because he loved his cousins dearly and wanted them to have a place, they would be able to celebrate the loves they had found.

It was ironic that he was now a cousin of the lady that he had so insulted. It was a warm and clear spring day, so he decided that a walk in Hyde Park was in order. He left his study and requested that Killion, the butler at Darcy House, fetch his hat, coat, and gloves. Once he had donned his outer clothes and taken his walking stick, his late father's favourite, he started his walk across Grosvenor Square. Darcy noted the nameplate on the house opposite his that read, 'Bennet House," he couldn't help but be swept up in his reverie, thinking about the past three months as he headed to the park's entrance and his destiny.

~~~~~~~/~~~~~~~

A little over four months ago...

As he had promised that he would, Darcy was in his carriage on his way to join Bingley at the estate that he leased in Hertfordshire by the name of Netherfield Park in early November of 1811. The estate was less than four and twenty miles from town, and his particularly good friend, Mr. Charles Bingley, who was five and twenty and had a large fortune from trade, had taken the lease on a good-looking estate near the town of Meryton.

Although he was but two years younger, Bingley relied heavily on Darcy's council. On the one hand, he knew that it would be better for his younger and more naïve friend to stand on his own two feet, but Darcy quite enjoyed the feeling of control it gave him when he directed others. Bingley's parents had died some two years previously in a carriage accident. His father had been a minor partner in Gardiner and Associates, a company that Darcy and his uncle both invested in. The company ran a phenomenally successful import/export business, owned a few ships, and invested heavily in new and emerging technology like the steam turbines being used in some cloth mills. Bingley had two sisters who would be there with him. The oldest of the siblings, Louisa, had married a minor country gentleman, Harold Hurst, a few months before the tragic loss of Bingley's parents. Louisa Hurst was a pleasant lady, albeit easily led by her younger sister, Miss Caroline Bingley.

Charles was the middle sibling. When Miss Bingley, now one and twenty, had seen Pemberley, Darcy's vast estate, for the first time, she had set her cap for Darcy and was determined that she would be its next mistress. Darcy had sat her down with her brother and older sister and explained as gently as he was able that she would never be more than the sister of his good friend, stating clearly that he would never offer for her. He had pointed out, in no uncertain terms, that he would never countenance any use of his name to gain access to the Ton. She had been terribly upset, more so by the loss of social standing and wealth that she never had. Thankfully, his dearest Mama had sat the young woman down and had a private *tête-à-tête* with her. No one would ever know what Lady Anne Darcy said to Miss Bingley, but it worked.

It was the influence of her late mother that had made Caroline Bingley as she used to be:

Mrs. Maude Bingley had always believed that she was destined for greater than being the wife of a tradesman. She had filled Caroline, her younger daughter, with all of her delusions about joining the first circles. She had drummed into her youngest's head that it was her duty to rise above their roots and propel the family to the top echelons of the Ton. The unhappy lady had been very envious and coveted that which she did not have.

Charles Bingley Senior worked day and night, which meant he hardly ever saw his children. No matter how hard he worked, no matter how much he increased their wealth, it was never enough for Maude. She was not a demonstrative woman, so the only way she had shown Caroline love is when Caroline emulated her mother in looking down her nose at those in their own circle, even those above them. The only ones good enough were in the circles to which they would never be admitted. It was Maude who put the idea into her daughter's head that if there was an opportunity for such a match that she should do anything and everything to secure him, regardless of his desires. Even after Maude and Charles Senior died in the tragic accident, Caroline behaved as her mother had taught her and kept the delusional dream alive, right up until that afternoon with Lady Anne Darcy.

Darcy had joined his friend to inspect the estate a month earlier where they had met the agent and local solicitor, a Mr. Frank Phillips. During the tour, neither man saw anything of concern as the house was large and very well maintained. There was room for thirty to be accommodated easily, and the housekeeper, Mrs. Claire Nichols, and the butler, Mr. Bernard Darling, were well spoken and seemed most efficient as the house and the estate appeared well run and was, in truth, well maintained.

As they rode along the fields of the estate as part of the tour, Darcy noticed a group of riders at a distance. They were riding very good-looking thoroughbreds, flying across the fields at full gallop. It was a large party and Darcy noticed that three were ladies; some of their hair had escaped their coiffure and he could see that two were blonde and one raven-haired. He did not ask Mr. Phillips about the group he saw racing across the fields; if he had, it may have altered the trajectory of his life.

They noticed that the estate was far larger than the portions that were available for lease, but the agent was tight-lipped about the owner and only stated that Netherfield Park was owned by a marquess who preferred to remain anonymous. *'It must be the family of a duke or one of his secondary estates. The society looks savage, far below what I am used to.'* Darcy thought to himself, ruminating on all he had seen as Bingley sat with the agent to sign the one-year lease. Since Ramsgate, he had withdrawn into himself and had regressed terribly. Even before the near disaster, Darcy had become very judgemental, believing that his opinion was more fact than conjecture.

Darcy was not a bad person; he had put up a defensive wall to protect himself from being hunted. He had escaped no less than three attempts to entrap him, and those along with the constant hunting of his person, had coloured his outlook on society. He only truly felt relaxed at Pemberley with his dear and beloved mother, Lady Anne, and his sister, his ward, of whom he shared guardianship duties with his cousin and brother in feeling, Colonel Richard Fitzwilliam.

Fitzwilliam Darcy, or William as his family and close friends called him, had been a very pleasant boy and had remained thus until his dear father passed some five years before, leaving him to inherit Pemberley, three secondary estates, and a vast fortune. He had been considered prime marriage material by the Ton even before he became master, but now he felt like the fox that was being hunted from all sides. He adopted his disdainful mask, became taciturn and stoic, and would never dance the first or more than one dance with any young lady, if he deigned to dance at all. Darcy's disdainful mask and stoic countenance was further reinforced by the dreadful act, committed against his sweet sister, Georgiana.

His mother, Lady Anne Darcy, had told both he and Richard that something did not feel right about Mrs. Younge, who they hired as a companion for the fifteen-year-old girl. Darcy was used to being in charge and did not consider her opinion important enough to sway his thought, so he followed his own judgement and hired the woman. Until the extremely near debacle at Ramsgate, his mother would spend most of her time at Pemberley, but now she was in residence wherever his sister was. While Darcy was with Bingley in Hertfordshire, his mother and Georgie's new companion, Mrs. Helen Annesley, were with his younger sister trying to help her recover from her near elopement. Mrs. Annesley's every character had been checked and rechecked. She was approved by Lady Anne, he and Richard as Georgiana's guardians, and Lady Matlock. His sweet, little sister had been lied to and manipulated by the profligate wastrel, George Wickham, and assisted in his scheme by his current paramour, Mrs. Younge.

His cousin Richard had wanted to hunt down Wickham and end the blackguard, but Darcy, in his infinite wisdom, had decided against that avenue; he did not want his private business becoming public knowledge, his and Georgie's names being fodder for the prolific gossips of the Ton was to be avoided at all costs. Both his mother and his cousin had pointed out that his inaction would put others in jeopardy, and in his arrogance, he had asked "why that should affect me?" He only cared that Georgie was safe and scandal had been avoided.

On his arrival at Netherfield, Darcy was met by Bingley and his younger sister, who was to be his hostess and mistress of the estate. If the Netherfield servants had known that the pleasant lady that was mistress had not always been so, there would have been in disbelief as they found Miss Bingley to be a very pleasant and fair mistress.

Darcy had first been led to his room to wash and change. After Carstens, his manservant, had helped him with his ablutions, he joined the two Bingley's and the Hursts, who had joined their brother in the drawing room before dinner.

"How was your trip to Hertfordshire, Darce?" Bingley asked affably.

"It was good, thank you, Bingley. Pity that the society here is somewhat savage." he added, his disdainful remark catching all in the room by surprise.

"Far be it from me to disagree with you, Mr. Darcy, but there are a number of people of quality here." Miss Bingley offered demurely.

"I do not believe so, Miss Bingley, but I have been here a short time. To whom do you refer?" he asked, already deciding that she could not be correct.

"There are the Bennet's of Longbourn, they..." she smiled, taken aback when he rudely cut her off.

"I know of the Bennet's of Longbourn. Their small estate

is entailed to the male line and will be inherited by a distant cousin who happens to be my aunt, Lady Catherine's vicar. People of quality? They are a poor family with many daughters and no prospects," he pronounced, sure that he had the right of it.

"I am sorry, Mr. Darcy but you…" Miss Bingley did not finish what she tried to say.

"Darcy will see for himself at the Assembly on the morrow Caroline. A number of the Bennet's will be there, and he will be able to judge for himself," Bingley interjected with a smile as if he was hiding a great secret that Darcy could not discern.

As they walked into dinner, Caroline Bingley held her brother back. "You must warn him how far he is from the truth, Charles. If he angers Lady Elizabeth, it could be unbelievably bad for us. You know how he can get when he has formed an opinion." Miss Bingley reminded softly.

'If I had followed Mama's dictates,' Miss Bingley thought to herself, 'I would have not listened to anyone, I would have been my own worst enemy! Instead, Lady Anne took the time to mentor me, a tradesman's daughter. Only Louisa knows that I maintain a correspondence with her for when I need to ask her questions or request advice, and in her grace, she answers me as honestly as she did when we had 'our chat' that first time at Pemberley.' Caroline Bingley recognised that rather than be accepted as a friend to some in the Ton as she was now, that had she followed the path that her mother had set her on; she could have well ruined herself and her family in the eyes of society.

"You will see Caroline, all will be well." Bingley took his sister's hand and patted it to calm her snapping her out of her reverie of the past. "Darcy is a gentleman after all, and he knows how to behave." Little did he know that what he had just uttered, would soon be disproved.

CHAPTER 2

Life had been good to the Bennet's since *she* had left the mortal coil, but as with all of God's creations, there is never all good or all bad. The one bad thing for the family was that Lord Thomas Bennet's brother and sister-in-law, the Duke and Duchess of Bedford had not been able to have any children. Lady Rose Bennet had been with child four times, but each one had been lost before the third month of her increasing. After that she never became *enceinte* again.

The family was one of the wealthiest in the realm outside of the royal family. In addition to the fifteen estates between both dukedoms and an enormous amount of liquid assets and investments, they owned the Dennington Shipping Line which is the largest shipping line in the realm with several shipyards in which they built many ships for His Majesty's Royal Navy, and the East India Company. Lord Thomas Bennet had lent Edward Gardiner the seed money to start Gardiner and Associates, and rather than full repayment he retained a ten percent stake in the highly successful company. Gardiner had paid back ninety percent of the borrowed funds well before either of them had expected profits. As a much-loved uncle to Ladies Marie and Jane, Bennet had loaned him the money interest-free. The connection and approval of the Royals made sure that no one outwardly derided their-closer-than-most connection to trade.

Luckily for the Bennet family and the ducal line, The Duke and Duchess of Hertfordshire had no problems bearing children. Less than a year after Lord Thomas had married the love of his life, Lady Sarah, their first son, Lord Thomas Hugh Bennet, called Tom, was born. He became the Marquess of Birchington and Netherfield. He was followed two years later by a daughter, Lady Elizabeth Rose Bennet, who looked like her mother, Lady Sarah Bennet, in colouring, and was gifted with vivaciousness, wit, and intelligence. She had her mother's raven hair and hazel eyes with flecks of green and gold that shone and changed when she felt more intense emotions. Just a little more than a year after Lizzy, Lord James Atticus Bennet, named for Lady Sarah's late father, was born. He became the Marquess of Netherfield so that in the future, as there was now, there would be a Duke of Bedford, inherited by Lord Thomas from his Uncle Sed, and a Duke of Hertfordshire, Lord James. Almost three years later, the last of the children that the couple had been blessed with were born, twin girls, Ladies Mary and Catherine. Unlike the previous set of Bennet twins, the babes were not identical. Lady Mary looked a lot like her mother and her older sister Lady Elizabeth, while Lady Catherine, who was called Kitty in private, had the sandy blonde hair and light blue eyes of her father and eldest sisters.

When the children were old enough, their papa's entrapment and first marriage were explained to them so that they would learn to always be careful and more circumspect. 'That woman's 'name was otherwise never mentioned as it was not worthy of being spoken. One unintended consequence of telling the story of the Duke's entrapment was that Elizabeth became quick to judge people's intentions. She was suspicious of people's motives, and she tended to sketch their characters very quickly; once her good opinion was lost, it was gone forever. The oldest two Bennet girls knew that the woman that bore them, and made their dearest Papa and Mama both miserable for a year, was the sister of their Uncle Frank and Aunt Hattie Phillips, and was also the sister of their much-loved Uncle Edward and Aunt Maddie Gardiner. The citizens of the area who knew the story respected the Duke's wishes and never mentioned the disgraced and still-hated woman by name.

When they spent time with the Bennet's, their uncles in

trade and their wives were never made to feel less than. Even though the children born from the union of Thomas and Sarah Bennet were not related to them by blood, the Gardiners and the Phillips were considered aunts and uncles by all of the Bennet children, and conversely the Gardiner and Phillips children considered the Bennet's their aunt and uncle. The Phillips had a son, Graham, who was four and twenty, that had followed his father into the practice of law, and a daughter, Franny, who was seventeen and was named after Hattie's mother. The Gardiners had four children, Lilly who was twelve, Edward Jr, called Eddy, was ten, May was six, and the baby, Peter, was four. At Christmastide, the three families gathered together to celebrate, they alternated between Bedford and Longbourn.

Ladies Jane and Marie, although identical in looks, were vastly different in character. Jane, who was older by four minutes, was of a serene temperament, always trying to find the good in everyone and everything. Those that knew her well would first say that she had a backbone of steel; so, any who tried to take advantage of her or anyone that she loved did so at their own peril. Marie was more like her younger sister Elizabeth in character, except she was not as quick to judge and forgave much more readily than her next youngest sister. While both Lords Tom and James very much took after their father in character, Tom had the same hair colour that his Mama, Lizzy, and Mary had, while James and Kitty had their papa's colouring. Lady Elizabeth Bennet was a beautiful, vivacious, intelligent young lady who loved to read and study far beyond the limits that were usually imposed on young ladies

The twins, Ladies Mary and Catherine, the latter of which had a love for cats which led to her being called Kitty, were seventeen and not out yet. Jane and Marie were four and twenty. Lady Marie was betrothed to Lord Andrew Fitzwilliam, Viscount Hilldale and heir to her papa's good friend the Earl of Matlock, and Lady Jane was being courted by his younger brother Richard, who was a colonel in the army, intending to resign shortly to claim his inheritance, the estate of Brookfield in Derbyshire. Some questioned why the two oldest Bennets were not yet married, and the answer was simple; Bennets married for one reason and one reason only: for the deepest love and respect. Marie and Andrew would marry in a month and it was an open secret that Richard Fitzwilliam would be proposing to his Jane soon.

Lord Tom was three and twenty, had no special lady yet, and divided his time between his estate of Birchington, one of the family houses in Town, Bedford, and Longbourn. He had learnt all there was to know about Bedford and the other estates that he would inherit one day from his uncle the Duke. He fervently hoped that his inheritance was many years in the future, as he and all the Bennet offspring loved Uncle Sed and Aunt Rose like a second set of parents.

Lady Elizabeth was one and twenty and so far after three seasons, no one had been able to catch her interest. Lord James was twenty and in his final year at Cambridge, which is why the lease offered on his estate, Netherfield was but for one year in length. He would take up residence at his estate after the Bingley's lease ran out in October of 1812.

Besides the various estates, His Grace the Duke of Hertfordshire and his sons owned several town houses in London. Bennet House, the Duke's preferred London residence was on Grosvenor Square in Mayfair. It was coincidently across the square from Darcy House, and had Mr. Fitzwilliam Darcy been of a more sociable nature, he would have known who the Bennets were before he committed one of the biggest social gaffs in recent history. The Bennets had invited the Darcys to events from time to time. After the fourth or fifth time the gentleman in question disregarded an invitation, he was dropped from the Bennet's lists. Thomas Bennet knew that he was his friend Matlock's nephew, but he had no interest in furthering an acquaintance that was clearly not desired by the other side.

On Russel Square, which the late Duke's grandfather had developed, were Birchington and Netherfield Houses, as well as Bedford House that belonged to the Duke and Duchess of Bedford. The Hertfordshire House on Portman Square was currently being leased due to Bennet's preference for Bennet House, and his brother preferred the house on Russel Square. The coming out ball for the twins and Elizabeth had been held at Bennet house, as would be done when Mary and Kitty came out the following year.

Lady Sarah's brother had married the love of his life, which meant Lord Cyril and Lady Pricilla De Melville were now the Earl and Countess of Jersey. They had two children, Lord Wesley, Viscount Westmore, who was one and twenty and the heir, and a daughter, Lady Loretta, who had just turned seventeen and would have her come out with her Bennet cousins, Ladies Mary and Catherine the following year. As would be expected, the De Melvilles and the Bennets were close and spent much time together.

In the House of Lords, the Dukes of Bedford and Hertfordshire and the Earls of Jersey and Matlock were a force to be reckoned with. Their wives were no less influential, even without the family ties to the royals. Lady Pricilla, Countess of Jersey was a patroness of Almacks, and close friends with the other patronesses: The Countess de Lieven, Princess Esternhazy, and Lady Cowper. Ladies Rose, Sarah and Elaine, although not patronesses, had almost as much sway at Almacks and were part of the leading ladies in the Ton. One did not cross anyone under their protection and survive unscathed.

~~~~~~~/~~~~~~~

The evening before the assembly, the Bennets of Longbourn were sitting in the drawing room discussing the new tenants at Netherfield. All seven Bennet siblings were home, as Tom had returned from Birchington a sennight earlier, and he had collected James at Cambridge for the term break.

"What do we know about James's new tenants," asked

Lady Elizabeth who loved to sketch the characters of new people that she met.

"There was no need to have Sir Randolph's investigators send me a report," the Duke replied with a conspiratorial smile.

"Why not, Papa," James asked. "I thought that you always investigated my tenants, so what is special about them?" James asked, concerned at this seeming lack of protocol that his father had himself established.

"The reason is simple," the Duke arched his eyebrow very much like his second daughter was wont to do. "Mr. Charles Bingley is a minor partner in Gardiner and Associates as was his father before him. I checked with Uncle Edward and he was able to tell me everything that I needed to know, along with providing a glowing recommendation."

"You could have started with that information, Thomas. I know you like to make fun with our children at times, but mayhap you could have let James remain calm," his beloved Duchess mockingly censured.

"Please, Papa," Mary and Kitty said together as they often did, "tell us what you know of them."

"Bingley is an ebullient and happy fellow. He is here with his two sisters and his brother-in-law. The older sister is Mrs. Louisa Hurst, who married Harold Hurst, a minor gentleman. Mr. Bingley is the middle sibling. His younger sister, who I believe is Lizzy's age, is Miss Caroline Bingley. I understand that she is a very personable and pleasant sort of lady. She was not always; thus, Gardiner reported that two or three years ago she used to be a voracious social climber who acted like she was of higher standing than she was.

"Uncle Edward does not know who, but someone took her under their wing and she changed into a lady that is a pleasure to be around. I understand that they were joined today by one Fitzwilliam Darcy of Pemberley and Darcy House." At the questioning looks from his family Lord Thomas Bennet continued his diatribe. "Yes, our neighbour from across Grosvenor Square, the one who could not bother to answer any of your mother's invitations.

"I know from my friend Matlock, who is his uncle," seeing the look on Marie and Jane's faces he confirmed their thoughts. "Yes, he will be your cousin soon, Marie, and yours too Jane if things proceed as planned." Bennet offered affably. "Reggie tells me that he can be arrogant and taciturn at times, but at heart he is a good and honourable man."

"Until we meet him, I will reserve judgement," Bennet's most judgemental daughter said.

"Do not be uneasy, Liz-bear," Lord Tom winked at his younger sister. "If he bothers you, I will call him out." Tom's statement drew laughter from the family.

"I am sure that he is a gentleman and a good man as uncle Reggie implies," Lady Jane interjected.

The family spent the rest of the evening in repose. The girls, all who had learnt from the top masters of their chosen instruments, along with their mother, Lady Sarah, performed some music, and not long after the last song was shared, the family retired for the night.

~~~~~~~/~~~~~~~

The following morning, Lady Elizabeth, accompanied by her companion Miss Anita Jones, walked into Meryton. They were discreetly escorted by two huge footmen in plain clothes, to avoid standing out. The one in charge was aptly named Biggs, for he was indeed large in stature. Elizabeth was dressed in one of her older day dresses, as she did not want to ruin yet another creation of Madame Yvette Chambourg, the Bennet's exclusive modiste, as she was apt to do. Lady Elizabeth enjoyed walking immensely. She was also fond of riding her stallion, Mercury, but finding the day pleasant enough, she opted for an alternate means of transport.

As she walked up the main street, she could see some men in regimentals. She had heard that a unit of militia would quarter in Meryton in about eight days. This, she supposed, must be the advance party of the Derbyshire Militia.

Wanting some ribbons for her dress, she entered the haberdashery with Miss Jones, while Biggs and his fellow guard kept watch outside. As she left the store, the three Netherfield gentleman were riding up the main street. Lady Elizabeth exited the store ahead of Miss Jones and stood waiting between her two guards, who had not yet moved from their post.

As he rode past, Darcy noticed the raven haired local that was leaving the store and he automatically donned his mask, which to Elizabeth Bennet looked like a sneer. She was offended and filed it away under "slights from unknown persons" in her mind. As he passed Darcy thought to himself, *'If that is an example of the 'people of quality' this savage town boasts, Miss Bingley was very wrong indeed. I knew that there were none here worth my notice; they are all below me!'* In his arrogance he believed himself to be right and never looked back. If he had, he would have seen the companion join her and the two huge men step in to follow her. Had he seen this, even he would have recognised that there was more to this lady than met the eye.

Darcy turned to his friend riding between himself and Hurst, "I knew how it would be Bingley; everyone in this backwater town is below me. What a waste of time. Mayhap I will stay at the estate tonight rather than joining you at the assembly for these savages!"

"Darce, you are a gentleman, correct?" Bingley frowned.

"Of course I am, Bingley," he retorted with indignation. "What kind of question is that?"

"Did you not agree to come to the assembly to see if you were wrong?" Bingley asked with a pleasant smile.

"I did, but I am sure I am right!" Darcy's lips pursed as he disliked having to make unnecessary efforts.

"So that allows you to renege on your word?" Bingley asked, trapping his friend as he called his honour into question.

"You have me there, Bingley. I did, in fact, give you my word. I will stand by it and join you as promised." Darcy knew that there was no way out, so he had to grin and bear it. *'I will not dance with anyone other than Mrs. Hurst and Miss Bingley, and even that is too much. How could I dance when I failed Georgie like I did? Mayhap I should not have blocked Richard from going after that wastrel. My dear mother warned me about Mrs. Younge and I did not heed her!'* As he berated himself for not paying heed to his mother, he was doing the same thing at Netherfield, only relying on his own beliefs. This night would change his life and it would take him some time so see the positive results for himself.

When Lady Elizabeth arrived home, she was fit to be tied and stomped into the Duke's study. "Hateful, insufferable man!" she spat out.

"Lizzy," her mama looked up in concern as she was sitting with her beloved Thomas and they had been talking before their daughter's unceremonious entry. "What has your equanimity so disturbed?"

"Some *man*," she vented her spleen, "sneered at me for no reason. I was coming out of the haberdashery and three men I have never met before rode past. I assumed they are from Netherfield, being the only new arrivals in the area. Granted, I was in one of my older day dresses, but is that reason to be unpardonably rude to one you have never met or know anything about their situation?" She huffed in indignation.

"No Lizzy, that is not the behaviour one would expect from a gentleman," the Duke saw the expression of vindication on his middle daughter's countenance, "however, do you know for sure if the sneer was directed at you? Do you know what was going through the man's head at the time?"

"Lizzy, I beg you, before you jump to conclusions, listen to your father. As much as I love you, and a mother could not love a child more, you do sometimes assume the worst and then act on your assumption as if it is fact." She reminded her and could see that her daughter was about to protest. "No, Lizzy, I ask that you think before you unleash that rapier wit of yours. You know that we will all support you if there is any reason to do so."

"All we ask, my Lizzy, is that you try to be a little circumspect. You know that we would never suspend any pleasure of yours, Liz-bear." Bennet smiled gently. Her parents had succeeded in calming their sometimes too quick to temper daughter. She kissed each on the cheek and went to her bed chamber to rest, knocking on Marie's door before she went to her own. Marie's lady's maid informed Lady Elizabeth that Marie and Jane were in the shared sitting room. On the entry of their younger sister, the twins looked up from the note that Marie was holding.

"What is that Marie?" their younger sister inquired.

"It is a note from Andrew," as she mentioned his name, she got the dreamy far off look in her eyes that she always did when speaking of her betrothed. "He and Richard will be delayed, they will arrive about half way through the assembly, but they will still be here."

"They will be guests at Netherfield. I gather that they know the tenants, so there will be no issue with them being hosted." Jane added, deeply pleased that her Richard would be dancing with her at this assembly.

"Lizzy, we can see that you are perturbed. What has so disturbed you?" Marie asked with concern.

Elizabeth shared her story with less asperity than she had given their parents with the first telling. When she was done, if she was looking for her sisters to disagree with their parents, she was disappointed. They gave her remarkably similar advice to what her parents had told her. On entering her own chambers, she pulled the bell to summon her Abigail, Jacqueline Arseneault, who she called Jacqui and spoke to in fluent French whenever she wanted to practice that language. Elizabeth spoke five languages fluently: French, German, Italian, Spanish, and, of course, English. When her Abigail answered the bell, Elizabeth asked her to help her out of her dress, then wearing only her shift, she pulled the counterpane over herself to rest for a while.

Lady Elizabeth was gently shaken awake by Arseneault at

a little before half after five in the evening. She bathed and was dressed in the hunter green gown with gold trim, one of Madame Chambourg's creations. Once she was ready, she joined the family for light repast and, shortly after, all except for the younger twins, who were not out, climbed into the two waiting carriages and left for the Meryton assembly hall.

At Netherfield, Darcy was waiting while his valet Carstens was putting the finishing touches on his cravat. As much as he would have preferred to stay at the estate with a snifter of brandy and his latest edition of Cowper, he had made a commitment and a gentleman always keeps his word. When he arrived in the entrance hall, the whole party was assembled and he heard Miss Bingley lamenting the fact that no matter how she tried, she could not get an appointment with London's premier modiste, Madame Chambourg. He did not hear everything, but she was telling her sister that she was sure that some Duke's wife and daughters all wore her gowns. He remembered that his mother and sister had only recently got an appointment with the exclusive modiste because of a friend of his Aunt Elaine's, she herself being the Countess of Matlock, and she too had required the same effort from her friend. Whoever that woman was, she was not to be trifled with, as she had influence few could match if even his aunt had needed that lady's assistance

Thankfully, they left on time as one of the things that Miss Bingley had learnt from Lady Anne Darcy was that fashionably late did not impress; it was just rudeness. From that day onward, Miss Bingley made sure that she was on time or even slightly early. As they arrived at the assembly hall, Bingley's driver had to wait for two exceptionally large and expensive looking coaches to move on. Had Darcy been attending, he would have noticed the crest of the Bennet family, the Bedford and Hertfordshire Bennets, not the ones that he had convinced himself were the occupants of the 'small, low-earning' estate that was entailed from the female line.

CHAPTER 3

When the Bennets entered the assembly hall, the conversation quieted as the host, Sir William Lucas, welcomed them with all reverence. By the time the Netherfield party entered, the Bennets had moved off to the side where they were partially obscured. Had Darcy been paying attention instead of thinking how insupportable it was that he had to be among these plebeians, he would have noticed that their party was being paid scant attention. There were no whispers about his reputed ten thousand a year or the size of his estates. He was so used to that phenomenon wherever he went that even though it did not happen, in his head he imagined that it did.

Bingley and his sisters greeted Sir William affably and thanked him when he asked if they would like to meet some of the principal families in the area. Bingley, his sisters, and Hurst answered in the affirmative, while Darcy, letting the dark thoughts about his sister and her suffering come to the fore, rudely walked away without so much as a nod to the host. Lady Elizabeth immediately recognised the man that had sneered at her earlier that day. She had been willing to try and do what her parents and sisters had urged her to do, to keep an open mind, but when she saw the way the hateful man treated Sir William, who was a sometimes silly and loquacious but harmless man, she was livid.

What she saw confirmed all her thoughts towards the unknown gentleman. She had never seen such arrogance, and the haughtiness was unparalleled, the way that man looked down on one and all. '*He looks down on our friends and thinks he is above everyone! Does the disdainful man not know that he is in the company of a Duke and Duchess? Who does he think that he is? I think that I am going to have to bring this proud taciturn man down a peg or two!'* As Lady Elizabeth was getting angrier, she did not see the pain displayed on the man's face, there for all to see as he again berated himself for his perceived failures which had almost caused his dearest and only sister to be ruined.

Lady Elizabeth was snapped out of her reverie when Sir William approached with the Bingley and Hurst party in tow. Lucas stopped and bowed to her parents. "Your Graces, Lords and Ladies, may I introduce the Netherfield party to you?"

The Duke of Hertfordshire inclined his head in agreement to the man that he had known for many years. "Your Graces, the Duke and Duchess of Hertfordshire, Lord Birchington, Lord Netherfield, Ladies Jane, Marie, and Elizabeth, it is my honour to present Mr. Charles Bingley of Scarborough and London to you." Bingley bowed deeply to the Duke and his family, "Mr. and Mrs. Harold Hurst of Winsdale in West Suffolk and Miss Caroline Bingley also of Scarborough and London." As they were presented to their graces and the family, each bowed and curtsied as their name was mentioned.

"Lord Thomas Bennet, Duke of Hertfordshire, Lady Sarah Bennet, Duchess of Hertfordshire, Lord Tom Bennet, Marquess Birchington, Lord James Bennet, Marquess of Netherfield, Lady Jane Bennet, Lady Marie Bennet, and Lady Elizabeth Bennet." As he named each member of the Bennet family, they inclined their heads. Bingley was speechless. He had never seen the likes of the beauties before him. He knew that a daughter of a duke would not be interested in the son of a tradesman, but he could not but admire the radiant beauties before him.

Miss Bingley approached Lady Elizabeth; this was a lady that one did not want to anger, based on what Caroline had heard about her. "Lady Elizabeth, do you object if I enquire of the gowns that you and your sisters are wearing are creations of Madame Chambourg?"

"I have no objection to the question Miss Bingley, and yes they are. You have a good eye," she said with a small smile.

"You have my thanks your ladyship; I have tried for many

a year to get an appointment, but she will not accept anyone that is not referred by one of her well-established clients."

"That is true Miss Bingley; mayhap one day someone will refer you." Elizabeth smiled almost as if to herself, as her mother and sisters were the most established clients that Madame Chambourg had.

While they were talking, Bingley, who believed that none of them would dance the opening set with one who was not an intimate, asked if any of the ladies had a set free in which he could pencil his name. Lady Jane, to his great surprise, told him that she was free for the first, while Lady Marie awarded him the second and Lady Elizabeth the third. The Duchess demurred stating that she would only be dancing two or three sets with her husband.

Across the hall, Darcy, whose view was partially obscured, could not understand why the Bingleys and the Hursts were spending so much time with one of the lowborn local families. He had to admit that the group, from what he could see of them, seemed to be better dressed than any others at the infernal assembly, but he was in no mood to think about what he saw, so he dismissed it. The first set was called, and Bingley was dancing with an ethereal blond beauty. A replica of her was led to the floor by a man who Darcy neither wanted to know, nor cared, who he was, and then the third lady in the group was led out by another young man.

While the participants enjoyed their dancing, Darcy was stalking back and forth along the far side of the hall so that no one would try to engage him in inane chatter. As he watched, the dancers seemed to enjoy their dance, which turned his mood even darker as he thought about how much he hated having to be there. The first set ended, and he was about to go do his duty and ask one of Bingley's sisters to dance when they were led out by some unknown men. That they happened to be the two marquesses from the Bennet line, he had not a clue. The identical blondes were dancing, but the dark haired one had taken a seat near him. '*Slighted already, poor country girl!*' he

SHANA GRANDERSON A LADY

derided. Before the set began, he was approached by Bingley.

"Come Darcy, I must have you dance. You cannot stand about stupidly the whole night; this is an assembly, not a wake." Bingley tried to use humour to get Darcy to relax. It did not work.

"I shall not, you know I will not dance with one that I am not acquainted with, and to dance with all of these people so below me, is insupportable. Be off with you Bingley, your partner is waiting," Darcy retorted.

"I have never seen so many pretty girls before," Bingley said dreamily.

"You danced with one of the only pretty ones here, now go dance with her twin who is waiting for you." Darcy tried to dismiss his friend.

"I could not be as fastidious as you for all the money in the Realm. Look Darcy, the twins' sister is sitting there, let me introduce you and you can dance the next with her." Bingley incorrectly assumed that by now Darcy knew which Bennets were at the assembly.

Darcy gave the lady a cursory look, "She is tolerable, but not handsome enough to tempt me.," He did not notice that around him everyone had gone silent in mortification and Bingley had turned white, "I will not give consequences to ladies below me who have been slighted by other..." As he was about to finish, he noted that no one was moving, and Bingley looked like he was about to cast up his accounts. "Bingley, what ails you? Are you sick? Come, let us leave this infernal place now."

"Darcy close your mouth. Do you have any idea who you have just insulted?" Darcy looked at his friend and realized he was not sick; rather he was livid with anger. '*What is going on here? What did I miss?* 'He made to ask Bingley what he was about when he heard an icy voice dripping with disdain behind him.

"Lower than you, sir? Do you have some unknown rank that places you above the daughter of a *duke*?" He turned slowly and saw that other than the woman's family, not one person was moving, and they were *all* looking at him with abject disgust and scorn. *'Wait did she day 'daughter of a duke'? Please God, do not let me have made such an error.'*

She looked at Bingley, "Mr. Bingley, will you please introduce this excuse for a gentleman to me and my family?"

"Yes, your ladyship.' "*God no! It is* those *Bennets!* 'For the first time in a long while, Fitzwilliam Darcy was scared.

"Your Graces, my Lords and my Ladies, Mr. Fitzwilliam Darcy of Pemberley and London. Darcy," his friend said his name with no little anger showing, "*Lord* Thomas Bennet, the *Duke* of Hertfordshire, *Lady* Sarah Bennet, *Duchess* of Hertfordshire, *Lord* Tom Bennet, *Marquess* Birchington, *Lord* James Bennet, *Marquess* of Netherfield, *Lady* Jane Bennet, *Lady* Marie Bennet, and lastly *Lady Elizabeth Bennet.*"

Darcy blanched. He could see the looks of pure disdain directed at him by all the Bennets, and everyone else at the assembly also silently staring at him. He had heard the stories about Lady Elizabeth Bennet, that she had implacable resentment and once crossed, she could and would make life a living hell. Said lady was now standing before him with a look of pure, unadulterated hatred in her exceptionally fine eyes. *'What have I done! I was worried about rumours of Georgie and Wickham ruining the Darcys in society, but that is nothing compared to what will happen if I cannot fix this,* 'he told himself. He had to admit to himself, before him was one of the most beautiful women he had ever beheld, with flashing angry eyes that saw through to his soul and caught him before he fell, then dropped him into hell when he realized the passion was hatred.

"I had not even had the displeasure of meeting you when I ascertained your selfish disdain for the feelings of others. This morning you were riding with Mr. Bingley and Mr. Hurst in Meryton, correct?" He nodded dreading what he suspected she was about to say. "I was exiting the haberdashery as you were passing, my two footmen were not dressed in livery so to not stand out and my companion was still in the shop. You, who had never met me, knew nothing of my circumstances, assumed based on my clothes!

"Have you never seen one that you are acquainted with dress informally when the situation called for it? Did that make them less than themselves and an object of derision for you to sneer at?' "*My God, my dear mother, when she works in her rose gardens at Pemberley, if one did not know she was the mistress of the estate, you would think her a servant by how she dresses, Oh Lord help me!* 'He begged in silent prayer, knowing that not even God could help him at this moment.

"What kind of '*gentleman*' refuses to be introduced to anyone in a new place, slights the host, and stalks off with his nose in the air as if the place was malodourous? You are no gentleman, sir. You may be a landowner, may even be wealthy, but in behaviour and manner, you are anything but what a gentleman is supposed to be!

"If all of that was not bad enough, when I *chose* to sit out the second set as there are far more ladies than men present, if you had bothered to look, you would have seen that easily enough, but you were too busy being arrogant and disdainful so that when Mr. Bingley tried to urge you to dance, your response was to insult *me!*"

The Duke considered stopping his daughter from flaying the man in public, but he remembered some of the things that his friend Matlock had told him about his nephew, so he did not interfere, thinking that the man needed to be taken down a peg or three.

"I was '*slighted*' by no one, I *chose* to sit out the dance so that others would have the opportunity to participate. Unlike you, I care about the feelings of others! Then again, without any knowledge of who I am, my family, or my situation, after you insult my looks you then vocally and publicly claim to be above me! You are so far below me that you would strain your neck severely to view the heights that we inhabit!"

Lords Birchington and Netherfield stepped forward

threateningly so that Lord Tom was inches from Darcy's face, with Lord James right behind him. Lord Birchington hissed, "If it were not illegal and would bring scandal to my family, I would call you out! Who do you think you are? I, too, observed the abject arrogance you have portrayed since you entered our assembly. You looked on our neighbours and friends as if they were dirt on your riding boots. Unlike you, they are all good, honourable people who have never done anything to deserve your disdain. I would suggest that you retire to my *brother* Lord Netherfield's estate. You are no longer welcome at this assembly!"

"I too would like to call you out," Lord James chimed in. "You are a guest of *my tenant* in *my house* and you strut around like a peer of the realm looking down on all, ignoring the actual peers in this hall! You are a disgraceful example of a true gentleman! You deserve whatever Lizzy unleashes to punish you. As my brother said, begone; you are not welcome here," the normally serene James added hotly. Like his sister Jane, woe the person that hurt anyone that he loved, and he loved his sister Lizzy very deeply.

The marquesses did not have to tell him twice. Darcy could see the disgusted looks directed at him, so made as creditable bow as he could, and then turned and walked out of the hall with as much of his battered dignity that remained. He summoned Bingley's driver and requested that he convey him back to Netherfield and then return to wait for the rest of their party. When he at last reached his chambers and Carstens had help divest him of everything except his breeches and shirt, he fell into a chair with a snifter of brandy in his hand.

'*How could I have been so very mistaken? Miss Bingley and Bingley both tried to warn me that there were people of quality in the area, but I would not let them finish. I made an assumption and substituted my own judgement for the facts!*' As he thought he made a painful realisation, '*Good Lord above, Collins said the estate that was entailed upon himself was Longriver in Herefordshire, NOT Longbourn in Hertfordshire! The Family is Benet des-*

cended from family in France, not Bennet! I thought he had nothing of worth to say so I did not pay attention as I should have. What will the cost be to myself and my family for this arrogant folly?

'*I would love to say that Lady Elizabeth was wrong in her estimation of me, but it is now obvious she was close to the mark. She does not know of my worry about Georgie, but as she pointed out, a gentleman would not behave the way that I have been. How am I going to explain this to Mama? Oh. No. Is it one of these ladies Andrew is betrothed to? One of the blond beauties, Mary, Miranda, no Marie, Lady Marie Bennet. I think that Uncle Reggie and Aunt Elaine are friends of the Duke and Duchesses, even Aunt Catherine admires them!*

"*Have I allowed myself to become such a man? Yes, I have been hunted relentlessly and had to suffer attempted compromises, but should it follow that it gives me leave to assume that everyone will treat me thus? I have developed this mask to scare anyone off to get some peace, but have I not become the type of person that I was trying to protect myself against? Mother and Father taught me right from wrong, but as an only child for twelve years I started to look down on those that I considered below us as I became spoilt. Then Georgie was born, and as a much older brother and heir, I did not amend my behaviour. I always see fault in others but have been blind to those in myself.*'

Darcy did something that he had not done since his beloved father died after falling off his horse and breaking his neck five years previously, he cried. He was not crying for a mistake or the massive error he had made that night, but for the realisation of the man that he had allowed himself to become. Once he had released the pent-up emotions, he made a pledge then and there that he would strive to become a better, less judgemental man. He knew that he had a mountain to climb, and it would start on the morrow when he would present himself at Longbourn and prostrate himself before the family to offer his sincere apologies.

~~~~~~~/~~~~~~~

As the music commenced once again at the assembly, the

Bingleys and Hursts gingerly approached the Bennets. "Your Graces, My Lords and Ladies," Bingley said tentatively with a bow, "on behalf of myself and my family I offer my sincere and deepest apology..."

He cut himself off as the Duke raised his hand, "What is it that you have done to apologise for, Mr. Bingley?"

"For Darcy, your Grace. He is my guest and my responsibility, and he insulted your family, especially Lady Elizabeth, and all of the good people from the area most grievously." He bowed again as he completed his statement.

Lady Elizabeth interjected, "You did not make him behave in the reprehensible manner that he did." She countered. Bingley and his party took comfort at her words, only to have the worry return as she continued. "Although it is true that we are judged by the company that we keep."

'I will kill the man! 'Miss Bingley thought. *'Of all of the woman to insult in the realm, he had to choose this one. I have heard that she is faithful to a fault to those she loves or counts as a friend, but heaven help you if you cross her. I have heard that she is not quick to forgive.'*

"We will not censure you for your friend's words or actions," said Lady Sarah, looking at her first-born daughter with a warning to withhold her piece, "however I suggest that you make sure that Mr. Darcy does not repeat his behaviour."

No one had noticed the two gentleman that were approaching them from the entrance to the hall, one tall with light blond hair and blue eyes, was very handsome and impeccably dressed in a fine form fitting tailored outfit, and the other not quite as tall, but much broader, with the same colouring. Though not quite as handsome as his brother, he dressed in his scarlet regimentals with the epaulettes informing one and all that he was a full colonel.

"Hello all," Lord Andrew Fitzwilliam, Viscount Hilldale intone., "Sorry that we were delayed but we did arrive sooner than we thought that we would." His eyes locked on those of his betrothed as he spoke, gratified to see her joy at his arrival followed by a shared look of pure adoration. A similar look was shared between Richard Fitzwilliam and Lady Jane Bennet, which was not missed by Bingley. *'There was no chance that a daughter of a duke would have accepted me;, she is an angel but I see that she is not available, based on the look that I just saw between her and the Colonel.* 'he noted, as he turned to greet Darcy's cousins.

Before he could, the Colonel spoke, "What was it that you were saying about William?" Seeing the questioning looks, he clarified with an amused chuckle, "Darcy."

It did not take long for the events of the day to be explained to the Fitzwilliam brothers, who were livid by the end of the retelling. "He is lucky that he did not offend Marie," the Viscount but out as he looked at his betrothed with such love even the married women in the room blushed, "and if he had insulted Jane, Richard would have run him through! Insulting you or anyone else is inexcusable, Lizzy, and on behalf of my family you have my sincere apologies for my cousin's ungentlemanly behaviour." He took his future sister's hand and bestowed a kiss on her glove.

"Neither you nor Richard are responsible for your cousin," interjected the Duke. "Can we forget this for the rest of the evening and enjoy the company of pleasant people?" No one was confused; the Duke had not suggested; it was an order and there were none that would dare gainsay him.

Richard approached his beloved Jane to request the next set, thinking how he could not wait to propose to her on the morrow, and she of course accepted while giving him her shy smiles that radiated love for this man in regimentals. Before they joined the line, she turned to Miss Bingley and Mrs. Hurst. "If you are not otherwise engaged, you should call on us at Longbourn on the morrow. Shall we say at two in the afternoon?"

Louisa Hurst answered on behalf of both, "We have no prior engagements; we will be happy to join you on the morrow. Thank you for the gracious invitation Lady Jane."

~~~~~~~/~~~~~~~

On their return to Netherfield, three irate and upset men found the object of their anger sitting in the library drowning his sorrows in brandy. Darcy looked up, and after a moment to focus his eyes, he believed his guilt was making him hallucinate his Fitzwilliam cousins standing next to a very out of character unhappy Bingley. As soon as Cousin Andrew spoke, he winced because he knew it was not an hallucination.

"William, how could you! Have you taken leave of your senses? What were you thinking?" Lord Hilldale fired off questions in rapid succession.

"I-I am afraid I was not thinking clearly. Worries for Georgie were on my mind and…" he got no further, as the cousin that was more brother than cousin cut him off.

"No matter your worry, how *dare* you behave the way you did to a sister of the lady I am courting, that I plan to propose to in the morning! You are only alive now as they do not hold your complete lack of manners and proper behaviour against *us*!"

Darcy dropped his head in shame, "Why did you not tell me, Richard?"

"I tried to, but you have been in your own world for the last three months since Ramsgate," Richard reminded him. Bingley looked on in confusion and was about to leave as the family obviously needed to have a private conversation when Darcy shook his head.

"I have been so intent on hiding my private actions and ducking the grasping women that hounded me that I lost the ability to see the difference between those who are like the former and not. Close the door please Bingley." Darcy's shoulders dropped in dejection. Bingley complied and then Darcy looked to his cousin and his sister's co-guardian who gave him a nod to proceed. "Have you heard me talk about George Wickham before?"

"I have. He is the one that was meant for the Kympton living?" Bingley verified his memory was correct and Darcy and his cousins nodded. "He is the debaucher, despoiler of maidens, gamester and the one that leaves debts and ruined girls in his wake?"

"That is Wickham. Two years ago, when the living became vacant, he had the temerity to write me a letter claiming 'his legacy 'as he put it. He claimed that his situation was desperate and that he was now willing to take orders and claim what was meant for him. He had received a one-thousand-pound legacy from my honourable departed father in addition to what I paid him. How he wasted four thousand in such a short time I know not, but I do believe that he was desperate, knowing his profligate ways.

"I refused him, reminding him that he had signed a legal document renouncing any and all claim to the living. He wrote a very abusive missive in return where he swore revenge for me 'stealing' what was his. I heard not from him for more than one and a half years until he inserted himself into my life three months ago. You remember Georgiana's first companion, Mrs. Younge?" Darcy swallowed dryly; relieved Bingley nodded. "She requested that she be allowed to take my sister to Ramsgate so she could take in the sea air while continuing her lessons. We have a house there and I could see no harm.

"Thither went Mr. Wickham as well, by design. I did not check Mrs. Younge's characters, which we later found out were falsified. She had a prior relationship with the bastard and was one of his paramours. Wickham imposed on my sister and convinced her that he loved her and she him and got a fifteen-year-old impressionable girl, my *sister*, to agree to an elopement. His aim was her fortune of thirty thousand and to exact his revenge on me.

"By pure luck, I decided to surprise Georgie and arrived at my house in Ramsgate two days before the intended elopement. When Mrs. Younge opened the door and saw me, she looked like she would be ill, so I was immediately suspicious. I walked into the drawing room and there was the blackguard holding my baby sister's ungloved hands. His reaction on seeing me was like his co-conspirator, but he soon recovered and informed me that he was engaged to my sister and that they were to marry. For a second Georgie radiated happiness, until she saw the look of pure fury on my countenance.

"I coldly asked the dastard who had given him permission to marry my underage sister and how he intended to support her. He gleefully ignored the first question, telling me that her dowry was more than enough for them. I wiped the smirk off his face when I informed him that I had convinced my father to add a clause that stated that without permission from her guardian or guardians, not one penny of her dowry would be released. At this Wickham denigrated my sister and myself, then ran out in anger.

"In my arrogant foolishness, I stopped Richard going after the wastrel, caring not that he was free to roam and hurt others. I only thought of my own family and not for the possible suffering of others. Even my dear mother told me I was wrong, but as you know, I always think that I have the right of it. Well, I thought that way before tonight." Darcy completed the recitation, and Bingley stood silent as he gaped at him.

"I understand that you are still worried about Georgie, William, but how does that give you licence to not behave as a gentleman should?" Andrew demanded.

"In hindsight, I know that regardless of who they were I should not have behaved as I did. Both Bingley and his sister Caroline tried to tell me who the principal members of the community were, but I refused to listen. I remembered parts of a conversation with Aunt Catherine and her vicar, Mr. Collins, and I assumed and would not hear what others were telling me."

"What did you assume?" Richard asked his cousin whose sufferings increased with the discussion rather than decrease.

"Collins is the beneficiary of an entail of a distant cousin's estate named Longriver in Herefordshire, and the family is named Bennet. Until tonight, and only *after* I returned from my abject humiliation, did I accurately remember the estate and shire names. I thought them too far below me for any consideration or condescension from me." Darcy admitted, the shame he was feeling easy for the others to see.

"I have heard about that family as well cousin, they are *Benet* not Bennet! Mayhap you should have listened better," Richard admonished his cousin.

"Even had that all been true, you had no cause to treat my neighbours thusly!" Bingley accused, his ire rising again.

"I will not dispute that. Lady Elizabeth has the right of it. I acted like an arrogant arse. I had selfish disdain for the feelings of others, and my behaviour was not that of a gentleman." He then explained the other understandings he had come to here in his moment of humiliated clarity. "I am so used to my income and wealth being discussed that I imagined the same was occurring here, where in truth there was nary a whisper about me and my wealth. What arrogance I have!" All three were silent for a minute, none ever thought they would see the day when the 'great Fitzwilliam Darcy' would admit fault even berate himself. They had never seen the proud man so humbled in his life.

"What are you going to do about it?" His cousin Richard asked with no trace of anger left in his voice.

"I will present myself to the Duke in the morning, explain myself, and beg forgiveness. There is naught else that I can do." Darcy replied quietly. The three men agreed with Darcy, and well knew that all but one of the family would be open to forgive him, if not right away. They equally knew that one lady would not. To earn her forgiveness would be very hard. They advised him to explain, but to not try to excuse his bad behaviour, as there was no excuse for it.

CHAPTER 4

Just after nine in the morning, three riders handed their mounts to the grooms that met them in front of Longbourn. Darcy felt his folly more and more as they rode the distance between the two estates. From the point that they entered the main gates, it was over a mile to the manor house. The house itself was elegant and large. He spied a large park that sported formal gardens which he was sure would be a riot of colours when spring arrived, if it were anything like the gardens his mother took particular care with.

Lord Hilldale knocked on the door which was opened by the butler. He informed the man that he and his brother the Colonel had come to see the family while his cousin, Mr. Darcy, had come to see his Grace. The normally unflappable Hill raised one eyebrow slightly as he heard the name of the third gentleman of whom there had been much talk among the family, none of it flattering. He directed the Fitzwilliams to the relevant drawing room, then returned and took Darcy's card while he requested that he wait in the entrance hall while he went to verify if his Grace was available. As Darcy waited, he could not fail to notice the understated elegance. Nothing was for show or to impress, this was a home to be lived in, not to display opulence and gaudy baubles like Rosings used to display until Anne was able to convince her mother to allow her to redecorate.

Mr. Hill returned and directed Darcy to the master's study. As he walked in, he noticed that the study was large and well-lit with natural light from the big windows that overlooked part of the park. He was about to bow and greet the Duke when he noticed that they were not alone. The Duchess and Lady

Elizabeth were seated on a settee to the right of the desk, the latter looking none too happy to see him again.

~~~~~~~/~~~~~~~

In the drawing room, after greeting and bowing to the two ladies, two girls, and two young men present, the Viscount took a seat next to his beloved while the Colonel headed directly to Lady Jane. After he enquired after her health, he moved his head closer to hers, "Will you please take a turn in the park with me, Jane?" They had agreed to use familiar names some months back.

With a light blush, she replied in the affirmative. She was about to ring for her companion when the younger twins volunteered to join them as their chaperones. The Colonel waited for his lady and her sisters in the entrance hall where they joined him within five minutes. They walked around a part of the park that was left to be as nature intended so it looked like a prettyish wilderness. After they walked for a while, Richard asked if they could sit on one of the benches, to which Lady Jane Bennet readily acquiesced. The younger twins sat on a bench that offered them a clear view of the courting couple but allowed them the privacy to talk without being overheard.

"Jane, I have a particular question that I would like to ask you." She nodded as she blushed becomingly to indicate that he should continue. "We have known each other for a number of years and I have loved you for many of them, but I never thought that you would be interested in following the drum. Two years ago, I inherited Brookfield in Derbyshire and a substantial fortune with it. Depending on your answer to my question, I may be resigning from the army and selling my commission." He got down on one knee and took her hands in his much larger ones.

"Lady Jane Ingrid Bennet, my one and only Jane, possessor of my heart, when I look ahead at life's journey there is not a version that I can imagine where you are not next to me. Not behind me, but next to me as an equal partner. Until you accepted my request for a courtship, I was not sure that you had any tender regard for me so at your acceptance, my love for you grew even more. Jane, I am a simple soldier not prone to long flowery speeches, so I will get right to the point. I love you with all that I am and need you for all I hope to become. Will you do me the ultimate honour of accepting my hand and consent to be my wife?"

Lady Jane had tears of joy flowing down her cheeks, finally hearing the very proposal that she had dreamed of, yet better than any version she had imagined. "Yes Richard, yes. I will marry you. How silly you were to think that you could not approach me sooner. I have been in love with you since you danced two sets with me at my coming out. Until you requested the courtship, I was afraid that you saw me only as a sister. You have made me the happiest of women and given me my heart's desire: you as my husband until death do us part."

Richard Fitzwilliam, his heart singing, stood and pulled his betrothed up until their lips met with just a brush. Jane sighed as she received her first kiss from a man not part of her immediate family. On hearing the sigh, Richard kissed her with his lips fully on hers, and had they not heard the giggles and 'ahems 'coming from Mary and Kitty, they may have enjoyed some fuller kisses. The lady twins swarmed their oldest sister and soon to be brother.

"How fun," Lady Catherine said with a giggle, "brothers marrying sisters. You should marry in a double ceremony!"

"That is a very good idea Kitty. Jane, Richard? You should talk to Andrew and Marie, and I am positive that neither Mama nor Papa would oppose you." Mary offered; her clear thinking often helped others find easier solutions than they would have devised for themselves.

"Calm down you two. We promise we will talk to Marie and Andrew, and *only if* they agree will we all talk to Mama and Papa." Jane laughed at the hope in her sisters faces knowing they wanted her happiness above all, and that Richard made her truly happy.

"I will go and ask his Grace for his consent and blessing as soon as he is available. I believe that my Cousin William is meeting with him now."

~~~~~~~/~~~~~~~

Darcy could not help but witness the frosty looks that Lady Elizabeth directed at him. Her parents did not look openly hostile, but neither were their looks welcoming. He bowed deeply to each, "Your Graces, Lady Elizabeth, I thank you for accepting this call from me. I am sure that I am the last person that you would be prevailed upon to socialise with today." He was met by silence, but the Duke pointed to a chair in front of his large oak desk where Darcy would be able to see the three Bennets in the room. "I am here to apologise unreservedly for my despicable behaviour, especially toward Lady Elizabeth, almost from the first moments I have been a guest of Mr. Bingley."

Before any other could speak, Lady Elizabeth said with no small amount of asperity, "Once you found out who we are, of course you would apologise; you would be stupid not to. No matter your faults, you look like an intelligent man."

The Duke gave his middle daughter a quelling look. "Let us hear what the man has to say before we *rush to judgement*." Lord Thomas Bennet emphasised the last knowing Elizabeth's propensity to do just that. It was lost on the lady that this trait was one she had in common with the hateful man. Lady Sarah put a hand on her daughter's arm to reinforce her husband's expectation that their daughter allows Mr. Darcy to speak.

"Thank you, your Graces, Lady Elizabeth," he inclined his head to each in turn. "Last night, before Andrew and Richard returned to Netherfield with Bingley and wanted to do far worse to me than the Marquess did in wanting to call me out, I had a long time to think. There is no excuse for my behaviour, *regardless* of your station or rank. I acknowledge that my late father taught me better, and my dear mother, Lady Anne, will be seriously displeased with me when she hears of my behaviour. And she will hear of it in detail from my own mouth.

"I do feel the need to tell you about a situation that was heavily weighing on me, has done so for the past three to four months. It is not to offer an excuse but am hoping to offer a better understanding of my mindset. Before I proceed, I need to ask your secrecy with regards to one part of the tale as if it became public, my fifteen-year-old sister would be harmed, and I would rather die that have her suffer any more."

The Duke looked first at his wife and they communicated silently as they were wont to do and then at his most volatile daughter. Yes, she was quick to temper, but she was also fiercely protective of anyone weaker than her that was hurt. "You have our word, on the honour of the entire Bennet family, please proceed Mr. Darcy." Lady Elizabeth nodded for him to be assured his confidence would be kept safe.

"Before I tell you, since my honoured father passed..." Darcy shared his experiences in society, and the mechanisms that he used to protect himself, while not always appropriate, they were effective. He explained how he had learned to adopt his mask of indifference that displayed the haughty taciturn man, and how the more he was hunted the more he withdrew within himself until he only listened to his own council, to his own detriment as had been on display the previous night.

As Darcy finished this portion of his recitation, the Duke asked him to pause and told him a very brief version of his entrapment, then suggested to Darcy, that he have a settlement drawn up like the one that had been used for the hussy that compromised him. The terms should be widely published in society so that any 'lady 'considering trying to entrap him would know that her life would be a living hell and that she would never have access to anything besides a small room and a pittance of a settled amount with almost no pin money. Darcy thanked the Duke who promised to have Sir Randolph send his solicitor a copy of the template that had been used in his first 'marriage'.

At that point, Darcy laid out his history with one George Wickham, ending with his planned revenge of stealing Miss

Darcy's fortune via an attempted elopement. When he was done, there was silence for several minutes.

Lady Elizabeth was the first to speak, "As sorry as I am for Miss Darcy that she was importuned by that kind of blackguard, and I accept that you were distracted by your worries, that neither excuses your behaviour nor makes it more acceptable."

"Andrew, Richard, and Bingley told me the same last night, and I agree. As I said before I shared all of this with you, it was not as an excuse, just in hope of your understanding. I know that I have a lot of work to do, and that I have major changes to make. In addition, I have amends to make to many who I have both intentionally and unintentionally slighted." He offered with great contrition and wanted to further clarify his character. "My parents taught me what was right but never demanded that I correct my temper. I was taught good principles but left to follow them in pride and conceit. The humiliation that I received last night, richly deserved and just, forced me to reflect on my behaviour and character. I at last saw myself through other's eyes, and what I saw was not very pleasant or gentleman like. Lady Elizabeth showed me how arrogant all my pretensions are, or rather, were." He hung his head as shame overwhelmed him.

"You may have heard, Mr. Darcy, that once someone has lost *my* good opinion, it is lost forever." Lady Elizabeth spoke before her parents could again waylay her; inwardly satisfied Darcy nodded in acknowledgement with his eyes on his shoes. "I have been accused of having implacable resentment. It may be because I am cautioned by what my beloved Mama and Papa suffered for a year before God took *that woman* away. Talk is not indicative of status, Mr. Darcy. We are all judged by our actions. This morning I have written to my Aunt, Lady Pricilla De Melville, Countess of Jersey, and Mama's sister. She will share my news with my other Aunt, Lady Rosamond Bennet the Duchess of Bedford, and her fellow patronesses. As bad as I feel for your sister and would like nothing more than rip the heart out of the blackguard and his paramour, you will find that not many will want your society.

"If you can indeed change, can become a better man even in the face of such adversity, then I will know that you meant your words and they were not offered just to placate us and rescue your reputation in society. Your actions will not be held against anyone else, not your friends at Netherfield, nor any of your family most especially your sister or mother. That is the only hope that I can offer you at this time, Mr. Darcy, the rest will be up to you. As a good Christian woman, I can do no less. You have made painful admissions this day, so at the very least, I must allow that you may be sincere and can *earn* my forgiveness. I suggest you use your time well." With that, Lady Elizabeth rose, as did Darcy, she returned a brief curtsy to his bow, then left the study.

As Mr. Darcy left Longbourn, Elizabeth watched him from her bedchamber window. For the first time that she could remember, she started to question herself, that mayhap she had been too hard on him. Did he in fact have redeeming qualities that she had been blinded by her prejudices to see? Unbidden, a thought popped into her head that he was the most handsome man that she had ever seen. She dismissed the thought with alacrity willing herself to think on something else.

She admitted to herself that she never expected the arrogant man to apologise, and certainly not in the fashion that he had. Her emotions were warring with each other and the more she thought about it the more that she could see the sincerity of his apology. She was sure that he would never have recounted his sister's trauma if it had not been completely true. She shook her head to try and clear it, she knew that she had much to think on.

Darcy had expected some repercussions, but not to the extent such as this. Strangely, or maybe not, it firmed his resolve. As hard as it would be, he would make the changes and be a better man, one worthy of the title 'gentleman'. He thanked the Duke and Duchess for their time and then left

Longbourn for Netherfield where he instructed Carstens to pack his belongings. Darcy found the Bingleys and Hursts in the drawing room.

"I need to apologise to all of you. In my arrogance and refusal to listen, I could have caused all of you to be tarred by the same brush I have been deservedly painted with. It will be easier for everyone concerned if I take my leave." If he had been expecting any disagreement with that statement, he would have been disappointed, as none was forthcoming. "My man is packing as we speak and my carriage is waiting for me. All I can do is beg your forgiveness and make the same promise that I made to the Duke of Hertfordshire and his family. I will change and work to correct my flaws, to become a man worthy of the appellation 'gentleman'."

"You know that I will forgive you, Darcy," Bingley looked him right in the eye as he said it, having seemingly matured overnight, "but you have work to do and only you can do it. You have to *want* to do it."

"I know that, my friend. It will not be easy, but I know what I have to do, and I will succeed." He stated firmly with a determined look in his eyes.

"We all wish you well, Darce. God be with you." Bingley nodded once at his friend. Darcy bowed to the four present, and then as his valet indicated that his trunks were loaded, he boarded his coach and headed back to London. As he sat in his comfortable conveyance, he had visions of a beautiful, fiery lady with the finest eyes that he had ever beheld.

~~~~~~~/~~~~~~~

There was a knock on the study door and the Duke called for the person to enter. Colonel Richard Fitzwilliam marched in and stood at attention in front of the desk. "At ease, Colonel," the Duke jested. "Please take a seat, Richard."

"Thank you, your Grace," he said as he sat. "Before I get to the point, is Darcy still alive?" he asked with a smile, only half serious but fully curious.

"He is still in the land of the living, but he has work to do.

You know Lizzy, she is quick to anger and slow to forgive. She wrote to my sister Pricilla this morning with a full report of last night and you know the rest. She will talk to her fellow patronesses and to Rose, and after that it will not be easy for your cousin."

"William will have to sink or swim. He made this mess; he needs to fix it for himself." Richard paused and looked the Duke in the eye. "I am sure that you know my purpose here today, your Grace, but in case not, let me be direct. I asked for Lady Jane's hand in marriage and she has accepted me, so I have come to you seeking your permission and blessing." He made sure to be specific in naming his betrothed as he was well familiar with the Duke's propensity to tease.

"How will you support her on what you earn as a soldier, and what will happen to my firstborn if you are called back to battle?" Bennet challenged. Richard knew why the Duke was asking this. A little more than a year previously he had been wounded in his left leg at the Battle of Buçaco. He was lucky that no major blood vessels or nerves had been damaged, but his leg had been badly broken, and he was only now cleared for full duty and could walk without a noticeable limp.

"Let me address the army first. Before I came to see you, I sent an express to General Atherton, my commanding general, to announce that I am resigning from the army. I will see him when I go to Town to have the settlement papers drawn up and to sign the papers necessary to put my commission up for sale. Aside from that, I believe that you are aware, I inherited the estate of Brookfield some months ago from an uncle on my mother's side who died as he lived: a confirmed bachelor. The estate is large and well run and has an income of just over eleven thousand a year. With the estate came a legacy of one hundred and twenty thousand pounds. Uncle Paul saved most of his money over the years, as he had no one to spend it on.

"Regardless of Lady Jane's dowry, I can keep her in the style to which she is accustomed. In the settlement you will see that I intend to leave her dowry under her control to use as she sees fit."

"Each of my girls have a dowry of one hundred five and twenty thousand pounds. We do not advertise the amount to keep the fortune hunters guessing. Besides, I have clauses built in, just in case. I never want one of my girls, or any of my children, to suffer from an entrapment. You have my consent and my blessing, Richard." Bennet stood and shook hands with him. "Welcome to the family, son. Have you discussed a wedding date yet?" Bennet asked, having a very good idea what was going to be requested. His first two daughters were identical twins, after all.

"We know that Marie and Andrew will marry in six weeks; we would like to ask them if we can have a double wedding. It was Kitty and Mary that made the suggestion. If they agree, we will inform her Grace that she will only have to plan one wedding." When the two men joined the family in the drawing room, there was no doubt what the announcement was even before the Duke made the betrothal official.

The two betrothed couples had a short conversation in which Marie and Andrew threw their unreserved support behind the idea of a double wedding and the girls' mother had no objections. Richard requested the use of the library or study to write and express to his parents and family who were at Matlock House.

At two that afternoon, the Bingley, and Hurst party were admitted to Longbourn, and were welcomed by all. It was refreshing to the Bingleys and Mrs. Hurst that they were not looked down on simply because of their ties to trade. Given that the Duke was a silent investor in Gardiner and Associates and the Bennet's shipping interests, it would have been overtly hypocritical to judge others by the means that they earned their money. Once they were informed of the new betrothal, the arriving party wished the couple joy and the Bingleys and Hursts joined the two marquesses to speak of horses and sport.

The ladies began to talk fashion, and of course about

Madame Chambourg. The five Bennet daughters invited the sisters to come view some of the modiste's creations in their dressing rooms. As they went above stairs, Miss Bingley and Mrs. Hurst could not but help notice that Longbourn, although a little smaller than the house at Pemberley, rivalled it in comfort, taste, and excellence of the furniture and artwork. The ladies repaired to the suite shared by Ladies Jane and Marie. The visiting sisters were awed by its size. Even though the suites at Netherfield were large by any standard they had seen or heard of, they looked small compared to the suite shared by Ladies Marie and Jane. The two occupants of the suite each brought out three or four gowns for the sisters to see. Miss Bingley and Mrs. Hurst could only marvel at the exquisite creations that the modiste had produced.

Lady Elizabeth got a glint in her eye, "How would you and Mrs. Hurst like a dress made by Madame Chambourg's assistant modiste, Miss Bingley?"

"T-t-that would be a dream, but how Lady Elizabeth?" The Bennet girls all smiled.

"It would be easy. When we are at Longbourn for longer than a month, the assistant modiste and two or three seamstresses work out of a shop in Meryton. No one knows that they are there as it is for our exclusive use. If you like, you may come with us and Mama tomorrow when we visit them," she offered invitingly.

"Yes, we would love to accompany you," Mrs. Hurst responded for both sisters. "We thank you for the very welcome invitation."

"Is Charlotte not joining us as well on the morrow, Lizzy?" Kitty asked and when Lizzy nodded, Kitty smiled. "I hope that Maria will come as well. I miss her."

Seeing the questioning looks from the sisters, Lady Marie explained. "Charlotte Pierce, Lucas as was, is married to Longbourn's rector, Mr. Christopher Pierce, these five years. She is three years older than Jane and me, and they have a son and a daughter." Seeing that the sisters did not remember the name

Lucas, she reminded them of their connections already introduced to the Netherfield party. "At the assembly you remember the master of ceremonies, Sir William Lucas?" recognition dawned and she finished, "Charlotte is his eldest, and we have been friends with her as far back as we can remember."

The ladies then returned to the drawing room, and after a most pleasant hour, the Bingleys and Mrs. Hurst said their farewells and returned to Netherfield

~~~~~~~/~~~~~~~

A dejected Fitzwilliam Darcy was drowning his sorrows with a bottle of brandy in his study at Darcy House on Grosvenor Square in London. He was still stunned and disbelieving, momentarily ignoring his oath to himself as he thought. *'How has my life come to this? Me, a Darcy, to be so ostracised from society even my own family cannot help me, all because of Lady Elizabeth and her implacable resentment,'* he lamented to himself, and then added at least some honesty. *'Me and my big mouth. Why did I have to say such a thing just to try to get Bingley to leave me alone? How was I to know that she is the daughter of a duke? I thought that they were the Bennets to whom Aunt Catherine's vicar is related and whose estate is entailed. I believed them far below me and behaved as such. Good Lord above, what have I done?'* He groaned in self-pity as he took a long swallow from the snifter in his hand.

'I had no idea that they were those Bennets. They have such connections and wealth as to make me look like a pauper. Miss Bingley tried to tell me I was wrong about them, but I dismissed her and look at the price I am paying! Bingley tried to tell me as well, but did I listen? No, the 'great, all-knowing Fitzwilliam Darcy' knew better! Not even Aunt Catherine will be sympathetic, and I admit that I appreciate her company much more as she has ceased her requests that I marry Anne. Lady Catherine, who seldom defers to anyone, does so to the Bennets. Lady Elizabeth's father is one of Uncle Reggie and Aunt Elaine's friends, and her mother is Lady Sarah Bennet, De Melville as was, sister to the current Lord and Lady Jersey. How will I ever recover?

'I at least know how I got confused. Aunt Catherine had told me that her new clergyman at Hunsford, not the brightest fellow but otherwise harmless, is a distant cousin of a minor country gentleman with an entailed estate of which Collins is the beneficiary. The cousin, a poor country squire, has a number of daughters and no son and his estate brings in less than two thousand per annum. The estate name is Longriver in Herefordshire. By coincidence, the name is Benet with one 'n.' Yes, it was the wrong estate, wrong shire, and the family has no connection between those Bennets and these. I assumed they were the ones the parson is a distant cousin of and the rest is history!

'Richard was right to have me send Georgie and Mama to live with them at Matlock House in the meanwhile. Mama warned me about Mrs. Younge, but did I listen? no, the great Darcy always knows best! Good Lord, Lady Elizabeth's older sister, Lady Marie, is Andrew's betrothed, so no wonder the family is upset with me, and rightfully so. And Richard is courting her twin sister, Lady Jane. I truly need to become better at listening to others. It gets worse and worse the longer I consider my actions. How was I to know that by insulting her I was insulting the royals? Why would I know that the Bennets are cousins of the royals? Both of her brothers, one the Bedford heir and the other the Hertfordshire heir, rightfully wanted to call me out!

'I could not have made a worse mistake if I tried. Yes, I was upset worrying about Georgie and what that blackguard Wickham almost did to her with Mrs. Younge's assistance in Ramsgate, but I should have guarded my words. How could I call the handsomest woman of my acquaintance 'tolerable but not handsome enough to tempt me, and then for good measure I added some tripe about not giving consequence to someone so far below me that had been slighted by others? What a dullard I am!

'Enough of this wallowing. I said that I would change, so it is time to start. There is no one to blame but myself. Yes, I had 'selfish disdain' for the feelings of others. I swear to you, Lady Elizabeth, that I will make real changes and you will see for yourself. Yes, talk is cheap, but I will act. In the morning I will go talk to Mother and

Georgie at Matlock House, then will start to make amends, ask for advice, and listen to the advice that is offered.'

With that, Darcy put the stopper back in the crystal brandy bottle and standing straighter than he had since he had caused the mess he was in, he walked up to his chambers with purpose to have a much-needed bath and to get some sleep.

CHAPTER 5

Darcy knocked on the door of Matlock House with no little trepidation. He felt as though he was walking into the proverbial lion's den. Other than his honoured mother, the Earl and Countess, Lady Catherine, and Anne were all in residence. The butler, Mr. Smythe, led him to the family sitting room and announced him. His mother, uncle and two aunts stared at him as if he had two heads on his shoulders. He was about to walk over to his mother and kiss her cheek when he caught the look in her eye and stopped dead in his tracks.

"*Have you taken leave of your senses?*" his Uncle Reggie thundered, "What possessed you, William? Do we need to send you to Bedlam?"

Darcy was so taken aback he blanched. He knew they would be angry, but this was far more than he expected. "Do you know what you risked with this reprehensible behaviour of yours, William?" his mother asked calmly, but he could tell by her tone that she was very upset with him. "Thanks be to God that their Graces did not hold your actions against your cousins. We received an express yesterday evening that Richard is betrothed to Lady Jane Bennet. Your uncle and aunt would have broken with you if you had affected either Andrew or Richard's chances with their betrothed. They have each made love matches with the best of ladies." He could see the look of disappointment in his mother's eyes and dropped his to the floor in shame.

"Where did you learn to act in this manner, William? You are no better than a thug with such behaviour. The Bennets could have ruined us all without blinking had they chosen to," Lady Catherine de Bourgh added with asperity.

His cousin Anne, who had been quiet up to this point interjected on his behalf, "Why do we not let him tell us what happened in his own words, and then we can berate him if needed," she suggested with sympathy, as she looked at the cousin who she thought of as an older brother. "From what I can see, he has been berating himself far more than any of us can."

"Anne has the right of it," the Earl said, assessing his nephew, his voice an almost normal volume. "Tell us all, William."

Darcy did as his relations asked. He related the events without glossing over anything, giving them the absolute and unvarnished truth. When he was done, there was some pride evident as he declared that he would change and correct his behaviours. Though there was a little sympathy for him for having to live with the consequences of Lady Elizabeth's anger, they would not alleviate his suffering. He would have to do the work and fend for himself.

It was decided that his mother and sister would live with the Earl and Countess at Matlock House until there was a resolution to the self-made mess that Darcy was in.

Before he returned to Darcy House, his mother pulled him aside. "William, you know that I love you as much as any mother has ever loved a child, do you not?"

"I do, Mama," he replied with, almost choking on the emotion of love he too felt for her.

"As hard as this may be for you, it may also be one of the best things that will ever happen to you. It has saddened me to see how aloof, haughty, taciturn, and proud you have become." Lady Anne held up her hand to stop the protest that she could see coming. "Look at how you considered no one's council but your own, you even dismissed Richard's advice after that blackguard that your late father supported nearly stole my baby from me. I told you something that in the characters that Mrs. Younge presented did not seem right; that I felt that she was not a good person, that she was not some-

THE DUKE'S DAUGHTER PART 1

one to be trusted with my darling daughter, but you ignored even *me*. You just admitted that the Bingleys tried to tell you about who the family was in the neighbourhood, but you dismissed them before they could speak, sure that *you* could not be wrong.

"I know that your life has not been easy since my George went to God. You had to assume great responsibility at the age of one and twenty, which would have broken a lesser man. Yes, you are hunted relentlessly by debutantes and their mothers, and I know that you had some narrow escapes from attempted compromises, but that does not explain the arrogance and disdain that caused you to dismiss anyone who you thought was below you. You are the best master and landlord; you treat our servants and tenants with respect; why did you think that no others below you deserved the same respect?

"You remember how my sister Catherine used to behave?" Darcy Nodded. "You have long heard us discuss that her way was not the way to relate to people, yet for some reason I see that same behaviour in you. It has led you to think that treating others who you decided were below you with disdain was acceptable. Do you not see the contradiction in your behaviour?"

"It will not be easy, my darling boy," she reached up and cupped his cheek, "but I will pray for your success every day and hope that the man that your father and I always believed that you would become will finally be seen. I love you, William; and I will be here to talk to you whenever you need me, but this is something that you have to do for yourself. There is no one that can do it for you." He kissed his mother on each cheek, collected his outerwear from the butler, then slowly walked back to Darcy House.

'*Mama is right! How did I become like the old Aunt Catherine? Mayhap I picked the most off-putting persona I knew to emulate in order to protect and insulate myself? Yes Mother, I have a lot of work to do and I am the only one that can do it!*'

As soon as he had divested himself of his outerwear, he

went to the study to write an express to Richard to convey his well wishes.

8 November 1811
Darcy House, Grosvenor Square London

To my cousin and brother Richard,
At Matlock House earlier I was informed of your betrothal. I give thanks to God that my thoughtless actions did not harm you and your prospects with your betrothed. I wish you and my future cousin joy. Please pass my best wishes for the future on to Lady Jane.

I can only but beg your forgiveness again, with a promise to you on my honour that I will become a better man; one who is a gentleman in all ways. There is a long and hard road ahead of me, but I will not waiver.

Just know that if you ever need anything from me, you but have to ask it. If either you or Andrew wish to use Seaview or Lake View Cottages for your wedding trips, you are welcome to either or both of them for as long as you may wish.

With all of my best wishes for your future,
William

~~~~~~~/~~~~~~~

Colonel Richard Fitzwilliam felt sympathy for his cousin, but he knew that trying to intercede on his behalf would not help him; this was a lesson William would have to learn on his own, no matter how difficult the path he needed to follow. He was walking with his betrothed, following behind Andrew and Marie who were walking with Elizabeth and Tom in the early morning before they were all to break their fasts at Longbourn. The group was headed up to Oakham Mount to see the sun rise this morning after he had received two expresses, one from Darcy and one from his General. His commander had wished him well, informed him that he had all the paperwork for the Colonel's resignation from the army ready, and added that the only thing needed was his signature. The plan was for him to depart for Town early Monday morning to see the

General, sign the forms, and to make it known that his commission was for sale. He had sent an express to the family solicitor with an outline of items he wanted in the marriage settlement, so while he was there, he would review the draft. If, as he expected, all was acceptable, he would have final copies the next afternoon, meaning that he could return to Netherfield on Wednesday. He planned to go to Matlock House after he left the barracks to inform his parents of the proposed double wedding that would be on Friday the 17th day of January in the year 1812.

Lady Jane looked at the man she loved and could see that he was deep in thought. "You look far away Richard, is something troubling you?" she asked, concern for her beloved Richard was evident in the depths of her question.

"No, my love," he assured her as he covered her hand on his arm with his, "I was just cataloguing all of my tasks I need and hope to accomplish while I am in Town."

"That reminds me, Richard, Mama said to ask you to carry an invitation for your family to return with you. That way we might all celebrate our betrothal and plan the wedding together."

"Does her Grace…" Richard started, smiling warmly when his wife cut him off.

"Come now, Richard, you know Mama and Papa have told you that there is no need for the 'your Grace' when you address them or speak of them. In six weeks or less you will be their son. Papa prefers for you to call him Bennet and Mama said yesterday that she prefers Mother Bennet," she reminded him in a mild and playful censure.

"I will try to remember, my love. Then does *Mother Bennet* know that both of my Fitzwilliam aunts and their daughters are currently in residence at Matlock House?" he said with a mischievous smile on his face.

"Andrew had mentioned that to Mama, so she made sure to tell me to inform you that all of your family," she looked at him and was suddenly a little embarrassed as she clarified, "*at*

Matlock House, are very welcome."

"Do not worry, my love. William would not expect to be invited to a family affair that includes the Bennets. I must tell you this, though, William may have behaved in a reprehensible way in Meryton, and most especially toward Lizzy, but when he gives his word, it is his bond. When he says that he is committed to change and better himself, I would stake my life on it." Richard soothed.

"As long as she does not think that you are asking her to forgive him before she sees proof of his changing herself, you may want to share that information with Lizzy. You know how obdurate she can be, but I can tell you that she was shaken by his apology." Lady Jane collected her thoughts for a few seconds. "She could not imagine that one with such a character as she had sketched for him was willing to apologise and prostrate himself as he did, or to accept full responsibility for his actions with no excuses. She will not admit it, but she is much more impressed by my soon-to-be cousin than she wants to be, and she does find him more than tolerable to look at."

While the six stood on the top of Oakham Mount, a hill and not a mountain by any stretch of the imagination, Richard and Jane stood next to Lizzy and Tom Bennet. "I received an express from your favourite person with best wishes to Jane and me on our betrothal." Richard offered, as he smiled with amusement.

"I would expect no less; he is your cousin after all." Lady Elizabeth sniffed, trying to feign disdain.

"Liz-bear, you realise that in six weeks he will be your cousin too, do you not?" Tom Bennet, Marquess Birchington teased his sister.

"We do not have to see or like all of our *family*, Brother. If you are not careful, I will place you in that category along with Mr. Darcy!" she retorted with a playful smile.

"There are some things that I must tell you about *our* cousin, Lizzy. And before you berate me for trying to influence you to forgive him before you are ready, I am not. I just want you to have the information. What you do with it is up to you. Are you willing to listen?" Richard asked carefully, following his Jane's advice knowing that she would never want to cause harm and only bring peace to those she loved.

"Do you think me so unreasonable that I would not listen?" Lizzy frowned as she looked at each of her companions and saw the looks that they were sending her and blushed a little, 'Do not answer that! Yes, Richard, I will listen."

"Thank you for your condescension, Lady Elizabeth," he gave her a faux bow. "In his express, Darcy gave me his word of honour that he would do what he needed to in order to correct his faults and be a better man; the man that we who know and love him believe that he can be. Before you repeat the 'talk is cheap' refrain, there is something that you must know, and Andrew will verify the veracity of what I am about to say." Viscount Hilldale understood where his brother was going, and he nodded his agreement.

"Darcy has never lied in his life. When he gives his word of honour, I would stake my life on the truth of his statement. It may not be easy for him, and it may take him longer than he would like it to, but he *will* do it. He will make a real change, not offer hollow words to placate you or anyone else. The other thing is that I know of no one that is more loyal to those that he cares for. Yes, he had a big blind area regarding those that he feels are below him in consequence.

"The irony is that he is the best master and landlord. He will do anything, bear any expense, to help those who are dependent on him and Pemberley or his other estates. You could ask any of his servants at Darcy House or his estates, and they and any of the tenants would give him such a flaming character that you would be sceptical and wonder if they were coerced to speak of him so. Anyone who believed that would be dead wrong. I think it is because he knows that none of them would ever try to hunt him for their gain and that he can be himself with them that helps him lower his mask completely when he is around them.

"None of what I have recounted to you excuses his behaviour here, nor his insults to you and the family. All I hope is that it gives you an insight into the man behind the mask. I trust that the good man that we all know is inside of him makes an appearance; the one we see when he is relaxed and not uncomfortable in society.

"Lastly, he is very shy. Even without being an object to be hunted, he is not comfortable around people with whom he is not acquainted. Before you point it out, his upbringing as a gentleman should have governed his behaviour, his mother and father, and yes, my mother and father and our aunt Catherine tried to curb his pride. He is now faced with the truth of what he has become and that is what he has to correct."

"You have given me much to think on, Richard," Lady Elizabeth stated as she turned toward the east to watch the sun rise.

It was a cold but clear day with no wind. They could see their breath as they watched the spectacular pallet of colours God had chosen to paint the sunrise with on that day. Once it was above the horizon, the six headed down the path and walked back to Longbourn for some very welcome hot tea and coffee before they broke their fasts.

After the family had completed their meal, the two Fitzwilliams joined the Bennet men in the billiard room for some friendly competition. It was good that the younger men were all friends and soon to be brothers as all four were very competitive. It was a source of entertainment for Lord Thomas as he watched the younger men try to act as if they did not care when they lost to one of the others. After observing for a while, the Duke returned to his study to address estate business.

~~~~~~~/~~~~~~~

The following morning after his trusted valet had shaved him and helped him dress, Darcy broke his fast, then departed for his solicitor's office. he broke his fast then Darcy departed for his solicitor's office. The first thing on his list was to have a settlement drawn up as his Grace had suggested. He would then allow Mr. Harrison Steveton, Esq, his own solicitor, leak the terms of the settlement so it would soon be widely known that if he was forced to marry any lady against his will, thanks to a compromise, that this would be the *only* settlement that he would use. His sister already had protection that would not release her dowry without a match approved by both Darcy and Richard Fitzwilliam.

The Darcy's had used Steveton and Son since Darcy's late grandfather's day. Both his grandfather and his father before him had always arranged an appointment, but the current master of Pemberley and Darcy House would arrive when it was convenient for him and expect to be seen without 'lowering' himself with the effort of making an appointment. He rapped on the roof with his cane and told the driver to return him to Darcy House. If he was going to change, he needed to change all his high-handed actions and arrogant presumptions, starting with this one. A very surprised Killion opened the door for the master who asked him to have his messenger sent to the study. When the boy arrived in his study, he nervously wrung his cap as it was the first time ever being there. Normally, the butler would bring him messages and he would return answers to the same. Darcy had never mistreated a servant, but like requesting an appointment, talking directly with the young lad was another step he wanted to take.

"What is your name lad?"

"K-Kip B-B-Black, Master," The nervous boy stammered.

"Kip, please take this message to Mr. Steveton at Steveton and Son and wait for an answer. Do you know where that is?" Darcy asked with a warm smile.

"Y-yes master, I does," said the scared but pleasantly surprised boy.

"Good. When you return, please bring the answer directly to me." The boy backed out of the study offering the best bow that he was able to affect before he made his way to the mews where the cob that he used to deliver his missives was waiting, saddled and ready to go.

A flabbergasted, but pleased Mr. Harrison Steveton was staring at the message the Darcy House messenger had just handed him as if it were a bewildering bit of news. He asked the lad to wait in the hall and then asked his clerk to have his father join him in his office. When his father entered, he observed that his son looked as if he was trying to puzzle some great mystery.

"What is it, Harrison? You look truly perplexed?" His father asked, the concern unmistakable.

"In the five years since Mr. George Darcy's accident, how many times has his heir requested an appointment, rather than arrive unannounced and demand our attention?" he asked his father with all the warmth and love that he felt for the man.

"As far as my recollection goes, never. Why do you ask?" his father asked with no little curiosity.

"Because I just received this," he said quietly as he handed his father the missive. After reading the short note, the father was as amazed and as pleased as his son.

"Mayhap it is true that he ran afoul of Lady Elizabeth Bennet as has been rumoured, and she has set her family and their connections after him? Maybe Darcy is finally trying to become more like his late father?" the elder Steveton chuckled.

"I know not, Father. All we can do is pray that he is finally looking at the way that he treats others not wholly connected to himself. When you return to your office, please ask the lad waiting in the hall outside my office to come in." The solicitor wrote a reply he handed to the boy which indicated that if it did not conflict with another meeting on his schedule, Mr. Darcy had an *appointment* at three o'clock that afternoon. As he watched the lad leave his office, the younger Steveton could only shake his head in continued amazement. He had never thought to see such a day when the 'great' Fitzwilliam Darcy requested, not demanded, but *requested* an appointment.

~~~~~~~/~~~~~~~

The Bingley coach arrived at Longbourn ten minutes before the time that Mrs. Hurst and Miss Bingley had been invited to join the Bennet daughters. They were shown into a very elegant drawing room where the ladies were already seated. The Duke was in his study and the other four men were in the billiards room waiting for Bingley and Hurst to join them. The men bowed and were directed thither by a footman. The ladies curtsied to one another and then the five Bennet ladies joined the two arriving ladies and walked back outside. There were two huge coaches waiting for them, the most comfortable coaches the two sisters had ever seen, each with the coat of arms of the Duke of Hertfordshire emblazoned on the doors. The two sets of Bennet twins rode in the first carriage while the two awed sisters were joined by Lady Elizabeth in the second vehicle. When Mrs. Hurst enquired whether Mrs. Pierce and her sister Miss Lucas would meet them in Meryton, Lady Elizabeth informed them that Little Emma Pierce had a low fever and her mother and aunt were looking after her, so they had conveyed their regrets. The carriages were impressive from outside, but that was nothing to the comfort inside. To say that the conveyances were well sprung was an understatement.

'*If I had not taken Lady Anne's lessons and advice to heart, I would never have been here due to the offences I too may have given to Lady Elizabeth. I would have been jealous of her beauty, wealth, and position, and would more than likely have done or said something that would have ruined me in society just as Darcy had done.*' Miss Bingley was snapped out of her reverie as she heard Lady Elizabeth ask if she was well.

"You have my sincerest apology, Lady Elizabeth. I am well and was but wool-gathering. Did you ask me something?" She inquired, chagrined that she has not heard the question.

"It is no matter; we are all lost to our reveries from time to time. I asked how long your brother and Mr. Darcy have been friends." The lady repeated her question without any hint of censure in her voice.

"Charles met Mr. Darcy in his first year at Cambridge. You know that our roots are in trade, yes?" Caroline

expected the distaste at her admission that she often saw when members of the first circles heard that their money was from trade.

"I do know that, but you have to know that I, none of us, will judge you based on that fact. Consider Mr. Darcy, if you will. He is a member of the first circles, yet I prefer your company over his. Your late father was, and your brother is now, in partnership with Edward Gardiner of Gardiner and Associates, is that not so?" Lady Elizabeth stated more than asked.

"Why yes, your Ladyship, how do you know that?" asked a surprised Mrs. Hurst.

"Did you know that my dearest Papa was entrapped into marriage by a despicable woman who died bringing Jane and Marie into the world?" Elizabeth asked bluntly.

"N-no, we did not," replied a very shocked Caroline Bingley.

Lady Elizabeth proceeded to tell the sisters a shortened version of the actions of *that woman*. "So, you see, Uncle Edward and Aunt Maddie are Jane and Marie's uncle and aunt by blood, and the rest of us born to our Mama count them as the same. The solicitor that brokered your brother's lease, is husband to Uncle Edward's older sister. After we have been to see the modiste, we will stop at the Phillips' for tea." Elizabeth informed them.

It was barely a mile into Meryton, so before the conversation could continue the carriages pulled up in front of the nondescript storefront that the Bennets owned which was kept for the modiste's use when the Bennets were in residence. "We will speak later," Lady Elizabeth stated. It was not a question.

Madam Chantelle welcomed some of Madam Chambourg's most important clients into the shop. They had notified her that they would be joined by two additional ladies so there was tea service for seven already laid out. If the Bennets brought someone with them or recommended that the modiste accept them as clients, they were accepted without question. With one simple action that proved their characters to their benefit, Mrs. Hurst and Miss Bingley had gotten their names on the list of clients that they had believed was very far out of their reach.

~~~~~~~/~~~~~~~

In the billiard room the two Bennets and two Fitzwilliams were not happy. Bingley had beaten all commers and was the only one who was unbeaten that afternoon. The soon to be ex-colonel belatedly remembered that their banished cousin had told him Bingley was one of the best billiard players he had played against. Richard had thought that his cousin was exaggerating, but he was not. In fact, he may have understated Bingley's skill with a cue. Hurst had not bothered to check his amusement with the frustration exhibited by the other men. He had seen it many times before from others who thought that they could match his brother's skill.

Tired of being bested, the men retired to an unoccupied drawing room where Lord Tom rang for Hill to bring them some libations. None of the men present believed in drinking to excess, but a snifter of the best French brandy or a glass of port would not hurt anyone. Once Hill had poured each man his choice of drink, he bowed and left them.

"Tom and James," Richard Fitzwilliam looked at his future brothers, "I understand that you two threated William, that is Darcy, with being called out if it were not Illegal."

"You heard correctly, Richard," James answered for the brothers with bravado.

"You are very lucky that it is illegal." He stated plainly, inwardly amused at the sceptical look both young marquesses sported.

"Of what do you speak, Richard?" Lord Tom frowned.

"Have you not seen the fencing awards on the walls in the club at Cambridge, nor the same for pistol mastery that cover 06' to 08'?" Andrew jumped in.

"We have. I personally did not look too closely and not at

specific years, did you, Tom?" James asked, suspecting that he now knew whose name was on the awards.

"I did not, brother," Tom Bennet looked at the Fitzwilliam brothers expectantly, hoping they would answer the open question.

It was Bingley who supplied it, "For the three years that he was at Cambridge, Darcy was *unbeaten!* Since he has graduated, his skill has only improved. Whenever he is in Town, you can find him at Angelo's. Even among the masters there are few that can beat him. With a duelling pistol at twenty paces, there is none that can match him."

"I have been in the army for nigh on ten years, and I only wish that I could come close to his level of skill with both weapons," Richard told the now somewhat pale Bennet brothers. "You would have been safe. I am sure that as he was so mortified at his behaviour that had either of you actually challenged him, he would have deloped."

"You mean that his apology was genuine, he is a man of honour?" James asked, his pallor returning to normal.

"Yes!" All four non-Bennet men answered simultaneously.

"William has a lot of traits that he needs to examine, but he has never been lacking in honour or honesty. I know that Lizzy wants to see proof," Andrew told the group, "but his word is his bond. I have known him since he was born and he has never lied nor gone back on his word once given. I understand why he adopted the mask that he wears, but I do not condone the behaviour that he adopted with it. That is his cross to bear, and his alone."

The room was quiet for a little while as the two Bennets assimilated the information that had been shared. Both marquesses came to the realisation that if he could fix his behaviour, Fitzwilliam Darcy would be someone worth knowing.

~~~~~~~/~~~~~~~

Darcy was shown into the younger Mr. Steveton's office. The solicitor was already standing and waiting for his single biggest client. They bowed and shook hands then both men sat.

"How may I be of service to you today, sir?" the solicitor asked as he made himself comfortable behind his desk.

"Before I make my request, Steveton, I need to make an apology," Darcy lifted his hand to stop the protests that were about to be offered by the man, "Ever since I took over from my late father as master of Pemberley, I thought myself above following the rules of your business that every other client follows, norms that my late honoured father used to follow as well.

"Even though I knew full well that you asked each of your clients to set an appointment, I disregarded that rule. As if it were my exclusive due, I would walk in when it suited me and would then have the temerity to be peeved if you were not able to see me when I deemed it time to do so. I understand that you set up the system so that you can give each of your clients the attention that their concerns need. Please pass my apology on to your father as well and believe that from now on I will behave with the same courtesy to you as all of your other clients do," Darcy bowed his head to reinforce his apology. Of all his clients, this was the last one Steveton ever thought would make such an apology. That he would humble himself before one that many considered a tradesman in such a way left him speechless. Could it be that his father was correct, that the son was finally becoming more like his late father?

Steveton stood and offered Mr. Darcy his hand, "I thank you on behalf of Steveton and Son for that heartfelt and sincere apology, Mr. Darcy. We are here to serve you, sir, and I dare say that you will see that the service will be much improved when we have time scheduled that we know is yours and yours alone. If you notify us in general terms what it is you wish to meet about, then we can be that much more effective in our service to you. I am also now at your service, sir. Please proceed and let me know how I can be of assistance today."

"The Duke of Hertfordshire gave me some welcome advice

on how to stop the attempted compromises from ever being attempted again. He suggested that I draw up a marriage settlement based on these points," Darcy reached into his coat pocket and handed the solicitor a folder sheet of paper.

The solicitor read the suggestions over thrice and then looked at his client with a broad smile, "I would have to agree with his Grace, this would be enough to make anyone thinking of compromising you run in the opposite direction. I have just one question: how would they know that this is what awaits them?"

"That is where you come in," Darcy smirked slyly. "I want *you* to let it 'slip' that I have had you prepare this settlement and that it is on file to be used if anyone tried to entrap me into an unwanted marriage. Most of all, make sure that the precise amounts are known as well." He thought for a second and then proceeded, "It could be a good way to get new business as I am sure that I am not the only one that huntresses have targeted. I have no objection if you decide to use this as a template for others."

"I can think of no lady in polite society who would want to chance being saddled in a marriage with such a contract; it is brilliant. If her male protector fails to sign, then her intended victim would be free with his honour fully intact," Steveton whistled at the ingenuity of the settlement. He imagined that there was a reason that his Grace had come up with such a plan, but he was not about to ask why. "I will have a draft ready on Monday if you would like to return after the Sabbath."

Darcy told Steveton that the appointment was acceptable, shook his hand, and left. After Mr. Darcy had exited, Mr. Steveton, Senior entered his son's office from an interleading door. "Yes, my old friend George Darcy would be very happy if he could see that his son is finally ready to make the changes that will have the man that his father always knew he would be emerge."

CHAPTER 6

After what was unanimously considered a good afternoon at the modiste, the five Bennet ladies, Mrs. Hurst, and Miss Bingley presented themselves at the Phillips' residence for tea. Mrs. Hattie Phillips and her daughter Franny who would have her eighteenth birthday on December the fifth greeted them warmly. Franny had the colouring of her late grandmother, sandy blonde hair like her cousins but she had green eyes rather than the trademark blue eyes of the Gardiners. Their colour was a contribution from her father. Franny did not know that she shared a name with the one that her cousins, the Bennets, referred to as *that woman*. Her mother and father had never informed her of her late aunt's name, so she never had questioned that she was not named after her late grandmother. Graham Phillips, who was a little more than six years older than his sister, knew the story, but like the rest of the family, the dishonourable woman's name did not cross his lips.

Mrs. Phillips was the opposite of her late sister. She was intelligent and gentile. Selfish, vain, and a gossipmonger were not terms anyone could ascribe to her and still be truthful. She apologised that the visitors had missed her son Graham who had returned to London. Thanks to his Uncle, the Duke, he had been accepted as a clerk in the chambers of Norman and James at the Inn of Courts under the supervision of Sir Randolph Norman himself to continue his studies and to become a barrister. The son's desire to be a barrister was in no way a rejection of, or a feeling of superiority to, his father who encouraged him in his endeavours with no rancour or envy. Graham Phillips wanted to broaden his horizons and felt that it would be advantageous to do so in Town. His parents and sister were justifiably proud of the Phillips heir.

The ladies sat and partook of the proffered tea and treats. After tea was complete, Lady Elizabeth drew Miss Bingley to one side of her aunt's sitting room where she could continue the conversation that had been interrupted when the carriage stopped. Caroline was not deficient of understanding, so she had no doubt that the middle Bennet daughter wanted to ask about Mr. Darcy.

"We were interrupted when we arrived at the modiste. Do you remember the question that I asked that you did not have a chance to answer? If you are uncomfortable answering, I will understand. It is not my intent to force a confidence," Lady Elizabeth said as she reached out and gave Miss Bingley's hand a companionable squeeze to reassure her.

"I have no scruples about answering you, my Lady," Caroline paused to gather her memories. "When Charles went to Cambridge, Mr. Darcy was entering his final year at the university. As we discussed, our family is in trade and as I am sure that you know, not all members of the first circles are as accepting and gracious as yourselves and look down upon, even denigrate anyone not of their circle."

"Just like the proud and arrogant *Mr. Darcy* did here in Meryton!" Elizabeth spat his name out with no little asperity as she was reminded of his abhorrent behaviour, but then her attitude softened when she remembered that her rush to judgement was not without fault.

"As much as I hate to disagree with you, Lady Elizabeth..." that lady interjected before she could continue.

"I would like it if you would call me Elizabeth, or Lizzy as my family does, Miss Bingley," Lady Elizabeth requested.

Miss Bingley was shocked. A daughter of a duke had just given her permission to call her by her Christian name, and not just any daughter of a duke, the fearsome Lady Elizabeth Bennet! "It will be my honour La... I mean, Elizabeth. I will do so if you call me Caroline. Does anyone call you 'Eliza?'"

"Only one is permitted to use that variant of my name: Mrs. Charlotte Pierce, the former Miss Lucas that was. She has used Eliza as far back as I can remember, so no, other than Charlotte. When my Christian name is used, I only answer to Lizzy or Elizabeth."

With the subject of preferred names settled, Caroline continued the long-awaited answer to her new friend's question. "As I was saying, as much as I hesitate to contradict you, Lizzy, when Charles started at Cambridge he was bullied mercilessly by some lordlings and their friends... that is, until Mr. Darcy stepped in and stopped it. He stood up to members of his own circle and defended the son of a tradesman. He let it be known that anyone who took any liberties with my brother would be doing the same to himself and his cousins.

"Lord Hilldale and the Colonel, then a Lieutenant, had left Cambridge but on a visit when they met Charles, they let it be known that like their Cousin Darcy they extended their protection to my brother. No one was in doubt that the threat against anyone who bullied Charles extended to the years after Mr. Darcy completed his studies until the day that my brother left Cambridge. From that day on, Mr. Darcy and Charles became a very unlikely pair of good friends. Mr. Darcy taught my brother the way of a gentleman and helped him become less naïve, to examine the motives of those who wanted to befriend him and to be able to judge if their intentions were pure. Mr. Darcy gained an ebullient and outgoing friend, traits that I am sure that you have seen the man does not possess himself." Caroline smiled as she had long loved these traits in her own brother.

Lady Elizabeth Bennet was silent for a long while. Between what the Colonel had told her on Oakham Mount and with the information that her new friend was revealing about Mr. Darcy, her absolute surety that she had sketched his character accurately further waivered. "I do not understand, Caroline. We all saw how he behaved here, how everyone seemed to be below him, how rude, haughty, taciturn, and arrogant that he was. How do I reconcile that with the man that you are describing?"

"I understand your confusion, Lizzy, and had I not known what I do of the man, I too would not have an explanation," Caroline said.

"Please explain it to me, Caroline, as it seems like there are two different men," requested a confused lady, something that was wholly new for her. In the past, she had been very sure of her judgements, and now she had to start questioning her propensity to jump to conclusions based on a short interaction with people. Had her mother and father not recently told her that she should reserve judgement until she had more facts?

"In a way, I think that you are correct. There are, in some respects, two Mr. Darcys. Have you heard that he is the best landlord and master?" Elizabeth nodded, "I have seen it and can verify the veracity of that statement. With anyone that depends on him, or who want nothing from him like the members of the Ton do, he relaxes and removes his 'mask.' When he saw Charles suffering, I believe that his protective instincts, which are indeed very strong, kicked in. Charles wanted naught but friendship from him, so he relaxed and let my brother know the real man behind the façade.

"I know better than most how he is hunted for his wealth and property. I am chagrined to admit it, but I was one of the huntresses," Caroline appreciated the disbelieving look that her new friend gave her, so she continued. "Lizzy, I can tell without fear of contradiction that you would not have liked the person that I was at seventeen, when I was a guest at Pemberley for the first time.

"I went to Mrs. Havisham's seminary for girls in town. Louisa had been there before me and warned me about the treatment that I as a tradesman's daughter would receive. I did not heed her words. I was shocked when everything that my sister told me was proved to be correct. Rather than look at the behaviour of the horrid girls and learn to be better, I started to emulate them! Like them, I put on airs and graces and ran away from my Papa's background as fast and as far as I could. In my delusion, I convinced myself that I was a member of the Ton and started to look down my nose at anyone that I deemed below me, which were all except those of the first circles.

"But when I accompanied my brother to Pemberley for the first time? Oh, Lizzy, you have no idea what a magnificent estate it is. All I saw was the wealth of the owner and how such a marriage would take me away from the stench of trade. I set my cap at Mr. Darcy and had the temerity to put on airs as the mistress of the estate while Lady Anne Darcy, Mr. Darcy's mother, was still mistress.

"It was about a week after; as I was acting like it was a *fait accompli*, that Lady Anne *invited* me for a *tête-à-tête* in her private sitting room. In my delusion, I thought that she was about to endorse a match between myself and her son. The truth could not have been further from the truth, even had I imagined becoming a member of the royal family! I was so very wrong, Lizzy!" Caroline Bingley flushed red at the remembrance of how she used to be but continued her tale, no matter how mortifying it may be for her.

She took a deep, fortifying breath and picked up her tale again, "She started by giving me a set down like I had never before received. She made me see that I had been living a delusion that would *never* be realised. Lady Anne did not stop there; she pointed out that the only reason that I, my sister, and brother Hurst were at Pemberley at all was as family to a friend of the master. It was not I that had been invited thither, but Charles. The lady did not just take me to task, for a good few hours, we discussed the causes of my behaviour and she helped me see that my aping the terrible things that the girls at the seminary did, would never gain me any true friends. and that chasing after a man for no other reason than wealth and position made me the worst kind of fortune hunting social climber!

"Lady Anne asked me to be honest with myself. She made

me look at my interactions with her son, to see that the more I had tried to be agreeable to him, the more that I had tried to demonstrate what a perfect wife and hostess I would be, the more distant he became. That is when I saw his mask for the first time. When we had arrived, he was aimable and affable, not nearly as much so as Charles, but nothing like the man that you saw here. My hunting of him *in his own home* forced him to don the persona that he uses to ward off unwanted advances from women in London.

"It was through that first conversation, and many subsequent ones, with Lady Anne that I saw the person I was in danger of becoming for the first time. Lady Anne is a mentor to me; we maintain a correspondence to this day and I will be forever grateful to her as without her caring enough to take me to task, I would still be the person I was then becoming, and more than likely be much worse than I want to admit. I guarantee you, Lizzy, you would not have liked that lady!"

Lady Elizabeth Bennet sat in silence for a long moment as she assimilated the information Caroline Bingley had just shared with her. The story caused her to further waiver in her firm opinions and character sketching. Surely if Caroline could have changed as she had, then others, herself included, had the capacity to change and learn! She silently considered all Caroline had revealed.

"Why, Caroline, do you think that Mr. Darcy did not find out who was in the area before jumping to conclusions and treating the people of Meryton the way that he did?" Lady Elizabeth asked, her question not nearly as simple as it had been to ask.

"My belief is that it is part of the protective persona that he has adopted. The more he became hunted, the more attempts of a compromise made, the more he withdrew inside of himself, relying only on his own council. I think he decided that the only one that he could truly trust was himself, so once he believed that he was correct, he did not look for the possibility of being wrong. Have you met his aunt, Lady Catherine yet?"

"No, I have not, though Papa and Mama have. Oh, If the Fitz-williams accept my Mama's invitation then all of them, including Lady Anne and her daughter, and Lady Catherine, will be with us at Longbourn for a time." Lady Elizabeth smiled hopefully.

"It would please me to no end to see Lady Anne again, and her daughter Georgiana. The girl is fifteen, extremely shy; for some reason the last time I saw her she was much shyer than I remembered, but she is very accomplished on the piano-forte." Caroline Bingley paused as she remembered what she wanted to say. "Yes, Lady Catherine. The lady that you will meet is nothing like the one she used to be. She used to be very much like the woman I was destined to become, multiplied by many times and with the confidence of rank. The same person that helped me see that there was a better way did the same with her sister, and, with assistance from her brother, it is now pleasant, most of the time, to be in the great lady's company.

"From what I now see, as part of his protective mask, Mr. Darcy began to behave in the most off-putting way that he could. On top of everything else, I saw a great sadness in Mr. Darcy which I had never seen before when he joined us here at Netherfield," Caroline concluded.

After the apology made in her Papa's study, Lady Elizabeth knew the source of his sadness, but as she did not have leave to share what they had been told, she said nothing on that score. "Do you believe that I was too harsh in my reaction to Mr. Darcy?"

"In truth, no, I do not." Caroline agreed and Elizabeth's eye-brows arched as she had not expected to hear that answer. "He needed a shock that would make him look at the man he was becoming. While I know that I will never be his wife, the way he was before you took him to task would have made him unmarriageable except to those who only wanted his fortune. Lady Anne shared that she will support her children in their chosen partners only as long as there is the deepest love and mutual respect between them."

"That is the Bennet credo as far as matches go, and why my oldest sisters did not become betrothed until the age of four and twenty." Elizabeth smiled warmly.

"He needs to feel the disapprobation toward his former behaviour. I am confident that the Mr. Darcy that I first saw at Pemberley, the one that took Charles under his wing, will be the one that rises from the ashes like a phoenix. It must not be too easy for him, and he does need to feel the weight of his past behaviour, but he *will* succeed. He gave his word, and once he had done so his honour was engaged, and he will not stop until he attains the goals that he has set for himself." Caroline nodded at Elizabeth to show she believed her words.

'*It seems that I need to look at myself as well,*' Elizabeth Bennet, told herself, '*Is not my quick temper and even quicker judgement a fault as was the pride and arrogance I saw in Mr. Darcy? Unless I want to become a hypocrite, I too need to make some changes.*' With that resolve taken, she turned to her new friend and took her hands in her own.

"I understand that what you have told me, especially about yourself, has not been easy, and that makes me appreciate it even more. You have given me much to consider about Mr. Darcy, but I am glad that you have confirmed that he is a man of honour. The best thing is that I have a new friend close to my own age in the neighbourhood, and for that I am very grateful." She squeezed Caroline's hand to emphasise her statement. A tear ran down that lady's cheek at gaining Lady Elizabeth as a friend, something that she would not have imagined in her wildest dreams.

~~~~~~~/~~~~~~~

George Wickham needed to get out of London as soon as was possible. He was being hunted by the father of one of his conquests, and his many had become unmanageable, so much so that he could not keep his lies straight any longer. Withers, known as Scar Face, who was the *Spaniard's* man, was after him, and Wickham knew that he would end up in the Thames if he could not pay in full. If only that prig Darcy had not spoilt his plans in Ramsgate, he would have thirty thousand at his disposal. The sad truth was that Wickham lied to himself as much as he did with others. He conveniently forgot that even if the scheme that his paramour had assisted with had succeeded, thanks to the restrictions on the Miss Darcy's dowry, he would not have received a single penny. Wickham had only twenty pounds left to his name and was at a loss as to what his next move would be when he spied an advert in a discarded newspaper from that day.

'*The Derbyshire Militia is seeking honourable Derbyshire men to become gentlemen officers and join its ranks. If you would like to serve King and country, please report to the Inn in Meryton, Hertfordshire on Wednesday, 13 November, 1811 at midday. A commission for an Ensign costs ten pounds; Lieutenant, twenty pounds; ...*'

He stopped reading due to the restriction of his funds. As much as his ego would have preferred a higher rank, with the twenty pounds he had, he had enough money to purchase the ensign's commission and still have a reasonable amount left over to live on until he could win some at cards from the unsuspecting dupes he would encounter in the militia. With a plan in place, Wickham hired a horse and rode toward Hertfordshire. Twelve miles outside of London he found a nondescript inn away from the main road where he was unknown. He paid for a room until the following Wednesday morning. As much as he hated to pay for himself, he knew that he needed to keep a low profile to avoid coming to the notice of anyone who may remember him and tell the wrong people if they searched this far from Town for him.

He kept to himself, did not meddle with any girls or women as was his wont, and refrained from joining any games of chance. He needed to be another nameless, faceless traveller. As a further precaution he had signed in using the name 'John Smith'. He would have liked to use his nemesis Darcy's name, but he knew that those seeking him would recognise that name and associate it with him. He was not going through all of this to be caught while trying to blacken his nemesis's name.

~~~~~~~/~~~~~~~

After Church on Sunday, where he got many looks of disdain and few that were willing to greet him, Darcy was sitting in his study at Darcy House determined that the next person that he needed to talk was his mother, again, after everything that she had been through, he needed to make this right, not just for her but for himself. He thought back to the near miracle that had kept his mother with them rather than passing as they had expected after she had given life to Georgie.

Lady Anne's first confinement resulted in the birth to her son Fitzwilliam Alexander Darcy, who, to ease confusion with her Fitzwilliam nephews, was called William by all of the family. After giving birth to her beloved son, she had become with child five times, with only one surviving until birth. The first four had been miscarriages that ended between the second and fourth months. They were difficult losses that sent her into the depths of depression for many months while her body recovered slowly, though it was never fully to the state that she had been prior to the pregnancy. The last one was the hardest, she had carried the babe to term, and then the baby boy had been stillborn. The accoucheur who attended her along with his trainee, Mr. Frederick Gillham, could offer no medical reason so chalked it up to 'God's Will'.

At the time, both physicians and Pemberley's midwife had all agreed that Lady Anne should not increase again as they were concerned that she would not survive another pregnancy. Six months later, once she had recovered from the depression, George Darcy and his beloved wife had a furious argument. It was the first time that the almost ten-year-old William had ever heard his parents fight. In the end his Mama had carried her point and his parents had agreed that they would leave it up to God in His wisdom.

When young William was eleven his Mama had informed him that she was increasing again. As much as he was worried for his mother, he had been excited about having a sibling as his circle of people he could play with only included his cousins on occasion and the steward's son, George Wickham, who was a year younger. As his playmate got older, the more his devious and deceitful nature was exposed to the boys they played with, but he hid it well from Mr. Darcy, his godfather.

Lady Anne had carried her baby for eight- and one-half months, and unlike the previous time this baby was active, providing proof that he or she was alive multiple times each day, most especially when the expectant mother tried to sleep. She entered her confinement, and a month after his twelfth birthday his mama gifted young William with a beautiful baby sister who was a small copy of her mama.

As happy as he was to have a little sister, William Darcy was beset by worry. His father looked so very grave and he heard talk that his mama had lost too much blood then lapsed into unconsciousness. Less than four and twenty hours after she gave life to her daughter, Lady Anne had a raging fever. The bleeding had ceased, but the physicians were concerned that she would be too weak to fight the infection after all the blood she had lost. The fever ravaged her for three days and Mr. Darcy had been prepared by the medical men that it was only a matter of time until she succumbed. That night, when it seemed that she was getting weaker by the minute, George Darcy had impulsively marched into the nursery and picked up his sleeping daughter. He was determined that his beloved wife would feel the presence of the life that she sacrificed so much to bring into the world before she was called home to God.

The baby, not yet named, woke as he placed her next to her ailing mama, and started to squall indignantly at being disturbed. For whatever reason, one they all attributed to a miracle from God, his wife's breathing started to gain some strength and that night the fever broke. She woke the next day begging for two things: water and to see her child. Young William, who had never seen his father cry before, watched as his Papa wept openly and unashamedly while he offered prayers of thanks to God *for bringing his beloved Anne back to him.*

The fever had broken when she awoke and his mama had gained strength every day from then on. They had named his sister Georgiana, combining the names of both of her parents. Two months later, Lady Anne Darcy was fully recovered, hale and healthy as she was before the miscarriages and stillborn birth.

Darcy would not fail to appreciate the gift from God that was his mother's presence with them, and he would never again reject her council out of hand. He had to become the man that both of his parents, indeed, all his family, would be proud of once again.

He was admitted to Matlock House by the butler. After he had greeted the family who were relaxing in the family sitting room, he asked for a private meeting with his mother. Once they were seated in the sitting room attached to her suite, Lady Anne addressed the drawn look on her son. "You asked to meet with me, William." Lady Anne sat back and waited for her son to speak.

"I have been such a fool, mother," Darcy started, and the lady's eyebrows arched as this apology was not what she had expected from her son, who had allowed pride and his judgment to overrule good sense too many times. "I must offer my deepest apologies. I have been behaving like a man who neither you nor my late, honoured father could have been proud."

"It is true that I have not been happy with your behaviour, William. To tell the truth, the way you have behaved toward those you deem below you who are not your family, friends, or dependants, has disappointed me greatly many times, but I have never stopped loving you as my son." Lady Anne agreed.

"Never have I doubted your love, Mama, no matter how unworthy of it I at times have been." He kissed his mother on both cheeks. "I had forgotten that your being with us today is a gift from God which I have been squandering. Well, no more! This is my oath as a Darcy and as a gentleman. At first, I was indignant at the reproofs that Lady Elizabeth flung at my door; but once I saw through my wounded pride and considered her words honestly, I saw them for what they are. They were nothing but the truth.

"Church today was the first time that I experienced the extent of the Bennet's reach. Those that would normally fawn all over me would barely acknowledge me and the rest did not even look at me," Lady Anne's son said, looking like her lost little boy from years ago.

"I know that the man both your beloved, late father and I believed you to be is inside of you begging to be released. In the steps that you have started taking, you are on a path that will lead you to where you *need* to go. As I said, I always loved you, but I did not always like the man that you had started to become. My prayer to God is that you are able to recover yourself, much as I did when everyone thought that all was lost." As his mother looked at him to see the depths of his soul, he was as certain as he was that he would draw his next breath that he would be the man that she and the rest of the world would be proud of.

"It shames me how I dismissed your feelings about Mrs. Younge. If I had but listened, then Georgie..." Lady Anne cut her son off before he disappeared down the deep and dark rabbit hole of self-recrimination.

"William, look at me, Son," she asked gently. Darcy raised his eyes to meet her cerulean orbs, the very eye colour that all three living Darcys had in common, the one that now looked back at him with all the compassion at her disposal, "if you self-flagellate from now until the second coming, will it change anything that had happened?"

"No, Mama, it will not," he agreed, knowing that she spoke the truth.

"I will not sit before you and tell you to forget the past. That would be an error as well. What I will tell you is to remember the past and learn from it. What is, is. It is only when we refuse to learn and grow that we are destined to repeat the mistakes of the past repeatedly." She again squeezed his hand. "What good would that be to anyone if we only remonstrated about the past and did not learn from it? Let me ask you a question, William. When you and Richard retained Mrs. Annesley, did you make a snap decision, or did you verify her characters *ad nauseum*?"

"Yes, Mama, we did the latter," the son smiled for the first time during this interview with his mother.

"If you were not able to learn, William, then rather than making sure that you did not repeat the same errors in every way that you could, you would not have checked, rechecked, then rechecked her characters again. That is exactly what I mean by learning, changing, and growing. You have made errors in your management of Pemberley have you not?" She challenged with a gentle smile.

"You know I have, Mama. Both you and Mr. Chalmers have seen me make errors." A truly chagrined Darcy admitted as he thought about an error he had made just after his dear father passed where he almost cost the estate the spring planting.

"How many times did you repeat said errors, my son?" His mother challenged him to think.

"As far as I know, Mama, never," he recalled as he smiled again because he could see what his mother was trying to teach him.

"Exactly, because you have the capacity to learn and change. You are one of the most intelligent men that I know, William. Because I have seen your capacity to change once you recognise the error of your ways, there is no doubt in my mind that you will be able to do the same in this case. It will not be easy, and I feel that Lady Elizabeth highlighting your relative insignificance in our world will only serve you in good stead. You my dearest and favourite son..." she smiled sweetly.

"I am your *only* son, Mama," he interrupted with his first genuine smile in a while, one that showed his dimples.

"As I was saying, Lady Elizabeth humbling you the way that she did will, I sincerely believe, be the making of you as a man, William. She has not made it easy for you, and she has forced you to look in the mirror at yourself with a critical eye. She

THE DUKE'S DAUGHTER PART 1

has done you and all who love you a great service, my son, who I love with all of my maternal power." As the relief flooded through him, seeing the rectitude of his mother's words, Fitzwilliam Darcy, master of Pemberley, Darcy House and three other estates, wept in his mother's arms for the first time since he had been a young lad as he released the tension that had been building inside of him for a long time.

He thanked God again, as he did every day, sometimes multiple times, that He had not taken her after Georgie was born. Once he was done and had put himself to rights, he offered his mother his arm and they repaired to the family sitting room to join the rest of the Fitzwilliams, de Bourghs, and his sister, Georgiana. Darcy made a very sincere and heartfelt apology to all present and was granted the same unqualified forgiveness by the rest of his family as his dear mother had. His young sister hugged him tightly and again tried to beg his forgiveness for her part in the Ramsgate debacle. Darcy quietly offered his sister the same advice that he had just received from their mother, to learn from but not live in the past.

"Richard and Andrew will be home on the morrow," Lord Reginald Fitzwilliam, the Earl of Matlock informed his nephew. Like his younger sister, he believed that his favourite, if only, nephew had turned a corner and things would be much better going forward.

"That will be perfect, I need to talk to them. I wrote to Richard wishing him joy on his betrothal to Lady Jane, but I would like to wish him thus in person," Darcy informed his uncle.

"The news of my Richard's betrothal is excellent news, but even better is that he has informed his commanding general that he is resigning from the Army and will sell out of his commission while he is in town organising the settlement," an incredibly happy and greatly relieved Lady Elaine Fitzwilliam, Countess of Matlock reported.

Before Darcy could respond with joy, his Aunt Catherine remonstrated him. "Your behaviour could have cost Richard his love, and you could have caused Andrew and Richard to lose ladies with dowries of one hundred five and twenty thousand *pounds* each!" she huffed but was not done, "not to mention that they are cousins to the royals!"

"Catherine," Lady Anne intervened as she could always calm her older sister, "no harm was done, and the important thing is that Andrew and Richard are marrying women that they love and respect. That would have been enough had they been daughters of a poor country squire and their dowries were but one thousand each!" She looked at her sister, daring her to gainsay her words which Lady Catherine did not.

"Richard will not have to go back to the war!" Miss Darcy, who even before Ramsgate, did not speak much unless spoken to, exclaimed, then remembering herself, she clapped her hand over her mouth.

"You are not the only one in the family who is excited, Georgie; we all are. If I were not so tired, I would stand and dance a jig," Lady Matlock said with a wink to her young niece. The image of the graceful Countess dancing a jig was enough for Georgiana to relax and smile.

"Speaking of settlements, there is a rumour going around that you have instructed Steveton to draw up an incredibly special one to be used should someone try to force you into an unwanted marriage. Is there truth to this?" Darcy's uncle asked, his grin the largest Darcy had seen in too long, directed at him alone.

"It is completely true, and it is a solution suggested by his Grace, the Duke of Hertfordshire, as much more elegant than my mask of doom." None present had ever believed they would hear him make sport of himself and so stared on in amazement. "Here Uncle," he withdrew a sheet from his pocket, "are my notes that I made when I met with the Duke to go eat my most humble pie." The Earl of Matlock took the paper from his nephew and after reading for a minute, he whistled as he passed the sheet onto the group of ladies who were looking on in question.

"No protector in his right mind would ever sign this, William!" Lord Reginald said with a guffaw that filled the room.

"That, my dear family, is the whole idea. Steveton will have the final copy ready for me to view tomorrow. After that, it will stay on file with him and will be the *only* settlement I offer to one who sinks low enough to entrap me," Darcy said with no little satisfaction.

"This is brilliant, William," Lady Catherine opined, "when we see his Grace at the wedding, I will have to thank him. Utterly brilliant!"

"What time do you expect them tomorrow, Uncle?" Darcy nodded at his aunt Catherine in agreement then refocused on his uncle.

"They will leave Hertfordshire early and are riding, so I would say that they will be here by nine in the morning, in time to break their fasts. Would you like to join in the morning, Nephew?" he offered. Darcy thanked his uncle for the invitation and gladly accepted it. As he walked back across the square to Darcy House, he felt lighter than he had in many years.

CHAPTER 7

Sunday evening, a very bored George Wickham almost gave into temptation to go find a piece of fluff and a card game. He just managed to stop himself as he was about to leave his room. *'This will all be worth it,'* he told himself. *'I will soon be able to charm the merchants out of everything I need, take as much money as I please from the simpletons in the militia, and when I am ready, I will escape and disappear. Mayhap I will go make my fortune in the Americas.'*

He had no idea how close to disaster he came. A man with a scar that ran the length of his left cheek, the very one known as *Scarface* who worked for an unsavoury man, the *Spaniard, whom* Wickham owed a large sum to, was at that moment canvassing the patrons of the same inn that he resided at. Withers' employer would not rest until he was paid in full or had Wickham's throat cut and his body dumped in the Thames. After three hours and no clue pointing to his quarry, the man set off, very unhappy that all traces of the man he was tasked with finding seemed to have evaporated.

~~~~~~~~/~~~~~~~~

Sunday evening the Netherfield party, the Phillips, including their son Graham who had come home to visit his parents Saturday afternoon, and the Pierces sans Emma and Paul, who were visiting their grandparents, aunts, and uncles at Lucas Lodge, arrived at Longbourn for an informal dinner. Once everyone had greeted one another with the prerequisite bows and curtsies, the younger men repaired to the billiard room while the younger ladies stayed in the drawing room with the Duke and his Duchess.

Graham Phillips had been born the same year as Tom Bennet and they were awfully close as friends and cousins, and not just in age. James too enjoyed spending time with his Phillips cousin. He was well known to both Fitzwilliam brothers and was soon chatting amiably with Charles Bingley and Harold Hurst after introductions had been made. He had heard that his cousin Lizzy had taken the Fitzwilliam's cousin to task about some atrocious behaviour. He was impressed that neither brother tried to make excuses for their cousin, saying that he made his bed and now had to lie in it.

In the drawing room Franny Phillips had not missed the way that Miss Bingley had looked at her brother. In the short time before the men left to the billiard room, she took note of the way that the lady had been appraising Graham with an admiring eye. Although not as beautiful as her Bennet cousins, Miss Bingley was a handsome, auburn-haired woman. From the impression that Miss Phillips had when the lady had visited her house with the cousins, she could tell that Miss Bingley was a genteel and pleasant lady. The fact that her roots were in trade was inconsequential for Franny, given that both her father and her uncle Gardiner were in trade as well. Franny decided that she wanted to get to know the Netherfield party better to determine if there was mutual attraction and affection, and, if things progressed, Miss Bingley would be worthy of her beloved brother.

Charlotte Pierce was sitting next to her friend, Lady Elizabeth. Their friendship had deepened when six years previously, Longbourn's vicar, Mr. Christopher Pierce had proposed to and married the then Miss Lucas. The Longbourn Church's parsonage was on the estate's grounds, so the two friends saw more rather than less of each other after Charlotte moved into her husband's house.

"Now, tell me Eliza, is that 'poor' Mr. Darcy still alive, or did you secretly slay him?" she half teased her friend.

"He is well and in Town, from what Andrew and Richard Fitzwilliam have informed us. He promised to correct his behaviour, and from all I have heard so far, he seems genuine in his desire to do so," Lady Elizabeth paused as she ordered her thoughts. "You know how hard it is for me to forgive, do you not?" Charlotte nodded her head, "It seems that Mr. Darcy is not the only one who needs to make some changes. I believe that I need to be more circumspect in sketching a character and not make such fast and irrevocable judgements. I have to learn to not let what happened to Mama and Papa all those years ago affect the way I react to things and colour my judgements."

"I am happy that you have reached this realisation on your own, Eliza. I love you as one of my best friends, even a sister of my heart, but I have long known that you are far too quick to make judgements. Knowing that nothing would change until you came to see things for yourself, I kept silent while hoping and praying you would come to the same conclusions." She gave her friend an encouraging look. "And while you may have been harsher than some would have been, the way that Mr. Darcy behaved while he was in the area deserved the strongest of reproofs, so I have no objection to your calling him to account. However, that you have come to the realisation that you need to be open to forgiving those who have wronged you is something that truly warms my heart."

Elizabeth appreciated that her friend Charlotte would always be honest and would not gloss over the truth or try and spare her younger friend's sensibilities. Charlotte began telling her friend Eliza how she missed her children, even though they would be home from Lucas Lodge on the morrow, when Hill announced that dinner was served. After he made the same announcement in the billiard room, the men joined the ladies to escort them into the dining room.

The married and betrothed couples sat as couples and the rest sat where there were open seats. Graham Phillips ended up next to Miss Bingley while his sister Franny was seated next to Mr. Bingley opposite them. Dinner conversation was as lively as usual in the Bennet household. The Duke and his Duchess smiled at each other from their ends of the table, for life had been good to them, particularly good. They had a wonderful family and their children, all seven of them, were kind, considerate, and honourable to a fault, just like their parents. It seemed that even Elizabeth was re-evaluating her propensity for quick judgement and anger, and if that were caused by her interactions with Mr. Darcy, her parents could not repine the result.

Miss Caroline Bingley felt like she had to pinch herself, that she was dreaming and would soon wake. She was seated at a table with a Duke, Duchess, two Marquesses, a Viscount and five Ladies! If she had imagined a scenario where she would be at dinner with peers, it would not have been this, not even in her wildest imaginings. She had hoped that the Bennets, when she met them, would at the very least not look down on them with disdain for their ties to trade. Certainly, routinely being in company with the family and having been invited to use Lady Elizabeth's Christian name was never a thought that had invaded her consciousness!

Graham Phillips was intrigued by the lady sitting to his right. She was very handsome. Her auburn hair tended toward red but suited her very well. She had light brown eyes and was a beautiful woman. She spoke well, seemed to be well read, and was not ashamed of her family and their roots. He had discovered by some subtle inquiries that Miss Bingley had a very generous dowry, but she was not of a vulgar bent to mention it or, heaven forbid, boast about it. She was not ashamed that they had a house on Gracechurch Street a few doors down from his Uncle Edward and Aunt Maddie and was considered a niece by the Gardiners. Yes, this was a lady that was worth getting to know; a woman worthy of being pleased. He was sorry that he would be returning to Town on the morrow, as he would have liked to further his acquaintance with the lady. At least he would have company on his ride. His soon to be Fitzwilliam cousins were returning to town, so they would ride together.

Caroline Bingley could not but notice the attention that

she was receiving from the younger Mr. Phillips, and it did not displease her. She was not attracted to his connection to the Bennets, nor that he would be a gentleman as a barrister. She felt warm when she looked at him, felt an attraction that to date she had never felt with any man before. She felt a stirring in her stomach that she could not explain, but it was a pleasant feeling of warmth all over that led her to blush becomingly.

"How long will your family be at Netherfield before you return to Town, Miss Bingley?" the object of her attraction asked.

"As we have been invited to Ladies Jane and Marie's wedding, I believe that unless business calls my brother to London beforehand, that it will be for the little season that we return, Mr. Phillips," Caroline replied demurely.

"It is good," he said as he gave her a meaningful glance that made the lady blush more than she had before, "that I will return at the end of next week and remain here until after the wedding. I enjoy my work in Town, but I find that there are many *attractions* in Meryton to draw me home."

Miss Bingley blushed scarlet at his statement, knowing full well that she was the attraction that he spoke of. "I am sure that *everyone* will be very happy to see you return Mr. Phillips." She surprised herself with her bold statement but felt that it was allowed after his.

Across the very same table Charles Bingley was forming an attraction to Miss Franny Phillips. She was not the typical 'angel' that he seemed to fall in love with so rapidly and then just as fast he was out of love with them. She had sandy blond hair and green eyes, vastly different from the bland, blond, blue-eyed ladies with willowy figures that he usually preferred. Miss Phillips had a fuller, but very pleasant figure. He knew that she would be turning eighteen very soon and would then be out in society. She was not vapid like most who had previously turned his head. She was an intelligent young lady, not unlike her cousin Lady Elizabeth, and he had learnt that she was well read and had good accomplishments. He had also learned that she had a respectable dowry, but none in her family was vulgar enough to discuss such matters in public. He decided that she was a woman worth getting to know, then they would determine if there was mutual affection and respect, rather than jumping into 'love' with an 'angel' as had been his propensity. No, this was a worthy lady, and so he would take his time to get to know her properly.

Like her younger sister, Mrs. Hurst was ruminating about how they, a son and daughters of a tradesman, were sitting in the dining room of a duke and duchess. *'If Caroline had not changed, I am not sure that I would have had the strength to do so. I, the older sister, used to follow Caroline's lead. I just did not have the energy or force of will needed to oppose her.*

'Whatever it was that Lady Anne said to her at Pemberley not only improved her life, but mine as well. I may not be on first name terms with Lady Elizabeth as Caroline is, but she and her family do not look down on us or disdain us for our roots. If ever there was a time to follow my little sister's lead it was when she made a change for the better. I can never repine how pleasant our life has been since.'

After dinner and after a brief separation of the sexes, the pianoforte was opened, and the harp placed next to it. Ladies Marie and Jane performed a duet first, the former on the ivory keys while the latter plucked the strings of the harp. The performance was excellent, but when Lady Elizabeth joined them in a song those who had not heard the Bennet sisters sing before thought that they were at the best performance they had ever had the pleasure of hearing. The voices of the three sisters blended in perfection, and when Lady Elizabeth had a solo, her mezzo soprano voice sounded like that of a herald angel. After the three completed the song, the applause was thunderous. Miss Bingley and Mrs. Hurst followed the Bennet sisters and did a very creditable job as they played a duet on the pianoforte. The sisters did not possess the same skill level of the Bennets, but their playing was heartily and sincerely applauded by all.

~~~~~~~/~~~~~~~

The Fitzwilliam brothers handed the reigns of their horses to the grooms waiting for them in front of Matlock House on Grosvenor Square. As they were about to enter the house, they saw their cousin William walking toward them.

"Good morning cousins," Darcy offered as he reached the waiting men, "this is good timing. Richard, I know I sent you a missive, but allow me to wish you joy. I am incredibly happy that my abhorrent behaviour in Meryton did not affect your relationship with *any* of the Bennets."

"We have forgiven you, William," his cousin Andrew informed him as he slapped his cousin playfully on his back. "Your harder task, a much harder one, is to earn Lizzy's forgiveness. She is not as quick to forgive as the rest of us."

Darcy looked chagrined, but it only increased his absolute resolution to become a better man, one who one and all would enjoy being with. "Do not worry so, William. I have informed Lady Elizabeth about you being an honourable man, and before we left Hertfordshire, I did detect a *slight* thawing in her attitude toward you," the Colonel informed him, giving him a sliver of hope.

The three men were welcomed into the breakfast parlour where the family was just sitting down with their plates filled from the bountiful offerings on the sideboard. The two Fitzwilliam sons shook their father's hand and kissed the cheek of each female relative ending with a kiss on each cheek for their mother. Darcy greeted all in a similar fashion with an especially warm hug and kiss for both Darcy ladies.

"I come bearing an invitation," Andrew informed the family with no preamble. "Their Graces have invited *all* of the family to join them at Longbourn so that the ladies may plan a double wedding." As he said this, he looked pointedly at his cousin William.

"As much as I appreciate the gesture, I must decline. This should be an enjoyable time for all of you, and until I have reached the level of amending my behaviour that I and *others* feel is acceptable, I will not be the one to cause any tension." He saw the approving looks of all his relations, except his baby sister, who did not look happy at his decision, "Once I have proven that I am worthy and a gentleman in all ways, it would be my pleasure to be in the Bennet's company again, if they so desire."

Lady Anne Darcy glowed with pride as she watched her son. This was the man that she had always dreamed of meeting. As a child he had been so much more affable and considerate of other's feelings. Lady Elizabeth may have very well been too severe on him, but Lady Anne could not repine what the lady had made her son acknowledge. Her set down had been the catalyst that her dearest son needed to put him on the path of self-discovery and character correction that he was now on.

Before her daughter could complain about her son's decision, Lady Anne looked at her son with the pride that only a mother could display without it seeming too much, "William, I believe that you have made a good decision. Like you, I hope and pray that it will not be long before you are seen for the man that I know you can be. I am so very proud to be your mother, my son."

The sentiment was echoed by all the adults at the table, causing Georgie to mute the protest that had been on the tip of her tongue. "When are we expected?" asked the Earl, "and will there be others visiting besides us?"

"On Friday morning, and her Grace, soon to be Mother Bennet, has issued invitations to her husband's brother and her own. I understand that the De Melvilles will bring their son and daughter, so Georgie," Richard looked at the girl that he was co-guardian of, "there will be several young ladies close to your age present. In addition, the Gardiners and their four children will be there, as will the Phillips family. I believe we will see a lot of the Bingleys and Hursts as they too have become somewhat friendly with the Bennets. And strangely enough, there seems to be true friendship between Lizzy and

Miss Bingley."

"W-who will be there?" Georgie asked timidly. As her daughter asked her question, the mother thought proudly of her protégé. Indeed, Miss Bingley had come far, and Lady Anne could not have been more pleased.

"Let me see," Richard continued, "there will be the Bennet twins, Ladies Mary and Catherine, called Kitty by friends and family," he winked at his aunt who playfully swatted her hand in his direction. "The twins are seventeen, Lady Loretta De Melville is just seventeen, and you will meet Miss Maria Lucas, who is newly sixteen and the sister of Mrs. Pierce, the wife of the clergyman who holds the livings at Longbourn and Meryton. So, sweetling, as you can see, there will be a good number of girls for you to meet and become friendly with."

"W-will they like me? W-what if they find out about my f-folly," she asked with her eyes on her slippers.

"They already know, Georgie," Andrew spoke gently. At her look of horror Andrew proceeded quickly, "William explained all to the Bennets when he informed them of the reasons that he was in a particularly bad mood the night of the assembly in Meryton."

"T-they will hate me," the sobbing girl cried.

"No, they will not, Georgie. In fact, they are looking forward to meeting you!" Richard countered her so abruptly that the crying girl looked up at Richard with disbelief. "They think that you were very brave to have informed William what was afoot. Yes, you did not observe propriety, but just as we do, they fully blame the blackguard and his paramour that manipulated a tender-hearted girl practically *half his age*." Seeing that his cousin was looking decidedly better, he added a little more as he would stake a substantial amount on being right. "I pity the wastrel if Lady Elizabeth ever meets him! The way that she took William to task will be *nothing* compared to the rage, and I dare say hate, that she feels for *that* man."

The last caused some laughter and a half smile from Georgie who had dried her tears. "T-they will accept me? They are looking forward to meeting me?" When she saw the nods of both Fitzwilliam brothers, she smiled her first genuine smile since Ramsgate and all in the room were choked up at the sight of it, because this meant their beloved Georgie was on the road to recovery. Lady Anne and the rest of the family who were invited to Longbourn could not wait to meet the 'fearsome' Lady Elizabeth Bennet. As soon as the family completed the meal, the Countess repaired to her study to compose an express to the Duchess of Hertfordshire accepting on behalf of all her family, adding her nephews' regrets that he was unable to defer the business that would keep him in Town.

Later that afternoon, the Earl, the Viscount, Darcy, and the now former colonel walked into Whites. The Fitzwilliams were greeted with warmth, but Darcy much less so. Once they were seated, they were approached by a particularly good friend of Andrew Fitzwilliam, Harold Smythe, the enigmatic and idiosyncratic Earl of Granville. Not one to blindly follow the mores of society, after greeting all the men with equal warmth, he sat down next to Darcy.

"Darcy, can you confirm the rumours that you have an iron-clad settlement in place in case anyone tries to force you into an unwanted marriage?" As Granville asked his question, all the surrounding men fell silent. Regardless of the message that for the moment Darcy was *persona non grata*, this was an answer the single men who had been hunted relentlessly wanted very much to hear.

"Not only will I happily confirm it, but I signed it before meeting my family at the club and it is now stored at Steveton and Son. I am anxious to see if any lady is dim-witted enough to test my resolve. If you would like one drawn up, please feel free to contact Mr. Steveton at his offices. He has my permission to show it to any gentleman who feels the need to protect himself in a similar fashion. The terms will be available for your perusal and he is more than willing to draw up one for any that ask for it," Darcy said, his amusement clear, which was as astounding to those present because before he would have answered gravely and with arrogance for having been questioned. If asked, he would have admitted that he was relieved that he had such a solution to ward off the huntresses.

"I will be making an appointment with Mr. Steveton as soon as he can accommodate me. Where did the idea come from?" the impressed Lord Granville asked, knowing the answer was one the growing crowd of listeners wanted to hear.

"That, your lordship, is confidential. If the source ever wants to be made known, that will be his prerogative, not mine." Darcy replied, out of respect for all involved, most particularly the duke.

One of the listeners forgot that he was not supposed to talk to Darcy and asked a question he wanted clarified. "It only settles five thousand on the lady, regardless of the dowry she brings? She forfeits her dowry and anything else to you irrevocably as your property? The rumour is that there is only five pounds of pin money a quarter, that she must pay all her expenses from this very pin money. Is this all true?"

"Yes, Mr. Barrington, those are some of the points in the settlement," Darcy confirmed, his smile a mile wide.

"Who would ever sign such a document on behalf of a woman under his protection?" asked the befuddled Harry Smythe.

"That, my Lord," Darcy answered with a glint in his eye, "is the point of the settlement. If the other side refuses to sign, then the gentleman is released with his honour intact." There were many nods of agreement from the listening crowd. Steveton and Son were inundated with appointment requests starting as soon as they opened the doors of their offices the next day, finding a line of messengers awaiting them with appointment requests, with Lord Granville's messenger first in the queue! It is safe to say that the firm of Steveton and Son had more work than they had ever had before.

~~~~~~~/~~~~~~~

At the inn twelve miles from Meryton one George Wickham was a bored man. Due to his decision to keep out of the public rooms and to himself, the *Spaniard's* man had left and moved on, looking in the opposite direction of which Wickham intended to go. He sat thinking about his life and how his misfortunes were always someone else's fault, but never his own.

'Only two more days and I will be free from this place. When I am established in the militia, I will be able to have as much entertainment as my heart desires! Stuck here in the middle of nowhere, me, George Wickham, in hiding! It is all Darcy's fault. If he had given me my due, I would not be in the straits that I am. He stole the living that my godfather meant for me to have all because of his jealousy that the old man preferred me to him. I will take care of Darcy as I did the old man.'

As he always did, Wickham constructed facts for the narrative he told himself and others. That he had refused to take orders and had received three thousand pounds in lieu of the living did not fit the image he wanted portrayed to gain the pity of others and the hatred of his nemesis, so it was conveniently forgotten. He also ignored the fact that he had received a one-thousand-pound legacy, which was less than he believed was his due, from old Mr. Darcy's will. He had left Pemberley that day with four thousand pounds, which he had managed to fritter away in less than two years, most of which was in the *Spaniard's* establishments. Also excised from his memory was the legal and binding documents that he signed which stated that he surrendered all claim to the Kympton living or any other living under Darcy's control in return for the pecuniary advantage that he had received that same day.

'Someone who was jealous of me told old Darcy that I had meddled with some of his servant girls. Who cares about servants? They are there to serve and I needed their service! The old man told me that he finally realised that I was not the man he thought and ordered me off Pemberley! How dare he? After all the time I put into making myself pleasing to him, he had the temerity to tell me that he would cut me from his will when his attorney was to visit him in a sennight.

'I could not allow that, so I waited until he took a ride, then frightened his horse in the forest. It could not have gone better. He was thrown and landed on a fallen trunk that snapped his neck. I do not allow people to cross me! And all that trouble for a measly one thousand pounds!

'I almost succeeded in getting the little mouse Georgiana to elope with me to gain her thirty thousand, which would have been a bargain of a price to take such a burden off his hands. Darcy should have been begging him to marry his sister so he would not have to deal with her simpering, but the prig arrived two days before and the mouse told him all. He owes me and I will find a way to get my revenge. Just you wait, Darcy! One day you will get all that you deserve.' Wickham scowled.

~~~~~~~/~~~~~~~

Tuesday evening found the Netherfield and Longbourn residents invited to Lucas Lodge, the home of Sir William and Lady Sarah Lucas. Although the knight was not the most intelligent of men, the Duke enjoyed his company. He was a very affable, ebullient, and social man who loved to repeat the story of his knighthood that he had received when he was the mayor of Meryton and had made a speech that had pleased King George. Mr. William Lucas had been summoned to St. James palace where he was christened Sir William Lucas. In a neighbourhood that had a duke, a duchess, two marquesses, and several ladies of elevated rank, the knighthood of Sir William was not of much interest to the population of the area, but as he was universally liked, no one ever pointed this out to him during his many recounting of the honour that he had received.

Once he had the knighthood bestowed on him by the King, Sir William decided that he was above being in trade any longer. He sold his store of all goods and purchased the small estate that was now named Lucas Lodge. If at the time he had exercised good sense, he would have asked his friend Edward Gardiner to help him invest and grow his capital. Unfortunately, as previously stated, good sense was not one of his attributes. The Lucas family was not destitute, but they were not well off and their situation could be described as genteel poverty. The Lucases had four children, the oldest Charlotte, thankfully married, and so no longer a burden on the family's stretched finances. There was also Frank, the Lucas heir, who was four and twenty, followed some years later by Maria, who was just sixteen, and lastly young John who was thirteen. Frank, whose full name was Franklin, against all the odds given his parents financial position, had attended Oxford and completed his studies with honours.

By some miracle, Oxford had been endowered with funds to help many sons of Meryton study, so Frank Lucas had been able to complete his education at no cost to his parents. What none of them knew was that the Bennets had made the donation to the school for the express purpose of making sure that Frank, and one day John, would be able to receive the gentleman's education that their father never did. Sir William did not begrudge the fact that his oldest son was far more educated than he himself and had handed the running of his small estate over to him some two years. The results had been incredibly positive for the whole of the family. Implementing new farming techniques that he had learnt about at Oxford, as well as others he had studied about, Frank Lucas had doubled Lucas Lodge's income after but a year. The jump was from seven hundred fifty to a little more than one thousand five hundred pounds, which to some may seem a pittance, but to the Lucas', it was an enormous sum.

As the family was used to living on far less, Frank Lucas, from that first year of the increased profits, took anything more than nine hundred pounds and invested it with Gardiner and Associates. In the year since he had invested the initial six hundred and five and twenty pounds, the value of their investment was climbing toward one thousand pounds. With his father's blessing, Frank intended to allow the funds to remain where they were to compound, and he would add anything above the number he set for each year. The Lucas family was by no means wealthy, but they were no longer so poor either. The Duke was incredibly happy that the investment he had made in the Lucas's education were bearing fruit.

The Colonel in command of the Derbyshire Militia was an invitee, as were three of his officers, Lieutenant Denny, and Captains Saunderson and Carter. They had come ahead of the main body of the officers and soldiers who would arrive on Thursday. The Colonel was expecting a few new officers to purchase commissions on the morrow as he had advertised in the London papers. The junior officers kept to themselves, somewhat intimidated by the Duke and his family. In the few days that they had been in town, they already knew to never cross Lady Elizabeth Bennet. Colonel Jackson Forster was talking to his host when Sir William mentioned that Lady Jane was recently betrothed to Colonel Fitzwilliam, and that her twin sister to Lord Andrew Fitzwilliam, Viscount Hilldale.

Colonel Forster excused himself from the host and gained the attention of Lady Jane Bennet, who was sitting with her sisters, Ladies Marie and Elizabeth, Mrs. Pierce, Mrs. Hurst and Miss Bingley. "Excuse me ladies, I just heard the most extraordinary thing." He looked at Lady Jane with amusement in his countenance, "Lady Jane, am I to understand that you have brought that scallywag Richard Fitzwilliam to heal?"

He saw the indignant looks on the ladies' faces and understood that his jest was not taken as such; somewhat afraid at the dark look being directed at him by Lady Elizabeth. "Before there is a misunderstanding, Richard Fitzwilliam and I are the best of friends. I was teasing, but I understand how what I said could be misconstrued if one did not know about the connection," the Colonel said as he inclined his head to the ladies who all visibly relaxed.

"In that case, as I can see you mean no harm to my betrothed, then yes, sir, I am Colonel Fitzwilliam's betrothed," Jane said with pleasure as the man she loved above all others filled her mind to the exclusion of all else for a moment.

"We met at Cambridge in our first year, both second sons

who needed to shift for themselves, although if I heard correctly my friend has resigned from the army and is now a landed gentleman in his own right."

"Your information is correct Colonel," Jane said, reassured as very few other than close confidants knew the truth of Richard's inheritance.

"I assume that you both joined the army after Cambridge?" Lady Elizabeth asked.

"You are correct, your ladyship. We both went into the regulars and gained field promotions; by the Battle of Buçaco I was a major and Fitzwilliam a captain." As the memories of the bloody battle in which he would have lost his life if it were not for his good friend washed over him, Forster shuddered just a little before continuing. "I know that he does not like to speak of it, but he was one of the heroes at Buçaco. I was seriously wounded, and he saved my life, and that of several others, including a Lieutenant General.

"He was himself wounded, and after he recovered, he was promoted to Lieutenant Colonel and I was declared unfit for the regulars, due to my wounds. Rather than leave the army, I asked to join the militia and was made colonel of the Derbyshire Militia and have been with them ever since."

"Richard, his brother Lord Andrew, the viscount, who is my betrothed," Lady Marie blushed as she thought about her beloved, "and the rest of the Fitzwilliam family will arrive at Longbourn on Friday around midday. Given the friendship between you, I am sure that Richard will wish to see you, Colonel Forster."

"That will be capital!" his whole face lit up and in seeing the genuine pleasure of the meeting on the colonel's face, even Elizabeth relaxed. Such an expression could hardly be fabricated. "I will be able to introduce him to my wife, Harriet, who will arrive in two days with the body of my unit. We married three years past and we have an almost two-year-old daughter, Matilda, who we call Mati," he said with obvious pride.

"When I write to Richard, I will let him know that you are here Colonel Forster." Jane smiled up at the man who obviously was genuine in his affection for her betrothed.

"Thank you, Lady Jane, it is much appreciated," the Colonel bowed to the ladies and returned to his officers.

CHAPTER 8

On Wednesday morning, George Wickham was up earlier than his wont. He packed his meagre belongings into his saddle bags then descended and made sure that he settled his account in full with the landlord. He wanted no one to have reason to remember him, and landlords always have an excellent memory about those who do not pay what they owe.

A half hour later he was on his way toward Meryton after casually informing the Landlord that he was going to London and then Leeds. He rode at a leisurely pace and arrived in the little market town about two hours later. He was early, so he went to the inn where the recruiters would be and ordered some food, as he had not yet broken his fast.

~~~~~~~/~~~~~~~

Since the rumours about the settlement that would be offered to one who entrapped him into marriage had been confirmed as fact, and he was certain of the effect of Lady Elizabeth's letters to her aunts, for the first time since he had been out in society Fitzwilliam Darcy was able to move about without the fear of being hunted. It was as liberating a feeling as he had ever felt. Several single bachelors who used to be hunted as relentlessly as he was had braved the disapproval of being seen talking to a *persona non grata* and thanked him sincerely for the trend that he had started; bestowing freedom for them to move in society with impunity and not having to worry about an attempted compromise.

As popular as he had become with single men of fortune, he had become much more unpopular with the huntresses and their matchmaking mamas and papas. At first those whose whole life revolved around marrying well, even if they needed to affect a compromise, rejected the rumours out of hand. It was not until the father of one woman who was interested in marrying the Earl of Granville, regardless of his thoughts on the matter, saw the settlement that he had to sign. His daughter publicly 'fell' into the Earl's arms with her dress magically ripped, for which he and his wife had been there to cry 'compromise' and demand that the Earl marry his shrew of a daughter. The Earl had said nary a word, except to hand the grasping father the card to his new solicitors, Steveton and Son.

When the man saw the settlement, and it was exactly as purported by the rumours, he refused to sign. He was told that he either sign the settlement or a document releasing the Earl with his honour intact, which he did with alacrity and practically ran out of the solicitor's office to the sounds of the Earl's rich laughter. As soon as the truth of the matter was confirmed, all huntresses and their handlers withdrew to lick their wounds, trying to divine new stratagems rather than attempting to be decent women that would attract a man for the right reasons.

Besides his changed attitude and the newfound respect that he afforded his solicitors, Mr. Darcy was exceedingly popular at Steveton and Son for the many new clients that had come to them due to the settlement. There was so much work that the older Mr. Steveton had added another solicitor and three clerks.

Mr. and Mrs. Killion, the butler and housekeeper at Darcy House, could not fathom the changes in their master. He had always treated them with respect and been caring of their needs, but he was also stoic, sometimes even taciturn. Now he seemed to smile more than not, and he looked much happier. The housekeeper felt that the change in the master was so extraordinary that she wrote about it to her fellow housekeeper at Pemberley, Mrs. Reynolds. Pemberley's housekeeper was in regular communication with the mistress and she had recently heard the tale from Lady Anne about the 'fearsome' Lady Elizabeth who took Master William to task, and the resulting emergence of the man that they always hoped that he would become. Mrs. Reynolds had been Pemberley's housekeeper since the young master was four, and before that she was under housekeeper for several years. The relationship between mistress and housekeeper was more of friends than employer and servant. There was never any impertinence and Mrs. Reynolds knew her place, but the two were remarkably close and Lady Anne knew that she could tell her housekeeper anything and that it would always remain in confidence.

The letter that Cheryl Killion received back assured her that all was well with the master, though it lacked any details of why Mrs. Reynolds knew it was so but informed her that what she was seeing was a positive not a negative. Darcy was waiting in his study for his uncle and male cousins to join him. When the butler announced the three Fitzwilliam men, the four repaired to the library. The butler bowed to the men, exited the library, and shut the doors.

"It seems that you have mitigated a lot of the damage to yourself in society with the abject adoration of many single members of the Ton," the Earl informed his nephew. "With the women who used to hunt wealthy bachelors, you are considered the devil himself." The four men laughed as they sipped their chosen drinks.

"My commission was purchased this morning, so all ties that bound me to the army are now cut," the newly minted Honourable Mr. Richard Fitzwilliam reported.

"Mother has never been happier," Andrew stated the truism.

"The same can be said for your aunts and female cousins Richard." Lord Matlock said in a gruff voice thick with emotion, "I include myself in the number happy that I never have to see you go into battle again."

"Me too," Darcy agreed with deeply felt relief and gratitude.

"And I," Andrew added, "thank God above that you came back to us in one piece after Buçaco. I am sure that Jane is ecstatic that she will not lose you to the army again."

"She is, very much so. In her letter today she informed me that that reprobate Forster is the commander of the militia that will be arriving in Meryton on the morrow. They will be encamped just outside of town until April, then they will move to the big camp at Brighton." Richard grinned as he teased about his friend in the same way as was done to him.

"Let us hope that they are all honourable officers," Lord Hilldale opined, "you know some of these militia officers are barely gentlemen, and some worse."

"I know that Forster does not stand for that kind. In fact, he makes all new officers sign a pledge of honour and woe to the man that breaks that agreement." Richard shuddered as he considered the punishment that Forster issued. "He is very skilled with the cat."

~~~~~~~/~~~~~~~

George Wickham strutted up to the table where the militia officers were seated. There were two men ahead of him and soon it was his turn. "Welcome Mr...."

"George Wickham, at your service, sir," Wickham gave the militia fool his most charming smile.

"Welcome, Mr. Wickham. I am Colonel Forster the unit commander, and this is my adjutant, Lieutenant Denny," the Colonel informed him as he indicated that Wickham should sit in the chair placed in front of the table where they sat. Wickham was somewhat apprehensive as he knew the Denny name from Lambton. He could only hope that this Denny did not know of his 'activities' in that area. He relaxed some when the adjutant did not react to his name.

"How may we help you, Mr. Wickham?" The Colonel asked professionally.

"I am here to join your unit, Colonel. I would like to purchase the rank of ensign." Wickham proffered the ten pounds to Forster.

"We welcome all, Mr. Wickham, but there are some things that I must tell you. If after you still want to join, then, as all gentlemen are, you will be welcome."

"I am here to join, so please, go-ahead sir." Wickham nodded once, thinking that the man was just overblowing his self-importance.

"My unit drills regularly. You can canvass any of my officers, so if you expect that your life will be strutting about in regimentals and attending balls and soirées, then this is not the place for you. There will be some society when one is off duty, but most of your time will not be so. I do not look with a kind eye on any man that breaks the code of conduct that each officer is required to sign prior to joining and receiving his commission. Any violations of the code will be met with severe punishment. I expect the highest level of professionalism from my officers." Forster paused so the man had time to assimilate what he had been told.

Wickham, who was used to lying, manipulating, and charming his way out of any situation, presumed, much like he always did, that the rules did not apply to him. "There is nothing you have said that discourages me, so I will sign the pledge and happily accept the commission in the Derbyshire Militia."

The blackguard signed, shook hands with the colonel and his adjutant, and was sent on his way to get fitted for his regimentals. Forster, who was a particularly good judge of character, did not get a good feeling from his new ensign. He decided to give him the benefit of the doubt but would have him watched.

As Wickham exited the inn and headed toward the camp where he would be issued his regimentals, he saw a carriage stop with a coat of arms that he did not recognise. A group of ladies exited the coach and entered a shop. He had never seen so much beauty in one place, and better than that? He could tell by the clothing and jewels that they were wealthy, very wealthy. If it were not for four huge footmen that watched the ladies like hawks, he would have approached them. As he walked toward the camp, he was almost salivating as he thought about how to charm one or more of the ladies into his bed. They seemed a little older than he preferred, but for that kind of wealth and beauty he would make exceptions.

As Lady Elizabeth and her sisters entered the modiste's store, Elizabeth who made it a point to be observant when she was off Bennet land most especially, turned and watched as the man that had leered at them continued on his path. Yes, she had said that she would try and reserve judgement, but that man made a cold shiver travel the length of her spine.

"Are you well, Lizzy?" Lady Mary asked her sister.

"I am, thank you, sister." She then turned to all four of her sisters "Did anyone of you see how that man was leering at us, or was I imagining things?"

"No, Lizzy, it was not your imagination. I, too, saw it," Marie agreed with her younger sister. "That is not a man who we want to know."

"Make sure that none of you venture out alone without at least *two* footmen, sisters," Lady Jane reminded them. All sisters nodded and agreed that they should mention the lecherous man to their parents.

The subject of their worry reported in and handed the Colonel's note to the men to issue him regimentals at the appropriate cost with the rank of ensign. He spied a captain he correctly guessed was part of the advance party. Once he was in uniform and looking very well in scarlet regimentals, he approached the Captain with his idea of a salute. Once he introduced himself, the man introduced himself as Captain Carter. With some subtle questions, Wickham learned the information that he craved. He had just seen the daughters of the Duke of Hertfordshire, who, if stories were to be believed, had dowries that made the mouse's look like a pittance.

On Thursday evening the Phillips' had a reception to welcome some of the officers, led by Colonel and Mrs. Forster. Harriet Forster was the oldest of four daughters, whose father was a country squire in Herefordshire with an entailed estate. When she was introduced to the Bennet daughters, they all laughed about the coincidence that her maiden name was

Benet but was spelled with one 'n'. The three oldest Bennet daughters looked at each other and smiled, as *hers* was the family that Mr. Darcy had assumed *theirs* to be. Mrs. Forster was a genteel lady who was between the oldest Bennet daughters and the middle daughter in age. She seemed to be a very sensible lady, one that the Bennets would not object to getting to know. The Duke and Duchess were sitting with Mr. and Mrs. Phillips, their discussion quiet and most amusing. All their sons had been invited to Netherfield to have dinner with Bingley and Hurst and so were not present. The three oldest were sitting with Charlotte, Miss Bingley, and Mrs. Hurst when Mrs. Forster approached them and asked if she could introduce a new ensign to them.

Before they looked at the man, Marie inclined her head in acquiescence. She immediately regretted her decision when she saw Lizzy staring at the man with disdain. It was the man from the street. The Bennet ladies signalled each other that they would wait and see what the man was about. "Ensign George Wickham, it is my pleasure to present Ladies Marie, Jane, and Elizabeth Bennet to you. Mrs. Pierce is the parson's wife, and finally, Mrs, Hurst and Miss Bingley of Netherfield. Ladies, I present Mr. George Wickham, the newest recruit in the Derbyshire Militia."

It was worse than she imagined. Lady Elizabeth was looking at a seducer of maidens, manipulator of young girls, leaver of debts, and all-round blackguard. She politely excused herself from the group and as unobtrusively as she could joined her parents, uncle, and aunt. She requested that her uncle ask the Colonel to join them. When he did, she spoke quietly so no one would hear her words outside of their small group. "Mama and Papa, do you remember the name of the blackguard that Mr. Darcy told us about?"

The Duke looked confused but answered, "Why, yes I do, George Wickham."

As soon as the Colonel heard the name, he almost yelled the name, but regulated himself just in time. "What is this man accused of?"

Between the Duke and his middle daughter, Forster was informed of the character of his new officer without mentioning Miss Darcy's name or anything that would identify the family. Lady Elizabeth then proposed a plan whereby she would mention something negative about Darcy in the debaucher's hearing and they would be able to gauge if he was the same man by his reaction. As she walked back to her group still being 'entertained' by Mr. Wickham, the Colonel quietly posted officers at each possible exit from the room.

As soon as the man took a break in his chatter, Lady Elizabeth asked, "You are from Derbyshire correct, Mr. Wickham?"

"Yes, my lady. I used to live in that county." He affected a sad mien.

"Do you know the Darcys, by any chance?" She inquired, and thankfully the rest of the ladies in her party did not ask any questions.

"W-why do y-you ask," he asked as his pallor changed to a shade of white.

"The disagreeable and rude man was here. He was run out of town," Lady Elizabeth laid it on thick to draw the man in.

'What luck! Darcy was here and they hate him. I will be able to garner much sympathy!' he told himself and then proceeded to unfold his version of events to the ladies. He was so enjoying himself that he did not notice that he was the only one talking and all were listening to him.

When he was done with what the Bennets knew to be pack of lies but for little kernels of truth here and there, Elizabeth drew him on a little more. "How despicable to ignore his father's wishes." The dastardly man looked incredibly sad and nodded his head in agreement. Just as he felt like it was all going his way, she pounced. "Ensign, you told us that your godfather put his desire that you receive the living in his will, did you not?" Thinking that he would garner more sympathy, he allowed that it was so. "Then why did you not seek legal redress?" she asked with feigned innocence.

His face fell as he tried to come up with a plausible excuse, "I did not want to harm the son in honour of my godfather."

Before he could spout any more contradictory lies, the lady with the finest eyes he had ever seen proceeded with her prosecution. "Could the reason be that you *refused* to take orders and were paid three thousand pounds then signed a *legal* document resigning all claim to the living in exchange for the pecuniary advantage that you received?"

"H-h-how could you..." he stammered, his mind reeling, and he could not fathom how the lady could have this knowledge.

"Not only that, but you also received an additional one-thousand-pound legacy from your godfather, leaving Pemberley with four thousand pounds. Please tell us how you wasted the money in two years and then wrote to Mr. Darcy demanding the living that you had no claim over?" She arched an eyebrow. "And 'Mr.' Wickham, pray tell us about all of the ruined maidens and debts that you have left around the country."

Wickham had no idea what had hit him, the chit knew all about him, but how, if she hated Darcy? To add insult to injury, she was *laughing* at him. He was about to lunge for her when he felt himself being gripped and restrained by two of the officers. The Colonel was about to speak when Lady Elizabeth told him one more thing.

"My sisters, the beautiful blond ladies here," she pointed at Ladies Jane and Marie, "are betrothed to the brothers Fitzwilliam. I understand that my soon-to-be brother, Richard, would like to *speak* to you." Wickham had been scared before, but now he was petrified. What he heard next from the Colonel would bring him pain, but at least he would be able to leave and be gone before Colonel Fitzwilliam got his hands on his person.

"You will be escorted to the camp where you will be stripped of your rank and you will not receive any returned money as stated in the Pledge of Honour that you signed. For untruths on said pledge, you will receive thirty lashes and be

sent on your way. Your name and description will be disseminated to all militia units, so I would not try to ply your lies
and manipulation with any of them if I were you," the terribly
angry colonel warned the dissipator.

Wickham was taken to the camp, stripped of his commission, then after his torso was made bare, he was bound
between two posts and flogged by the Colonel. He passed out
before the tenth lash was administered and soiled himself.
Later that night, he came to with his possessions unceremoniously dumped next to him. They had put salve on his wounds,
but he knew with the imminent arrival of the Fitzwilliams
that he needed to get away. He took his rented horse and somehow made it out of Hertfordshire. He found an inn and used
the rest of his funds to get a room for a week and have the
local apothecary attend him. Through the haze of his pain, he
had discovered one that he needed to revenge himself on and
hated more than Darcy. He made an oath that he would get his
revenge on Lady Elizabeth Bennet, come what may!

<center>~~~~~~~/~~~~~~~</center>

Fitzwilliam Darcy was happy that his mother and sister
would be joining him for dinner at Darcy House on Thursday.
It was very gratifying to see how happy his young sister was at
the prospect of meeting all the Bennets the next day. He knew
that no matter how disenchanted Lady Elizabeth had been
with him, she would never be unkind toward his sister. In
fact, he was certain that after his revelation of Ramsgate, that
the lady would be protective of Georgie, which could only be
counted as good for her self-esteem and self-confidence.

As he sat in the study waiting for them, he let his mind
drift back to the lady who had taken him to task. He knew, as
he was not blind, that the words that he had used to get Bingley to leave him be were the furthest from the truth he could
have possibly uttered. Not only was Lady Elizabeth handsome
enough to tempt him, but she was also, in fact, the most handsome woman of his acquaintance. Her older twin sisters were
what some would call classically beautiful, but Elizabeth, as

he thought of her, was magnificent. She had wavy, sometimes curly, raven coloured hair that he recalled had some lighter brown that you would only see when the sun hit it just so. Her eyes, those bewitching, fine eyes were hazel with green and gold. Depending on the lighting or the sun, her eyes could seem to be any one of those colours. The night that she had been so angry with him at the assembly they had looked green to him as they flashed at him in anger.

He knew that she was the first lady that he could ever have any kind of tender feelings for, and he knew without any having to tell him that his chance of ever winning her heart was tiny and to climb that mountain would take a lot of work. More work than he was putting into correcting his behaviour and the way that he related to those who he was not already acquainted with or seemed to be below him in society. He knew that he had made strides in his quest, something that he was doing for himself. It was important to him that Lady Elizabeth Bennet see for herself that he was not just 'paying lip service' as she had intimated. The changes he was making were not for her or anyone else, but for himself.

He heard the knocker and then the opening of the front door. As he hurried out of his domain to greet his ladies, Killion welcomed the mistress and Miss Darcy home. His sister flew into his arms and received a bear hug for her trouble, then he kissed his mother on both cheeks. Georgiana repaired to her chambers to find some things that she required and was followed by her companion, Mrs, Annesley. Mother and son walked into the study.

"I cannot remember seeing you look happier since before my George passed, William," his mother stated with obvious joy in her eyes.

"It is the best that I have felt in many a year, Mama. I feel as if a millstone has been lifted off my shoulders. Besides the work I am doing to banish the proud, arrogant, and taciturn man that I was, being able to be in society without the worry of being hunted like a fox is liberating," he agreed with a big smile on his face. "Did you hear that a woman attempted to compromise Lord Harry Smythe, the Earl of Granville, so he was the first to use what is now being called 'the Darcy Compromise Liberator?"

"We did hear that." Lady Anne laughed. "Andrew informed us, and he passed on that Granville is so appreciative, he would do anything for you."

"I do not need anything; peace of mind is enough." Darcy then recalled that he wanted to tell his mother something. "I leave for Pemberley on the morrow. It is just me and Carstens, so we will travel hard, and I will be home by Saturday evening."

"It may be for the best, William. I know that Richard would have wanted you to stand up with him, but he understands your position and respects you for what you are doing," Lady Anne agreed.

"I will be sad to miss both his and Andrew's wedding, Mama, but it *is* for the best. I will not chance myself taking attention away from the couples getting married. My plan is to return to town just after the weddings, and I understand that everyone except the newlyweds will be here by then."

"We will miss you at Christmastide, William," his mother stated softly as she held her son's hand.

"As I will miss you and Georgie, Mother," he promised as he held her hand tighter in return.

"I wish that you could find someone who could give you as much happiness as your father gave me," Lady Anne admitted.

"The funny thing is, I think that I have found the very lady, but whether she will ever see me as more than the proud, arrogant horse's behind that I was. We will have to see," he said wistfully.

"William are you referring to *Lady Elizabeth Bennet*," asked his astounded mother.

"Yes, Mama, I am. If I can get her to see the real man that I am, that I will be, then I may have a sliver of a chance to win her heart." William offered a rueful smile.

"From what I have heard of her from the Fitzwilliams, if you can climb the mountain that you will need to, she may be your perfect match." She smiled sadly, having little expectation of her hopes coming true, but hope she would as it would mean her son had a woman who would never be cowed by him, challenge him, and love him fiercely were he to win her.

CHAPTER 9

The Duke and Duchess had informed their family that Uncle Sed and Aunt Rose, and Uncle Cyril and Aunt Pricilla and their children had to attend a soiree in Town that day so they would only arrive on the morrow. The first to arrive on Friday morning were the Gardiners.

Edward Gardiner had met Miss Madeline Lambert in the market town of Lambton in Derbyshire, the daughter of the vicar of the local church. There had been an instant connection and it was not many months later that they had married. Along with their other family and friends, the Bennets had been at the wedding. The Bennets had stayed at Snowhaven, the Earl of Matlock's estate in Derbyshire. After their wedding trip, the Gardiners had moved into the house on Gracechurch Street near Gardiner and Associates' warehouses. Lilly was born two years after they wed, followed by Eddy, then May, and lastly was Peter.

The three younger children were the first to alight from the carriage and they ran to Tom and James Bennet, who were firm favourites, especially for the boys, and May loved to be picked up by her strong cousins and hugged tight. Lilly, who was approaching her thirteenth birthday and had just moved from the nursery to her own bedchamber, exited at a much more sedate pace, but like her siblings were overly excited to see her Bennet cousins, especially Elizabeth. After greetings were exchanged, the Gardiners were shown to their chambers in the family wing, and Miss Lilly Gardiner was well pleased that she too had a bedchamber and was not shown to the nursery like her siblings.

It was just before midday when four more carriages drew

to a halt in the circular drive at the entrance to Longbourn. The first two came to a stop under the large overhang that would protect one if there was precipitation. Two contained family while the last two held Miss Darcy's companion and the personal servants of the arriving party. Lord and Lady Matlock, and Lady Catherine and Anne alighted from the first conveyance, and they were followed by the Fitzwilliam brothers and Misses de Bourgh and Darcy. Lady Anne looked on with appreciation as Lady Elizabeth went to her timid daughter and immediately started to make her feel welcome and at ease.

After changing and washing from the road, the Fitzwilliams, Darcys, de Bourghs, and Gardiners joined everyone in the largest of the drawing rooms. While they were busy with their ablutions, the Netherfield party and the Phillips had arrived. Those who had not been introduced previously were presented to those that were unknown, and after a lot of bows and curtsies they all found seats as the Duchess rang for the butler to bring some pre-luncheon aperitifs.

With a small glass of sherry in hand, Lady Anne, who had been happy to see her protégé Miss Bingley so readily accepted by all, sat down next to Lady Elizabeth. "Lady Elizabeth, allow me to express my gratitude at the way that you welcomed my Georgie and put her at ease." She placed her hand on Elizabeth's arm to stay her response. "William told us that you all know about Ramsgate, so Georgie was very worried that she would be rejected because of her folly. She was still worried even after William reassured her. I can see how all your family accepts her with no judgement. That she is sitting with your younger sisters and participating in the conversation warms my mother's heart more than I can say."

"It was very easy for us, Lady Anne. She is but a fifteen-year-old girl, he is almost thirty. With the combined lies and manipulation by that man and the companion, Miss Darcy stood no chance. God's hand must have guided your son to arrive when he did to save his sister." Lady Elizabeth squeezed Lady Anne's hand in a show of understanding for what the mother had endured almost losing her daughter to such a rake. Just as she was about to let Lady Anne know about Wickham's comeuppance, there was a loud guffaw from the Earl of Matlock.

"Lady Elizabeth drew him in and then closed the trap? How I wish I had been there to see it," the Earl said with glee.

"Of what are you talking, Reggie?" Lady Catherine asked. Though she was reformed, she still liked to be part of any conversation.

"I was informing your brother of what had befallen that wastrel, George Wickham, but yesterday, Lady Catherine," the Duke explained.

"**Wickham is here?**" Richard Fitzwilliam bellowed then instantly apologised for raising his voice.

The Duke explained that the wastrel had departed with his tail between his legs the night before and shared what had happened the previous day. He went on to tell them about his punishment and expulsion from the militia. When Miss Darcy had heard her tormentor's name she had blanched. Seeing her discomfort, both Ladies Mary and Kitty had each taken a hand. By the end of the Duke's recitation, her pallor was restored, and she was feeling much better, wasting no sympathy for the pain that the seducer had suffered.

"I wish I had known that he was in the area," the former colonel growled. "As happy as I am that for once he had felt some consequences to his actions, the man will never accept that his own actions are the cause of all of his ills, and once he recovers, he will be hell bent on revenge." Richard was only sorry that he was not the one to be able to deliver the punishment that the blackguard so richly deserved. "I will go see that incompetent officer, Forster, on the morrow and see if he had an idea where Wickham slunk off to."

"We always have at least two footmen with us when we are away from home." Lady Jane informed her betrothed. "That should give anyone who tries to approach us pause. You have seen the size of the footmen Papa retains as bodyguards for us all."

Richard was mollified to some degree, but he also knew that angry men, especially ones such as Wickham, were never wise. He kept his concerns to himself, promising himself that he would do everything within his power to protect his beloved Jane. Luncheon was announced and would be held in the formal dining parlour. It was not a formal meal, but there were too many to comfortably sit in the family dining parlour.

At lunch, Lady Anne sat with Lady Elizabeth to her right and Miss Bingley on her left. "She leaned toward Miss Bingley, and in a soft voice that only that lady could here she asked, "Was my William as bad as I have been told while he resided in the area?" Miss Bingley simply nodded decisively.

'I need to have a conversation about this with Lady Elizabeth. Anyone who can cow and humble my son and leave him with a tendre for her is well worth knowing.' Lady Anne smiled to herself as she looked to her right with approval.

After the meal was completed, the two mothers of the betrothed individuals, along with the other matrons, met with the two couples in one of the smaller drawing rooms while the older men retired to the Duke's library for port, conversation, and chess. The younger men headed to the billiard room while the ladies, under the watchful eyes of footmen and companions, took a turn around the extensive park. The three younger Gardiners, to their supreme delight, were taken to have pony rides.

Once tea had been served in the drawing room where the couples were meeting with the ladies, the Duchess looked at them and then asked, "You are all sure that you want a double wedding? It is no hardship to plan two separate weddings if that is your desire." Lady Sarah paused and looked at both of her eldest daughters and their suitors again. "I want to make sure that you are not choosing this just to cause *less trouble*, because I can assure you that all we care about is what you genuinely want. It is your day or days, not ours."

The four had discussed their desire to have a double wedding extensively before the men had returned to town, so

Marie gave Jane an almost imperceptible nod, designating her very slightly older sister their representative. "I promise you that it *is* what we want. Marie and I have done most of the things that marked our progress from girls to women together, so we always spoke of a double wedding from the time that we became aware that was a possibility for us." Jane Bennet paused and looked at the brothers, "It is not only *our* desire, Richard and Andrew are the closest of brothers, so they have no objection to being married in a double wedding, either."

Elaine Fitzwilliam looked smug, "I told you that none of the four would ever do anything that they did not want to do. Lizzy is not the only strong willed one between our children." The Countess's tease produced some giggles from the ladies and wide smiles from both of her boys. Men, yes, but they would always be 'her boys'.

"Well, if that be the case," Sarah Bennet said with a smile, "let us plan a wedding." She looked at her soon to be sons-in-law and saw the looks of horror on their countenances at the thought of being trapped planning their nuptials, so she gave them the relief they so desired. "Andrew and Richard, go join my sons and the other young men in the billiard room; I dare say we will manage without you here." Neither man needed to be told again. Each kissed his betrothed's hand and could almost be accused of running out of the room. As the footman was closing the door after their rapid exit, they could hear laughter emanating from the room they had just escaped.

~~~~~~~/~~~~~~~

At an inn in Essex, George Wickham was writhing in pain. Not even when he had fallen from a horse as a lad at Pemberley and broken his arm had he experienced such excruciating, ever present pain from the welts and cuts on his back. The apothecary had given him more of the salve to stop infection and to try and ameliorate the pain, but it did little. The only way that he could sleep for any amount of time was after a dose of laudanum. When he slept, he dreamed of exacting his revenge and retribution on that Bennet woman. When he was awake wracked with pain, his vengeance, and the pleasure he would take in exacting it, were all that he could think about.

How had the woman taken him in like that? He was the one that did the deceiving, he was not supposed to be the deceived. To make matters worse for his bruised and wounded ego, she had *laughed* at him. He had never been so humiliated, and if that was not bad enough, he had been flogged, and it had cost him ten pounds! After paying the apothecary and for his room for a week, he barely had four pounds left. The only thing he could do with that was ride post back to London, to Edward Street and Mrs. Younge.

He knew that Karen Younge was not happy with him after their plans were spoiled by the arrival of the stuffed shirt in Ramsgate. Not only had they not realised the mouse's dowry, but she had been summarily dismissed without any further pay. With the little money that she had; she took the lease for a big house on Edward Street that she converted to a boarding house. She accepted anyone, even ladies of the night, some of whom plied their trade from their rooms. If she got a cut, Mrs. Younge had no scruples about what transpired under her roof.

Wickham knew that she was doing well for herself. She was certainly not flush with blunt, but she was making a profit which was far more than himself. So as soon as he was able to go to Edward Street and to Mrs. Younge's bed, he would go.

~~~~~~~/~~~~~~~

Early Saturday morning, before the sun made its presence known, Darcy was on his way to his beloved Pemberley. He was starting to feel like the new man that he was becoming. He would never be as affable and ebullient as Bingley or his cousin Richard, but he would be pleasant to be with, regardless of the status of the persons he was around. He was keen to talk to his good friend, Mr. Patrick Elliot, who was the rector who held the livings of Pemberley, Kympton and Lambton. Elliot would not mince words and always tell him the absolute truth as he saw it.

Yes, he was taught good principles, but he followed them in pride, arrogance, and conceit. All his hauteur has disappeared when Lady Elizabeth placed a mirror in front of him. That had forced Darcy to see himself through the eyes of another. The experience had showed him how insufficient were all his pretensions, that he was not yet the man he needed to be to please a woman worthy of being pleased. And Lady Elizabeth, Elizabeth deserved to be pleased.

The truth was that even with the drubbing that he had received at the tip of the rapier that was her sharp tongue, now with hindsight, he could see that she was angrier with him for his treatment of her friends and neighbours than with the way she was treated. His statement to Bingley had just been the last straw that had unleashed her temper against him, and what a magnificent woman she was.

The fact was he was sick of civility, of deference, of officious attention. He was disgusted with the women who were always speaking for, looking for, thinking of his approbation alone, and hunting him, and then if all else failed, attempting to force his hand. Lady Elizabeth roused and interested him because she was so unlike them. He could never hate her for taking him to task regardless of the pain that it had occasioned him. He had long owned that he had deserved everything that she had hurled at him, and he knew, whether she was willing to see it or not, that he was no longer that man.

Darcy felt so much at peace with the man that he was becoming that he easily did something that he almost never did in a carriage, he fell into a deep and restful slumber. Carstens, sitting on the rear facing seat, could scarce comprehend that the master was asleep and looking like he was no longer carrying the weight of the world on his shoulders.

~~~~~~~/~~~~~~~

On Saturday morning, rather than a gallop on the back of Mercury, Lady Elizabeth decided to take a ramble. The Netherfield party, which included the Fitzwilliam brothers as guests who, for propriety's sake, were not sleeping in the same house as their betrotheds, were invited to spend the afternoon. Elizabeth was sure that Andrew and Richard would not wait that long and would be at the house to break their fasts with the rest of the Longbourn residents. She would not wake Miss Jones, but Biggs and another mountain of a footman were waiting for her. As she walked past the small drawing room, she noticed that the door was half open and sitting within was Lady Anne Darcy.

"Good morning, Lady Anne. I see that I am not the only one who rises before the sun." Elizabeth smiled warmly at her.

"I trust that you had a restful night, Lady Elizabeth." The elder lady inclined her head to the younger.

"Rather than ride this morning, I am taking a walk. Would you like to join me?" Elizabeth offered.

"Yes, I would like a good walk. Will you wait while I repair to my chambers to prepare?" Lady Anne asked. Elizabeth nodded and seated herself while Lady Anne ascended the stairs on her way to her chambers.

It did not take Lady Anne long to return with her pelisse and warm gloves. Living in Derbyshire her whole life, the cold of winter did not daunt her, especially the milder winter in Hertfordshire. For the first ten minutes the ladies walked in companionable silence while the huge footman trailed them.

Elizabeth, looked to her companion, and opened the dialogue that she was sure they would need to have sooner or later. "Are you not angry at me for the way that I spoke to your son?"

"This may sound counter-intuitive, but I think you may have done him and his family the biggest of services, whether that was your intent or no," Lady Anne replied as she squeezed one of the younger woman's hands to prove truth to her words.

"From things that Richard and Caroline have shared with me about your son, it could be that I misjudged him somewhat. I will never be sorry that I took him to task for the behaviour that he displayed while he was briefly in the neighbourhood, however I may have been too severe in the punishment that I visited on him," she admitted to the man's mother.

"As much as I love him, he needed the blow that you delivered. After the tragedy that took my dearest George, William had all the responsibly of Pemberley, Darcy House, and our other estates thrust upon him when others of his age were enjoying a grand tour or some such thing. I have never told William this, but I do not believe that my George's death was an accident. Like his son and daughter, he was born in the saddle and one of the most accomplished riders that I have ever seen, William included. There was no proof to the contrary, even though there were signs of another horse close by. It could have meant anything as the family and many on the estate ride in the forests, but my suspicion is that his godson had a hand in his accident."

"*George Wickham*?! I thought that your husband protected him. Why would he want to hurt the man that was trying to secure his future?" Elizabeth was astounded by Lady Anne's suspicions.

"George did not know that I knew he was going to cut Wickham out of his will. His eyes had finally been opened when reports of his godson's meddling with maids and other servants reached him. I have never told another of my suspicions. William was in enough pain without my adding to it." A tear ran down Lady Anne's cheek as she spoke about her beloved husband that had been taken away from her and his children far too early.

"Enough maudlin thoughts, back to William," Lady Anne directed the conversation as she dabbed her eyes with a silk square. "You may have been severe on him, but in my opinion, he needed it. With the wealth and power that he commands, there are few who could make him feel the consequences of his behaviour. Do you know when I knew that the man that I believed he would always be was emerging?"

"I have no idea, when?" Elizabeth asked, offering an open smile.

"When he refused to join us on this visit and for the wedding. He left for Pemberley this morning where he will keep busy and then return to town for the little season after the wedding." Lady Anne returned her smile.

"From everything that I already heard, and with what you have added, I can tell that he is sincere in his quest to change his behaviour. I am more than willing to let it be known to my aunts, and through them the Ton, that your son is forgiven," Elizabeth agreed.

"I appreciate that you are willing to do this. You realise that just like William, you are changing too." Seeing the look of question on Elizabeth's countenance, Lady Anne clarified her statement, "You have been known for your implacable resentment and unwillingness to forgive once someone had offended you. Do you not see that you are changing and growing just like my William is?"

"It is hard to argue with your logic. How did you know that he was changing just because he declined the invitations to visit now and attend the weddings? That he was not just protecting his pride at having to face me again?" the younger lady challenged.

"It is simple, he put the needs of others ahead of his own. You may have heard that he has always been the best master and landlord?" Lady Elizabeth nodded to acknowledge that she had. "He was quite different with all of society, even his family. His needs and desires came first, and like you, he was very quick to judge and would rely on his own council above all others.

"His main concern was that his presence would in some way detract from the enjoyment of the rest of us. Rather than be selfish as he was in the past, he is becoming selfless. This may sound strange, and it is up to you to act as you see fit, but I would request that you leave things as they are until a week or two before the weddings." The ladies headed back toward the warmth of Longbourn, having had enough exercise for now. "As much as I love my son and wish that he were here, he needs to feel the full weight of his folly so that he will never be tempted to fall back into his old ways," Lady Anne added.

"Will he not be sad to be alone at Christmastide?" asked a concerned Lady Elizabeth.

"No, dear, he will not. The Fitzwilliams, de Bourghs, Georgie and I will arrive at Snowhaven a sennight prior to Christmas Eve. I will write to William to inform him so we will all be together for the holidays. We will leave before twelfth night to return to Longbourn for the final wedding preparations, and he will be at Darcy house a day or two after the wedding."

"Will Andrew and Richard spend the season with the family or here?" she inquired.

"Lady Elizabeth Bennet," Lady Anne playfully admonished her, "you are a highly intelligent young woman. Do you think that either of my nephews would agree to be separated from their betrotheds for a day, much less ten of them?"

"No, I do not suppose that they would," said a smiling Elizabeth, pleased to see Lady Anne had a similar sense of humour to hers.

As they entered the house and were divested of their outerwear, Lady Anne again turned to Lady Elizabeth. "I also want to thank you for befriending my protégé. I have spoken to her and your friendship means the world to her."

"Caroline is a pleasure to know. She was completely honest about who she used to be and your role in putting her on a good path. You could not have bestowed your friendship and advice on one that appreciates it more than she," Elizabeth replied with genuine warmth.

After their conversation that morning, Lady Elizabeth knew that she liked Lady Anne very well and Lady Anne knew that if her William could ever win her heart, Lady Elizabeth would be perfect for her son and the ideal sister and daughter-in-law. Her opinion of Fitzwilliam Darcy was shifting and he was no longer to be hated and despised. Her thoughts as she watched him leave her home returned to her. Elizabeth now fully believed that he was an honourable gentleman, and regardless of his prior behaviour, deserved the appellation 'gentleman'.

Later that morning the house party was completed when the Duke and Duchess of Bedford, and the Earl and Countess of Jersey and their son and daughter arrived. Longbourn was a large house, so even with over thirty guests in residence there were still many unused bed chambers. After they changed out of their travel attire, the Duke of Bedford joined his brother and the other older men in the library and were soon joined by their other brother-in-law, the Earl of Jersey.

When the men were comfortable with their selected libations in hand, Lord Sedgwick Bennet looked at his brother. "Did you hear that Granville used your settlement that you gifted to Darcy?"

"Yes," added Lord Jersey, "worked like a charm, it did."

"I must apologise, Hertfordshire. William told me that he got the idea from you and I forgot to mention that it saved Granville from an attempted entrapment."

"We had other things to discuss, Matlock, so as there would have been no occasion to think about it so there is nothing to forgive." Lord Reginald Fitzwilliam inclined his head to his host.

The three men who knew of the tale informed the rest and Lord Thomas Bennet felt a deep sense of satisfaction. As much as he hated the time that he had been married to *her*, it had given him Jane and Marie and now he was able to make the lives of many bachelors tolerable in society. He knew of the Earl of Granville, and when he saw him during the season, he would disclose the source of the settlement.

CHAPTER 10

George Wickham, still in pain but much improved compared to the days immediately following his flogging, sat in the dark and musty smelling living room of Mrs. Younge's boarding house on Edward Street. Karen Younge had first wanted to deny him entry as she was still peeved after his last scheme had gone so very wrong and she had ended up worse off than before. She had relented when he showed her the welts on his back from his flogging. At least they were closed now, so the threat of serious infection had passed. She had given him two cushions to place at his lower back so he would not lean back and add to the pain from his 'unjustified' punishment.

"Karen, I swear to you, we will be rich this time. The thirty thousand that we missed when the prig arrived is nothing compared to what we can get this time," Wickham cajoled as he gave his paramour his most charming smile.

"What is it this time, George? If you remember, the last time you had a 'cannot fail scheme,' it failed," she responded with not a little scepticism.

"We will get one hundred thousand this time!" he said with confidence, and as he usually did, he began to suck Mrs. Younge into his scheme. "Have you heard of the Duke of Hertfordshire?"

"Yes, I have. He is brother to the Duke of Bedford. Filthy rich family, but how will you get money from them? Do you have something on one of the dukes?" she asked, her interest peeked at the exorbitant amount that Wickham had mentioned.

Wickham proceeded to tell her about the daughter Lady

Elizabeth Bennet who needed to be humiliated and at the same time make their fortunes. Neither knew about the royal connection and that any attempt to harm a relative of the royals was treason, for which there was but one punishment. He needed time to recuperate and when he spoke about the season his accomplice confirmed that the Bennets were always in Town for the season.

Karen Younge was not lacking intelligence; she just could not resist the good-looking rake in her sitting room. "George, you said she is always escorted, how can you do this on your own?" She asked a very pertinent question.

"Once I am better healed, I will have to approach the *Spaniard*."

"He will kill you! Do you not owe him close to ten thousand?" asked a very worried Mrs. Younge.

"Yes Karen, I owe him money. Killing me will get him nothing. If he assists me, at little cost to himself, then he will receive double the amount that I owe him; trust me when I tell you that he will not give up the chance to receive such a sum."

"You know him better that I, but I agree that very few would turn down the chance to earn such a sum."

"I will ask him to allow his hunting dog, Victor Withers, help me. He came to the inn that I was staying at before I joined the militia." Wickham shuddered as he remembered how close Withers had come to catching him. He almost had not recognised it was him leaving the inn until he saw the scar in the moonlight.

~~~~~~~/~~~~~~~

It was a week before Christmas and there was a fresh layer of snow in Derbyshire. It had snowed for two days, but this day, although cold, was clear with little wind. Darcy looked out across the park from his study. He loved winter at Pemberley. Until the letter from Aunt Elaine had arrived a sennight previously, he was resigned to spending Christmas alone. He had been filled with happiness when he read the invitation and had responded affirmatively without delay. He would join the family, minus Andrew, and Richard, at Snowhaven in but two days' time. He would not be alone; he would be with his family. He would miss the brother of his heart, Richard, but he understood why he was staying. If he, too, had a Bennet daughter but days from the alter, he would not be willing to leave her side for so many days together.

His family had been invited to join the party at Longbourn, but they had demurred, and Darcy saw his mother's hand in the decision. In her letters she had told him how proud she was of him and had hinted that he would not be alone over Christmastide. He now understood her reasons for saying such and loved her even more for it.

Darcy had made significant changes here at Pemberley. His servants from his housekeeper, butler, and steward on down could not but help to notice the difference in the master. He had always been good to them, but not to those not dependent on him who he viewed as his social inferiors. Something had changed; and while they were not sure what it was, it was most welcome. Mr. Darcy had started accepting invitations to dinners and other gatherings in the neighbourhood with those who he had always refused to associate with before. In early December he had done something that he had not done since before his honoured father had passed; he attended an assembly in Lambton and from all reports, other than the first set, he danced almost every single one!

Cheryl Killion, wife to Darcy House's butler and the housekeeper of Darcy House, had written that something significant had happened that had caused the master to start behaving in a much more acceptable manner to all, not just his employees and tenants. Mrs. Killion had mentioned that she heard that it was somehow connected to one of the Bennet family, but she knew no more than that. Mrs. Hannah Reynolds would have loved to know what the catalyst for the change in the master, but she would not pry. She would not allow anyone under her to gossip about the family, and she held herself to that same standard. The master had rung for tea and the housekeeper delivered the tray to the study herself and prepared her master's tea, just the way he liked it.

She was about to leave when the master asked her to stay for a minute. "I was a very proud and arrogant man, was I not Mrs. Reynolds?"

This was the last question that Mrs. Reynolds had ever expected. She had been through so much with the family, the near death of Lady Anne, her master's accident, and much more. The three Darcys treated her almost like a member of the family when in private.

"Do I have your leave to speak freely, Master William?" she asked carefully. He nodded his consent, hoping that her opinion would not be too harsh. "Outside of Pemberley and Darcy House, I am afraid you were such, Master William. But why dwell in the past? I am one of many who has seen the changes in you, and all of them are positive. I see the man that we all hoped that you would become in the boy that used to be."

"Would it be an impertinence to ask what caused the introspection, Master William?" she asked quietly.

Darcy asked Mrs. Reynolds to sit and then shared the tale of his abhorrent behaviour in Hertfordshire, the set-down delivered by Lady Elizabeth Bennet, and the societal consequences that he was paying in the wake of his actions. Mrs. Reynolds did not respond as she absorbed all the additional information that she had just been told.

"That lady sounds like a spitfire, sir. She may have been too harsh in the consequences that she had wrought, but on the other hand, would you have changed like you have if there was little or no consequence?" She knew that she may have overstepped with the last question, so she held her breath as Darcy had an inscrutable look on his countenance while ruminating on her question.

"That was a fair question, Mrs. Reynolds, and I think we both know that answer. It is possible had there been no or hardly any consequence that I would have dismissed her charges and rationalised it in some way. She is magnificent, you know," he said with a wistful look.

It struck the housekeeper that her master had tender feelings for the lady. If he was able to redeem himself in her eyes, and if she were ever of a mind to reciprocate his feelings, was a whole other question.

The next day Darcy visited his friend Patrick Elliot, and his wife Emily, at the parsonage on Pemberley's grounds. Patrick invited his patron and friend into his study after Darcy had greeted his wife and their almost two-year-old daughter Grace.

Darcy unfolded the whole for his friend who after listing and thinking for a while, gave his friend the unvarnished truth as he saw it. "The lady's reaction may have been too harsh William, but" Elliot stayed his friend with his hand, "it is about time that someone had to gumption to call you out for your behaviour Darcy. You had become someone that I was not starting to recognise, and I cannot be anything but pleased that you have started to make corrections and emends for your former behaviour.

"God works in mysterious ways and I believe that He has sent you a message that you have been wise enough to heed. I am confident that once this Lady Elizabeth sees that you have made real change that she will forgive you fully.

"How is it that you have feelings for her now Darcy?"

"It is hard to explain Elliot, but besides the fact that she is a beauty, the passion and fire that I saw in her attracted me like no other. She did not care about *what* I had, just *who* I was as a man, what my character was. I am sure that she will never consider me as such, but if I could win her..." Darcy's speech faded as he thought about the lady as he seemed to be doing more and more. Not long after the men parted, and Darcy returned to the great house.

~~~~~~~/~~~~~~~

On the afternoon of Christmas Eve, the three elder Bennet sisters, two Bennet brothers, and their cousins Franny and Graham Phillips, were welcomed at Netherfield by Mr. and

Miss Bingley. By now the Netherfield ladies were on familiar terms with all the Bennet daughters and with Franny Phillips. Miss Bingley, as the hostess, received the arriving party in the drawing room. As soon as the Fitzwilliam brothers saw their betrotheds, they sat down next to their respective lady and were soon deep in conversation. Both couples were most excited with less than three weeks before their wedding. It did not take long for Bingley to find his way to the now eighteen-year-old Miss Phillips, who was officially out in society.

Graham Phillips took a seat next to the settee where Miss Bingley and Lady Elizabeth had settled, next to the end where the object of his affection was seated. Elizabeth did not miss the becoming blush that her friend displayed as he sat, nor the look of joy that both wore at the proximity to one to another. Louisa Hurst sat down next to Elizabeth, and her husband and the Bennet brothers took themselves to the billiards room.

"Have you heard from Lady Anne yet, Caroline? Did they arrive at Snowhaven safely?" Elizabeth smiled as she was sure that her friend's thoughts were elsewhere and did not hear her.

"Please accept my apologies, Elizabeth. Did you say something to me?" Caroline asked in embarrassment as her attention had been very pleasantly engaged by another.

Elizabeth smiled, wondering how long it would take the two unofficially courting couples to come to the point and who would act first. She repeated her question and added that no apology was required.

"Yes, I received a letter from Lady Anne two days ago. They all had arrived two days prior to her sending me the missive. Mr. Darcy was to join them the day that she wrote to me and she expressed her and Georgiana's joy at soon seeing him again," Caroline reported.

"It gives me pleasure to hear that. I have grown to like both Lady Anne and Georgie very well. I almost think of Lady Anne as another aunt now," Lady Elizabeth said with a smile that reached her fine eyes. Talking about the Darcy matriarch caused her to think about the time that they had spent together.

Lady Elizabeth Bennet had grown awfully close to both Darcy women while they and their family were at Longbourn. She and her sisters had helped Georgiana recover and regain her self-confidence. As soon as the young girl saw that what her brother had told her, that none of the Bennets judged her, she had started to emerge from her shell. Lady Anne, Elizabeth, and Georgie had braved the cold with almost daily walks and rides. When they rode, they were always joined by Mary and Kitty, as well as either Tom or James. Her betrothed sisters and their fiancés chose to spend time in the warmth with one another and demurred often when asked to join a riding party. Anne de Bourgh, who could not countenance the cold, did not venture outside for either walks or rides unless she was bundled up with a good number of heating bricks in one of Longbourn's phaetons.

The younger Bennet twins had become best friends with Miss Darcy, and it had not taken above one day before all the young women in residence, Anne de Bourgh included, were calling each other by their familiar names. Elizabeth truly liked Anne as well. She had a very sharp and dry wit and was a keen observer of all. Before Lady Anne departed, Elizabeth had asked her if she should call off the hounds yet to which the lady had reiterated her stance that she had expressed the first time that Lady Elizabeth had made the same offer.

Elizabeth was snapped out of her reverie when her friend squeezed her arm, "What was *your* excuse for wool-gathering, Elizabeth," Caroline teased.

"Sorry, Caroline. I was ruminating about Lady Anne and Georgiana and how close I am with them now. The family were all known to us except for the Darcy ladies," she paused as she thought about it for a moment. "Is it not strange? A little above a month past I thought that the name Darcy was synonymous with arrogance and pride, and then I met the ladies of the family. It has been a valuable lesson to me not to judge too quickly and that there may be circumstances and facts that I am unaware of that effect one's behaviour."

"Do you regret being so severe on Mr. Darcy," Louisa Hurst asked.

"I did, Louisa, but after consulting Lady Anne, and with her advice we decided that he needs to feel the weight of his behaviours. As soon as I see him in Town, I will offer my full and unreserved forgiveness. I have already asked my aunts to let it be known that he is no longer to be excluded from society when they return to London after twelfth night." Elizabeth explained to the sisters and her cousin Graham.

"Lady Anne informed me that she had asked you to wait to let him off the hook, but until you spoke about it now, Elizabeth, I did not feel it was my place to converse about it," Miss Bingley told the lady sitting next to her.

Graham Phillips, who had been looking at Miss Bingley longingly while the ladies were conversing, excused himself to go join the men at billiards. In fact, he wanted to talk to Bingley to request a private interview with Miss Bingley. The more time that he spent with the lady, the more he was sure that she was the one for him. She was no fresh debutante as she was already approaching the age of two and twenty, and he was sure that if she accepted a courtship that it would not be a whim or to say that she was in one to get a leg up on her friends.

He knew that the lady was thoughtful and selfless. She was certainly not lacking in intelligence and had a wit that could be pointed at times, but it was not a negative for him. She was a pretty woman, and her bearing was always that of a confident lady who knew what she wanted from life. She always dressed appropriately, not like some who would dress to try and display their wealth. He knew that she had a dowry of twenty thousand, but not from her. Miss Bingley was not one to make vulgar pronouncements. They both had roots in trade but had not allowed their roots to define who they were. Her brother was on the path to become a landed gentleman, her sister had married a pleasant gentleman, and one day soon he too would be a gentleman when he became a fully licenced and practicing barrister. He had not even told his parents yet, but Sir Randolph was so impressed with young Phillips's work ethic and the results of his work that the great man had offered him a position with Norman and James.

Phillips found Bingley, who had just gone to see if his guests needed anything, with the rest of the men in the billiards room. Lord Birchington was playing against Mr. Hurst while Lord Netherfield and Bingley chatted. He caught Bingley's attention and indicated that he would like to talk to him, so Bingley joined him in the hall.

"Bingley, I am requesting your permission for a private interview with Miss Bingley." He held his breath so he would not immediately react in case he was about to be denied.

"As I hope that we will be brothers one day anyway, I will not deny your request. What is it that you are asking of my sister Phillips?" Bingley arched a brow, but his smile was not as hidden as he intended.

"I will be requesting a courtship. I know that Caro...Miss Bingley is careful in all that she does, so I do not want to rush her if she is not ready to accept more." Then Graham realized what Bingley had said, and he suddenly saw all the time that the man spent talking to Franny in a new light, "Brothers? Franny?"

"My hope is to request a courtship with your sister soon. I take it that as you are asking my sister for a courtship, and we will be brothers if things go as you would like, that you do not object to my courting Miss Phillips?" Bingley teased.

"There would be no objection from me. Aside of the fact that I like and respect you, I am no hypocrite. Be warned, my father will not be opposed, but he will tell you that he wants Franny to have at least part of a season before you declare yourself." Seeing the downcast eyes of his hopefully future brother, he gave him some advice, "Talk to my father at Longbourn on the morrow. It may only be a matter of three months to wait, so no long faces. It is Christmas Eve after all." The two men headed back to the drawing room.

~~~~~~~/~~~~~~~

George Wickham and Karen Younge had just celebrated the eve of the Son of God's birth in their own unique way, with copulation. Wickham felt little pain now, and the scars from the flogging, although still red and raised, were no longer scabbed.

"I love you, George. Why can we not forget the revenge and make a life together and be happy?" his paramour asked him as she kissed his cheek. She had aimed for his lips, but he had turned his head.

"If you love me, Karen, you will not ask that of me. It is not only about revenge, but we also need money. We deserve to live in style, and with such a sum that we will have, even after that blood sucker the *Spaniard* is paid, we will still have more than double than we would have gained from the mouse's dowry," he felt a chill run down his spine as he thought about what would be done to him if he did not pay his debt. "This is one debt that I cannot run out on; that man is relentless. He will keep on looking for me no matter how long it takes."

"Will you not be in danger when you go see him after Christmas?" asked his worried lover.

"As I told you," he said with no little impatience to be having the same discussion again, "as he stands to gain more than twenty thousand, he will not touch me. Especially when I propose that he have that scar faced Withers stay with me until we have the money in hand."

"Sorry, George, I cannot help but worry. I love you, and if anyone ever took you away from me, I would not rest until I took a loved one of theirs from them!" When Wickham saw the look of determination on Mrs. Younge's face, he believed that she was completely serious. She was not a woman one wanted to cross in the wrong way, especially with that cutthroat brother of hers that was the leader of a band of smugglers somewhere in Cornwall.

~~~~~~~/~~~~~~~

151

Bingley signalled to Caroline that he wanted to talk to her, so she politely excused herself and met him in the hall where she saw Mr. Graham Phillips waiting as well. She could not say that she had fallen in love with him yet, but she had never enjoyed the company of a man that was not a family member the way that she did with Graham. Each time that he approached her she felt a flutter and a fission that was not unpleasant. Could that which she dreamed of for some weeks now be happening? She hoped so.

Her anticipation and excitement increased when Charles asked her if she was willing to have a private interview with Mister Phillips. She did not trust herself to speak, so all she did was nod very adamantly. Bingley told them that he would allow ten minutes in the study, and that the door had to remain semi-open.

Graham indicated that Miss Bingley should sit, and once she did, he pulled his armchair close to her. "Miss Bingley, Caroline, if I may call you thus," she nodded her agreement, "from the first day that we met I have felt an attraction to you. I hold you in very tender regard and there has never been one before you that I have ever felt as attracted to as I feel with you. I will not dissemble and tell you that my feelings are deeper than they are at this point. I am not yet in love with you; however, I can honestly say that I am moving in that direction. So more than anything, if you agree, I would like to court you so we can get to know each other better. If, as I suspect, that you are not indifferent to me, a courtship will allow us the time to find out how well we suit and the depth of our feelings. I expect the courtship to end in the natural conclusion, unless you decide that I am not the man for you.

"Your selfless nature, the way I have noticed you treat the servants with respect and kindness even when you think no one is observing you, have only increased my tender feelings for you. Lizzy accepted you as a friend far faster that I have seen her do before; that says a lot for your character. In short, I see only pros, no cons.

"That Caroline, was my long-winded barrister way of asking you if I may court you." As he looked into her eyes, he could see joy reflected at him, a particularly good sign indeed.

"Mr. Phillips, Graham, there is nothing that I would like more than to accept your offer of a courtship, but…" Graham's stomach fell, was she about to refuse him? "I must tell you of my past, of who and what I used to be. When I was younger…" Caroline did not want any secrets between them, so she shared all with him. She wanted him to know all and then if he still wanted to make his request, she would know that it was done with his eyes open. She informed him how she used to look down on others who were in fact above her, her social climbing and fortune hunting days, and how it had all ended with her visit to Pemberley and Lady Anne Darcy taking the time to mentor her. Once she was done, Graham visibly relaxed. She was not rejecting him, she felt that he needed to know of her past and she was giving him an honourable way out in case he chose it before any courtship was made public.

"Caroline, there is nothing you have shared with me that changes anything. Do you think that you are the first person who has erred? I care not about who you *were*, only who you *are* today! What you told me only makes you more estimable in my opinion. The ability to acknowledge our own foibles and then correct them is not a trait that all have, and I respect you even more than I did before. Unless you have a *good* reason to deny my request, I would very much like to court you, Miss Caroline Bingley."

"In that case," the lady responded as tears of joy fell from her eyes shining with tears, joy, and relief, "I would like nothing more than to be courted by you Graham." He took her ungloved hands in his and bestowed light kisses on each of her inside wrists. Both would have liked to kiss, but they did not know how long they had used of the allotted ten minutes and Graham did not want to rush her. It was good that they waited as they heard Bingley clear his throat as he entered his study.

"Well?" he asked.

"Oh, Charles, I am so happy," his younger sister gushed before Phillips had a chance to formally request consent for the courtship.

"I take it that Phillips requested a courtship and you accepted Caroline?" Bingley smiled at the happiness radiating from his sister.

"Yes, he did, and I did. I am so happy; oh, I do not deserve to be so happy! Why cannot everyone be so happy?" the normally sensible lady babbled.

"In that case, you both have my heart-felt consent." Bingley chuckled. "Let us hope that we all find that happiness you want us to find, dearest sister."

"I thank you for permission to win the heart of your sister, Bingley, and I hope that we will be brothers with both of us being granted our heart's desire." Phillips winked at his friend.

"You will need some patience, Charles. Franny told me that her father has decreed that she will have three months of the season at the very least before any possible suitor," she looked directly at her brother, "declares himself."

"That is news that Phillips imparted to me already, but thank you, Caroline. Let us go inform the rest of our guests. Phillips, will you ask the three in the billiard room to join us please?" Bingley was keen to return to the drawing room. Although he had heard about Franny's father's decision regarding anyone declaring himself, he was resolved to request a meeting with the man on the morrow at Longbourn.

Miss Francine Phillips was not the prototypical lady that Bingley had fallen in love in the past. Ladies Jane and Marie were the exact physical types with whom he would have fallen in love with and called 'his angel' before he had matured in the last year or so. He had fallen in love with alacrity, and out of the state just as fast several times since he finished Cambridge. Once he started to mature and become a much more resolute man who thought before he acted, he realized all had been infatuation, not love. Additionally, he was now aware that physical attributes were no indicator of character and compatibility.

Franny was a very pretty, young woman, and that was the last thing that Bingley had noticed. He was attracted to her sense of fairness, character, and intelligence before he took an in depth note of her physical beauty. In short, the lady that he was losing his heart to was pretty on the outside and even more so on the inside. The way that he felt about Franny Phillips was incomparable to his past infatuations. For all those in his past it had been quite easy to persuade himself that he was not in love with any of them as soon as he was not in their presence, but he knew that there was no living being that would be able to separate him from Franny. Charles Bingley was in love, deep, irrevocable, romantic love for the first, and last, time in his life.

Once everyone returned to the drawing room, Bingley asked everyone to charge their glasses with the champagne that the butler distributed and drink a toast to the courting couple. There were many wishes for future felicity, hugs for Caroline from the ladies, and back slapping from the men for Graham; And for those watching for it, it was hard to miss the look of longing that passed between Franny Phillips and Charles Bingley.

CHAPTER 11

Darcy could not remember a Christmas where he had felt as happy as he did at the one being celebrated at Snowhaven, and if he had it certainly was not since his dear father had been taken from them.

He was listening to his family regale him with tales of their sojourn in Hertfordshire with their Graces and family. He was jealous of the time that they had all spent with the Bennet's, especially of one Bennet with fine eyes. He was sure that he had made the correct decision. If he had returned to Lady Elizabeth's company too soon before he felt that most of the areas, he needed to address for his quest for betterment was done, it could have been more detrimental to his case than not.

The difference in his baby sister was nearly indescribable. She had regained her self-confidence, and, if the recounting could be believed, she was no longer shy in company. She would still be quiet with people unknown to her, but she would no longer sit with her head down hoping to not take part in a conversation without being directly addressed. Even when she was, one had been lucky to receive a monosyllable as an answer. And his aunt Catherine could not stop singing the Bennet's praises. She extolled their breeding, rank, and wealth, although the others in the family knew those were not the attributes that they truly admired in the family. It was true Lady Catherine was a softer version of herself, but sometimes, most especially when she was not thinking about it, her beliefs on the distinction of rank being preserved came to the fore.

His mother seated herself beside him on the settee and

squeezed his hand, "William, I hope that you know how proud I am, all of the family is, at the changes that you have made in your behaviour." She looked into the distance, thinking about her late husband, the love of her life. She missed him all the time, but more so at Christmas, as it was one of his favourite holidays.

"Thank you, Mama," he answered, and in recognizing the look from Christmases past he added, "I too wish that Papa was still with us."

Lady Anne wiped a single tear as she again looked at her son, "You know, William, that if it will be too hard for you to not be at your cousin's weddings there will not be *one* who will not want you to attend."

"I appreciate that Mama, but I will stand by my decision. I refuse to allow any chance of distracting from the day that is all about my cousins and their brides," he answered resolutely. "My one regret is that I will not get to stand up with Richard. We spoke in Town and he understands why I feel that this is the only course of action for me to follow at this time." he added wistfully.

Lady Anne knew not to importune him on that particular subject any longer. "I understand that you have offered the boys the use of Seaview Cottage and the Lakeview House, near Lake Windermere, for their wedding trips," his mother glowed at the generosity of her son, especially as he had self-exiled himself from their wedding.

"It was not a hard decision, mother. As you know, Richard and I are like brothers and Andrew has always been a good friend and cousin to me, so it was the very least that I could do after potentially jeopardising things for them with my behaviour." Darcy blushed as he gave a nonchalant shrug, trying to convey it was the least he could do.

"William, my son, I love you but you need to learn a philosophy that Lady Elizabeth has adopted. 'Think only of the past as the remembrance gives you pleasure.'" She offered gently.

157

"Are we talking about the lady for who once her good opinion is lost, it is lost forever?" he asked, not able to reconcile the philosophy with what he knew of Lady Elizabeth.

"Do you think that you are the only one who has learnt and grown after she confronted you?" she raised an eyebrow in question.

"That would be an arrogant assumption, would it not be?" he offered with a half-smile, his arrogance again checked and his mother nodded her head, "I am interested to know what had changed with the lady."

"Elizabeth understands now that she was too quick to anger and judge. She acknowledges that if she does not allow that people can change and earn her forgiveness then that is not following the precepts of Christianity." Lady Anne paused, "His Grace told you about his entrapment, did he not? Of course, he did as that is what led to the settlement that all fortune hunters and dishonourable members of society now hate with a passion." The last elicited a dimple revealing smile from her son.

"The story of Lord Thomas's entrapment and the year that he was forced to be separated from Lady Sarah was told to all of the Bennet children, but Elizabeth used it as a cautionary tale that imbued her with suspicion and led to her propensity to judge and not forgive. She sees that is not the best way and like you has changed and will continue to do so.

"Do not misunderstand me, William. Your behaviour in Hertfordshire warranted the severest of reproofs. I believe with all of my heart that had you merely received a 'slap on the wrist' that it would not have been the impetus for you to change as Lady Elizabeth's set down and subsequent punishment has been." She took her son's hand again as she wanted to make sure that what she was saying would not be seen as a censure of him.

"Look at how much happier you are now. Thanks to the settlement, you can go out in society without feeling like a fox surrounded by hounds and hunters. And I will tell you this,

William. If you were not an innately good person, you would not have made any changes. You would have blamed anyone but yourself. You know one who is like that." She stated, tensing at the very thought of the man she suspected of the most horrible of crimes.

"Wickham." he spat the name out. "That is one thing I am very sorry I did not witness. To see Lady Elizabeth, humble that dastard. He did the right thing to preserve his life by slinking away to lick his wounds before Richard returned. My cousin would not have shown restraint if he had seen the blackguard again."

"I cannot disagree with you, William. Do you think that his exposure and punishment made that that, oh I do not want to use unladylike language, that man," both mother and son smiled at her regulating her speech instead of saying what she truly wanted to. "Not for one moment do I believe that *he* became introspective and asked what he had done wrong. Like he always has, he will blame everyone except himself. I loved, I still love my George and will never understand why he had such a blind spot for so long."

"I know not, Mama." Darcy admitted, long having felt his father preferred his godson's company to his own.

"Did your father tell you that he was going to break with the man before his accident?"

"No, he did not." Darcy frowned.

"He received proof that Wickham had meddled with some of the maids. I do not know if my George confronted the seducer before he was taken, but I do know that he intended to." Lady Anne always got maudlin thoughts when she talked about her beloved husband's passing.

"As father left no notes about a meeting, we will never know," Darcy replied quietly as he processed the information and wishing his father would have talked with him about this and many other things before he had ridden that day.

~~~~~~~/~~~~~~~

After Christmas dinner, the men were sitting in Longbourn's library indulging in tobacco and libations. Bingley approached Mr. Phillips to ask him if they could talk.

"As your sister will hopefully soon be my daughter, it is a request that I happily grant," said Phillips senior as he tossed the contents of his snifter back and placed the empty glass on the nearby side table. The two men then found two armchairs out of earshot of the rest of the men.

"Mr. Phillips, it cannot have escaped your notice that I have been paying Miss Phillips a good amount of attention," Bingley started tentatively.

"Yes, neither my wife nor I have missed that, Bingley. What are your intentions toward my daughter?" Phillips asked, adopting his best prosecutor's attitude.

"My intentions are entirely honourable, sir. I care deeply for your daughter," Bingley stated emphatically.

"I expected no less, my boy. What is it that you wanted to talk to me about?" his beloved's father cut right to the issue.

"If you allow me, I would like a private interview with Miss Phillips and request a courtship from her." Although Bingley was nervous with anticipation, he managed to make the request calmly.

"You know that I want Franny to have at least part of a season before you, or anyone else, declares for her, do you not?" Mr. Phillips senior asked, his brow arched in question.

"Yes, sir, I do. But I wanted you to know that I am in earnest. I love your daughter, and if my fondest wish is granted, I will make it my life's work to make her happy." Bingley spoke, his voice almost trembling with the depth of his emotions.

"There is no doubt in my mind that you are sincere, nor am I insensitive to the fact that my wife and I have not missed that Franny holds you in tender regard." Phillips thought for a little while, "Here is what I will agree to. We will be in Town after Jane and Marie marry. If you still feel as you do, you may declare yourself in early March." Phillips saw Bingley cogitating and pre-empted him, "No, my boy, not at the Netherfield ball but at the end of that month. That way my girl will have part of a season before she is officially courting." Bingley could see that there would be no additional flexibility.

"You have my gratitude, sir. Thank you." Bingley felt immense relief as the wait would be less than he had originally thought, if not as short as he had hoped.

Caroline Bingley was sitting with Lady Elizabeth, Franny, and Mrs. Madeline Gardiner and Mrs. Gardiner was congratulating Caroline on being courted by Graham. She loved her niece and nephew and believed that Caroline and her nephew would be very happy. She was as excited from what she could see and the snippet of conversation that she had heard, she was reasonably sure that Franny would not be single for too much longer, so both of the Phillips children were finding their matches in the Bingley family.

Mrs. Gardiner could not believe that the woman sitting with her niece was the same person that she had met some years ago when Mr. Bingley, Charles's father, had purchased a ten percent stake in Gardiner and Associates. She thought back to when she had first made their acquaintance.

Caroline Bingley had her nose in the air as if there was a bad smell in the room. She had been very disappointed when her father had purchased a townhouse on Gracechurch Street not far from the Gardiner's house as Caroline had felt that their house should be in Mayfair. They were wealthy, after all, and as she let one and all know, she had a dowry of twenty thousand pounds.

Things had only gotten worse when the young lady joined her older sister at the pretentious Mrs. Havisham's Seminary for Ladies. Daughters of members of the Ton had looked down on and derided the Bingley sisters for their roots in trade. The lesson that the older took away was that it was sad that some used standards other than one's character to judge them, while Caroline tried to emulate them and started to treat people that she deemed below her worse and worse. It became harder to bear the young lady's company and pretentions for any length of time.

Louisa Bingley, now Mrs. Hurst, did not display the same airs and graces as her younger sister while the middle child, Charles, had always been affable and pleasant to be with. Louisa had married Harold Hurst a month after the three siblings completed their mourning period. The Bingley parents had died when tragedy struck and their carriage overturned on the way back from York-shire four Christmases ago. Hurst had a townhouse in London, not in the area that most members of the Ton resided, but closer than Gracechurch Street so Caroline, who had become Miss Bingley spent most of her time with the Hursts until her new brother re-stricted the amount of time that she could spend at his home.

No one was sure what happened, but the Miss Bingley who had invited herself to join her brother on a visit to the Darcy Estate in Derbyshire, Pemberley, was not the same one that returned to Lon-don. She had changed, seemingly overnight to a pleasant young lady with impeccable manners with whom one wanted to be around. There was never a mention of her dowry again and she no longer tried to hide her roots in trade from the world.

Madeline Gardiner, Aunt Maddie to the Bingley siblings, was brought out of her reverie by the young ladies laughing softly at something. She decided that the mystery of what happened to change Caroline into the young woman that she had grown to love, almost like another daughter, would re-main a mystery until and unless Caroline decided to reveal all to her. She would not ask or try to force a confidence, and re-gardless of how it came about she loved the pleasant young lady that had emerged. She held her in as much esteem as she did her nieces and nephews. The fact that Miss Bingley had been accepted as a friend by the Bennets and her niece Lizzy, specifically spoke volumes to who Caroline was now.

"I am sorry, Caroline, what did you say? I was wool-gather-ing," Mrs. Gardiner said a little chagrined that she had missed what was said to her.

"I was asking if you will return to Town before Jane and Marie's wedding, or will you and Uncle Edward wait until after the wedding?" asked a smiling Caroline Bingley.

It had been a revelation for Elizabeth and the rest of the Bennets when they found out just how close the Bingleys were to the Gardiners. That they were business associates was well known, but it was only when the Gardiners arrived to visit that the strength of the connection was revealed. Elizabeth and the rest of her family were impressed that once the Bingleys had become aware of the familial connections that they had not tried use their connection to the Gardiners in any way to their advantage.

"Edward needs to attend to business, so we will go to Town after the New Year and return some days before the wedding in time for the ball that your Mama," she looked at Elizabeth, "informed us she is planning for two days prior to the nuptials."

"Luckily, Madam Chambourg herself was in Meryton this last week to oversee my older sisters' wedding gowns. The final fittings will be after the New Year which leaves more than enough time for any adjustments to be made." Lady Elizabeth turned to Caroline, "I hear that you and Louisa are on her list of clients now. I wonder how that came about," she teased her friend.

"You are excused from giving me a gift for the rest of my life, Lizzy. Not in my wildest imaginings did I ever think that Louisa and I would ever be added to her list of accepted clients," Miss Bingley gushed.

"It was my pleasure, Caroline," Elizabeth smiled playfully at her friend.

The local visitors left before supper, and it was a very contended group that found their way into their beds that Christmas night. Lady Elizabeth Bennet did not understand why, but she felt pangs of regret that Mr. Darcy would not be attending her sisters' weddings. She did understand that why he had decided not to attend and wished that she had not been so harsh with him in the past.

~~~~~~~/~~~~~~~

Two days after Christmas, George Wickham was shown into the dingy office of the *Spaniard*, Juan Antonio Álvarez. Álvarez had been in London for over twenty years. He had left the ship on which he was a crewmember when he was two and twenty after the ship docked in Portsmouth. With the help of José, a friend from his hometown, they had broken the lock on the strong box in the captain's day cabin and made off with all of the ship's funds, unconcerned that the money was meant to pay their fellow crewmates. Showing the lack of loyalty, which was one his hallmark traits, when they were away from prying eyes, Álvarez had requested that his friend check to see how much they made off with, and as soon as José turned his back, he had cut his friend's throat in a way the murdering criminal liked to call 'a permanent smile'.

Álvarez disposed of his 'friend's' body by pushing his mortal remains into a river. José was the first victim he interred in a watery grave, but not the last, by any means. His first destination was Leeds where he used the blood money to purchase a piece of property, he turned into a gambling hall. He was smart enough to know that there was a lot of money to be made from those insensible enough to gamble away their fortunes.

After four years he owned three gambling houses and two houses of ill repute where tables were available for the 'patrons' to play games of chance. He was ruthless, and it was not long before all who came in contact with him learnt not to cross the Spaniard. By year eight he had doubled his empire and was raking in a very respectable profit, earned almost entirely from illegal and immoral means each year. In his gaming houses he gave a new 'client' a taste of winning to suck them in and then would fleece them for as much as they wanted to lose. If cheating was needed to increase his profits, so much the better. By the tenth year he had sold his empire in Leeds for a very healthy profit and moved to London. He bought a number of properties in St. Giles, Hackney, and Stepney, again opening gaming houses and houses of ill repute. He had no interest in being in the areas that the Ton inhabited; he did not need or want the scrutiny.

No matter how much money he had, Álvarez knew that as

a foreigner of low bastard birth he would never be accepted in British society, so he contented himself building his London based empire. George Wickham had come to his attention when he had started making large wagers in one of his gaming houses. He had his man in charge check and it was discovered that the man had between three and four thousand pounds and was a bad card player to boot. The dealers were instructed to initially let him win a few hands, and then over a number of months they took it all. It was not many months more before Wickham was deeply in debt to the *Spaniard*. With the original amount, plus the compounded 'fees' and interest that had been added, the sum that was owed grew from the original five thousand pounds to now exceed ten thousand.

Wickham was unceremoniously shoved into Álvarez's office by Scarface. Neither man could believe that after evading them so effectively for so long that the idiot they were staring at walked into the lion's den.

"Are you mad, Senior *Jorge*?" Álvarez asked in his heavy Spanish accent. "Do you 'ave my money? If no, your life, she is over."

"I do not have it *today*, but if you hear me out you will see that I will be able to get you double what I owe you if you help me attain my goal," Wickham tried to convey confidence, but he was very worried that he may have erred. "Will you hear me out?"

"You are still alive, no?" Álvarez stated with deceptive ease as he cleaned dirt from under his fingernails with a dagger.

"Have you heard of the Duke of Hertfordshire?" Wickham challenged and got a nod from the man, "I was recently acquainted with his daughter, *Lady* Elizabeth. The lady's dowry is more than one hundred thousand pounds."

"What of it," Withers, Scarface to those on the street, asked.

"With a little help, I intend to take her and then demand a ransom from her family." Wickham smirked.

"'Ow much, *Jorge*?" Until Wickham mentioned the size of the dowry and ransom, the *Spaniard* was getting ready to order his death and disposal.

"One hundred thousand pounds!" Wickham announced triumphantly. The amount of one hundred thousand pounds hung in the air like the smoke from the cigars that Álvarez liked to smoke.

"What make you think you able do this *Jorge*?" The *Spaniard* demanded. He had heard of the Bennets and was well aware that the sum that Wickham mentioned was not a hardship for them, and he was not one to pass on an amount such as this.

"That is where I will need some help and funding from you, Mr. Álvarez." Wickham could see that he was on very thin ice, so he proceeded before an objection could be raised. "I will not need much, just a supply of coin to pay a group of urchins to watch her when she comes to Town. There needs to be a good number of them, or the Duke's guards will notice the same two or three hanging around Bennet House."

"You expect the boss to trust you, Wickham?" Withers demanded.

"No, which is why you should be with me to help and to keep an eye on things to make sure that all is being done as promised and I am not trying to double cross Mr. Álvarez." Wickham offered the gambit he hoped tipped the scaled in his direction.

"Before I agree, 'ow much will I 'ave from this?" The *Spaniard* challenged. Wickham had been willing to go to thirty thousand, but he decided to offer lower so there was some room to negotiate.

"Twenty thousand; which is double what I owe you now," Wickham proposed with affected confidence.

Álvarez knew that it would take a few months, but he saw merit in the plan. Besides, he was even now hatching his own plan that would cut Wickham out after the girl was taken, literally and figuratively. Yes, he would dispose of them and keep all the money for himself, with a little to Withers. Scarface would be integral to his alternate plan succeeding. Thus, the scheme was agreed to. He would fund the hiring of the urchins necessary to watch the quarry and ascertain her schedule, and Scarface would be with Wickham to help execute the actual kidnapping. His avarice overruled any pause that he may have taken to consider possible problems. Until closer to the kidnapping, two of his toughs would be with Wickham, one awake always, so he would have no time to slip away again.

Wickham was accompanied back to Edward Street by Withers and the two men. The men would stay at the boarding house for free, much to the displeasure of the landlady who lost two rooms to rent out in the deal, until the Bennets arrived in Town and a full plan with a date the kidnapping was to occur was in place. When the plan was that far along, Withers would replace the two ruffians. George placated his lover, Karen Younge, convincing her that the presence of the men was a necessary evil and that she should keep her eye on the prize, which was the magnificent fortune that they would soon have. He thanked his lucky stars that the *Spaniard* had not balked at the amount that he had offered. He, who would do what he had to do to cheat or steal, did not consider that there was an ulterior motive for the quick acquiescence. His own greed and desire for revenge blinded him to things that should have been plain for him to see, especially when dealing with someone of his own ilk.

George Wickham was feeling better than he had been since his humiliation and subsequent flogging. He was sure that it would not be too long before he would take his revenge in full on the woman who thought that she was so much better than he. Wickham's fragile ego had always been his Achilles heel, and it would be again.

~~~~~~~~/~~~~~~~~

Two days after Christmas, the Fitzwilliams, de Bourghs, and the two Darcy ladies started the journey south to Hertfordshire while Darcy headed north to Pemberley. Even though he would have preferred to travel with his family south,

His relationship with his Uncle and Aunt Fitzwilliam was

better than he could remember. He had thought that because he always paid the deference due to his family, all was well. He now knew better. They had not been comfortable with his behaviour outside of the family circle. It was with no little shame when he recalled that Uncle Reggie had tried to talk to him a few years past, and just as he had cut off Bingley and Caroline in Hertfordshire, he had done the same with his uncle. As he sat in his carriage for the short ride from Snow-haven to Pemberley, he thought back on the conversation he had with the Earl the evening after Christmas.

Being the only two men present, the Earl and his nephew had retired to the master's study to enjoy their cigars and brandy. For the first ten minutes they had sat in silence, puffing on their cigars and sipping the French brandy then Darcy had opened the conversation. "Uncle, where did you acquire this excellent French Brandy? With the war I had thought it was all but impossible to procure."

"It is thanks to my connection to the Duke of Hertfordshire." His uncle had replied with a nod when Darcy looked at him questioningly, not understanding how his Grace helped acquire French brandy. "Have you heard of Gardiner and Associates?"

"I have, Uncle Reggie, but I do not see the connection between an import export trading company and his Grace." Darcy admitted somewhat perplexed.

"William, you are much less arrogant and haughty than you used to be, but the last bit there lets me know that you have some work left to do. The Bennets themselves are in trade. Do you know that they own the Dennington Line Shipping Company?" Seeing the look of surprise on his nephew's face he chuckled. "Before you ask, there are many peers who have interests in trade today, there are many of us who have seen the future and it will be us seeking favour from tradesmen soon enough.

"You have made great strides and it makes my sister Anne, all of us, very proud as we see you fighting to become the man that all of us, including my late brother George, knew that you could be." Not the type of men who usually discuss topics so emotionally charged, the two men had sat for a few moments in silence.

"I know that the Bennet family is wealthy, but I did not know the extent of their interests. How do they connect to Gardiner and Associates?" Darcy's voice was gruff as he tried to maintain his composure.

The Earl then explained the connection via 'she who is not to be mentioned'. He informed Darcy that Bennet did not hold her brother and sister responsible for the abhorrent actions of their sibling and father, and that the Gardiners and Phillips' were considered to be full members of the family by all.

"Gardiner and Associates have sources on the continent, and I would guess in conjunction with Dennington Line Shipping they are able to acquire almost all that most of us would not have access to." Darcy mused, his conjecture confirmed when his uncle nodded, "You know that Bingley is one of my best friends and he is in trade, and I have invested in some of his ventures."

"That, William, has been the contradiction that was you until Lizzy tore into you," the Earl said with a smile as he thought about the vivacious young woman that would soon be sister to his sons. "You treated your dependants at Pemberley, your other estates, and Darcy House as well if not better than most, but disdained any others that you thought below you. You are close to the Bingleys, but even now, and mayhap you did not realise it, when you mentioned the words 'trading company' you got a look of distaste on your countenance. Fleeting, true, but it was there.

"All I am suggesting is that you need to work on schooling your features toward kindness rather than judgemental. It will take work, but I know that you are determined, and I have yet to see you fail to realise a goal that you have set for yourself," the Earl squeezed Darcy's shoulder to reinforce his pride in how far his nephew had progressed to date.

Darcy was snapped out of his reverie when the coach passed Pemberley's gatehouse and the keeper, Burris, doffed his cap to the master. Yes, he had made much progress, but he wanted to be even further along before he was again in company with the lady that filled his thoughts if not otherwise engaged during the day and inhabited his dreams at night, Lady

Elizabeth Bennet.

CHAPTER 12

Wickham was becoming impatient; why was that *woman* not yet in Town? He had used some of his dwindling personal coin to have a rider go to Meryton to sniff around when there was no activity at Bennet House after Twelfth Night had passed. He was mollified when the rider returned and informed him that the family was planning a wedding for about ten days hence so their arrival in London would be delayed.

What he had no way of knowing was that the Bennets would not be in Town for any length of time until the end of March and would return for the Bingley and Philips engagement ball at Netherfield as well as spending some weeks with friends who had estates close to London. It would only take a little patience; the question was how much tolerance would Álvarez show before he cut his losses. If he did that, George Whickham was under no illusion as to what sort of 'cutting' would take place.

He was very happy to have an expected time to report to the *Spaniard,* so the man did not vent his spleen at him. Wickham knew that when he was angry with someone, the chances of their survival were very low indeed. The two toughs that had been installed at Edward Street were a necessary evil. They were dirty and smelled like they had never bathed, but there was nothing that could be done until Withers replaced them. At least *Scarface* bathed once or twice a week.

~~~~~~~/~~~~~~~

It was three days before the double wedding in Meryton. All that could be done had been done. Lady Sarah Bennet, with the able assistance of Ladies Elaine Fitzwilliam, Anne Darcy, and Catherine de Bourgh, had completed all of their tasks well ahead of the upcoming ball and weddings. Their cousin, Queen Charlotte, had sent each couple an exquisite Ming Dynasty vase as a gift. Along with the gift was a note that offered the use of her vicar, the Archbishop of Canterbury, to officiate the wedding, but the family had politely demurred. When the gifts had arrived, very carefully transported by royal couriers, all of the ladies had exclaimed at the beauty of the Queen's gift. Even the men had been somewhat impressed. The Prince, Princess, and their retinue would arrive some hours before the ball on the morrow and would remain until they witnessed the marriage of their cousins on behalf of the family.

Due to the royal presence, and with so many peers of the realm in attendance, there was not room for all four and twenty principal families of the area. The local populace would be represented by the Lucases, the Longs, the Gouldings, and the Purvises. Of the four families, the Bennets were closest to the Lucas family. The oldest son, Frank, was a friend of both Marquesses and Lady Elizabeth. The younger daughter, Maria, now Miss Lucas was an intimate of Ladies Mary and Catherine as they were very close in age. Georgiana Darcy, who had been in residence since just after the New Year, had grown close with Kitty, Mary, and Maria, as well as the three elder Bennet sisters, all of whom were instrumental in helping her voice her preferences and offer her own opinions in conversation. The youngest Lucas, John, although he was a little older than Eddy Gardiner, was fast friends with the Gardiner heir.

Louisa Hurst and Caroline Bingley had assisted whenever the Duchess needed their help, and Caroline was as happy as she had ever been. Her courtship with Graham Phillips had given them the opportunity to know one another more and had only deepened the feelings between them so she was sure that she was in love with him. He had not yet told her how he felt, but she was sure that her love was requited, and hoped that he loved her as fully as she did him. Lady Anne Darcy looked on her protégé with pride and happiness for her. She felt that Caroline deserved all the happiness she was about to attain.

Anne de Bourgh, between their first visit and the current one, had become close with the ladies of the house, especially Lady Elizabeth. She had also gained a deep friendship with Charlotte Pierce, nee Lucas; they were true kindred spirits and Anne was now enjoying the comfort of having a sister of her heart. She was not as close to Caroline Bingley and Louisa Hurst, but they all got along well so formal titles had long since been abandoned for informal address. The wedding was the first time her friends would have the chance to meet the man who was courting her, Mr. Ian Ashby who was the second son of the Earl of Ashbury from Surrey.

Some would conclude that as Anne de Bourgh was the owner of the unentailed estate of Rosings Park in Kent, that Mr. Ashby was a poor second son looking to make his fortune by marriage. They would be very wrong. Ashby had inherited the large and prosperous estate of Sherwood Park from his maternal grandmother as well as a large monetary legacy. His estate's income was a little larger than Rosings Park's. Ian Ashby had no need to marry for money, he had more than enough of his own. Besides the connection with Anne, his father was a close friend of her uncle, the Earl of Matlock, and was well known to the Bennets and De Melvilles. Both Ashby and his older brother, Viscount Amberleigh, Lord Stephen Ashby was a good friend of one of the grooms, Lord Andrew Fitzwilliam, Viscount Hilldale. In fact, Ashby was standing up for Lord Hilldale.

Lady Catherine, once her sister Anne had helped her accept that there would never be a union between her daughter and her nephew William, had not stood in the way of the budding romance between Ian Ashby and her daughter. She even allowed, though only to herself, that her future son was much better suited in disposition and interests to her daughter than her nephew ever would have been. The two had been courting for six months, a period set by herself. Even though Lord Matlock was Anne's guardian, he had agreed to the courtship term after his ward had told him that it was agreeable to her.

Lady Catherine's sister Anne, her brother Reggie, and her sister-in-law Elaine had all told her that she was more than welcome to stay with them for as long as, and whenever, she so desired. As satisfying as it was to know that she would be welcome with her siblings, she could not look forward with equanimity to the approaching time that Anne would leave her. In no way did the mother begrudge the daughter her happiness; she was simply scared of being alone. She would miss seeing Anne almost daily, much more than she was willing to admit to anyone. Lady Catherine had wanted to keep Anne at home a little longer even though she knew that it was a selfish desire, and did not look forward to the time when she would be alone in her daughter's manor house.

Lady Catherine de Bourgh was certain that Ashby, who would arrive later that day, would propose to Anne before they all departed Hertfordshire. When she had still ascribed to the delusion that Darcy and Anne were 'formed' for each other, she allowed no word on the subject of Mr. Ashby from her daughter. It was only after her illusion was dispelled that she had listened to her daughter, and as much as she used to believe that love was not needed in marriage, that it was a plebian concept, she could not deny that Anne loved her suitor.

The six months had passed so quickly and Lady Catherine, who used to intimidate others, was nervous about what her future would be like. As she was sitting in her sitting room at Longbourn considering all that had passed and what was yet to come, there was a soft knock on the door. She called for the person to enter and watched as her sister and her namesake entered the room.

"Mama," Anne de Bourgh said softly, "why are you in your sitting room and not with the rest of us?"

"Anne," Lady Catherine offered them a sad smile when they both replied. "It was nothing," she said not looking directly at either.

"Catherine," her sister said sympathetically as she sat and

took one of her hands, "I know that you will be happy for Anne, but you are worried about being alone after she marries, are you not?" Lady Catherine nodded while a few tears dripped down her cheeks.

Her daughter handed her a silk handkerchief as she sat down on the other side of her mother. "Mama, please look at me," she asked, "*Never* think that you will be abandoned when I marry, that is if Ian asks me," she said with an impish smile as one and all knew it was a when and not an if. "You will be welcome to live with us, if that is your desire. And do not forget that both Aunt Anne and Uncle Reggie have issued open invitations for you to spend as much time with them as you choose to," Anne squeezed her mother's hands and then hugged her.

"I do not deserve to be loved as you all love me," Catherine said as she wiped her tears and sniffled.

"*Catherine Pauline Fitzwilliam de Bourgh*! Do not say things that are patently false!" her younger sister admonished her with a playfully aghast look.

"The way that I used to..." she got no further as her daughter interrupted her.

"That is the point Mama, *used to*. You are not the same person that you used to be," she soothed. "Yes, you still like to be in control," Anne winked at her mother as she teased her, "but there is none other than I would prefer as my mother, and I know that you have never done anything out of malice. Everything that you have done was out of love and fear. You know Mama, you were the way you were because you were afraid that if you did not control all of the minutia that something bad would happen to me and those that you love." Lady Catherine nodded acknowledging the truth in her daughter's statement.

"If Reggie, Elaine, and I did not love you Catherine, would we have taken the time to try and help you change the way that you were toward others? Look at where you are, you are in their Graces' home, a wanted and very much included part of the celebration of our nephew's nuptials three days hence."

"I am sorry Anne and Anne," she looked at each as she said their names, "I allowed myself to be consumed by maudlin thoughts and made assumptions that at heart I knew were not true. I thank you both, and if you are sure that you want your older, but not always wiser sister with you after my daughter's suitor gets to the point and marries her, I would like to visit with you, my younger and much wiser sister, for some months so that I do not impose on Ashby and Anne at the start of their marriage."

"Your company will never be an imposition, Mama," Anne kissed her mother on both cheeks, and after Lady Catherine put herself to rights, the three joined the rest of the ladies in the drawing room.

~~~~~~~/~~~~~~~

Lord Sedgwick and Lady Rosamond Bennet, the Duke and Duchess of Bedford, would have the honour of being part of the receiving line at the ball later that night. The Duke of Bedford was some years his brother's senior. The Duke's wives, although Lady Rose Bennet was seven years Lady Sarah Bennet's senior, were as close as any sisters. Lord and Lady Jersey, Cyril and Pricilla De Melville, Lady Sarah Bennet's brother and sister-in-law were also part of the closely knit family circle. They were seen almost as another set of parents by the Bennet's children, and they were a very much-loved Aunt and Uncle. Cousins Wesley, Viscount Westmore and the heir to the Earl of Jersey and his sister Lady Loretta were very close to their Bennet cousins. Lord Wesley, Wes to family and friends, was not quite a year older than Lord James Bennet and had recently graduated from Cambridge. Ladies Catherine and Mary thought of their cousin Loretta, or as they called her, Retta, who was about six months younger than the youngest Bennets, like another sister. The three cousins had requested that they have their come out together even with Retta being a little younger, their mothers granted the request with pleasure.

Georgiana Darcy had met Lady Loretta on her first visit to

Longbourn the previous year, and she had felt an instant affinity to the young lady. It was not just that they were closer to one another in age; they were of similar disposition. Both were somewhat shy, and both were well read and intelligent. It was not long after they met that Lady Loretta was calling Miss Darcy Georgie and being called Retta in return. Shortly after, they considered one another their closest friend, and when the Darcys had travelled north for Christmas, the two kept up a very active correspondence. They were both overjoyed to be back together again for the whole of the fortnight before the double wedding.

In the billiards room where the younger men had gathered, Graham Phillips approached the man that he hoped would soon be his brother. "Bingley, may I speak to you in private?" Bingley nodded and the two found an empty parlour near the billiard room.

"How may I be of service, Phillips?" Bingley asked, fairly sure he knew what he was about to request.

"I am sure that you have not missed that my courtship with your sister Caroline has been progressing very well." Graham hedged and Bingley allowed that it was so. "I am in love with your sister and would like your permission to have a private interview with her."

"Even if I were a blind man, I would not be able to miss that the tender feelings are mutual. I have never seen Caroline light up the way that she does when you enter a room," Bingley sighed, certain that his younger sister would accept an application for her hand from this man with alacrity. "It has not escaped my notice that you have never once asked about her dowry. Do you know how much she has?"

"No Bingley I do not, nor would I care if she were penniless. Whatever the truth, I would not want to marry her any less than I do now. I am not a very wealthy man, but I am comfortable and well able to support myself and a wife. My parents have gifted me a legacy of fifteen thousand that my Uncle Thomas and Aunt Sarah matched. In addition, I have the use of one of Uncle Thomas's smaller townhouses on Portman Square for as long as I need it, rent free. I will soon move from being a clerk to a fully-fledged barrister, and as you may know I have been offered a true position with Norman and James, so my prospects are good," Phillips took a breath and looked Bingley in the eye, "I hope that you see that your sister's dowry or lack thereof, had no influence on my decision to offer for her."

Bingley extended his hand, safe in the knowledge that his future brother wanted to marry Caroline for the right reasons. After the men shook hands, Bingley spoke the words that Graham had been waiting to hear with bated breath. "Yes, Phillips, I will grant you your interview. I will go and summon Caroline, wait here. *Never* hurt her!"

"I would sooner die than ever cause her a moments pain!" Phillips looked at him aghast at the thought of Caroline hurting. Bingley nodded and left the room, leaving a somewhat nervous young man pacing in the parlour. It seemed like a lifetime, but in a few minutes the man who had become a good friend returned with his sister in tow.

"You have ten minutes, and the door will remain partially open," Bingley stated letting them know that his terms were not negotiable.

'*Please, God, let this man that I love beyond reason propose to me. I know that I deserve happiness, I will remember Lizzy's advice to think only of the past as it gives me pleasure,*' Caroline Bingley told herself as she watched the beginning of her dream coming true when the man that she loved above all others took her hands in his and got down on one knee in front of her. Her heart felt like it was beating as fast and hard as a galloping horse.

"Caroline, from the first moment that my eyes beheld you I felt an invisible magnetism that drew me to you. I find that any version of my future that I imagine requires you in it. The more that I got to know you, the more I was captivated by your kindness toward others, your unselfishness, and the way that you care so deeply for everyone's feelings. Your treatment of the servants in your brother's home impressed me. I watched you treat them as people who deserved respect, not some dirt on your slipper as many do. I watched your interactions with them when you had no idea that you were being observed so that I knew I was observing the real you, not some contrived person to impress others."

"Miss Caroline Heather Bingley, I love you with all that I am and would like to, no I need to ask you to be my helpmeet and accept my hand in marriage because without you my life will be empty. Will you marry me, Caroline?"

Tears of joy flowed freely down her cheeks as she heard the words she had once thought she would never hear from any man, never mind one that she loved so deeply. Momentarily overcome with emotion she was unable to speak so she nodded emphatically, not wanting Graham to misread the situation or think that she was about to refuse him.

"Is that a yes, Caroline?" he chuckled, her blush and her eyes already telling him she loved him, her nod making his heart soar.

"Yes, yes, as many times as you need to hear me say it, yes Graham, I will marry you. I too love you and felt the attraction from the first time that we met. I am so very..." Whatever she was about to say was lost as her betrothed had stood up and his lips descended to hers, brushing them so Caroline Bingley experienced her first kiss from a man that was not a family member. After their lips touched softly, Phillips drew back to make sure that his fiancé did not object to his action. Rather than objection, he saw a look of unadulterated pleasure, her lips parted and begging for more and being a gentleman, he obliged his lady.

The kisses got deeper and more passionate as her arms wound around his waist as if by their own volition, and then she felt his tongue probing her lips. The sensation was wonderful, so she did what came instinctively and opened her mouth and welcomed his tongue with her own. They would have kept kissing had they not heard Bingley clear his throat before he knocked on the door to announce that he was entering.

By the time he made his way into the parlour, the couple was standing a respectable distance one from the other although the swollen lips and heightened colour of both did not require a soothsayer to tell him what had taken place.

Bingley lifted an eyebrow as he surveyed the inhabitants of the room and there was no missing the look of pure unadulterated bliss on both. "Is there something you want to ask me, Phillips?"

"Er, yes there is. Your sister has done me the greatest honour and accepted my proposal of marriage. I request your permission and blessing to marry this wonderful woman." His betrothed blushed at his characterisation of herself.

"Is this what you desire, Caroline," he asked despite knowing the answer to his question.

"Yes, Charles, with all my heart it is what I want." Caroline smiled at him.

"In that case, Phillips, you have both my consent and my blessing," he took his soon to be brother-in-law's hand and they shook again. "Welcome to the family."

The three entered the drawing room and none within missed that something significant had taken place. Phillips had requested that he be allowed to inform his parents before an announcement was made, however, the announcement was superfluous.

"Graham, are you *betrothed*?" Hattie Phillips blurted out as the joy of the moment overtook her.

"Yes, Mama, we are, although I had hoped to inform you, Papa, and Franny in a less public setting..." he admitted.

Anything else that he was about to say was lost in a sea of congratulations. "We could celebrate your betrothal at the ball tonight Caroline and Graham," the Duchess offered.

"We thank you, your Grace, but tonight is not our night," Caroline Bingley said decisively. "This night is to celebrate the wedding of Ladies Jane and Marie to the Viscount and Mr. Fitz-william."

"Caroline is correct and is one of the reasons why I wanted to inform Mama and Papa privately. I had intended to request that Bingley not make a public announcement until after the weddings," Graham informed his family.

"I could not agree with my son and soon to be daughter more," Frank Phillips added. "Have you two discussed a wedding date yet?"

"We have not, Mr. Phillips," Caroline answered.

"You are to be our daughter," Mrs. Phillips said as she took her new daughter's free hand, the other being firmly held by her older sister Louisa. "We will never replace your late Mama or Papa, but we would be very honoured of you would call us Mother and Father." Caroline was deeply moved by the warmth of her new mother's declaration that she choked up as she nodded her acquiescence.

"I am so very happy for you, Caro," Louisa Hurst told her younger sister with tears in her eyes. She had seen the looks of love that Caroline sent toward Graham, and the ones that he sent her, and could not have been more pleased for her baby sister.

"There is an easy solution," Charles Bingley informed everyone. "It will be my honour to hold an engagement ball at Netherfield. What say you all for about a month from now? The newlyweds should have returned from their wedding trips by then and Hertfordshire is close to town so it will be no hardship to return."

"That is an acceptable option. I agree with Caroline, this time is for Jane and Richard and Andrew and Marie. It is laudable that Caroline and her betrothed do not want the focus of the celebration to be on them," Lady Anne Darcy proudly said seeing clear evidence of her protégé's sweetness.

Lady Elizabeth hugged her friend and added her voice to the growing number of well wishes that the couple received. An hour before luncheon as the well wishes were flowing, Mr.

Hill announced a new arrival, "Mr. Ian Ashby of Sherwood Park in Surrey."

Ashby was introduced to their graces and the rest of the family which included the younger men who had joined the rest in the drawing room. Lord Hilldale vigorously shook the hand of his good friend who would be standing up for him in less than three days, welcoming him warmly. He was accompanied by his twenty-year-old sister, Lady Amelia Ashby. Amelia had light brown hair and was tall for a lady. She had intriguing light green eyes with a full womanly figure. Tom Bennet, Marquess of Birchington was struck dumb when he saw Lady Amelia, lovingly called Amy by her family.

James Bennet, Marquess of Netherfield, who had one term left at Cambridge was enthralled with Georgiana Darcy. She was tall, blond and had cerulean eyes like her mother, brother, and the Fitzwilliam brothers. He knew that she would not be out for at least another two years, but that she had received permission from her guardian, Richard Fitzwilliam, to be at the ball until the completion of supper and was allowed to dance with men in the family party after her mother had plead her case. Kitty and Mary had received the same permission from Lord Thomas. They would be eighteen in March, but were still six weeks distant from their coming out ball that was being planned by their mother and aunts. They would take their curtsy before their cousin, the Queen, on their birthday with the coming out ball to be held on Saturday the 14th day of March.

It was not lost on James how Miss Darcy blushed whenever he paid her attention. The first time that she had visited Longbourn just after Jane and Richard's betrothal, she had been introverted and hardly spoke a word unless addressed directly. The girl that was before him now was not the same person other than in physical looks. She was self-confident, talked without being forced to, and was much more outgoing. This Miss Darcy commanded James's attention. He no longer saw a girl, but an attractive and intelligent young woman.

Lord James approached Georgiana where she was sitting and talking to Mary and Kitty.

"Miss Darcy, has anyone requested the first set for the ball tonight," he asked as she blushed scarlet at the meaningful question.

"No, my Lord, no one has." She looked at her mother who gave her a slight nod of approval for her agreeing her daughter could dance with him though he was not strictly family. "None of my sets have been claimed beyond the third with Richard and the fourth for Andrew."

"In that case I request the first, Miss Darcy," he gave her a half bow as he made his request.

"In that case, niece," her uncle Reggie interjected, "I will claim the fifth set. I would ask for the supper set, but you know that your Aunt Elaine would never forgive me," he winked at his niece as he smiled at his own joke.

"It is yours, my Lord Uncle," Georgie smiled back at her uncle who she loved like a father.

"As it seems that your second is open, may I request that set Miss Darcy?" Lord Tom snapped up her last open set other than the supper set. Miss Darcy nodded her acceptance and then the Marquess turned to the newly arrived Lady Amelia. "Your ladyship, if you are not otherwise engaged would you grant me the first set?"

Lady Amy Ashby, who could not help but feel an attraction to the handsome marquess, accepted his application. Ladies Mary and Kitty would dance the first with their father and Uncle Frank respectively and then they would be squired by other family or close friends until they left the ball with Maria Lucas and Georgiana after supper. Lady Elizabeth would open the ball with her friend Frank Lucas, which would be followed by her soon to be brothers and other family members. She had agreed to dance the supper set with Humphry Goulding, another friend from the neighbourhood who she had known from an early age.

A nervous Ian Ashby approached Lady Catherine as she

watched the young people filling up their dance cards. He sat down next to her and spoke quietly so only she could hear, "Your Ladyship, before I make this request to Lord Matlock, I want to respect your position as Anne's...Miss de Bourgh's mother and ask your blessing for me to request a private interview with her to request her hand in marriage."

"It speaks of your respect and love for Anne that you would apply to me before my brother. Just look after my precious girl, Ian, she means more to me than anything else." She collected herself and continued, "You have my heartfelt blessing to make your request of my brother." Ashby gave the woman that he hoped would soon be his mother-in-law a half bow and proceeded to where the Earl of Matlock was sitting with the older gentlemen.

"Lord Matlock, may I have a brief interview with you please sir?" he asked respectfully.

"Hertfordshire, may we use your study?" the Earl asked the Duke.

"By all means," Bennet agreed, "as long as you do not duel in there or otherwise disturb my books." He smirked.

As soon as the door was closed, Ashby got right to the point. "Some six months ago you granted me your permission to court your niece, Miss de Bourgh." The Earl nodded his agreement with the statement. "Our courtship has progressed, and I am now seeking your permission for a private interview with your niece."

The Earl decided to have some sport with the man, not unlike his friend Bennet had done when his sons had requested to wed the two oldest Bennet girls. "I did not realise that you were interested in Georgiana. You know she is not out yet, do you not?"

"W-what? Miss Darcy? No, my Lord, I am requesting permission to talk to Miss Anne de Bourgh." It was only then that Ashby saw the broad smile on the Earl's countenance and he realised that he was being sported with.

"Go to it, young man," Lord Matlock gave his ascent as he

slapped Ashby on the back. "Wait here, I will bring Anne to you. The door *will* remain open!"

A very short time later, Anne de Bourgh entered the study, and the door was but partly closed. Ashby had waited long enough so did not feel the need for flowery speeches so he took her hands, dropped to one knee, and asked her to marry him, telling her that she was the love of his life and his lady accepted without delay. They agreed that they would get married in April, though they would discuss the matter with Lady Catherine before settling on a final date. Just before her uncle returned to the study, Anne thanked her betrothed for honouring her mother by requesting her permission to speak before going to her Uncle. Lord Matlock's permission and blessing were given without delay, and so the second betrothal became official at Longbourn that day.

There was another round of hearty congratulations and the Countess of Matlock stated her intention to hold an engagement ball for her niece and soon to be nephew at Matlock House at the end of February. Ian and Anne followed the example set by Caroline Bingley and Graham Phillips, which meant there would be no announcement or mention of their betrothal at the ball. After luncheon, the Netherfield party, now including Ian Ashby, returned thither to rest as those staying at Longbourn retired to do the same.

CHAPTER 13

Longbourn was ablaze with light on the cold January night of the wedding ball. There were torches alight along the length of the drive to help guide carriages safely, at the end of which an army of footmen and grooms waited to tend to the arriving guests. If there was precipitation, none of the guests would be affected thanks to the oversized overhang that could accommodate at least two conveyances at a time. The receiving line was ready just outside the huge ballroom that was sparkling with the reflected light of thousands of wax candles in the twelve crystal chandeliers and numerous wall sconces. At the head of the line were the Duke and Duchess of Hertfordshire, the hosts, followed by Lady Jane, the Honourable Richard Fitzwilliam, Lady Marie, Lord Andrew Fitzwilliam, the Duke and Duchess of Bedford and the Earl and Countess of Matlock.

Prince Edward and Princess Elizabeth had arrived some hours earlier that afternoon along with a contingent of royal guards. Their Highnesses were resting and would make their entrance just before the first set. If it were not for the close familial relationship between the royals and the Bennets, the Regent and the Queen would not have sent representatives of the family to a ball and wedding outside of London. The royal cousins sent two almost priceless Ming Dynasty vases as wedding gifts for the two cousins who were marrying.

Sir William and Lady Sarah Lucas were among the first denizens of Meryton to make their way through the receiving line. Sir William, normally ebullient and ready to regale one and all with the story of his investiture to the knighthood, was awed by the number of peers present at the ball. It was a good mix of people from lowly country squires and merchants from the market town to peers and royalty.

Lady Elizabeth Bennet was far more subdued than her wont at an event where there was dancing, considering that she was one who loved to dance. The more that she had examined her way of sketching characters based on few facts, her quick temper, and her habit of making snap judgements, the less she felt good about herself. That was until she had the conversation with Lady Anne that morning. As she sat waiting for the ball room to fill up, she thought back to the conversation she had had with Darcy's mother, who she now called aunt and was called by her familiar name in turn, that morning when the two had taken a ride.

They had been well bundled up against the cold and were accompanied by Biggs and Johns, in addition to other footmen and a groom. Security had been increased on all of the family ever since Richard's warning about the probability of Wickham seeking to avenge himself against Lady Elizabeth. Miss Jones had been given the week off to spend with her uncle, the local physician and apothecary, and his family. The ladies had not planned to ride for very long because even though there was no precipitation that day and the wind was almost non-existent, it was a very cold day morning nonetheless. By mutual, if silent agreement they stopped on a flat area in one of the fields below Oakham Mount.

"I feel very guilty that because of my actions that your son will miss the wedding," Lady Elizabeth had said, her head down, feeling ashamed of her actions.

"Elizabeth. ELIZABETH Bennet!" She was lost in her thoughts but hearing her name the second time with raised voice snapped Elizabeth's out of her reverie. "Enough of this nonsense. You need to learn to follow your own advice about the past! The decision to miss the wedding was William's, and William's alone.

"Before we came to visit you the first time, it was made very clear to him that the invitation included his person. He chose to stay in town. I personally asked him multiple times if he would not relent and come to the wedding, but he told me that he would do

nothing to divert attention from the couples who are about to wed."

"Do you not see Aunt Anne," Lady Elizabeth insisted, "he made this decision because he was worried that I would let my temper run wild again and so it would be me that would actually have diverted attention from Jane and Richard and Marie and Andrew!" *Lady Elizabeth paused for a moment, then added, "After the way that I humiliated him publicly, how is it that he is so honourable to place my feelings above his own?"*

"That is who William is; who he always was. He just needed to be reminded of his true self, and you, my dear Lizzy, applied the pressure that cracked the façade. I have told you before, although as you now acknowledge, you were quick to anger and judge and employed implacable resentment against those who you felt wronged you or those that you love; William needed this. I want to believe that he would have arrived at the realisation that he could not continue to behave as he was on his own, but it could well have been a long time in the future," Lady Anne assured Elizabeth.

"This has been a positive for both of you. Both have identified and acknowledged faults and both of you have taken steps to correct said faults. How can that be a bad thing? You make me feel as proud of you as I am for my William. I finally saw the son at Snowhaven during Christmas that I used to see before that dreadful day when my beloved George was taken. There is no fortune large enough to repay you for the part you have played in being the catalyst for his transformation. He is not the only one who has changed; you have as well and it will bode well for both of you in the future."

Elizabeth thought about Lady Anne's words, "I see the truth in your words Aunt Anne. You should know that a fortnight ago, before they arrived, I contacted Aunts Rose and Pricilla and let them know that Mr. Darcy had been forgiven by me and to make sure that the Ton knows that he should be treated as anyone else in society and no longer ostracised. I am looking forward to debating Plato and Socrates with him, as I have heard that he studied both extensively."

Lady Anne Darcy gave her companion a warm smile, "He will

enjoy that above all else, Lizzy." As they were about to return to the warmth of the house, Lady Anne added, "I am in your debt for your help in drawing Georgie out. Not only have you helped give my son back to me, but my daughter as well."

Lady Elizabeth had felt a lot better after replaying the conversation in her head. She resolved that as soon as they arrived in Town three days hence, she would ask her Papa to send a note to Darcy House requesting that Mr. Darcy attend them at Bennet House and she would give him her complete and unreserved forgiveness and ask for his for her own precipitous judgements. Lady Anne Darcy had absolved her of guilt, but regardless of being told that she did not need to proffer one, she felt like she owed Mr. Darcy an apology.

It did not take long before Longbourn's ballroom was filled to capacity. A number of friends from Town and other locations would be hosted at Longbourn and Netherfield, thanks to Mr. Bingley volunteering his home until after the wedding breakfast two days hence. When the line for the first set started to form, it was led off by Jane and Richard, then Marie and Andrew, then followed the rest of the dancers. Elizabeth enjoyed dancing with her friend, Frank Lucas, and as per normal they bantered back and forth about nothing of great substance. Frank held no illusions that the raven-haired beauty that was 'little Lizzy' who used to beat him at everything from tree climbing and running to fighting would ever be more than a friend. It was not just about rank; Frank knew that she was far more intelligent than he was and that he would never be able to match her wit.

Ladies Anne and Catherine were seated next to one another, and neither lady missed the becoming blushes that Georgiana Darcy was exhibiting as she danced with the future Duke of Hertfordshire. Lord James was discretely giving her equally tender looks. The sisters agreed that they would have to keep a weather eye on the situation as Georgie was still two years away from her come out.

Further up the line, Lord Tom was enjoying his dance with

Lady Amy Ashby immensely. They had spent some time talking before the ball and the more he was around her, the more that the Marquess of Birchington was impressed. She was very light on her feet and there was no fawning over him like so many were wont to do as soon as they found out that he was heir to the dukedom of Bedford. For the first ten minutes of the set, they had danced in companionable silence.

"Lady Amelia, will you be returning to Town after the wedding or are you and your brother returning to Surrey?" he asked, hoping it was the former and not the latter.

"We will be at Ashby House in London, my Lord. We will join my parents, brother, and sister for the rest of the season," Lady Amy replied with a becoming blush. She was surprised by her attraction to the very good-looking man that she was dancing with.

Lady Amelia Ashby had survived two seasons without anyone piquing her interest though a number had called on her, but she had never agreed to more than the first call. Too many of them saw her as a way to increase their wealth and connections, not as the intelligent and vibrant woman that she was. Until she met the Marquess of Birchington, no man had ever caught her interest. They had only met that afternoon, but if he requested to call on her in Town, she would not object, she might even be so forward to ask him to have dinner if he was staying in town alone.

Lady Amy realised that she had not heard what he said next while she was lost in her thoughts, "I am sorry, my Lord, I did not hear what you said. Do you mind repeating it?" she asked, embarrassed but wanted to talk to him.

"I thought that mayhap my conversational skills were not up to the standard that you are used to, my Lady," he teased with a smile.

"Not at all, my Lord," she blushed with embarrassment after being caught wool-gathering on the dance floor again.

"The question, my lady, is whether you would permit me to call on you in London?" Lord Tom repeated, pleased she was smiling at him with her eyes wide and locked on him and no-where else.

"I would be both happy and honoured to receive your calls, my Lord." They enjoyed the remainder of their dance then Lady Amy was returned to her brother and future sister after the set was complete.

Georgiana Darcy had enjoyed dancing very much, especially the first set. She felt feelings that she had never felt before and as yet could not understand what they portended. Before the supper set was called, Lord James Bennet approached her and asked if she had a name pencilled in for the supper set. She shyly informed him that she did not, so James wisely applied to his new brother Richard for permission to dance a second set with Miss Darcy. After reminding him that his young cousin was still two years away from her come out, Richard granted James's request.

Lady Anne Darcy was ambivalent about what she was seeing. After hers and her sister's observations as her daughter danced the first, here was the Marquess leading her onto the dance floor again. On the one hand she was very happy that her Georgie was maturing before her eyes, but it also made her sad. Georgiana was her baby after all; and though she knew that one day she would marry and leave home, it had always been theoretical and many years in the future. It would still be three to four years before anyone would be allowed to declare for Georgiana if she had a say in the matter, but it was no longer many years in the future. If it were eventually to come to pass that Lord James and Georgie decided that they fit one with the other, Lady Anne knew that there could be no objection to James Bennet, not because of his title, wealth, and connections, but from all she had seen these last weeks, she knew he was a good and honourable young man.

For supper James and Georgie joined a table where the younger Bennet twins, Mariah Lucas, Lady Loretta, and their respective partners for the supper set sat under the watchful eyes of a bevy of companions. Lady Elizabeth, who had partnered with Humphry Goulding, sat with Reverend and Mrs. Pierce, Lord Tom and Lady Amy who had danced a second set, Caroline Bingley and Graham, and Bingley and Franny Phillips. As would be expected, the conversation was lively and Ladies Elizabeth and Amy found that they had much in common and ended up talking to each other more than their escorts. Lord Tom did not feel left out as he loved to watch his younger sister's mind work and was very much impressed that Lady Amelia could match her wit and was close to Lizzy in intelligence.

At the end of the meal the five girls who were not out yet were shepherded out of the ball room by the companions. Maria Lucas would spend the night with Ladies Mary, Kitty, Loretta, and Miss Darcy. As much as he would have wanted to, Tom Bennet did not request a third set from Amy Ashby which was a regret to both, but both understood that it already said much that he had danced the opening and supper set with her. It was close to five in the morning when the last head found the pillow and entered dreamland.

~~~~~~~/~~~~~~~

Fitzwilliam Darcy had arrived in Town that morning, deciding to leave his solitude at Pemberley a few days earlier than he originally planned. He was questioning his decision to not attend his cousins' weddings, but he would follow through with what he had stated he would do. His word was his bond, and the last thing he wanted was to appear like a man without resolution to the Bennets, especially not to Lady Elizabeth.

His mother had written to him to inform him that the lady had told her aunts he was forgiven and that there should be no further negative social impact. The Countess of Jersey had informed her fellow patronesses of Almacks, and soon it was common knowledge that Fitzwilliam Darcy of Pemberley was no longer *persona non grata*. Darcy had taken a walk in Hyde Park before the fashionable hour, but even with the small number of persons he encountered he could see that it was true as he was greeted cheerfully by one and all.

His reinstated status had been further evidenced when he went to Whites that afternoon. Among all but those whose daughters would have to find another way to gain a husband due to 'the settlement', he was welcomed like a returning hero. He humbly accepted the accolades, not revealing the true source of the terms set out in the document as he did not have his Grace's permission to inform anyone that it was his and not Darcy's idea.

The night before the double wedding found him sitting in the Darcy House library reading *Tom Jones* by Henry Fielding for the fifth time. The book was very special to him as he had read it the first time with his father when he was ten years old. Whenever he read the tome it made him feel close to his honoured departed father and he felt the comfort that came with the feeling of his presence associated with the book. He had ordered a tray for his dinner which Mrs. Killion had delivered to him in the library, and now he was sitting comfortably sipping a snifter of brandy. He had decided that becoming maudlin about missing the wedding on the morrow achieved nothing other than making him feel sorry for himself, so he concentrated on the book and let the pleasant memories of his interactions with his late father wash over him.

~~~~~~~/~~~~~~~

That night before they went to bed, Lady Sarah joined her eldest daughters for *the talk*. Although the Duchess was not their mother by blood, she was their mother in deed. In their hearts they both knew that there was no better mama in the whole of the known world. "Before I begin, do you prefer that I speak to each of you separately or together?"

"You know us Mama," Jane spoke for the two after a silent communication with her sister only a twin would understand, "we have no secrets one from the other and choose to listen to you together."

With her daughter's decision made, the duchess proceeded with her mission to elucidate her daughters. "This is your last night we have sole claim of you as daughters living under our roof. Tomorrow your husbands will have the honour, and I dare say pleasure, of your protection, though you must know that all of us will protect and love you all of your days," the Duchess said wistfully. She wanted them to be as happy as humanly possible but would miss her oldest children more than she cared to admit to anyone.

"Both Andrew and Richard truly understand and love you my dear daughters. If they did not, there are many men in this family who would take them to task," the last was said with a smile as Lady Sarah teased her girls. "Your father and I are equally happy and relieved that your marriages will be true partnerships with men who not only love and cherish you but respect you. Tomorrow night will be your wedding night and I need to talk to you about what to expect in the marriage bed," their Mama offered softly. With a blush rising in their cheeks, Jane and Marie nodded for their mother to proceed.

"The intimacies of the marriage bed are not something to be feared, especially not with someone who loves you the way that your betrotheds clearly love you. This implies that the marriage bed will be a wonderful, even pleasurable experience for both of you. Anyone that advises their daughter to 'lie back and tolerate' the relations between man and woman has no idea of what they speak. Do not be afraid to tell Richard," the Duchess looked at Jane, "and Andrew," she looked at Marie, "what you like and do not like, and let them know that you want to know the same from them. Just like you want your marriage to be true partnerships, the same is true of the marriage bed. My wish for both of you is that you will discover that it is as pleasurable to give as to receive, and that you are never ashamed of the relations that you will have in private with your husband. A good relationship in the marriage bed enhances your marriage as a whole and gives a depth of joy that cannot be harmed by anyone.

"I will not lie to you; there will be some pain and blood the first coupling, but thankfully it is only the first time that this should happen. The pain will be but a moment and marks your becoming a woman in every sense of the word. Richard and Andrew care very much about your wellbeing, so if you need to stop for a moment then or at any point, I am sure that they would understand. Neither man would ever force either of you to do that which is unacceptable to you. That is why telling each other what you enjoy, and do not enjoy, is so very important.

"If you never think of your relations with your husbands as a chore, they will never be so. No matter what anyone else may say, both the husband and wife deriving pleasure from the marriage bed is a good thing and does not make the wife a wanton, nor is it a sin to love your husband as only his bride can. I believe that each of you will take much pleasure in your marriage, both what happens out of and within the marriage bed. Never be afraid to be spontaneous, and regardless of what society professes, night-time is *not* the only acceptable time for relations with your beloved husband. Whenever you have privacy and you both desire the same thing, it is never wrong.

"In the future when you are with child there is no reason to stop having relations with your husband, until and unless you feel it is too uncomfortable for you as you near your confinement. Remember that it is a partnership, and like any good and equal partnership the shared experience of love, passion, and pleasure will be very fulfilling. Do you have any questions for me, Jane? Marie?"

Once both brides had stopped blushing, they looked at each other and then chorused, "No, thank you Mama."

Jane added, "Truly. You have helped us look forward to our wedding night with pleasure and not fear." Both girls stood and kissed Lady Sarah on her cheeks and she hugged each one with all of her might. After their mother left the chambers, the sisters discussed what their mama had imparted long into the night.

~~~~~~~/~~~~~~~

Friday morning, the 17th day of January in the year of our

Lord 1812, was a cold and clear day but for some wisps of snow-white clouds. The ceremony at Longbourn's church was to commence at half after the hour of nine. Longbourn's rector, Mr. Christopher Pierce, had met with both couples the previous afternoon to make sure that everyone was familiar with the order of service and to answer any questions that the couples may have had.

Not only did they like their rector, he had the very good sense to marry their Charlotte, thus elevating Mr. Pierce in the estimation of the family. Unless there was a royal decree, all five Bennet girls intended to marry from Longbourn with Mr. Pierce officiating.

Ladies Jane and Marie had dressed in very similar gowns for the whole of their lives up to this day, so they saw no reason to deviate on this most important of days. Both had silk gowns created by Madame Chambourg, the difference was that Jane's was white while Marie's was cream. Both had short-puffed sleeves with a clear organza overlay. The veils, also organza, matched the colour of the bride's dress with pearls sewn in for lustrous affect. Elizabeth was to stand up for Jane, while Franny Phillips would do the honours for Marie. Peter and May Gardiner had been appointed ring bearer and flower girl respectively.

By quarter after the hour, the congregation was all seated knowing that with the two royals present that anyone late would not be allowed in by the cadre of royal guards around the perimeter of the church. The grooms were waiting, Andrew on the left and Richard to the right of the altar. Ashby was to the right of and a step behind his friend while Colonel Forster in full dress uniform was there for the former colonel. The Duchess of Hertfordshire, escorted by Lord Tom, took her seat in the front pew, and they were followed in by Lord James with Lady Mary on one arm and Lady Kitty on the other.

The brides stood in the vestibule with their attendants, and the dukes of Hertfordshire and Bedford. In keeping with his status as a second father, Uncle Sed was to walk Marie down the aisle while Jane would be on her father's arm. Lord Thomas Bennet was normally not an emotional man, but on this morning as he and his brother were about to give his first-born daughters away to men who deserved them and would protect them with their lives if need be, he could not but be overcome. He looked at his two beautiful daughters and owned that they had grown into strong women who would from this day forward be under the protection of Andrew and Richard Fitzwilliam and no longer his.

The door opened with Peter and May proceeding Lizzy as the young girl dropped rose petals. Lizzy was followed by her father with Jane on his arm. Next came Franny Phillips followed by Lord Sed Bennet with Marie on his arm. As each entered the church, he or she made a bow or curtsey to the Prince and Princess. Lady Elizabeth smiled at Caroline Bingley and Charlotte Pierce who were seated next to each other as she slowly walked up the aisle. Both her older sisters had teased her with a reminder to walk at a sedate pace rather than the pace she set when she took her rambles about the countryside.

Lady Elizabeth stood on the right near Richard. As the Duke of Hertfordshire and Lady Jane arrived at the head of the aisle, Richard approached them. After the Duke kissed his daughter's cheek and lowered the veil, Lord Thomas Bennet handed the treasure that was his oldest daughter to Richard Fitzwilliam. The same process was repeated as the Duke of Bedford handed his niece to Lord Andrew Fitzwilliam. Once both dukes had taken their seats, the parson began the wedding service.

"Dearly beloved, we are gathered together here in the sight of God, and in the face of this congregation, to join together...

It was not long before both brides and grooms had recited their vows and Mr. Pierce closed the ceremony:

"Forasmuch as *Lord Andrew* and *Lady Marie and Richard and Lady Jane* have consented together in holy wedlock, and have witnessed the same before God and this company, and thereto have given and pledged their troth either to other, and have declared the same by giving and receiving of a ring and by joining of hands; I pronounce that each couple be man and wife together, in the Name of the Father, and of the Son, and of the Holy Ghost. Amen.

"God the Father, God the Son, God the Holy Ghost, bless, preserve, and keep you; the Lord mercifully look upon you with his favour, and so fill you with all spiritual benediction and grace, that ye may all so live together in this life, that in the world to come ye may have life everlasting. *Amen.*"

The four followed Mr. Pierce into the vestry to sign the register with the two dukes and maids of honour as their witnesses. The new Fitzwilliam sisters signed the name Bennet one last time and it was official. "I finally come before you, Janey, I am after all a viscountess now!" Marie teased her elder sister.

"Your Highnesses, your Graces, my Lords and Ladies, Lord Andrew and Lady Marie Fitzwilliam, the Viscount and Viscountess of Hilldale, and The Honourable Mr. Richard and Lady Jane Fitzwilliam," Hill intoned as he introduced the newlyweds upon their entrance to the ballroom where the pre-wedding ball had been held, now the location of the festive wedding breakfast to celebrate their wedding.

The young couples were congratulated by one and all. Lady Anne Darcy was standing next to Lady Elizabeth Bennet; she looked over at the younger lady who had become like another niece to her and smiled as she leaned close so no one could hear her words, "We are related in fact now, Lizzy, and you realise that you and William are cousins now, do you not?"

"Yes, Aunt Anne, well I know that!" Lady Elizabeth let out an unladylike huff. "You are not the first to point that out to me in the last few days, and I dare say my brother Richard will take every opportunity to tease me about your son and the Bennets now being connected through the marriages to my sisters."

"You are not upset at the connection, are you Lizzy?" Lady Anne asked worried that the young lady had changed her mind about William.

"Not at all, Aunt Anne. In fact, it pleases me greatly." Her smile reached her eyes so Lady Anne knew it was genuine. "I have gained more than your son as my cousin this day, I now get to claim Aunt Catherine, her Anne, and your Georgie as relations in fact rather than just in my heart. I do not repine the connection to any of my new relatives." Lizzy promised softly.

Lady Anne was happy for her son, although she had no way of knowing if Elizabeth and William would ever be more than cousins. She did know one thing, neither she nor anyone else would push them in one direction or another. If they were to become any more than cousins, that would be up to them, and them alone.

Both dukes and the Earl of Matlock made speeches welcoming all of the new family members. Both Lord Thomas and his older brother sent a not too subtle warning, disguised as humour, to the Fitzwilliam brothers of what would happen to them if they ever hurt either Jane or Marie. The two Marquesses and some other male relatives added their own more direct messages to the two grooms. No one believed it was necessary; the adoration that flowed between each couple was very easy to see, even to an unromantic eye.

By one in the afternoon the newlyweds had said their farewells. Lord and Lady Hilldale headed to Town where they would overnight before heading toward Brighton and Seaview Cottage while Richard and Lady Jane Fitzwilliam headed north, starting their almost four-day trip that would bring them to Lakeview House in the Lake District. Richard Fitzwilliam had reserved the biggest suite at a very respectable coaching inn three hours north of Meryton.

After the rest of the family had returned to the ballroom to continue the celebration, the Duke and Duchess of Hertfordshire stayed outside in the same spot where they had wished the daughters and new sons Godspeed for their travels.

"Will it ever get easier to see our children leave Longbourn, Thomas?" Lady Sarah asked forlornly.

"I would wager not, my love," Lord Thomas said as he hugged his beloved wife close to him. "My hope is that although we will let them go when the time comes, we will always love them as we do now, so it will never be easy to say goodbye to any of them."

"We did gain two very honourable sons, Thomas. Either one of them will do anything in his power to make our girls happy," she sighed, "Jane and Marie will be missed, but we will see them often enough. In fact, they will be at the Netherfield ball and then they will be in London with us for the season."

Thomas Bennet, Duke of Hertfordshire, who after all these years still loved his wife to distraction, hugged her close and kissed her soundly before they turned to re-enter the house. As they walked inside the Duchess was heard to say: "Oh my, Thomas, you make me feel like a newlywed again."

CHAPTER 14

Darcy was tingling with anticipation. The Bennets had arrived in town the morning after the wedding and were at Bennet House just across Grosvenor Square, and his mother and sister were back at Darcy House where they belonged. The house felt so much lighter with them in it, especially with his newly self-confident sister. Lady Anne and Miss Darcy were in their chambers washing the dust of the road from their persons when Killion knocked in his study door holding a salver that had a note on it. Darcy broke the seal of the Duke of Hertfordshire and with no little trepidation opened the missive.

18 April 1812

Mr. Darcy,

If it is convenient for you, could you please come to Bennet House at two o'clock this afternoon.

Sincerely,

Lord Thomas Bennet, Duke of Hertfordshire

It was short and to the point, and Darcy hoped that this was the day that he would receive the forgiveness he craved from the very lady for whom he had a tender regard but he did not want to assume anything. He would just have to wait until he walked across the square to find out what the Duke wanted to meet with him about. After all this waiting, it was these minutes that seemed to pass very slowly.

~~~~~~~/~~~~~~~

At last Wickham received good news from one of the waifs, he reported that the Bennets had arrived at their townhouse that very morning. Now he could have the family watched in earnest to learn the lady's schedule. Before he could celebrate, the boy who had reported they had arrived told him that he had been close enough to hear two servants discussing that the family would soon return to 'something shire' for a ball and that they would not be at the house to stay until early March for a 'coming ball'.

Wickham's first instinct was to strike the bearer of the bad tidings, but he restrained himself. He needed the boy and his friends if he was to glean the information that he so desired. Rather than punish him, he gave the beaming lad a shilling and told him to inform his friends that they were to start regular rotations so that no one boy would be noticed continuously hanging about the environs of the house.

"At last, I have some positive news to report to the *Spaniard*," he told his paramour, leaving out the not so good news part.

"I am so happy to hear that, George. The sooner we put this cesspool behind us the better," Karen Younge stated with a look of distaste.

She had bought into Wickham's delusion that this was a fool proof plan and was counting the money that they would receive after paying Withers and Álvarez. What she did not know is that her *lover's* plan was to take the money and disappear, leaving her behind. He wanted young maidens, not an old piece of leather like Karen Younge. He would have all the money needed to have a stream of them at his beck and call. He was spending the money in his head, as he always did when he hatched one of his hair-brained schemes, long before he had any in hand.

Mrs. Young was only six and twenty and for the most part still had her looks. The truth was that she was never married. She had adopted the 'Mrs.' appellation as she believed it gave her a certain gravitas that an unmarried woman did not have. She was too blind to see that Wickham felt nothing for her beyond what he felt she could do for him. She had lied to herself so much that had he told her his true feelings for her, the chances were that she would not hear it.

An hour later Wickham was standing before Álvarez in his office. "The Bennets arrived today, Mr. Álvarez."

"Zat is at least the progress," he said, "'ow long before you able to 'ave plan?"

"One of the boys heard that until sometime in March the family will not have a set schedule as they will be attending some events that are outside of London," Wickham saw the scowl on the *Spaniard's* face. "My source says that they will then be here for the remainder of the season. I will have the lads in rotation going forward, by early April we will be able to act."

"You 'ave until tenth day April. Either you bring girl, or you no live!" Wickham understood that there was no room for negotiation in the man's decree. At least he was still alive and had two months left to complete his mission.

~~~~~~~~/~~~~~~~~

All three Darcys were seated in the music room. Georgiana was playing the new Broadwood grand pianoforte that her brother had gifted her when she had turned fifteen. Like her mother, Miss Darcy was a very skilled pianist. Surprising to all the talent had skipped Lady Anne's sister, Catherine. As much as the lady claimed that she would have been a 'proficient had she learned' the instrument, the truth was that she, at but ten years of age had given up her lessons in disgust as she just did not have an ear for music, all of her claims to the contrary notwithstanding. Thankfully the kinder, nicer version of Lady Catherine de Bourgh very seldom made such outrageous claims any longer.

While his sister softly played, Darcy showed the note to his mother. "William," she said after reading the short missive, "this is your chance to start over with Lizzy. I will share something with you now, and I can only pray that you will not be in high dudgeon after my disclosure."

"Mother," he said as he took her hand, "no matter what, you know that I love you too much to be angry at you."

"When we visited Longbourn the first time after Richard's

betrothal..." Lady Anne proceeded to inform her son that Lady Elizabeth had been willing to forgive him then and inform her aunts that he was to no longer be publicly 'punished'. She also revealed her own reaction and requested that the lady hold off, and her reasons why she had made the extraordinary application. On completion of the recitation, her son sat very still. When he spoke, his answer was neither vituperative nor was it acerbic. His mother had anticipated a harsh reaction, yet she did not receive even a mild rebuke.

"Mama, you were completely correct in your judgement. I cannot but agree," his mother let out an audible sigh and squeezed her son's hand in appreciation of his response. "As I was then, it is highly probable that had there been little or no consequence, that I would have rationalised that I had done nothing so very bad and would not have been forced to confront my shortcomings. So no, Mother, I am not angry. I know that what you said was because of your love for me and always wanting what is best for your children. You knew that I needed a jolt to make me see the truth, that I needed to make meaningful and real changes, and were willing to risk my displeasure so that I would have a chance to become the man that you, my honoured, late father, and the rest of the family knew that I could be. Your love for Georgie was the reason that you begged me to check Mrs. Younge's characters. I know that your motives are pure, and I can only be ashamed of my past behaviour and wanton blindness."

"William, your reaction to what I told you is ample proof that you have addressed all of Lizzy's reproofs and amended your behaviour," she smiled at her son with all of her maternal love and pride shining in her eyes. "When you put the needs of others ahead of your own desire, by deciding not to attend us to Longbourn and the wedding, I was sure that you would succeed. When Lizzy told me what she wanted to do, I felt that it was not yet time to take the pressure off of you. You know what Elizabeth says about the past do you not?" He nodded with a small smile. "Well then, let us pledge, all of us Darcys, that we will honour that credo and move forward looking to the future. Yes, all people need to learn from past missteps, but it is not necessary to live in the past. Our decisions can change our todays and tomorrows, but there is nothing that any of us can do to change the past."

Darcy stood and hugged and kissed his mother and sister before asking Killion to bring his hat, gloves, and coat for the short walk across the square in the direction of what he hoped would be a new beginning with the Bennets.

On being admitted to Bennet House, Darcy was relieved of his outerwear by the butler, Thatcher, who then showed him to his Grace's study where the Duke was waiting for his caller. The Duke's study was a little larger than his own and like his, contained shelves with many tomes on them. After politely refusing refreshment and extending the usual pleasantries, the Duke, as was his prerogative, opened the conversation.

"Mr. Darcy, the reports that we have received have impressed us greatly. It seems that you took my Lizzy's set down to heart and are a better man for it," Lord Thomas said with genuine feeling. "The fact that you are now the hero to many members of the Ton who are bachelors, especially Lord Granville, is an added benefit for you, I am sure." The Duke said the last with a smile.

"I thank you, your Grace. I appreciate your kind words more than I can express. However, the changes that I have made, am still making, were not to impress anyone, but for me to become the man that my parents always believed that I would be." Darcy delivered the message unambiguously, that he had not made cosmetic changes for appearance. "As to my being a *hero*, it is you who deserve the credit, your Grace. As you never gave me leave to disclose the source of my information, I have had to live with the credit of it when it rightly belongs to you."

"Believe me, Mr. Darcy, I am very happy for you to receive the credit and accolades."

"Thank you, your Grace," Darcy inclined his head to show

his thanks to the Duke. "If your family is home, I humbly request an audience with them so I can proffer my apology to the family."

The Duke agreed to the audience, and Darcy followed him to the family sitting room where the family was assembled. When they entered, everyone rose, and the expected greetings and courtesies were exchanged. Darcy did not miss that Lady Elizabeth did not look him directly in the eye. When the family sat, he remained standing.

"I would like to offer my unreserved apology for my behaviour when we first met. I cannot look back on the way that I held myself without abhorrence. I deserved every word that Lady Elizabeth..."

He was cut off by a very contrite looking Lady Elizabeth. "Please do not repeat what I said then. I too owe you an apology Mr. Darcy, no matter who told me that I do not. Your behaviour was not what it should have been, but neither was the way that I acted. It was my way to rush to judgement and I allowed my temper to get the better of me. I want you to know that I have forgiven you without any reservation."

"I thank you sincerely for your forgiveness, Lady Elizabeth," he gave her a shallow bow, "although I do not believe you owe me any apologies, I offer my complete forgiveness nonetheless. What did you say that night that I did not deserve? I had acted in a way that caused Lord's Tom and James to want to call me out! No Lady Elizabeth, it is I that must thank you."

"Thank me?" the incredulous lady asked. She was shocked that the man would thank her after the way she humiliated him.

"Yes, my Lady. Without your reproofs and the added weight of my ostracization from society, I would not have been willing to look at my behaviour and make the changes that I have made, and will continue to make for the rest of the time that God grants me on this earth. My mother, sister, and my family have always loved me, but now they are proud of me like they never were before. So yes, Lady Elizabeth, I must thank you. I am a better man than the one that all of you first met in Hertfordshire, When I attempted to apologise at Longbourn you pointed out that talk is cheap, so I decided to act, not talk." He smiled as he said the last, his dimples revealed to the Bennets for the first time.

The man standing before them in the family sitting room, other than physical resemblance, was not the man that they had seen in Meryton. For once in her life Lady Elizabeth Bennet was speechless, so it was left to her mother to respond for the family.

"Mr. Darcy, you have all of our unreserved and complete forgiveness." Lady Sarah looked at her family and there was no dissention. "We missed you at the wedding *Cousin,* we trust that there will be no more *family* events that you will choose to miss." The Duchess raised her eyebrow in challenge as he had more than once seen Lady Elizabeth do.

"Thank you, your Graces, Lords and Ladies, I believe going forward we should look to Lady Elizabeth's philosophy about the past for guidance," he said as he looked at the lady who had a light blush on her face.

"I thank you for your graciousness, Mr. Darcy," Lady Elizabeth said, "It speaks to your character that regardless of the possible punishment, you made the changes that you felt were needed. You could have sunk into an ennui or become despondent or become angry and vituperative, but you did not. I too add my sorrow that you missed standing up with Richard, but as you said, it is in the past *Cousin*. My hope is that all of us can start over and move forward without looking back. I think that as we are in fact now family, that you should address us as such." There were nods of agreement from all of the Bennets.

"Your words are very meaningful, Lady...Cousin Elizabeth. I thank you and would enjoy being address as William or Cousin William by all of my new relatives." Darcy felt the final weight lift off of his broad shoulders. He had no illusions, his new cousin was very far from the possibility of having the same feelings for him as he already had for her, but they were now on a friendly footing. He believed that as long as he kept to the narrow path that he had chosen for himself; he was confident that his friendship with all of his Bennet cousins would grow. This was a good start to a better understanding between them, a very good start.

Before he left, the Duchess issued an invitation for the Darcys to join them for dinner after church on the morrow. The party would include the Jerseys, Bedfords, Matlocks, and the de Bourghs. Darcy thanked Lady Sarah sincerely and told her that he would send a note as soon as he had made sure that his mother and sister had no prior engagements. He unknowingly gained more approval from the Bennets for stating that he would ask rather than assuming and accepting the invitation without consultation.

~~~~~~~/~~~~~~~

At the Bingley townhouse on Gracechurch Street after church on Sunday, brother and sister were sitting and thinking of the people that they loved. Bingley was envious that he had to wait to find his happiness, but in no way envied Caroline her happiness and that she was already betrothed to the man that she loved while he was not allowed to declare himself for another six weeks. His envy was only about the timing; he could not have been happier for his sister. Bingley loved his kind and generous younger sister as much as any brother could love a sister. He was aware that her change for the better was connected to Lady Anne taking Caroline under her wing, but no more than that. Frankly, the details were not important. He would be forever in Lady Anne's debt for the magic that she had worked on his younger sister.

Said sister was sitting on a settee lost in her reverie. '*If you had told me that my life would be like it is now, even before Charles leased Netherfield, best thing he EVER did, I would have thought someone had lost their mind.*

'*Here I sit, friends with Lizzy and all of her sisters; accepted by* the Bennets and all of their family; and soon I will marry the man of my dreams. I, the daughter of Harrison Bingley, tradesman, is warmly welcomed in the houses of dukes and earls. Thank God this is not just a dream.

'I cannot wait for Monday morning to get here, I am joining Lizzy, Louisa, Lady Anne, Aunt Maddie, Lady Loretta, Georgie, and the younger Bennet twins and we are going to Madam Chambourg's shop to look at designs for my wedding dress! **Who would have guessed that the Bingley daughters once so snubbed are clients of Madam Chambourg and she, the most exclusive modiste of the Ton, is making my wedding dress!** After the modiste, we will go to Gunter's, and lastly to Harding, Howell, and Company. How exciting it will be to be in a store with departments so we can see wares that would normally need five or six shops to accomplish.

'Uncle Edward has offered for me to look through his new bolts of material for my trousseau and my wedding dress. All of the ladies will join me to turn the warehouse upside down on Tuesday. What fun we will have!'

The Hursts were soon expected and would spend the rest of the day with their brother and sister. The Hursts went to the church in the parish where Mr. Hurst's townhouse was located. It was not long before Harold and Louisa Hurst arrived and joined them in the drawing room before dinner.

In Mayfair, the Darcys had just arrived at Bennet House where the butler and a footman had relieved them of their outerwear. Darcy had noticed a young boy outside, seemingly watching Bennet House, but he did not think more of it as it was not uncommon for poor waifs to beg on the square hoping for some largess from one of the wealthy residents of the area. All three Darcys were warmly welcomed as they joined the large party in the drawing room. Georgie went to sit with Ladies Kitty, Mary, and Loretta while her mother gravitated toward their sisters, the Duchesses and Lady Jersey. Anne de Bourgh was conversing with Lady Elizabeth. Darcy envied his cousin talking to the only woman who had ever interested him beyond mere civilities. The two Dukes and two Earls had retired to Lord Thomas's study for a pre-dinner brandy.

Darcy decided that he hoped to get to know the two Marquesses better so he joined the group that included the two Bennet brothers and their cousin, his now as well, Wesley de Melville, Viscount Westmore.

"Welcome, Cousin William," Lord Birchington, as the eldest of the three, spoke first.

"I thank you Cousin Tom. Cousin James, I trust you are well?" Darcy did know who the third young man, also a new cousin, was, but as the lowest ranked man it was not his place to ask for an introduction.

"Tom, would you introduce me to our new cousin, please?" Lord Wesley requested with no little amusement.

"Wes, this is our cousin, Fitzwilliam Darcy of Pemberley, who is called William, Cousin William, Lord Wesley de Melville, Viscount Westmore." The two shook hands.

"You are the one who was on the receiving end of Lizzy's ire were you not," Lord Wes said with a smile.

"Yes, Cousin Wes, the very one. I can honestly say that I am a better man for the experience!" Darcy said with a smile.

"Can we drop the 'cousin' before our names? We all know what our relationship one to the other is. I for one do not need reminding each time we address each other." Tom suggested and all four agreed.

"William, Richard informed us about your skill with the foil and pistol after Tom and I threatened to call you out," James assessed Darcy. "When I returned to Cambridge, I found the awards on the walls of the clubs. You were unbeaten with a foil!" James said the last with reverence.

"I do practice a lot," Darcy admitted modestly.

"Andrew and Richard informed us that you are a regular at Angelo's." James wondered if this was still true and Darcy nodded to allow that it was so. "When do you go next, William?"

"I plan to go tomorrow while my mother and Georgie are spending Pemberley's hard-earned funds." His three new cousins enjoyed discovering that Darcy had a dry wit as all three had decided that this was a man worth knowing.

"Would you object if James and I join you…" Tom started.

His cousin Wes interjected. "I too would like to be there, if that is agreeable to all of you."

"I would be happy for all of you to join me, I will be there at eleven. Or if you like, you are welcome to come to Darcy House by half after ten and we can go together." All three agreed that they would meet Darcy at his home at the suggested time. "New opponents are always welcome," Darcy agreed with a sly smile. His three challengers smiled too, though sure that someone with the skill that their cousin had would make quick work of any of them with a foil.

In the study the four older men were just finishing their snifters when Lord Thomas turned to his friend, Lord Matlock. "I am very impressed by your nephew, our new cousin, Matlock," Bennet said with admiration, "I cannot think of another that would have attended to Lizzy's reproofs the way that William did. Most impressive."

"I agree Matlock," the Duke of Bedford added while his brother-in-law Jersey nodded in agreement. "When I first heard the story, my first reaction was revulsion at Darcy's behaviour. But the way that he has reacted shows a depth of character that few possess. I agree with my brother; he is a most estimable young man."

"If I could, I would kiss Lizzy for shocking his prior bad behaviour out of him. We are all very proud of him and seeing the unbridled joy in my sister Anne watching her true son emerge once again. It is naught but a gift from God Himself!" Lord Matlock said with much approbation for his nephew.

"He performed a miracle of sorts," Bennet agreed with a wide smile.

"To what do you refer, Thomas?" the Earl of Jersey inquired with a bemused look on his countenance.

"Lizzy forgave him, and she too has changed and learnt from the experience," Bennet informed his family with fatherly pride. "Her anger at the time was righteous, but she has learned not to sketch a character on far too little evidence, to control her temper, and not make snap judgements.

"Matlock, your nephew saved Sarah and me having to have that talk with Lizzy. For too long she used what happened to me when I was entrapped as justification. I am very pleased with this unintended benefit." The Duke thought for a moment, "To be fair, I believe your sister Anne's influence had a big part in Lizzy's changes."

"My sister has that effect sometimes," Reginald stated. As much as he missed his friend and brother-in-law George Darcy, every time that he prayed, he thanked God for returning his baby sister to them. He knew how close Anne had come to passing, and if one were to talk of miracles, his sister being alive was a daily reminder to Reggie Fitzwilliam of God's grace.

Even though there were a good number of peers present, seating for lunch was informal. Lady Elizabeth ended up seated next to her cousin William. The agreement to drop the appellation of 'cousin' during address as adopted by the four young men, was quickly taken up by all. Darcy could not believe that he now had permission to call the lady by her familiar name. Yes, things were definitely improving between them.

During the meal the conversation was as convivial as one would expect when family shared a meal. Darcy was not willing to call her Lizzy...yet; he hoped that they would arrive at a point that they would both feel comfortable with him using the shortened version of her name. They canvassed some books that they had enjoyed, and both were very pleased to discover that the other had similar tastes in books. They had found common ground; both were bibliophiles. Elizabeth discussed her father's libraries at both Bennet House and Longbourn and the collection of rare first editions that the Duke owned. She was equally amazed when Darcy described the library at Pemberley. There was no boasting or improper pride, just a description of what was. Lady Anne pointed out that if anything, her son had understated the scope of the library. He explained to the lady that his ancestor, Pierre D'Arcy, who had come to England's shores with William the Conqueror, had brought a considerable collection of books with him and that after he had anglified his name to Darcy, he started collecting tomes in the English language as well. The library was the work of many generations.

'*The thought of this man showing me his library is not abhorrent,*' Lady Elizabeth admitted to herself. Things were changing, she could see herself becoming her cousin's friend. If one had asked her if that possibility existed in November of last year, the middle Bennet daughter would have recommended the person be consigned to Bedlam.

"A thank you is owed to you, Elizabeth," Darcy said, when he saw her questioning look, he clarified, "Well, to you and your sisters. Georgie is back as she was before the blackguard tried to seduce her. In fact, she is far better than she used to be. Your vivacity is rubbing off on her, Cousin, and I for one could not be happier."

Lady Elizabeth inclined her head and accepted the praise on behalf of her sisters and cousins who had all worked to draw Miss Darcy out, but the thought of the source of their Georgie's pain gave her an opportunity to ask a question few others could answer. "Richard warned us that the seducer will more than likely try some ill-advised scheme to avenge himself on me. Should I be concerned about him?"

"You never go anywhere without guards, do you?" he asked with no little concern.

"No, William, I do not. When we go out, if I am on my own, then my companion Miss Jones is with me and four footmen guards. If I ride Mercury without others, I then add a groom to that number. I am negotiating with Papa for as few as possible with me on my morning rambles. Two days a week I like to take a walk in Hyde Park. I am begging Papa's indulgence to have only Biggs and Johns walk with me, at least then I would have the illusion of solitude."

"His Grace finds some mountain sized men. I assume Biggs is not a small man." Both smiled as he was correct.

"Yes, he is aptly named as he is one of, if not the biggest, footmen that we employ as guards." Elizabeth agreed with a playful smile.

The two were joined by Lady Anne, Georgiana, and Anne. As soon as talk turned to the shopping expedition on the morrow, Darcy made a tactical retreat. They had been so absorbed in their conversation that they had not noticed they were being observed by all at the table with them, the concern growing into amusement the longer their family watched, though all missed the look that passed between Lady Sarah and Lady Anne, both of them aware of Darcy's attraction to their Lizzy, and they had seen the spark that had ignited in her eyes as she had talked to him.

CHAPTER 15

Monday morning the ladies rode in three coaches to Madame Chambourg's. There was as much excitement at spending time with one another as they were about the shopping to come. The four younger girls and Miss de Bourgh were in one carriage, and Lady Anne, Madeline Gardiner, Lady Elizabeth, Louisa Hurst and Miss Bingley in the second conveyance while the third housed companions and some of the guards not riding on the back of the first two carriages.

It was a short ride to the modiste's shop on Bond Street. As they were entering the shop, Miss Bingley and Mrs. Hurst noticed the looks of envy on some ladies faces, just like they used to have when they thought that they would never be accepted by as clients for this particular Madame. They had three hours during which no other clients would be permitted entrance. One did not 'walk in' at Madame Chambourg's, one had an appointment or the lady, regardless of rank, would find herself removed from the list of clients irrevocably. One lady, and one lady only, committed the cardinal sin of trying to enter without an appointment over ten years prior. That lady was never **allowed entry** again no matter the entreaties she or anyone else made on her behalf. No one ever broke that particular rule again.

The four younger members of the group who were not yet out, looked through fashion plates lovingly. Mary and Kitty asked one of Madame's assistants, the one who was in Meryton when the Bennets were in residence at Longbourn, if they and their cousins could view the gowns for their coming out ball. The gowns for the presentation were being made at the modiste's as well, but everyone knew that the gowns the

Queen required would only be worn for the many practices, which the Bennet twins had started a month before, as well as on the day of presentation. The girls agreed that it was a wonder that they had never heard of one being presented that had tripped over the hoops or the train as they backed out of the presentation hall following their curtsey to the Queen.

Lady Anne and Madeline Gardiner were playing the role of mother of the bride and helping Caroline select the pattern for her gown, with assistance from Louisa, Elizabeth and Anne.

"I want something elegant, not overly ostentatious, and more along the lines of the wedding gowns that you created for Ladies Jane and Marie," Caroline told Madame Chambourg.

"*C'est sûr, ce sera mon Plaisir,*" the modiste said. She remembered that not everyone was fluent in French like the Bennet ladies. Madame spoke perfect English, just accented. "Yes, it will be my pleasure," she translated, "just select the pattern and style and then when you go to *Monsieur* Gardiner's warehouse, he will send me the fabric that you choose."

"We thank you, Madame. We will inform you if my soon to be cousin finds something that she likes," Lady Elizabeth said.

By the time that the ten ladies left the shop, Caroline had chosen a style from one of the modiste's **own unique** drawings. Colour and fabric would be decided at the warehouse on the morrow. The carriages bore them to Gunter's and none of them paid attention to the waif that was closely watching their movements.

~~~~~~~/~~~~~~~

Darcy was invited to meet at Bennet House to join the other three who would accompany him to Angelo's rather than depart from his home. When he arrived, he was shown to the Duke's study. On entering he saw Lord Thomas Bennet, his sons and his brother, Lord Sed Bennet, his uncle, Lord Jersey, and Lord Granville.

"Now that Darcy is here, please repeat what you told us Granville," Lord Thomas instructed.

"A night or two ago I was at White's and a rather unscrupulous rake and fortune hunter was boasting that he would get a copy of the settlement to be used once he entrapped an heiress by compromise. I mentioned what I heard to Matlock and here we are." Granville paused and drew a breath. "I thank you, your Grace, for giving Darcy permission to use and disseminate the draft of the settlement, but it was never meant to be used as the unscrupulous man intends." Seeing the questioning looks he added the name, "Joseph Beckman." All the men nodded, Beckman was known as a dissolute rake, gambler and fortune hunter, in the ilk of Wickham.

"Will he be at White's this afternoon, Granville?" Lord Sedgwick Bennet asked.

"Yes, your Grace, he will be," Lord Harry Smythe agreed.

"Let us all meet at White's this afternoon, gentlemen, and have a little 'chat' with Mr. Beckman in a public setting surrounded by his peers. I doubt that there are many who would like to oppose the houses of Bennet, De Melville, Fitzwilliam, Darcy, and Smythe, especially after we remind him that most of us are related to the royals. After our *tête-à-tête* with that scoundrel, he will be lucky to find a servant that will want to come near him!" No one witnessing Lord Thomas Bennet's resolution could doubt that Beckman was about to be ruined.

"He will be there some time after two in the afternoon, your Grace. What say you we meet at the club at two?" Granville asked and there was agreement from all. Joseph Beckman had made enemies of some of the most powerful men in Society.

After the meeting, the younger gentlemen headed to Angelo's. The full name was Angelo's School of Arms and was founded by legendary fencing master Domenico Angelo in 1758. The school, or club, was now run by the founder's son, Henry Angelo, who now was getting on in years so more of the day to day running of the school was being passed to his son, Henry II. The school always did very well, as learning to fence was an essential part of a gentleman's education, and the better the master, the more gentlemen wanted to join the school or club.

The founder was the first to emphasize fencing as a means of developing health, poise, and grace. Domenico Angelo literally wrote the book on fencing when he published 'L'Ecole d'armes' in 1763. As a result of his influence, fencing changed from an art of war to a sport. Angelo's fencing academy established the essential rules for posture and footwork.

George Darcy, while sparing with his son at a young age, could not help but notice his natural talent so at the ripe old age of eight, Fitzwilliam Darcy commenced training in the art of fencing with Henry Angelo. Henry's father, who passed in 1802, had said that he had never seen anyone in all of his years of training with as much natural talent as the Darcy boy. Domenico assisted with young Darcy's training until the boy was twelve, when the founder retired completely. In the last four years before his retirement, Darcy was the only student that the old master trained. By the time Darcy was fifteen, he was routinely beating Henry II, who had grown up in the school, and occasionally he achieved what no other student had--he bested Henry Angelo from time to time. The older he got, the more he beat the master until now it was rare for Mr. Darcy to lose to any of the Angelos.

When the four cousins walked into Angelo's, they found Bingley and his brother-in-law Hurst fencing against one another. Neither man would test their skill against Darcy since they had lost to him innumerable times in the years that they had been friends. It was not missed by anyone that Darcy was welcomed by Henry Angelo and his son Henry II.

"Welcome, *Signore* Darcy. I see you have brought some victims; I mean partners to spar with today," Henry the father smiled. He had seen many a young buck challenge the school's best student and very few had scored a single hit, never mind bested Darcy.

Lord Tom Bennet decided to try his hand first. Within seconds, Darcy had landed the first of the three hits he would need to win the match. The Marquess was stunned for the master had barely said '*en guard*,' when, in a flurry of parries and ripostes, the hit was scored in the middle of the elder Bennet son's chest. The match was over before it started, and Darcy scored the next two hits just as fast. Lord Tom, who was very skilled in the art of fencing, had not come close to his opponent with his foil. Seeing the level of skill that Darcy possessed, it was little wonder that no one else was fencing; they were all watching the unbeaten school's champion display his mastery of the foil. Neither James Bennet nor Wes De Melville fared any better or lasted any longer than Lord Birchington had.

By the time they left the club to return to Bennet House with some minutes to spare before the agreed time, the Bennet brothers had a full and clear understanding why Richard and Andrew had told them what a huge folly challenging Darcy had been. There was no doubt that based on the masterful display that they had just witnessed at the dulled point of Darcy's foil his skills had, at the time, been understated. Using that measure, they were left with little doubt that his skill with a pistol was better than had been stated.

~~~~~~~/~~~~~~~

The oldest of the boys watching the Bennets reported the lady's movements that morning, including the large number of footmen that accompanied her and other family members whenever they left the house.

"At the modiste on Bond Street, you said there were at least four of those big footmen near the door?" Wickham interrogated the boy.

"Yes guv'ner," the lad replied.

"Did one of your cohorts check the back?"

"I dunno what a ca'ort is. We look'd an there were two of them huge men near the back door." The young man frowned, hoping he had answered right.

Wickham dismissed the urchin, feeling his confidence in his plan's ability to succeed dwindle. How could he take her if she was so well guarded at all times? There were a surfeit of men watching her, not the normal one or two that one could often convince to leave a post for an ale or three. He knew that his only hope was to find some weakness in her security he could exploit before the tenth day of April was upon him. He did not know how yet but he *had* to succeed; failure was not an option that he cared to entertain.

His paramour noticed that he was in a bad mood and when she tried to enquire as to the source of his melancholy, he stalked off in high dungeon after helping himself to some of her coin. With one of the toughs trailing him, he headed to the closest tavern to drown his sorrows. Yes, he would get his due. Why should he have to work for what he wanted? Look what happened to old Darcy when the old man had tried to cross him. The same would happen to anyone else who tried to deny George Wickham his 'rightful' due. As he always did, he conveniently ignored the fact that he had run from Ramsgate with his tail between his legs.

He could never challenge Darcy face to face. George Wickham was a coward and the only way he had been able to exact his revenge on the father was to hide like a rat in his hole as he waited until the man and his mount were close enough for him to throw a sharp stone at the mount's rump that had caused it to rear up. Never in all of his delusions did Wickham imagine that he could ever face Darcy and win. He remembered well the thrashings that he had received from his then friend the two times that he had pushed the stoic boy too far. His knowing that Darcy was superior than he in every way that counted was the basis for his hate and jealousy of the man he thought of as a prig.

~~~~~~~/~~~~~~~

Just after two Mr. Joseph Beckman strutted into White's as if he owned the place. Unbeknownst to him, he was barely tolerated and on the cusp of having his membership revoked. Boodle's had already chosen to deny him now. As he walked toward the betting book to see if there were any wagers listed that he would like to bet on, he heard his name being called.

He turned and saw that the Duke of Hertfordshire was summoning him. He preened like a peacock at the honour of being invited to join such illustrious company.

Mr. Beckman was a gambler, a bad one, he needed to compromise Miss Lavinia Ashton sooner rather than later. He needed her thirty-thousand-pound dowry to pay off his debts and if there was a little left for betting on card games and horse racing, so much the better. He was going to use the settlement that he had heard of so that he would not have to spend too much of his ill-gotten gains on its previous owner. As he approached the group, he saw more peers in one place than he had ever seen before, and two of them dukes! He did not observe that they were sitting in the centre of the room and everything could be seen and heard by all other than the passing thought that all would see honour being bestowed on him.

Without preamble Lord Thomas Bennet launched his attack. "Mr. Beckman, were you in this venerable institution a few days past boasting how you planned to use Mr. Darcy's settlement to make sure the woman you plan to compromise will receive almost nothing?" Beckman went white. Before he could think of an answer, Mr. Darcy, who he knew was lethal with all weapons, stepped forward.

"That settlement has one purpose and one purpose only. It is to protect *against* entrapment, not *enable* it!" Darcy said acerbically. "You are no gentleman, sir. You gamble away your future and then think that the way out is to force an innocent lady into an unwanted marriage. As if that is not bad enough, you have the temerity to want to use *my* settlement to hurt the aggrieved party! You disgust me." Darcy had not spoken softly. Every conversation in the club had ceased and all eyes and ears were on the scene playing out in front of them. By now Beckman had gone weak at the knees, and if it were not for supporting himself on the arm of a chair, he would not have been able to stand.

The Duke of Hertfordshire spoke again, "It did not take much to discover that your intended victim is Miss Lavinia

Ashton. A note of warning was dispatched to her father before we came here." The Duke paused for a moment, "Your name will be mud from now on. No one in polite society will ever receive you again. An innocent lady paying for your own folly? No, sir, it will *not* happen." Beckman was then approached by the manager of White's who informed the fortune hunter that his membership was summarily revoked and that he would never be admitted again, under no uncertain terms. The man, quaking in his boots, was led out of White's by two large footmen.

Lord Sedgwick Bennet addressed the watching crowd: "Let it be known that any who tries to use Mr. Darcy's settlement against a lady, for any other reason than the woman tried to entrap the man, will be ruined in society by all of us that you see here before you. Make sure that any who think that they can cross us knows that they would be crossing the royal family in addition to us."

For a full five minutes there was silence at White's after the Bennets and their party left. It did not take many days for the salient message that was delivered to be disseminated throughout the Ton. Joseph Beckman would never show his face in polite society again. He would be forced to sell his estate in Essex to pay his debts. The irony was that Lord Thomas Bennet purchased the estate at a vastly reduced price, using Frank Phillips as his agent so the identity of the purchaser was never revealed to the seller. Beckman left England shortly after the sale, never to be heard from again.

The effect of the show of force at White's had the intended result, no man dared consider, let alone speak, of using the settlement for any purpose other than its intent, which was to stop compromises. Miss Ashton was safe, as were other unknown ladies who would have been targets of those from the same ilk as the disgraced Beckman.

~~~~~~~/~~~~~~~

The ladies stood in awe as they looked around in Harding, Howell, and Company Department store at 89 Pall Mall in St James's. There were four main departments spread over two floors. On the ground floor was one that sported fur coats, muffs, fur lined accessories, and fans. The department that shared the ground floor boasted jewellery, ornamental articles in ormolu, French clocks, and a vast assortment of perfumery necessary for one's toilette. On the first floor one found a haberdashery; including silks, muslins, lace, and gloves, as well as the department for millinery and dresses. It was a cornucopia of wares to peruse and purchase, if something caught their eye.

The younger girls convinced Mrs. Gardiner to accompany them and their companions to the first floor, while Lady Anne escorted Lady Elizabeth, her niece Anne, and the current and former Bingley sisters. Mrs Jenkinson, Anne's companion, and Miss Jones trailed behind them. Both groups were under the watchful eye of two footmen. Biggs was trailing the group that included his Lady Elizabeth while Johns was one of two near the front entrance while two more men were at the rear of the merchant's store.

There was much to admire at Harding, Howell, and Company, and had the ladies not been clients of the best modiste in London they may have been more interested in the ready-made gowns and dresses that were on display. The ladies were there for the experience and camaraderie of being together more than to purchase items unless something called out to one of them and they could not resist the pull.

"It is still hard for me to believe that we will be cousins in March, Lizzy," Caroline Bingley said as she looked at her engagement ring that had belonged to her betrothed's grandmother Gardiner. It was a gold band that had a larger diamond in the centre with four small diamonds surrounding it. It was not the most expensive ring, but to Caroline Bingley it was perfect.

"The whole family welcomes you, Caroline," Elizabeth said with meaning.

"You do realise what that means, do you not, Caroline?"

Lady Anne asked cryptically.

"I am not sure what you mean, Lady Anne?" the normally quick but now baffled woman asked.

"As you will be our cousins as well, I think it is high time that you call me Aunt Anne like your cousin-to-be does," Lady Anne elucidated Miss Bingley.

Mrs. Hurst and Anne de Bourgh also smiled as the information penetrated Caroline's besotted brain. "It is fun to see my baby sister so in love that she cannot use that quick mind of hers effectively," Louisa Hurst teased her younger sister, which earned her a playful slap on the hand.

"Do not forget about me," Miss de Bourgh added playfully, "I am a cousin too!"

"Aunt Anne, Anne, I must plead that my brain was addled," Caroline laughed at herself, "Oh my, the extended family will be so large, and..." The lady's pallor changed as she looked almost distressed. "W-we will be distantly related to the royals!"

"Yes Caroline, you are correct. However, as the connection is distant, neither the Regent nor the Queen will be inviting you to family dinners...just yet," Elizabeth teased her friend. It worked; Caroline's pallor returned to normal. The ladies enjoyed two hours at the establishment before they returned to Bennet House where they met the men who informed them of what Beckman had intended to do and the consequences of his behaviour. The ladies were very gratified that the men had let it be known that any who tried to use the settlement for nefarious reasons would be ruined and ostracised, just as had happened to the fortune-hunting rake.

~~~~~~~/~~~~~~~

Wickham was not happy. The report he had just received from the boy had angered him so that, in his inebriated state, he had hit the messenger because he did not like the message. It cost him half a crown to placate the rascal and stop him from leaving and taking all his brothers and friends with him.

He had gone to the tavern to drown his sorrows only to

return to receive more bad news. When the object of his revenge-obsession went out with family there were even more guards. The lad had reported that the excursion to Harding, Howell, and Company had eight footmen that watched the group, and, like at the modiste's, two were posted at the entrance and two at the rear! *'How am I to get my hands on the harridan and save my neck?'* Wickham asked himself. He needed something to go his way soon or he was a dead man.

Luckily for him, Karen would forgive his pique from earlier and welcome him back into her bed. That was something at least. If only she was younger...

CHAPTER 16

Lady Sarah Bennet was very happy. She was in her sitting room reading a letter she received from Marie before descending to the breakfast parlour.

20 April 1812
Seaview Cottage, near Brighton

My dearest Mama,

Before you berate me for writing you a letter while on honeymoon, I promise that this is not a long missive.

Mama you were so very right! Being with a man who loves you as Andrew loves me is one of the best experiences in my life! Other than telling you that EVERYTHING you told Jane and myself was very accurate, thank you, Mama, for preparing us to be the ladies that we are today. I cannot imagine that there is a better mother anywhere!

Seaview Cottage is not a cottage! It is three times larger than Lucas Lodge, sits on a bluff, and has a very private beach that one can only access from Seaview's land. We are close to Brighton, but I doubt that we will be spending very much time there. I suppose if Cousin George opens the Pavilion while we are here it will be rude to not, at the very least, send him a note.

Please give our love to all of the family including my new parents-in-law as Andrew has declined to write any correspondence unless absolutely necessary.

With all of my love,

A deliriously happy Marie

The duchess shed a few tears of joy as the contentment her daughter conveyed was palpable. It was in this state that her beloved husband found her.

"Sarah, are you well?" the Duke asked with concern.

"I am very well, my beloved husband," she said with a smile that gave truth to her words, "I am just overjoyed. I received a short note from Marie. Oh Thomas, our girl is so very happy. I could feel her joy as if I were experiencing it myself."

"That is a relief, my love," her husband replied with a small smile. "I suppose we will have to allow Andrew to live if our girl is so happy." The Duke's sardonic wit was on display and both laughed quietly at his ridiculous statement. "You have not heard from the other Fitzwilliams yet, have you love?"

"No Thomas. *If* Janey writes to me, given the distances involved, I do not expect a letter for at least another week." The Duke gave his Duchess a toe-curling kiss, and after she put herself to rights, they descended to break their fasts with as much dignity as they could muster.

~~~~~~~/~~~~~~~

Fitzwilliam Darcy was falling in love. The more time that he was around Lady Elizabeth Bennet, the more he felt himself falling into its clutches. Yes, she was beautiful, the most handsome woman that he had ever beheld, but she was so much more. Lady Elizabeth was loyal, intelligent, well read, kind and compassionate, as well as charitable to a fault. She used to be quick to anger and slow to forgive, but like he had changed, so had she.

The way that her fine eyes flashed and seemed to change shades and even color when her moods shifted. When they debated, he hated it more when the hour determined the end, than his wish for it to be, he felt like he wanted to never stop debating with her. His mother had been correct when she had said that he and Elizabeth had much the same taste in books. They had already debated Plato, Socrates, Descartes, Machiavelli, and others. One thing that he had already discovered in their short time as cousins was that if she felt like extending the debate, she would express opinions that were not her own so that they would be able to continue it. He had never met her like, and if he had not been so sure that she would laugh him out of the room he would have declared for her already. Some of her hair always escaped her coiffure and it delighted him to see some of her raven curls hanging down her neck. This was a woman who deserved to be pleased by one who knew how to please her.

As he was sitting in the library at Darcy House, he admonished himself for his thoughts of declaring for Lady Elizabeth before she was ready to hear such a declaration from himself. Who knew if she ever would be? '*You are supposed to be an intelligent man, Fitzwilliam Darcy. Unless you are reasonably sure that she is receptive to you and has tender feelings toward you as well, if you do anything precipitous you will undo all of the good that is your friendship with Elizabeth—Lady Elizabeth—has wrought. Slow down, man! Nothing good will come from trying to force something that does not yet exist,*' he berated himself. He was correct, Lady Elizabeth Bennet did not abhor him as she had in Meryton after his performance there, but at this time it was a budding friendship on her side, nothing more, yet anyway.

What he had no way of knowing was that the lady in question was sitting in her chambers at Bennet House thinking about him. Far from dislike him, she considered him a friend and her treasonous heart reminded her how handsome he was and that it was possible that he could be more than just a cousin who was a friend. She knew that she was far from ready to consider anything more at this point so her head overruled her heart, for the present.

He had been amazed when his mother relayed information to him about the charitable works of the Bennet family as a whole, and specifically those supported by the one that he loved. She had told him that the family, in conjunction with both dukes, had a foundation that was working to improve the lives of the common man. Their foundation was slowly opening and fully funding schools, hospitals, clinics, and orphanages around the country. The schools were for both girls and boys to teach them to read, write, and do sums. If they found any promising young men with aptitudes and the drive for further education, they would receive a scholarship to an institution of higher learning so they may one day aspire to be a steward or enter the law.

The orphanages were not workhouses. The children were treated as children, not slaves. Rather than having the young children enter the work force as soon as may be, they were educated and nurtured. Only those who would truly care for their charges were employed, and the children's well-being was the focus of all Bennet Foundation orphanages. The governors did not primp and preen to curry favour with benefactors while diverting most of the funds to their own wallets, the bulk of the funds was used to assist those in actual need. One of the stated aims of the Foundation's orphanages was to place children in loving homes where there were those who could not bear their own or simply had a big heart and wanted to take in additional children. Before placement was authorised there were extensive investigations of prospective adoptive parents undertaken with periodic unscheduled visits.

Unlike so many in the Ton, the Bennets did not do what they did for recognition or accolades. They believed that to those who much is given, they have a responsibility to take care of those who cannot do so for themselves. A few who had applied to the Foundation for help had tried to hoodwink them when there was no actual need, only evidence of avarice or indolence. Those cases were exposed with alacrity, sent away with a flea in their ears, and publicly exposed, which discouraged others from trying to take advantage of the largess of the Bennet family.

With the ownership of the Dennington Shipping Lines, their shipbuilding yards and the connection to Gardiner and other merchants, those who wanted to learn a trade were trained and offered well paying positions as they became available. The girls for whom higher education was not an option were prepared for good service jobs that the education they received assisted them in attaining. The schools, clinics, and hospitals were separate from the orphanages. The schools were open and free of tuition to any servants, tenants, or their children that wanted to be educated in the area in which the school was located, while at the same time created employment opportunities for the local populace. Darcy now understood why the denizens of Meryton were so loyal to the Duke of Hertfordshire and his family. The Foundation had built a hospital, an orphanage, and two schools in the area. Not only did they provide many well-paying jobs, but thanks to the school and the hospital the quality of life of many in the area had been made far better.

As if what her family did was not enough, Lady Elizabeth had founded, with her family's full support, Haven House, a charitable organisation for which his Aunt Elaine and his mother were board members before ever knowing the name of the founder or the family that was the home's major benefactor. Madeline Gardiner was the chairwoman of the charity and represented the family who remained anonymous.

Lady Elizabeth Bennet had started Haven House when she was but fourteen. She had been visiting the Gardiners and saw some girls who looked to be her age begging, one of them with child. She had approached them, handed over all the money that she had on her person, which had been a vast sum for girls who had naught. Once she gained their confidence, she asked them how they had ended up in the straights that she found them. Elizabeth Bennet had been aghast at the stories of abuse and seduction that these young, pitiful girls had told. Knowing how men invariably were not held accountable for their actions while women suffered the scorn of society, young Lady Elizabeth had marched the girls back to the Gardiner's house. Madeline Gardiner had not been as surprised as one would have thought when her niece returned home with the two timid, hungry, cold, and dirty girls in tow, even if one was with child. They were the first of many who inhabited what became Haven House.

The physical building was located near Cheapside. The Bennets had purchased a property, torn down the abandoned warehouses, and had the very large house built. The purpose of the house was to give a place for young girls who had been seduced, ruined, or worse, and then abandoned by deceiving blackguards. It was an irony that at least three current residents were victims of George Wickham's seductions from various parts of the country.

Haven House could host up to one hundred girls comfortably. There were dining areas, sitting rooms, classrooms, and administrative offices. More importantly, there was a hospital wing where girls could be taken care of during their confinement and be assisted by competent midwives, nurses, and, when required, an accoucheur. One of the best known accoucheurs in London was Sir Frederick Gillingham. He and the physicians he was training to become accoucheurs would volunteer their time at Haven House to help out as needed. The house had a permanent staff of five and thirty that included a contingent of footmen who were ex-soldiers, employed to keep the residents safe at all times in addition to their normal duties. The staff was augmented by a cadre of volunteers of which both Ladies Anne and Elaine were part.

If the girls were with child, then they were cared for in every way until their confinements, and until and after they were delivered. If the mother could not take care of her child, which was most of them, the babe was transferred to the nearby Foundation orphanage that was only for babes. No girls were ever forced out after she had delivered her babe. In some cases where the abuse had been particularly bad, the girls were allowed to stay for as long as she felt that she had a need.

There were classes that taught the girls at Haven House skills that they would need to seek gainful employment; they were supported and educated until they found good situations for themselves, a process that the employees and volunteers helped them with so that they were never on their own and left to fend for themselves. The employees of Haven House were determined to keep them off the streets and away from the brothels once they moved on from their time at the Haven. Aside from reading, writing, and sums, music, arts, and other accomplishments were taught by masters hired by Haven House so that girls would be able to learn the skills needed to be governesses or companions. Some of the former residents of the house chose employment at Haven House to work with and support others in the same situation that they had been in when they were offered sanctuary. Once Lady Anne discovered who the founder was, she and the Countess of Matlock had convinced Lady Elizabeth to accompany them on their next visit to the Haven the following week.

When Darcy heard his mother tell the story of how the fourteen-year-old Lady Elizabeth was the impetus to create Haven House, and of her tenacity in convincing her family to provide the considerable finances needed to build and fund the project, he would have dissembled if he said that he was surprised. He had already seen first-hand that once the lady set her mind to something, nothing would divert her from her course, except for herself.

The information only added to the respect and tender feelings that he had for the lady. He had requested and been granted permission to accompany the ladies to Haven House when they went on their next visit. The fact that his new cousin would be one of the groups that would be at the house had no influence in his decision. He wanted to see how he could assist, either materially, physically, or both.

~~~~~~~/~~~~~~~

As the Darcys prepared to leave Haven House to join the ladies on their foray to Gardiner and Associates warehouse, Lady Anne could only shake her head at the faraway look that she saw in her son's eyes. She was as certain as she could be, that her William had finally lost his heart. Her concern for him was that she was unsure if the lady would find and keep it. Only time would tell. The Darcys made the short walk to Bennet House where Miss Bingley and Mrs. Hurst were presently visiting the Bennets. Madeline Gardiner would join them at the warehouse which was well within walking distance from her home.

Anne de Bourgh would not be with them as she and her mother had returned to Rosings Park in Kent earlier that morning to take care of business that Anne, who had been mistress for almost a year since her full inheritance on her five and twentieth birthday, needed to attend personally. One of the duties was to welcome the cleric at the Hunsford Church home and wait on his new wife. He had been invited to go view the estate that he would inherit and had met the Benet's second daughter, Harriet Forster's sister Miranda, and two months later married her thereby securing the future of his cousin's wife and any unmarried daughters if Mr. Collins inherited Longriver prior to all of them marrying.

This day it was only four ladies who headed to the warehouse. Miss Darcy remained at Bennet House with her new cousins, Ladies Mary, Kitty, and Loreta. Georgiana was sad that Lord James had returned to complete his studies at Cambridge even while not fully grasping the depth of her growing feelings for the Marquess.

Mr. and Mrs. Gardiner welcomed the ladies to the warehouse and introduced them to a clerk, Mr. Peter Hobbs, who would be at their disposal to help them retrieve any bolts of fabric that they desired to inspect. Mr. Hobbs led them to the back area where new goods that were not yet available for public sale were processed, allowing Caroline Bingley the pick of fabrics that no other had seen, never mind owned. As the ladies were searching through the newly arrived silks, muslins, satins, and other fabrics, Biggs, Johns, and the rest of the footmen guards were keeping watch, which was as they usually did.

Biggs noticed the same ragamuffin watching their party at the Gardiner and Associates warehouse that he had noted at Madame Chambourg's earlier in the morning. He was sure that he had seen the boy hanging around Bennet House as well. It could have been a coincidence; but Biggs did not believe in coincidences. He walked nonchalantly in the direction of the scruffy boy, trying to look innocent as the lad leaned again a wall that gave a good view of the interior of the warehouse. He noticed that the closer he got the more suspicious the boy got. Just before Biggs reached his huge hand out to apprehend the scalawag, the boy ducked and took off in a sprint between two buildings which no one larger than himself would be able to fit through. Biggs berated himself for not having some of his men help him to trap the boy. He would make sure that they would be on higher alert from now on.

The ladies were unaware of the disturbance outside and had a very good time looking through fabrics. Caroline Bingley settled on a light green silk which Mr. Hobbs took charge of having sent to the modiste's shop. Louisa Hurst, Lady Anne, and Lady Elizabeth all selected fabrics for themselves that would join the one that Caroline chose on its journey to Bond Street.

"Caro did you see that hideous orange colour? Who would wear something like that?" Louisa asked, her nose in the air in a teasing way.

"I know that colour would look horrendous on me at least, Louisa. I am much happier with the softer tones that I use for my dresses and gowns," Caroline agreed, shuddering as she tried to imagine herself wearing the colour that did not suit her at all.

"Mayhap it would look good on me," Elizabeth said as she held some of the offending fabric to herself. It looked as bad on Elizabeth as it would have on Caroline, even though they had very different colouring. This caused the ladies to laugh raucously, Lady Anne and their Aunt Madeline included.

Once Elizabeth brought herself under regulation again, she asked her aunt, "Aunt Maddie, why would Uncle Edward order that fabric in that horrid colour?"

"It does not suit us, Lizzy, but there are those who it does, or they think that it does. So as long as there is a demand, Edward will bring some in," she explained.

Miss Bingley, Mrs. Hurst, and Mrs. Gardiner farewelled Ladies Anne and Elizabeth who were returning to Grosvenor
Square. The Bingleys and Hursts would be dining with the
Gardiners that evening; Hurst and Bingley expected an hour
prior to the meal. As Elizabeth followed Darcy's mother into
the coach, she noticed that Biggs and his footmen were looking around for something, but she dismissed it as them just
being ever vigilant.

~~~~~~~/~~~~~~~

Wickham was livid. "Your brother was almost what?"

"Sorry guv'ner, some'ow one of 'em big men s'pcted sum-
min and almos' caught 'Arry," the leader of the group of boys
said nervously.

"I should kill you! How can you be so useless?" Wickham
raged. "If you have spoilt this, I will kill all of you." The coward had no problem threatening malnourished, underweight
boys.

"Ah tolds you we needed more 'elp so's they don' see a same
boy too ofen, but you say we don' need more," the boy said
with some conviction, even knowing that speaking the truth
may earn him a punch or worse.

Wickham thought about what the lad said and stopped his
visceral reaction, which would have been to strike out of the
boy. The *Spaniard* had given him enough money to double the
number of watchers, but he had saved some for himself, just
in case. He admitted to himself that it was short-sighted. He
had to change his plan to throw the guards off the scent and increase the number of boys significantly.

"Here is what we will do. Until early March, some of the
boys need to be sent to the area to beg, but they are *not* to
watch for the lady or pay attention to anyone in particular at
Bennet House. Harry cannot be used, but I want you to find
ten more boys from St. Giles. You will all get paid the daily
amount that we agreed on, each and every day," Wickham told
the ragamuffin as he thought out his new plan.

"'Ow comes we don' need to watch 'em, guv'ner?" the confused lad asked.

"I want them to relax. After today they will be watching for any boys watching them," Wickham said with a smile. "With different boys begging in the area, they will get used to seeing them near those swanky houses. It is very important that your friends understand that they are *not* to follow them *at all*! For now, those are your orders. Do you understand them?"

"I does, guv'ner," the boy reported and smiled as Wickham handed him the coin for that day's work for him to pass on, after his cut of course.

Wickham did not like the delay, but after what happened earlier that day, he knew he had no choice. If he pushed forward now, the guards would be on heightened alert, and that would only hurt his plans. He would tell the *Spaniard* that they were away from Town for a few weeks. Wickham was sure that the added boys and the plan to make the footmen relax for the next few weeks would help him in his dastardly quest to avenge himself on the woman who had so humiliated and laughed at him publicly.

That night when he crawled into his lover's bed, he was in a decidedly better frame of mind about his plans, Karen Younge misinterpreted his mood as an increasing love toward her. Wickham knew only how to love one being on earth, himself.

CHAPTER 17

Wickham's scheme to have the Bennet's guards relax worked, at least partially. Over the following weeks until the day that they all decamped for Hertfordshire, thus making the lie that Wickham told Álvarez partially true, Biggs noted that he never saw that same waif again and there was no one that he could tell, young or old, that was paying any particular attention to the Bennets. Since the near miss of catching the youth outside the warehouse, none of the guards, all on high alert, had detected anyone following them to any of the places or events that their charges had attended.

Lady Sarah Bennet, Duchess of Hertfordshire could not have felt more contented. She had received a letter from Jane, expressing similar sentiments to the one from Marie. The felicity that her daughter was finding in her marriage to the Honourable Mr. Richard Fitzwilliam was plainly evident from the joy that sprung from her words. The Countess of Matlock had been Sarah Bennet's good friend for many years, and now the Duchess had grown very close to her friend's sister-in-law, Lady Anne Darcy, and counted the other sister-in-law, Lady Catherine de Bourgh, an intimate as well.

The mistress of Bennet House had just instructed the housekeeper to have the family packed for their removal to Hertfordshire as she sat in the east parlour that was the recipient of the morning sun, which was at a premium in the winter. She thought back to what Lady Catherine had related when she and her daughter Anne had returned from Rosings Park ten days earlier.

The Duchess, her sister Rose Bennet, the Duchess of Bedford, Lady Catherine and Lady Anne were all taking tea together at de

Bourgh House, and Lady Catherine seemed to be amused about something.

"What amuses you so, Catherine?" her sister Anne asked.

"It is my, no Anne's, parson," she said with mirth.

"Now you have to share the story, Catherine," Rose Bennet instructed, always one who had loved humorous stories.

"The cleric who has the living at Hunsford is not the smartest man in the world, but neither is he deficient. He is very deferential to anyone above him in rank, truly an out and out sycophantic to Anne and myself. He informed Anne and I that he had received an invitation to visit the estate, named Longriver, that was entailed on him in Herefordshire, but he was considering responding in the negative due to some disagreement between his late father and the current master of the estate."

Anne Darcy, seeing the quizzical look on her friend's countenance, nodded her head. "Yes, Sarah. This is the family that my William thought so below him and assumed was your own. Not only do the shires and the estate names resemble one another, but they too carry the family name 'Benet' but theirs is with one 'n' not two as is in your family name," she said with a wide smile, illuminating her son's mistake. "You met the eldest former Benet daughter, now Harriet Forster who is married to Richard's friend, the one who stood up for him." Lady Sarah nodded in remembrance.

Lady Catherine continued her tale, "Anne advised him that he should let bygones be bygones and offer an olive branch. She allowed him a month to be away from his parish, and I added that he should set an example for his parishioners and marry. I also pointed out that he could further heal the breach by marrying one of his cousins, thus securing the family's future and removing anxiety that they would be turned out of their home on the death of the father." Lady Catherine paused to take a breath, "I did feel that he should marry, when he was so inclined, but what I said to him was said in jest. I should have taken his character more into consideration as he decided to follow my advice as if it were a command from God Himself."

"He did not!" Rose Bennet gasped in amused surprise.

"He most certainly did," Catherine agreed, trying to contain her mirth. "We just welcomed his new wife, Mrs. Miranda Benet Collins, to Hunsford. Being the oldest, unmarried daughter, Collins proposed to her after knowing her for barely a week. Evidently, she decided that marrying him was a price that she could bear in order to secure the future of her mother and younger sisters.

"The mother, a very kind and sensible woman to hear tell, was very concerned about the future as the father is a little indolent and had not prepared for the future as he should have, and she did not want to be a burden on her married daughters or relatives. Miranda, who loves her mother dearly, saw the opportunity to relegate her mother's worries to the past and so accepted him.

"She will be the making of him. We already saw a difference when we met with them. He is still respectful, but not sycophantic. If he strays, then a look or touch from his wife redirects his attention. Anne and I believe that the improvements bode well for his parishioners and his life in general. We, the weaker sex? I think not!" Catherine laughed with her friends. "How many men would be useless without a strong woman behind them?"

"Very true, Catherine," Lady Sarah agreed. "You may have been jesting with him, but it seems that your joke has improved the lives of quite a few!"

"I agree with Sarah, sister," added Lady Anne. "It has worked out well for all concerned and who knows, the Collinses may yet find felicity in their marriage."

"You could have the right of it Anne; only time will tell." Catherine nodded once in support of her words.

Lady Sarah returned to the present as she thought about how sometimes the most unlikely couples came together. She could not help think about her middle daughter and the possibility that she may have started to develop tender feelings for William Darcy. Something that not too many months ago had seemed to be an impossibility! The Duchess had not missed how their cousin watched Elizabeth with evident adoration in his eyes. As perceptive as her daughter was, Sarah Bennet was sure that Lizzy had not noticed the way that she was viewed by Fitzwilliam Darcy.

The subject of her mother's thoughts, Lady Elizabeth Bennet, was relaxing in her sitting room while the family's trunks were being packed for a return to Longbourn to attend the ball to be held at Netherfield on fifteenth day of February in honour of the betrothal of her friend and cousin. She was very excited; her sisters and their husbands would be attending the ball. It would be the first time that they would see their sisters since they were married. Elizabeth could not fully understand the way that her feelings for her cousin by marriage, Fitzwilliam Darcy, had changed.

'*Who would have thought that we would become friends? Certainly not I,*' she admitted to herself. '*After the words that I flung at him, by rights he should have hated me. Instead, he has addressed the deficiencies in his behaviour and has become such a better man. Yes, I took a long and hard look at the way that I treat people that I felt had wronged me and I too have made changes. Would I have been able to forgive one who spoke to me in the fashion that I spoke to him? I do not know the answer to that.*' She sighed, hoping that she would have been able to react the way that her cousin had.

'*Yes, his behaviour was horrendous, and he had deserved being humiliated, but am I the one to judge others? It shows the depth of his character that he was able to both forgive me, as well as address and correct the reproofs that I laid at his door. That is in the past now, and we have both leaned from our mistakes. Aunt Anne must have the right of it, he was always this man, he only needed a jolt to shock him enough to see it for himself. The real question is, how do I feel about him now that I have seen the man that he is, not the one I assumed him to be?*'

'*I do consider him a friend now; and he is my cousin.* Do I feel more for him than as a cousin and friend? Can I say such so fast? *If I am honest, he is one of the most handsome men that I am acquainted with, but it goes much deeper than that. I have seen for myself with his interactions with ours and other servants that what Aunt Anne, Richard, and others said about him being the best* master is nothing but the truth. Even when he does not know that he is being observed he treats his servants with respect and kindness.

'I know that he has a charitable heart. He made a very large bequest to fund New Haven House after we all went to visit Haven House for the first time. He wanted to remain anonymous stating that his aim was to help, not just to receive accolades for his donation. I only know about it as I was reviewing the books and I saw the bank draft before Aunt Maddie deposited it. Ten Thousand Pounds! That is one year of Pemberley's reported income!

'I also appreciated his dry wit when he allowed himself to be comfortable with his company, and how loquacious he can be once he feels so with his company. It was not aloofness that I saw but shyness, just like Georgie used to be. We enjoy many of the same books, and when we debate, he respects my opinions and does not dismiss them just because of my gender. How many men would accept being trounced at chess by a lady and take it in stride like he has? When we play, he plays to win. He has never been condescending or allowing me to beat him just to placate me,' Elizabeth sighed. The man he was again highlighting the error and speed at which she would sketch characters in the past.

A few days prior, a large group of the younger set that included her brother Tom, cousins Wes and Retta, her younger sisters, and Anne de Bourgh had joined Darcy and his sister at Covent Gardens to see *The Taming of the Shrew*. Elizabeth had not missed that cousin William had enjoyed the play as much as she had. It seemed their tastes for the works of William Shakespeare were in alignment, like many other things.

She was not willing to admit to herself, never mind any other, that the feelings that she had for Fitzwilliam Darcy were transitioning from friendship to being of a tender nature.

Not long before midday the family were in their coaches, and, with a cadre of footmen guards and outriders, they left Town for their estate.

~~~~~~~/~~~~~~~

Expected at the ball outside the Bingley and the Bennet parties were the leading families from Meryton were the newlywed Fitzwilliam couples and the Matlocks who were excited to see their sons and daughters in laws, the Bedford Bennets and the De Mellviles had accepted invitations as well.

There were many happy tears shed when mothers and daughters reunited. Elaine Fitzwilliam had always dreamed of a daughter; now she had two and by extension three more as she counted Jane's and Marie's sisters as surrogate daughters as well. When said sisters joined the group surrounding the older, former Bennets, there were more hugs and tears. Lady Elizabeth could not but miss the glow of happiness and something else that as a maiden she could not fathom in the expressions of her older sisters.

At the same time that the ladies were welcoming one another, Darcy was being bear-hugged by his cousins. First Andrew, followed by a much longer embrace with Richard. Both thanked him profusely for the use of his properties for their wedding trips, which he demurred as nothing more than they deserved. As Richard slapped him on the back, he looked at his cousin and saw a relaxed mien and contentment that he had never thought he would see in Darcy.

"William, I missed you at my wedding," he held up his hand to stay the explanation that he knew was about to be uttered. "I accept that you did what you felt was the honourable thing, and I understand why. You were, however, missed. I had to request that the reprobate Forster stand up with me! I had to settle for a scoundrel as my support on the most important of all days," he teased with a huge smile. Rather than be maudlin about his cousin not being with him, he used his humour to express his feelings.

"Love you too, Rich," Darcy said as he slapped his cousin's back.

"Am I blind, or are you and Lizzy friendly to one another now, William?" Andrew asked, not believing his own eyes.

"We are Andrew. Your sister forgave her wayward cousin,

and even apologised for her quick temper and the misjudgements that she made of me," William informed his cousins, amused at their shocked expressions.

"Our Lizzy, the one sitting with our wives, *forgave* you *and* asked for your forgiveness?" Richard verbalised the disbelief of both Fitzwilliams. They were happy at the apparent maturation and growth of their wife's younger sister.

"She did, as did I. I begged forgiveness from all of the Bennets and am now much closer to Tom, James, and Wes." Darcy added with a wide smile. "The three young men came to Angelo's and fenced against me."

"Did you allow them to last above a minute?" Richard asked, vastly amused.

"Tom lasted almost two minutes, while Wes and I barely a minute!" reported a chagrined Marquess of Netherfield, a chorus of guffaws heard from the six men.

Like had been granted them for the prewedding ball, the young ladies who were not out yet were allowed to attend the Bingley's ball until after the meal and were only to dance with men from the family or preapproved family friends. Georgiana Darcy blushed deeply as she granted her cousin James's request for the opening set.

Darcy was not sure that Lady Elizabeth would accept him for the opening set, but he decided that nothing ventured, nothing gained. Lady Anne Darcy silently wished her son luck as he approached the object of his affection, correctly surmising what he was about to request.

Darcy sat down next to Elizabeth and looked at her. The intensity of his gaze caused a flutter in her stomach that she was not willing to acknowledge as yet. "Lady Eliz...Cousin Elizabeth," he opened their conversation in his deep baritone voice, "the last time I had an opportunity to request a set from you, in my stupidity I did not take the pleasure in your company for the dance. I do not want to make the same mistake again. May I have the pleasure of your company for the first set, Cousin?"

In response she gave him the very impertinent look with an arched eyebrow he most loved. "It so happens that set is open, William. And as I intend to dance as much as I am able at Caroline's ball, I suppose that I will have to accept you, so I do not have to sit out the night," she teased, her expression giving away that she was very pleased he had made his request.

"If I may be so forward as to request the supper set as well, your ladyship," he said with an amusing bow. "After all, we need to continue our debate on Descartes, and what better time for such a discussion than at a crowded and noisy meal at a ball," he teased her in return.

"I will grant you that set, sir." Then she leaned in and said so that only he could hear. "I would not try and ask for more than two sets were I you. It would be sad to have to refuse you before all of our family," she said with a smile, but the message was received.

Later that day, Ladies Elizabeth and Anne were taking one of their walks with Biggs and some footmen trailing until they found a bench they preferred, Lady Anne Darcy related something to Elizabeth that few knew.

"Elizabeth, I want to share something with you. It is a secret that none but I and your cousins, the royals know. Before I tell you, I need your promise that you will not reveal what I am about to relate to anyone who does not already know about what I am about to tell you. Can you give me your word of honour?"

"I swear it, Aunt Anne, you have my word of honour," Lady Elizabeth gave her solemn promise.

Lady Anne looked off into the distance and then began the extraordinary story. "Lizzy, do you know that if my George had been interested in a title, he would have been the Duke of Derbyshire?"

"I had no idea, Aunt Anne. How can that be?" Elizabeth asked incredulously.

"In '76, before my darling George courted me, he was not yet twenty and was out riding when he came across some anarchists trying to kill King George III. You have heard how his Majesty used to like to travel to see different parts of the country, have you not?" Elizabeth nodded that she had. "The brigands had felled some trees that had separated the bulk of the royal guard from the King, the guard that remained with his Royal Majesty had been killed, but not before killing all but one of the attackers. As George came up on the scene, he saw the anarchist raise his pistol to get ready to kill the King.

"He had no idea it was the Monarch. He had his horse charge and ran over the murderer before he was able to pull the trigger. The blow from his mount was so mighty that the already wounded man was killed instantly. It was only then that my George realised who he had saved. It was not many minutes later when the delayed royal guard arrived and secured the King.

"King George III wanted to confer the dukedom of Derbyshire, which was vacant due to the last Duke passing with no heir, on my soon to be husband, and told him that as he was in his debt. He made a cryptic remark about George saving more than just him that day and that he would grant him anything that he desired. George was never interested in a title and had but one request, for the King not to order him to accept the title. As much as the King wanted to confer the Dukedom on my George, he did as he promised and never ordered George to accept the elevation." Lady Anne had a look of sadness as she thought about, and missed, her beloved, late husband.

"When we met some years later; there was an instant connection, and after a short courtship, he proposed to me. He only told me the story after we married, swearing me to silence. No one in the family knows that my late husband saved King George's life, not even my children. The King told my George that he would record everything about the encounter in his royal journals and that only his queen and heir and successor had access to read his private writings."

"You should be a duchess and William should be a marquess!" an astounded Lady Elizabeth stated.

"Only if George had accepted the King's offer. As he did not, we are as we have always been," Lady Anne said as she hugged the woman who she suspected had tender feelings for her son.

"It seems that the son had inherited the father's sense of honour." Another piece of the puzzle that was Fitzwilliam Darcy just fell into place. The ladies stood and arm in arm returned to the warmth of the manor house.

~~~~~~~/~~~~~~~

George Wickham was very relieved. The *Spaniard* had thought that when he told him that the Bennets were away from town for an event in the country that it was a delaying tactic, which it was, so he had dispatched *Scarface* to verify independently. The gods had been with Wickham as Withers had returned and informed Álvarez that the family was away from town for an event and that they would be attending a house party, returning to Town in early March to attend the wedding of a cousin. The intelligence that Withers had been able to glean stated that from that point on all indicators were that the victim and her family would remain in London for the season.

"You lucky, *Jorge*. If you lied to me, you no leave here alive," Álvarez said menacingly. Wickham thanked God for the reprieve. He had not thought that the *Spaniard* would verify his information as he had, so the Bennets' exit from Town had just saved his neck. "B'cause they away, I give you until end April, but I swear if you no 'ave 'er by then, you die!"

Things were finally going Wickham's way. Even the constant reminders of his flogging in the scars on his back did not put a damper on his spirits. Mrs. Younge did not understand why the man that she loved was so happy. As she had on previous occasions, she assumed that it was his deepening love for her. She did not know that Wickham had promised to give *Scarface* a thousand pounds extra if he would 'get rid' of his paramour once they collected the ransom. The man who was going to be double-crossed was planning a double cross of his own.

~~~~~~~/~~~~~~~

The morning of the Netherfield Ball dawned clear and cloudless. It was still cold in the early morning in Hertfordshire in mid-February, but not unbearably so. The younger, unmarried residents of Longbourn took an early morning ride, the newlyweds not willing to leave the warmth of their respective spouse's arms so early. Those riding set out to see two smaller neighbouring estates that the Duke of Hertfordshire had recently purchased.

One, Bennington Fields, bordered Netherfield Park, while the other, Purvis Lodge, was next to Longbourn. Both families had relatives in the Americas who were doing very well for themselves and had decided to join them there. The estates were both medium to smaller estates but had good bones. Bennington Fields would be annexed to Netherfield, the manor house available for when additional guests needed to be housed if the main house was filled. The small house at Purvis Lodge would be torn down and the park added to Longbourn. It had a good piece of arable farmland that would expand the acreage for farming at Longbourn.

After the riders viewed both properties, they returned toward Longbourn, and in an open field they gave their mounts their head. Lady Elizabeth and Darcy led the pack, neck and neck as their horse's hooves thundered across the field and followed closely by Lords Tom, James, and Wes. The other young ladies trailed behind by a little and they were followed by the escorts. Biggs had recommended to his master, who whole heartedly agreed, that just because they were on home ground did not mean that they should relax their vigilance.

A little before the end of the field, the riders slowed to trot as both Darcy and Lady Elizabeth claimed that they were the first to arrive at the marker point for the end of the gallop. The truth was that it was practically a tie. The riders allowed the horses to cool down as they trotted back toward Longbourn's extensive stables. Neither would admit it aloud, save perhaps themselves, but both Lady Elizabeth Bennet and Mr.

Fitzwilliam Darcy were looking forward to the ball with more anticipation than either had ever felt before for a like event. Darcy at least was willing to acknowledge, to himself and his mother only, that he was irrevocably in love with the raven haired, beautiful, middle Bennet daughter. Elizabeth knew that she had growing feelings for him, but just how deep, she was not willing to acknowledge yet, even silently to herself.

CHAPTER 18

While Louisa Hurst knew that her younger sister was eminently able to plan the ball but two hours away from commencing at Netherfield Park, she had insisted that Caroline sit back and relax, to not expend any energy planning the ball. It was in her and her Graham's honour, so Louisa felt that it would not be right for Miss Bingley to plan her own ball, though Louisa knew her well and would be able to make it feel like it was a ball planned with her sister in mind.

Netherfield was awash with light when the first carriage arrived. The torches were lit to guide drivers to the drop off point, and there was a large number of footmen on hand to assist the riders as they alighted in their finery. The receiving line was composed of Bingley, the betrothed couple, Mr. and Mrs. Phillips and Mr. and Mrs. Hurst. The party from Longbourn arrived and traversed the receiving line. Lady Elizabeth gave her friend a hug and they admired each other's ball gown while Darcy shook hands vigorously with his friend Bingley. Elizabeth was followed by Lady Anne who hugged her protégé as she whispered how proud she was of Caroline in a way only she could hear.

The couples, led by Caroline and Graham, lined up for the first set. Both Lady Elizabeth and Darcy seemed preoccupied, as if they were pondering some great mystery. The Duchess of Hertfordshire and Lady Anne Darcy gave each other knowing looks as both could have told their children the answer to the mystery that had them so consternated. Even if her stubborn, middle daughter could not see what seemed to be inevitable, Lady Sarah could.

For the first ten minutes of the set there was no talking,

but Elizabeth noticed that her handsome partner was a very accomplished dancer. She decided that there had been enough awkward silence between them. "Come William, we must have some conversation," Elizabeth said archly.

"Do you make it a practice to talk while you dance, Cousin?" Darcy returned.

"If we go half an hour complete in silence, we will engender more talk than us dancing the first, William," she challenged.

"What would you like to discuss, your Ladyship; I would not suspend any pleasure of yours," he volleyed, anxious for her reply.

"I could remark on the number of couples dancing and the elegance of the dress, and you could remark that private balls are more enjoyable that public ones," she teased with a light tinkling laugh, one that he had grown to love. He repaid her gift with a dimple-revealing smile, one that Elizabeth loved to see, though the after affects were not something, she was sure she would ever get used to.

"James is again opening the ball with Georgie," Elizabeth observed, becoming more serious as they parted and moved down the line. When they came back together, she finished her thought. "I have never seen him pay attention to any lady in this marked a fashion before. If memory serves, he danced the supper set as well at the pre-wedding ball."

"They did," Darcy confirmed. "She is not sixteen yet and will not come out for two years. My mother and I desire that she have at least one season until someone declares himself."

"That should not be a problem for James. He will only graduate Cambridge in May," The dance separated them again as they circled other dancers. Once they were facing one another again, Lady Elizabeth picked up where the dance had forced her to pause. "Then he is to leave for his Grand Tour. He will only be one and twenty in early June, so I do not believe that he would consider proposing to Georgie, or anyone else, for at least three years. That is assuming that it would be something that either of them chooses."

After another sashay down the line, Darcy nodded his head. "That is good to hear. I would never push Georgie into an alliance, regardless of title or wealth, unless it was her desire and there was love and respect between them."

The first dance of the set came to a close and they stood waiting for the next one to commence. "I am glad to hear that as we Bennets will never marry without the deepest love and true and mutual respect." Elizabeth agreed.

Lady Sarah leaned over to talk to the three sisters sitting next to her, all current or former Fitzwilliams. "If I were a betting woman, I would bet that those two will set aside their stubbornness and acknowledge what most can already see," She said loud enough for only her friends to hear.

"They will." Lady Catherine sighed. "There was a time when I tried to claim that William and my Anne were 'formed' for each other, until my baby sister set me to rights." The two blood sisters smiled at one another. "If you had told me that I would be speculating about your Lizzy and our William making a match last year, I would have ordered the carriage to take you to Bedlam," she teased. "But one would have to be wilfully blind and ignorant to not see what is happening between those two."

"I will not be unhappy to gain Lizzy as a daughter to share with you, Sarah." Lady Anne took her friend's hand. "They are both very stubborn, and very different in some ways, but so very alike in others. I, like Catherine, would not have believed the changes in William, but I always hoped to see them. My thanks go out to Lizzy for giving me my William back."

"Lizzy was not the only one who thought he was the worst kind of gentleman," the Duchess shared. "We all felt that way after our first meeting. We are very happy to find out just how wrong we were. My sons have gone from wanting to call William out to thinking of him as a friend. It is not just Lizzy that he has won over. I would be very happy to share him with you as a son, Anne.

"Richard has always thought of William like a brother, if

those two," Lady Elaine inclined her head toward the two who were busy with the second dance of the set, "ever see what is as plain as the noses on their faces, I too will gain another son and daughter. As Anne knows, I have considered William and Georgie honorary children for many years now."

"What think you of James and Georgie, Anne?" asked her sister Catherine. "This is the second ball that he has requested the first from her."

It would not have surprised Lady Anne to know that her answer was eerily similar to the one that her son had given to Lady Elizabeth. The four matriarchs all agreed that there was a lot of time before either would be ready to enter the marriage mart, so they would just keep their eye on things for now. Mrs. Gardiner joined the four and they were soon talking about more mundane issues.

~~~~~~~/~~~~~~~

Caroline Bingley felt as though she was floating on air. She was at the head of the line at her own engagement ball, dancing with the man that she loved above all others to whom she would be married in about three weeks. Her brother was dancing next to them in the line with Franny Phillips. As happy as she was for herself, she felt sympathy for her brother. The end of the mandated time that he had had to wait to declare himself to Miss Phillips was fast approaching. Charles would be the last Bingley sibling to complete his path to a love match. Although this was a night of celebration, Caroline could not help but think about her late mother with mixed feelings, sad that she was not there to witness her daughter's wedding but not sorry to no longer be under the mother's bitter influence.

As she danced with her love, Caroline realised that her mother's naked ambition which led her to lavish all of her time on her while ignoring Charles and Louisa was not love. She had only been trying to live vicariously through her daughter. As sad as it was, Caroline had no doubt that her mother would have been disappointed with Louisa's husband, and post Lady Anne Darcy's mentoring, Caroline would have caused Maude Bingley an apoplexy. She missed her parents, but it was not an ache that one would feel for a loved one. Maddie and Edward Gardiner had been more like true parents than her own.

As the set was coming to an end, Caroline banished all maudlin thoughts from her head and took her friend Lizzy's advice and looked at the present and to the future. She had the love of an excellent and honourable man, and most ironic of all that she was now accepted into the very circles her mother presumed to aspire to. The behaviour that she had learned at her mother's feet would have banished, and possibly ruined, her and her family. Yes, God moved in mysterious ways.

~~~~~~~/~~~~~~~

Darcy did something after the first set that he had never done before, he asked ladies to whom he was introduced at the ball, and with whom he was not well acquainted, to dance. This was a departure from his past actions. Andrew was heard asking his brother who the spirit inhabiting William's body was and where was his poor cousin being held captive. The result had been a guffaw from his brother and peals of laughter from their wives.

"We should not have fun at his expense. This is a big change for William, and I think we can thank our *sister* for putting him on this path," Andrew, Lord Hilldale opined.

As Jane watched her younger sister dance with Frank Lucas, she said, "Yes, brother, she may have been the impetus for him to change, but he is not the only one who has changed. Lizzy has made her own positive changes, and I believe it bodes well for their future."

"Then you have seen the same thing as I, Jane?" Marie asked with a cryptic smile.

"I have, Sister; though only time will tell," Jane answered with a smile of her own.

"Of what do you talk, my beloved Jane," asked Richard, who noticed little that was not directly related to his much-loved wife.

"We are talking about Lizzy and William," Jane elucidated her blind husband and brother.

"What of them?" Andrew did not show any more insight that his younger brother.

"Are both of you blind, husband?" Marie asked as she playfully slapped her husband's arm with her fan. Seeing the clueless looks from both men, she decided that they needed to have the situation explained to them. "Do neither of you see the way that they look at each other? Not only that, our sister agreed to dance the *first* with him."

"The supper set too," Jane agreed.

"You are both so mawkish. Are you trying to insinuate that our sister Lizzy and our cousin William have developed a tender regard for each other?" Richard looked from one sister to the other in disbelief.

"That is *exactly* what we are saying!" Marie replied, exasperated at the wilful blindness of their husbands.

Both men searched their memories and arrived at the realisation at almost the precise moment that each other did. Suddenly the looks, the shy interactions, how each seemed to seek the other out in company, made sense to the brothers who were too focused on their own wives to see blossoming love in others. The brothers, Richard especially, grinned mischievously as they considered how much they could tease the stoic and reserved cousin.

Their wives could see their devious minds at work. Jane being older spoke for both after some silent communication that only twins understand. "If either of you tease William or Lizzy, it will be a long while before the ice melts in our bedchambers!"

The fate that was alluded to would be too high a price to pay to tease their cousin, so the two pledged that they would behave with regard to William and Lizzy.

Caroline Bingley danced the third set with Mr. Darcy. While they danced, she gently canvassed his seemingly closeness with Lady Elizabeth. He would not delve into the subject, but he did not need to. She could not miss the way that every time he thought he was not being observed his eyes would find her friend. She also could not miss that the surreptitious looks were not his alone. As much as she had set her cap at Darcy for a brief time, she could see without any doubt in her mind that if he was able to capture their Lizzy's heart, they would be ideal one for the other.

The Bennets and their family were aware that to try and force a confidence or push Lady Elizabeth before she was ready would only engage her stubborn nature with full force in the opposing direction, so they sat back and watched the couple who did not yet know they were a couple. Lord Thomas Bennet and his brother shook their heads watching the undeclared courtship before their eyes. Neither brother could comprehend how the two had gone from Lizzy not wanting to be around the man to where they were now friends, and if she would allow herself to see it, much more. Elizabeth's father and surrogate father were not unhappy at the development. There was no doubt that Darcy was an honourable man who would not trifle with Lizzy, so if they ever got to the point, the suit would have the full support of both dukes.

~~~~~~~/~~~~~~~

At the time of the ball, George Wickham was trying to find an exit from his predicament in case his 'perfect' plan did not succeed. After searching his scheming brain, he came to the realisation that there was none. The *Spaniard's* men, although louts, were dogged in their dedication to the duty that they had been given.

The two had split the day into two twelve-hour shifts and one of them was awake and near Wickham at all times. They had gone so far as to nail the windows shut in the chambers that he shared with his paramour, cutting off that route of escape. Any time that he was not in Karen's chambers, they were with him. When he imbibed, they would sip a drink, but never more than one or two so they were always alert. Wickham surmised that their boss either paid them very well or that they were afraid of him and did not want to end up in the Thames with a permanent 'smile', or a combination of both.

No, there was only one option, and it was not failure. Soon intelligence would start being collected again. They would find something; all he needed was one chance. He was not a religious man, but that night he prayed for divine intervention in his dastardly quest so he could save his own neck. Even in his prayers to God, he was purely selfish. He had delayed long enough, he had to go to her, as distasteful as it had become to him. He needed Karen Younge's assistance, so having her discover that he had no true regard for her would be disastrous at this point, so he took a deep breath, tipped the contents of his glass down his throat, and headed to Mrs. Younge's bedchamber to do his duty.

<center>~~~~~~~/~~~~~~~</center>

Upon completion of the supper set, Darcy led the lady that owned his heart to be seated. They ate at a table with his married cousins, the betrothed couple, and the couple who were aching to make their courtship official. They were joined by Mr. and Mrs. Pierce. Lady Elizabeth's friend Charlotte sat on her other side while Darcy, after canvassing what foods she preferred, left to fulfil his mission.

"Eliza, am I wrong that Mr. Darcy's company is not as distasteful as it once was?" her friend asked with an arched brow.

"You are not wrong, Charlotte," Elizabeth offered no more.

"Come now, Eliza. How do you explain the thawing between the two of you?" Mrs. Pierce asked, not satisfied with her friend's glib answer.

"We apologised to each other and both granted forgiveness. We are cousins now, after all, and I dare say that we have become friends."

"Friends, Eliza?" Charlotte challenged.

"Yes, Charlotte, *friends!*" Elizabeth gave her a quelling look that her friend recognised well. Eliza Bennet had told her in no uncertain terms that the subject was closed.

The men returned with sumptuous fare for the ladies then sat down next to the lady with whom each had danced the previous set and Elizabeth turned to Miss Bingley. "Are you enjoying your ball, Caroline?" The answer was obvious from the look of contentment on Caroline's face.

"Yes, thank you, Lizzy. I am most decidedly enjoying the ball." She looked at her betrothed. "Though I think that I will enjoy the celebration in a few short weeks even more!"

"I could not agree with my fiancée more," Graham Phillips agreed as he looked into his beloved's eyes. "That will be the best of days for me as well."

"I wish that Papa would relent and let Ch..., er, anyone that may desire to declare for me to do so," Miss Phillips said with a tinge of petulance.

Bingley took her hand under the table and squeezed it in solidarity with her. She was the woman that he loved beyond the capacity he had believed existed in him. Yes, he would have liked to have been allowed to ask for her hand already, never mind request a courtship, but he would honour her father's wishes. He would not, could not, put his beloved in a position where she would have to choose between him and her father.

At a table across the room, the Dukes and their Duchesses were seated with the Matlocks and Ladies Anne and Catherine.

"My Anne would have enjoyed this ball immensely," Lady Catherine opined. "She is in town with Mrs. Jenkinson. She was not feeling well when we left and I advised her that her health was more important than the ball. If it were more than a trifling cold, I would have remained with her."

"Have Anne and Ashby set a date for their wedding, Catherine?" Lady Rose Bennet asked.

"They have, Rose. They selected Saturday the 21st day of March, and she will, of course, marry from Rosings," the proud mother reported.

"You must let us know if we can be of assistance, Catherine. We are all family, after all," Lady Sarah Bennet offered genuinely.

"Anything that you need Catherine, all you need do is ask," her brother added, Reggie doing something that he had not done in many years, he winked at his sister and was rewarded with a giggle just as she had when they were younger.

"Is everything ready for Anne's engagement ball, sister?" Lady Anne asked her sister-in-law. "It is less than a fortnight. I apologise if I have been remiss, Elaine, but please inform me if there is anything that you need me to make my namesake's ball a success."

"There is no reason to apologise, Anne. You know that I would not have been recalcitrant in requesting if I had the need for assistance." All who knew Elaine as the force of nature that she was nodded in agreement. "The plans are all made, the invitations will be sent out as soon as we arrive back at Matlock House, and all that is needed is for chef to start making enough white soup."

"I cannot believe that the Georgie that I see here tonight is the same one that we met last year, Anne," the Duchess of Hertfordshire stated.

"You do not know how it warms my heart, Sarah," Lady Anne smiled with love for her daughter. "I credit much of her recovery to your daughters, most specifically Lizzy. She has become the best of friends with Kitty, Loretta, and Mary, but it was Lizzy that drew her out and showed her that even though she knew about Ramsgate there was no judgement, only love and acceptance." A tear of gratitude rolled down Lady Anne's cheek.

"Our Lizzy, when she is not delivering a set down," Lord Thomas smiled at the family elders gathered, "has that way with people. I, for one, was not surprised that she was able to draw Georgiana out the way that she did."

"Whatever the reason, I have never seen my Georgie happier or more self-assured and self-confident. I used to despair for her having no company but Mrs. Annesley, William, and myself. Now look at her; she revels in her connection to girls of similar ages. The other girl, the one with the light brown hair with curls, that is Maria Lucas, is it not?" Lady Anne asked.

"Yes, that is Maria," Lady Sarah agreed. "She is a good sort of girl, mayhap not the most intelligent, but a loyal friend and she would never do anything to harm anyone."

At the end of the dinner hour, Ladies Loretta, Mary, and Kitty, along with Misses Darcy and Lucas, wished their parents good night together as Sir William and Lady Lucas had joined the Bennets' table toward the end of the meal. Sir William's wife, Sarah Lucas, was an acquaintance of the Duchess but not as close as her husband was to the Duke. The loquacious knight had long ago realised that company like those at the Duke's table had no interest in hearing about his knighting, so he remained silent on the subject in their presence.

Soon after the farewells, the young ladies retired from the ball and were escorted back to Longbourn by companions and guards. Maria Lucas had been invited to overnight with her new friends, and, with permission from her mother, had readily accepted the invitation.

Lady Elizabeth turned down all applications to dance the final set, a waltz, without consciously knowing that her heart had communicated to her head that if she were not to dance the final set with her cousin William, then she would not dance with another. The man in question did not ask any lady to dance the final set for the same reason. At the end of the ball, the Bennet Party was one of the first to leave as they had no desire to keep their hosts from retiring any longer than necessary.

As Caroline Bigley lay down in her bed, she could not but think of the kiss that her betrothed had managed before the Phillips party departed. Graham had pulled her aside into a darkened parlour near the entrance and had bestowed a toe-curling kiss full of passion and promise. Caroline felt that the days between this one and the one on which she would resign the name Bingley and replace it with Phillips could not pass fast enough.

CHAPTER 19

Wickham felt relief; one of the young scallywags begging near Bennet House had reported that the family had returned. The Bennets' return to London would relieve a little of the pressure being applied by the *Spaniard*, at least temporarily. As impatient as he was to get his hands on her, he acknowledged that he must wait to make sure that the family's guards further relaxed.

He openly admitted to himself that as soon as he received the ransom, he would make the virago that humiliated him pay. He would show her what a real man was and would consider returning her only once she was well and truly broken and irrevocably ruined. He salivated at the thought of punishing the woman for exposing him and laughing at him in public. She would pay for his flogging, for his being cheated out of the mouse's dowry by the prig, all of it. She was the personification of all of the ills in his life. Like he always managed to do, he forgot to lay the blame in the only place that it belonged—with himself.

~~~~~~~/~~~~~~~

After the ball, the Fitzwilliams headed north to introduce their wives to the estates that would be their homes. The Viscount and Viscountess were to Hilldale in Staffordshire, while the Honourable Mr. Richard and Lady Jane Fitzwilliam's estate was Brookfield in Derbyshire. The Matlock heir's estate was west while Richard's was north of Snowhaven.

The plan for both couples was to leave their estates, meet at an inn they often used to trade horses, then travel together into Kent for Anne de Bourgh's wedding in March, arriving at Rosings a week before their cousin's nuptials. As the older former Bennets were not as intimate with Miss Bingley as their younger sister Elizabeth was, and Caroline understood that they needed to see their new homes so would miss her wedding, while Anne also understood them missing her engagement ball for the same reason.

They spent one night at Snowhaven to show their brides their childhood home. The manor house consisted of the old Matlock Castle which gave the impression that it had welcoming arms extending from the castle walls reaching out on either side of the drive. The two wings had been added over the years to increase the living space and the number of chambers for family and guests. The construction was completed by the current Earl of Matlock. Unlike many others, the Fitzwilliams had not permitted their castle to fall into a state of disrepair.

The castle and lands had been presented to the first Earl of Matlock in December 1485, as Sir Fredrick Fitzwilliam, a knight, had supported and significantly helped the winning side in the Wars of the Roses. As his reward, he had been elevated and presented with the title of Earl of Matlock, and gifted with the Matlock Castle as well as the vast Snowhaven estate.

Andrew and Richard Fitzwilliam loved and were justifiably very proud of their home, just as their parents were. Andrew informed the two brides that the land was flatter at Snowhaven than Pemberley, as Snowhaven was further from the peak district. There was an ongoing friendly rivalry between the Fitzwilliams and the Darcys as to whose estate was the better. Richard informed them that as Lady Anne grew up at Snowhaven, before she married their late Uncle Darcy and moved to Pemberley, she tried to remain neutral, most of the time. If pressed, however, she would admit a clear preference for Pemberley.

The Derwent River ran through Snowhaven, whose water flowed from the split with the Trent River in Derby. One of the Fitzwilliam ancestors dug a canal that fed into a manmade lake to the right of the manor. Jane remarked that her Uncle Edward would be happy to hear of the fisherman's paradise as he was an avid angler. In the front of the manor was the formal garden with a complex maze that the Fitzwilliam siblings and their cousins loved playing in, hiding from each other in their younger days. Marie noted that their next youngest sister would be pleased when she visited the estate and saw that nature was given free rein in the surrounding woodlands where Marie was certain Lizzy would discover many paths where she could indulge her love of walking and riding.

The long serving housekeeper, Mrs. Loretta Sherman, welcomed her boys' home and could not but be amazed at the beauty of their wives. She confided in the butler, a Mr. Hugh Hopkinson who had taken over the past five years ago, that the sisters looked so much alike that she could not tell them apart and hoped that Masters Andrew and Richard were able. Knowing their beloved brides as they did, neither brother had ever made that error, but they were assisted by the sisters who took to having the coiffures done differently and never wore the same outfit at the same time to try and reduce the possibility of confusion.

Before dinner the brothers introduced their wives to the maze. They walked the paths inside for almost an hour, revealing the secret of how to find the way out to each lady. They retired soon after having decided that they needed as much 'rest' as possible.

~~~~~~~/~~~~~~~

In the ten days since returning to town, the Darcys had been included in invitations to the Bennets quite often. They had attended dinners, musical soirées, a play, and two balls before the end of February. At each ball Darcy had danced the first set with Lady Elizabeth, and at one their second set was the supper set and at the other it was the final set. With every encounter that they had, feelings deepened on both sides.

There was no doubt for Darcy; he was irrevocably and deeply in love with his dearest loveliest Elizabeth, which is how he thought of her. The lady admitted to herself, though to no one else, that she had feelings beyond friendship for her cousin William, but was not yet willing to admit more. At least three times a week, Darcy, on his mount Zeus, joined Lady Elizabeth, on her stallion Mercury, to ride. It was, of course, never just the two of them. Lord Birchington had joined them on each of the rides, and his sister, and Ladies Loretta, Mary, and Kitty were part of the party for some of them. Lord Wes had also joined them the last time they rode out.

The morning before the engagement ball for Anne de Bourgh and Ian Ashby, Lady Elizabeth requested an interview with her father. After he indicated that his middle daughter should sit, the Duke started the conversation, "Yes, Lizzy, you requested this meeting?"

"I did, Papa. There is something that I need to request from you," Lizzy stated without giving her father an idea of what it was that she desired from him, although he felt like he had a reasonable idea.

"If it is in my power to grant," Lord Thomas saw his daughter's countenance light up thinking that she had just received a blanket yes. "Unless it is something that puts you in harm's way or I deem unreasonable." He had guessed correctly, for as soon as he added his conditions his Lizzy's face fell in disappointment.

She nevertheless decided to press on with her request. "Papa, you know how much I enjoy my solitary rambles," she reminded him, her eyes pleading for him to understand.

"Not entirely solitary, Biggs or Johns trail you."

"*Almost* solitary. If I want to take a walk now, I have Miss Jones, Biggs, and at least three more of his men. And they are not trailing me, they are close by!" she huffed in frustration, not understanding why father did not comprehend why the feeling of independence was so important to her!

"It had not escaped my notice that you chafe at the restrictions and all of the extra guards, Lizzy. I hope that you understand that I take the responsibility of protecting all of my family still under my roof serious, in the extreme," her father told her firmly but with understanding. "I have spoken to William as well as all of the Fitzwilliam men. They all agree, my Lizzy, that Wickham is like a wounded bear free among the crowd. As much as he envies and hates your cousin, when you humiliated him publicly and had the temerity not to believe his well-practiced lies, and then added the insult of laughing at him, you likely became his primary object of his revenge.

"He is one, from everything that your brothers, Reggie, and William have told me, that does not have the capacity to accept his part in anything that has ever befallen him. In his twisted mind, it is always someone else who bears responsibility. Until I *know* that the man is no longer a threat to you or anyone else, I will not relax the vigilance."

Lady Elizabeth felt like stamping her foot in frustration, but stopped herself knowing that a petulant childish display would change nothing. She needed to attempt a bargain. "In all of the time that I took my rambles with Biggs or Johns trailing me, did anything happen other than the prick of a bramble, Papa?"

"No, Lizzy, it did not," he answered and carried right on as he could see that she had a retort ready. "There is a difference. There was never a credible threat against you or the family then, Lizzy. Surely with your intelligence you can comprehend the difference."

"I do see the difference. Would you agree to my walking three times a week with only Biggs not trailing me as far as he used to?" his daughter asked hopefully.

"Not alone, but I will agree to twice a week, no Miss Jones, and three footmen," her father countered.

"I accept your terms, but please make it two footmen, Papa." While the Duke considered her request she added, "I suggest Biggs and Johns. They are both very quick for huge men and are crack shots with those pistols that almost no one knows they carry always within reach. They could trail me, but half the distance that Biggs used to at Longbourn?" Lady

Elizabeth asked hopefully.

The Duke of Hertfordshire considered his daughter's plea seriously. With both Biggs and Johns escorting her, with their cat like reflexes and proficiency in all types of combat both armed and unarmed, he decided that he could live with the compromise. "I agree..." Lady Elizabeth let a most unladylike whoop, "on condition that your mother has no objection. If my dear wife agrees, then we will see about trying things out after Caroline's wedding."

"Papa..." she cut off any objection that she was about to make as she knew that once her father made a decision like this that she would only argue her way out of any compromise, "...you have my sincere thanks." She kissed her papa on the forehead.

"Away with you now, Lizzy. I need some peace and quiet to consider my correspondence," he gave her a light pat on the posterior and sent his much happier daughter on her way, believing all would be well. Although he did not know it yet, father and daughter had just given Wickham the opening that he was looking for.

The following day was the ball at Matlock House. That morning the usual group took a ride in Hyde Park, including Lord Wes and the four younger girls. They were escorted by three companions, two grooms, and ten footmen. They rode slowly through the park not above a canter, most of the ride at a walk or trot. Galloping in Hyde Park was not looked upon with a friendly eye by those in the Ton.

Darcy came up alongside Elizabeth as they were following the Serpentine. He felt more daring than he had before any previous ball where he had danced with his beloved Elizabeth. "Am I too late to reserve the opening set with you, Lizzy?" he asked hopefully.

"You are not, William. The second, third, and fourth are reserved for Tom, my father, and Uncle Sed. Other than that, I have none spoken for, so, yes, the first is yours," she answered with a noticeable blush that encouraged him.

"Then may I be so bold as to request the supper...and the final sets, your ladyship?" He held his breath as the lady ruminated on his request.

"You are aware, William, that I do not dance three sets with anyone outside of my immediate family, are you not?" He had a chagrined look on his countenance and nodded his head, expecting a refusal. Mayhap she would dance no sets with him! "There is a saying, 'nothing ventured, nothing gained'. You were daring, William, so yes; I will dance all three sets with you tonight."

Darcy felt an indescribable feeling of immeasurable happiness. "You have my sincere thanks, cousin," he said with a bow of his head.

"Do not thank me yet, William. I am warning you any gossip mongers will be sent to you for comment," Elizabeth teased, and oh how he loved it when she teased him.

"You have a deal, Lizzy. Any person wanting to gossip may meet me at Angelo's anytime that they wish," he retorted with a smile that showed his dimples and made Elizabeth warm all over.

~~~~~~~/~~~~~~~

In Staffordshire and Derbyshire, the new viscountess and her sister were becoming familiar with their respective estates. They had 'inspected' the master suite at each estate very thoroughly, much to the delight of their husbands.

Hilldale was an estate that was comparable in size to Netherfield Park before Bennington Fields was purchased and annexed to James's estate. The houses were of similar capacity though Hillsdale's manor house was one not as tall by one story. The manor house had two wings that made the house look like half an 'H' so that the house was able to accommodate about eight more guests than Netherfield could. Lady Marie Fitzwilliam was very happy to see the sizable garden. Like her mother, she enjoyed nothing better than exercising her green thumb. She would not tread on the head gardener's toes, but like she had at Longbourn she would request a bed that was for her to do as she wished.

Marie took an instant liking to the housekeeper, Mrs. Mavis Payton, who had been in her post for over ten years, starting when the current Earl still held the title of Viscount. The rotund housekeeper's husband, Amos Payton, was the butler who had been in his post for almost the same length of time as his wife had been in hers. Mrs. Payton made Marie feel very welcome after there had been no Viscountess since the current earl had ascended to his title these seven years. Marie had been well taught how to run a house by her dear mother. She knew that she needed to work with her housekeeper, not arrive on her first day and make gratuitous changes simply to show her authority.

While Lady Marie met with the housekeeper and cook during the day, Lord Andrew rode the estate with Mr. Peter Gibbs, the steward, who had taken up his post one year before Andrew became the Viscount. The man was eminently qualified and extremely efficient, however Lord Hilldale, like all of the others in the extended family, did not believe in being an absentee landlord. As was family tradition, the tenants' needs were always addressed when issues were brought to the steward's attention and servants were treated with respect. The latter explained why the servants who served at any of the extended family's properties were often generational employees.

Richard and Lady Jane Fitzwilliam's estate was closer to the peeks, not as close as Pemberley, but close enough so that when the conditions were good, a southern portion of the peeks were visible. Richard had informed Jane that Pemberley was ten miles northwest of them and much closer to the Peak District. Brookfield was somewhat larger than Hilldale, and had a well-developed and prosperous horse breeding programme. With the increased size of the estate coupled with the horses, Brookfield earned about three thousand more than Hilldale per annum. Brookfield thoroughbreds were sought-after horses, and fetched a healthy price when sold. It was

Richard's intent to expand the programme to start breeding horses that would be used by the cavalry. His own horse had saved him during the battle of Buçaco, so this was his way of making sure that others would have the same quality of mount he had had.

The estate's steward was a Mr. Murray Lefroy who had studied alongside Pemberley's current steward under his predecessor, old Mr. Herbert Wickham. Edwin Chalmers had become the steward after Mr. Wickham senior passed, and two years later when Richard had sought a steward for his inheritance, his cousin William had recommended his under-steward, Lefroy. The housekeeper, Mrs. Mavis Ross, was promoted three years previously. The butler, who had been an underbutler at Darcy House, a Mr. Joshua Durand, had wanted to be closer to his ailing parents in Kympton. When Brookfield had needed a butler, Durand had applied for the position, and with glowing recommendations from Darcy's butler Killion and the man himself, the then Colonel had offered him the position.

In the marriage settlement, Lady Jane's substantial dowry was left untouched, but Jane had insisted that the approximately ten thousand a year generated by the dowry be used as needed by them. A smaller estate on the western border of their estate had been offered for sale. In consultation with his then betrothed, Richard had purchased the property and absorbed it into Brookfield. The house, with some minor repairs, would serve as a dower house, and until needed could be used for additional guests. The land included in the purchase added four new tenants to the expanded estate. The master and his steward were riding out to inspect the tenant farms on the added land to assess their state of repair and to schedule any repairs or improvements that were needed.

Jane was very happy with her new home. It was between Netherfield and the much larger Longbourn's manor house in size. The family wing had ten suites with two bed chambers each and four single chambers. They could easily house forty guests without employing the dower house.

On the journey north, Jane and Marie had discussed that it was hard being so far from their parents and siblings, they discussed inviting their siblings to spend time with them at various times after the season each year so that they would not miss seeing them for too long each year. They had always known that it was the woman's lot to leave her childhood home for that of her husband when she married.

<center>~~~~~~~/~~~~~~~</center>

Matlock House was awash in light. The Darcys and Hertfordshire Bennets had been invited to arrive an hour before the first guests to acquaint themselves with Ashby's family. They were introduced to the groom's parents, the Earl and Countess of Ashbury, and Viscount and Viscountess Amberleigh, Ashby's brother and sister-in-law. They had all met Lady Amelia Ashby at the ball held before the double wedding in Hertfordshire, and the Marquess of Birchington was especially happy to see her again.

Lord Tom Bennet had vastly enjoyed her company on and off the dance floor the night they met. They had been to the theatre and taken a walk in Hyde Park on two occasions. Not a few debutants who had seen them together were unhappy that the handsome Marquess seemed to be 'off the market' and would have loved to discredit Lady Amelia Ashby somehow, but they could find naught to achieve their catty aims. Like his cousin William Darcy, Lord Tom Bennet had escaped an attempted entrapment or two.

The Marquess of Birchington's feelings had not waned during their separation, and had only grown since his return to Town. It did not take long for him to secure the same three sets that Darcy had been granted by his sister earlier that day, and had not missed the pleasure with which the lady received his request. Lady Gillian Ashby, Amy Ashby's proud mother, was very happy that her daughter had finally found a man who interested her, knowing her daughter's feelings were not connected to Tom's wealth or titles, but that there seemed to be tender feelings on both sides.

Lady Elizabeth was sitting and talking with Ladies Anne and Catherine. "It seems that my brother has gone and lost something and that Amy has found and decided to keep," Elizabeth observed. She was happy for her older brother and had never seen him express any marked interest in a young lady before.

"She is not the only one who has found..." Before her sister Catherine could complete the sentence, Lady Anne gripped her arm and inclined her head toward Elizabeth, reminding her sister that none of them were to push William and Elizabeth together, allowing it to happen by their own design, if that happened to be their choice.

"Did you say something, Aunt Catherine?" Lady Elizabeth asked. Thankfully she had been distracted so she did not pay attention to what the older lady was saying.

"Nothing, Lizzy dear," Lady Catherine prevaricated. "I was remembering something, but it had no relevance to our discussion."

"I cannot but agree with you, Lizzy. How old is Tom now?" Lady Anne asked to distract their young friend from what her sister had almost blurted out.

"He will be four and twenty this May, Aunt Anne," Elizabeth answered as she watched her brother. The truth was that she felt envious of her brother as he was not afraid to display his preference, but then that was the man's prerogative, was it not? She had a reasonably good idea that William was not indifferent to her, but her head and heart were still at war, so she was not willing to admit that he was more than her good friend at this point. Whenever her head told her that, her heart whispered 'you lie'.

"Lady Amelia has had two seasons has she not, sister?" Lady Catherine verified.

"Yes, Catherine, I believe you are correct. She had a marquess, two earls, and a few viscounts calling on her, but I hear that she was never interested in any of them. She is much like you, Lizzy. She wants more than to be a bauble on a man's arm. She is too intelligent for that."

"That is why Amy and I found a kinship when I met her at Longbourn," Lady Elizabeth agreed. "She is a very able chess player if not quite at my level. She will be able to beat Tom from time to time without too much trouble."

"Time will tell," Catherine de Bourgh opined. "It could be that your brother is not ready to settle down and take a wife yet."

"As we have not discussed the subject, I have no knowledge one way or the other, Aunt Catherine." Elizabeth looked to where Anne de Bourgh and Ian Ashby were sitting, talking with their heads close together and ignorant of all others in the room. "Anne looks deliriously happy with her betrothed. How well they look together."

"Lizzy has the right of it, Catherine," Lady Anne agreed. "I have never seen my namesake radiate pure joy and love like I see in her when she is with Ian."

"I agree, Anne. My daughter has never been happier," Lady Catherine said wistfully. She knew that she would still be part of Anne's life, but she would nevertheless miss seeing her on an almost daily basis.

After all the guests had been shepherded through the receiving line, Lord Matlock asked all present to drink a toast to his niece and soon to be nephew. Darcy then came to retrieve Lady Elizabeth for the opening set. They joined the line, and while awaiting the opening bars of the music Darcy looked at his partner. "Have I told you, Lizzy, that I have seen no one more handsome that you are tonight? You are definitely handsome enough to tempt me to dance," he teased, his smile spreading as he twisted the offensive words that he had uttered in Meryton.

"Why thank you, William. I dare say that the same can be said of you," she said with an impertinently arched eyebrow. The music began and neither felt the need to talk. They both enjoyed the company of the other and did not need inane conversation to pass the time.

A little farther down the line Miss Bingley was partnering her betrothed. "I am in such anticipation, Graham. It is less than ten days until we say our vows to each other," Caroline said with a very dreamy look.

"Soon we will never have to be parted again, my love." Graham reached up an touched her cheek lovingly while his eyes displayed all of the love her felt for his betrothed, "I love you so very much, my Caroline," he spoke quietly as he gave her a look that reflected the depth of the love he felt for her.

While they went down the line separately, Caroline thought about the tour of his home, which soon they would share the previous day. When they came back together, she remarked, "I found the town home that your uncle gifted you to be delightful." As a wedding gift, Lord Thomas and Lady Sarah Bennet had gifted the house, which was not part of the entail of the properties belonging to his dukedom, to their nephew and his bride.

"It is hard to fathom that the Bennets were so generous. They allowed me to stay at the home for more than three years, never accepting a penny in rent and now this," Graham's voice was filled with gratitude. "Are you sure that there is nothing that you want to change other than your chambers, Caroline?"

"There is no need, Graham. Anything else would have been change for change's sake. Our home is perfect, so other than updating some furniture and the colours in my chambers, there is no *need* for any other changes." Graham had no doubt that most others would have demanded wholesale changes just because she could. Not his Caroline, she was too sensible for that.

Two couples over, Bingley was dancing with Miss Phillips, who were also counting the days until their siblings wedding because a day or two after the time restriction imposed by Franny's father would expire. As much as Charles Bingley was impatient to declare himself, his dance partner was even more impatient to receive the addresses of the man that she loved beyond the capacity that she had believed possible.

The Marquess of Netherfield was dancing with a young woman who intrigued him. He understood neither of them was ready for anything but friendship as cousins, but he hoped that she was feeling similar stirrings as he as he had not missed that every time, he looked at her or spoke to her she would blush most becomingly.

At the head of the line, Ashby could not have been happier. In less than a month he would be able to take his Anne home to Sherwood Park. There was a time when he believed that Lady Catherine would do all in her power to separate them, but then all had changed. There was now open approbation for the match which Anne's mother had blessed. They planned to live most of the time in Surrey, but would be at Rosings Park at least a fortnight every three months as well as a full month at Easter when the whole family had a standing invitation to spend Eastertide in Kent.

Anne felt as deeply about her betrothed as he felt for her. With only less than a month left, she could not wait for the time to pass so that she would be her Ian's wife. Anne was relieved that her mother would stay with her brother and then her sister after the wedding rather than in the large manor house at Rosings Park alone. Lady Catherine would join them for their first fortnightly sojourn at the estate in Kent in three months after the newlyweds had returned from their wedding trip and Anne had established herself at their estate in Surrey. Although she had invited her mother to live with them once they returned from their wedding trip, she could not repine the fact that they would have three months on their own at the start of their union.

The ball passed, as balls do. When William Darcy came to claim Lady Elizabeth Bennet for the final set, the third that they would dance that night, there were some very knowing looks exchanged by their family members. The gossips had a double dose of delight, because in line up for the waltz, the

Marquess of Birchington and Lady Amelia Ashby were right next to them.

CHAPTER 20

Wickham was growing restless, but thankfully his self-imposed moratorium on observing his prey was mercifully coming to an end. Another day or two and the waifs would be deployed with more than double the number so that they could be rotated regularly and make sure that they would be unobtrusive. He could not afford another mistake like the one where that stupid rascal had almost been caught by one of the Bennet guards.

He was mindful of the deadline that Álvarez had imposed, but, was confident that he would achieve his aims before the end of April. He felt no remorse for the plan that he had in place to double cross Mrs. Younge. He tolerated her because he had no other options, and it was expedient. He did not give her any thanks, but he was well aware that had he not been expelled from the militia when he was, then he would have been in the little backwater town when Colonel Fitzwilliam arrived the next day and he was not at all sure that he would have survived that meeting.

Until he could rid himself of Karen Younge, he had to play the role of her lover. The service put a roof over his head, gave him warm meals, and she provided coin for him to patronise the local tavern. What she did not know is that her blunt was also funding his visits to a brothel, one with young prosti-tutes as he preferred. Soon he would have wealth beyond his dreams. He was only sorry that there was no way to slip away before he paid the *Spaniard*. His desire to live overrode his de-sire to double cross Álvarez.

~~~~~~~/~~~~~~~

Darcy could not hide it anymore, nor did he desire to, he

was head over heels in love. His tender feelings had been enhanced for Lady Elizabeth when he had been one of the parties that visited Haven House between the two engagement balls. He remembered the day with pleasure and admiration.

All three Darcys had met the Countess of Matlock at Bennet House just after ten in the morning. Ladies Elizabeth, Kitty, Mary, and Loretta had been ready, and the party departed with guards, companions, and attendants on schedule.

Upon arrival at Haven House, Darcy could not but be impressed. There were two structures on the property of which the larger one housed the inhabitants of the Haven. The second, smaller building housed the clinic and hospital where the babes were birthed. The house was six stories, four above the ground level and one below. Below was the kitchens, pantry, cold room, and the offices for the housekeeper and her two under-housekeepers. The ground level was where the music room, administrative offices, classroom, dining parlours, and the public room were located.

The first, second, and third floors had the chambers for the inhabitants. On each floor there was two suites of rooms, each with two bedchambers for an inhabitant and a 'big sister' so there was always a person nearby who could help the girls if needed. The fourth floor was where the female staff's chambers were. The men that were employed at Haven House had chambers above the hospital so that way they were close by but did not sleep in the same house as the young ladies who had already been traumatised by men. There were always at least six guards on duty patrolling the outside grounds, and four footmen on the ground level at all times.

When they arrived, they were met by the administrator, Miss Ethel Cookson, and Mrs. Gardiner, who was the chairwoman of the facility. As always, when Elizabeth Bennet visited Haven House, the two girls that had inspired her, Clara and Ellie Steele were on hand to welcome her. Clara had been just shy of her fifteenth birthday when she gave birth to a stillborn son. Ellie was her younger sister, and as they could not return to the father that had abused them after their mother passed, they had been accepted for positions at the Haven. Clara was one of the senior maids and was in training to be an under-housekeeper while nineteen-year-old Ellie was one of the big sisters that live among the girls to help and guide them.

Both were aware that 'Miss Lizzy' and her family had been instrumental in finding them a place at the Haven, but neither knew the truth of the depth of the family's involvement. As they were guided on a tour by Miss Cookson, Darcy could not fathom how someone would abuse a girl as young as twelve. The administrator explained that they gave sanctuary to any girls in need, not just those with child. They had girls who had been abandoned for lack of family resources, physical and, or sexual abuse, and then there were those who had been seduced by manipulative liars who promised marriage and disappeared as soon as they took that which they wanted.

The administrator was dumbfounded when Lady Elizabeth disclosed her and the Bennet's role in creating and the continuing support of Haven House. The Steele sisters cried many tears of appreciation to think that their plight had been the genesis for the remarkable lady's drive to make a difference. While the ladies were talking to the Steele sisters, Darcy approached Miss Cookson.

"Miss Cookson, I find that I am very much impressed with the work that is done at Haven House and I would like to be a benefactor on an on-going basis," he quietly spoke with the administrator. He did not do it to impress the lady that he loved, he just wanted to make a positive difference. He did not then know that Lady Elizabeth Bennet had a very keen sense of hearing and had heard what he said.

"We have been thinking about a second house as we currently have to turn girls away. The need is so great," the lady explained sadly. "I have not presented the plan to Maddie, Mrs. Gardiner, for the board's consideration yet."

"Do not request the funds from the board." Darcy requested, nodding when she looked at him with obvious question. "I will fund the purchase of the property and any construction or renovation that is required. In addition, I will pledge an annual amount of four thousand pounds for the costs of maintaining the new

house."

"Mr. Darcy, I appreciate your offer, but that amount of money, are you sure, sir? I would not want you to do something that is beyond your means," she stated bluntly. "I intend no insult, it is such a generous donation, and if that is your desire, Mr. Darcy, then we will gratefully accept your beneficence."

"I will tell you a little secret Miss Cookson, my reported income if far below the reality. I appreciate your candour, but this will not hurt me or any of my other commitments." He wrote his information for her and told her to contact him as soon as she found an appropriate location for 'New Haven House', as the two dubbed it.

Darcy could not know it, but he had just shot very high up in the estimation of one Lady Elizabeth Bennet. In one of the classrooms, Miss Darcy heard one girl talking to another, and her blood froze when she heard what was being said.

"'E tolds me that if I really lov's 'im, I would lie wif 'im before the wedding." The girl explained.

"That is exactly what he told me, Jenney, and I, a gentleman's daughter, fell for his lies just like you did." The other girl admitted to her friend.

A timid and shaking Georgiana, holding her mother's hand and with Elizabeth's arm around her, approached the girls who became silent and gave a curtsy to the highborn visitors. "D-do y-you s-peak of a George Wickham?" she asked timidly, sure that she knew the answer.

"Yes, Miss, how would you know that?" The one who identified that she was gently bread asked incredulously.

With her mother and Elizabeth's support, Georgie shared her own history with George Wickham. One was heavy with child while the other, Jenny, had given birth some months back. Both had been rejected and cast out by their families. Georgiana's story brought to light that although what the girls had done was wrong, they had been lied to by a practiced manipulating seducer, the very worst kind of man. After that day, Miss Darcy would occasionally visit the girls with whom she could talk about what no one else could understand, and she maintained a correspondence with both women, and with her brother and mother's hearty approval. They belonged to the same club, even though she had been fortunate enough to be saved by her brother before she had allowed the black-guard to take her virtue.

Once word was disseminated that the lady that founded and worked so hard to create the Haven was at the house, Lady Eliza-beth was swamped with gratitude from the girls that had a chance at a good life rather than in the brothels or begging then dying on the streets. Elizabeth requested, on behalf of her family, that their contributions not be transmitted beyond the Haven's walls which she received a solemn promise that her request would be honoured.

As Darcy ruminated about that day, he knew that besides the work that was being done at the Haven, Georgie's meeting two of Wickham's victims, had helped the two girls with the healing process and allowed Georgie to use her experience to help others. Two days previously he had met Miss Cookson to view two large homes, one next to the other, just off Grace-church Street and close to the Haven that had been offered for sale. The houses were judged to be just what they needed and had been purchased. New Haven House had a home. They would need some renovation, but once done they would be able to house thirty to forty girls and the needed staff between them. The vision was to offer the homes to girls who had birthed babes and were ready to take their first steps back in society. The New Haven would be an intermediary step in the recovery process where the girls would have more independ-ence but still be well protected.

Darcy was unaware that his new cousin was cognisant of what he was about and how much his actions had unwittingly softened her heart toward him. The fact that he did every-thing quietly without seeking glory for himself made him all the more attractive to Lady Elizabeth Bennet.

~~~~~~~/~~~~~~~

The day that she had dreamed about had arrived! Caroline Bingley loved her brother and his name, but she felt like she was floating on clouds as she considered that but a few hours she would be taking the name of Phillips when she married her beloved Graham. Even though she saw very little of her father, she could not help but miss the fact that he would not be walking her to her betrothed and that it would not be her papa that would be giving her away in but three hours. The wedding breakfast would be at the Gardiner's town home. Both the Bennets and the Darcys had volunteered their own homes, but Caroline did not want her guests to have to all be transported to Mayfair when the church was within walking distance and she had her longest ties to the Gardiners and their home.

She heard a soft knock on her door. Louisa and Madeline Gardiner entered her room to fuss over her and help her as she prepared for her wedding. Miss Bingley was very grateful that her friend Lizzy and Lady Anne had joined them the prior evening for a lady's dinner. Louisa, Aunt Maddie, and Aunt Anne had sat with her for 'the talk' later that evening. Similarly, to the way that Lady Sarah's revelations had calmed her daughters about the wedding night, Caroline too felt calmer, though in truth now that the fear was gone, she anticipated what was to come.

Her dress of light green silk was hanging ready for her to wear after she had bathed. Madam Chambourg had made her the perfect dress with an empire waist and puffed sleeves and an organza overlay that made it shimmer. It was low cut, but not to the point that it displayed Caroline's womanly assets, and had a short train. Louisa would stand up with her, she was not only her sister, but was also her best friend. Even when Caroline used to behave badly, Louisa never gave up on her sister and was the least surprised when Caroline worked toward making the efforts to be the woman she was now.

Graham Phillips had spent the night before his wedding at the Bingley's home just a few doors down from the Gardiners. The previous night, the men had gone to White's. Luckily none had over imbibed so the groom would not have to contend with a pounding headache as he waited for his bride in the church. Graham's very good friend from both Eton and Cambridge, Mr. Hench Wetherspoon, was standing up for him. They were both clerks at Norman and James and on track to become fully fledged barristers in the near future. The younger Phillips remembered what his new Fitzwilliam cousins had advised him, to break his fast as it was unlikely that he would not eat at the wedding breakfast.

Charles Bingley was excited; he would declare himself for Franny Phillips in two days and that was something that he could not wait for. The house was full as he was hosting his Aunt, Uncle, and cousins from Scarborough, his late mother's brother, and relatives from his father's side as well. Their Uncle Toby was a long-time favorite of the three siblings. He was an equal partner with Bingley in their carriage works business in Scarborough, responsible for the day-to-day workings.

The time was near so those in residence at the Bingley townhouse made the short walk to the church. They were met outside by the Phillips, both Bennet families, Darcys, Lord and Lady Matlock, and Hurst. Mrs. Hattie Phillips hugged her son and kissed him on both cheeks. A mother could not be prouder of her son than Hattie was of hers. Charles Bingley greeted all of their friends then walked over to the Gardiner's house to collect his younger sister. Everyone took their seats except for Lady Elizabeth. She decided to await the bride so she could greet her friend before she made the walk down the aisle.

Edward and Maddie Gardiner and the three older children entered the vestibule and after greeting their niece and cousin, Mr. Gardiner accompanied his son and daughter to their pew while his wife made sure that young May understood what her duties of flower girl were.

"Caroline, you make a stunning bride, I am so happy that in no time at all we will be cousins," Elizabeth offered as she had never seen her friend look more becoming.

"Thank you, Lizzy. I appreciate your waiting to see me before I go to meet my Graham," Caroline said demurely. "It is thanks to you that Madame Chambourg created this gown for me."

"Stuff and nonsense, Caroline. You deserve everything on your own merit." Lady Elizabeth did not want to delay the ceremony, so she gave Caroline's hand a squeeze and joined her Aunt in finding their seats.

At the appointed time, May Gardiner walked up the aisle dropping red rose petals just as she had been instructed and, was followed by Louisa Hurst. There was a pause and the congregation stood, then Miss Bingley entered from the vestibule on her brother's arm. Caroline Bingley almost had to pinch herself because just below the altar stood the perfect, no, the *only* man for her. A man she loved and who loved her in return for no other reason than for who each were. She was very much looking forward to the wedding trip which would be a fortnight at Darcy's Seaview Cottage near Brighton, thinking of the exclusive time that she would spend with her husband. They arrived at the top of the aisle then Charles put her hand on her beloved's arm, and they took their place in front of the vicar while he signalled the congregation to take their seats.

The ceremony was as it should be with no objections, surprises, or delays, and before she knew it, Mrs. Caroline Phillips was in the vestry with her new husband and their attendants who would be their witnesses as she signed the name Bingley one last time. It was done, and legal, and she was irrevocably his. They would never have to leave each other again. Mrs. Hurst, Mr. Wetherspoon, and the rector left and gave them a few minutes of privacy which they employed to bestow very passionate they did not have to suppress now that they could claim one another.

They exited into the waiting, congratulatory arms of their family, led by Franny and her parents. Both Bennet brothers and their wives welcomed Caroline into the family. She, the daughter of a tradesman, was now related to dukes, duchesses, and other peers, and they were now distantly related, through marriage to the Darcys and de Bourghs.

It was a short walk across the road to the celebration being hosted by the Gardiners. Maddie Gardiner had the doors opened so that the formal dining room and two large drawing rooms made an area with ample space for the celebratory meal. Graham was very happy that he had taken the advice to eat before he had made the walk to the church. He asked his new wife if she was hungry and she informed him that she had followed the same recommendation of taking some nourishment prior to the wedding ceremony.

For a little more than two hours the newlyweds circulated among their friends and family. When it was time, Caroline was accompanied upstairs by her two sisters and her friend who was now her cousin.

"I never believed that I deserved to be so happy, oh why cannot everyone be as happy as I am today?" Caroline gushed.

"You deserve every bit of happiness, sister," Louisa admonished her. "Do not ever think you are less deserving than any other. I am so proud of you, Caro, and I know that Graham will always treat you as you should be." She then turned to her sister-in-law. "Thank you for sharing your brother with us, Franny."

"It is only fair," Miss Phillips replied as she looked at that faraway place only those in love can see, "as I hope that very soon you will be sharing your brother with our family."

"Very true," Elizabeth said as she held her cousin Franny's hand. "Quite often one marriage begets another."

"Are you referring to Franny and Charles?" the new Mrs. Phillips asked. "Or mayhap are you thinking of yourself?"

"*Caroline!*" Elizabeth gave her a playful smack on the shoulder while blushing scarlet. "I was *only* referring to my cousin and your brother."

"Methinks the lady doth protest too much," the bride said playfully. She saw that Lady Elizabeth was about to unleash a response, so she pre-empted her. "Peace, Lizzy. You who love to tease should have recognised the endeavour."

"You are correct, Caroline. I know not why I am so sensitive when teased about William." She admitted.

"Do you not, Lizzy?" Franny asked as she escaped the slap aimed at her hand.

"What are the plans for today, Caro?" Louisa asked, and Elizabeth appreciated her changing the subject. "I still cannot comprehend his Grace's generosity in gifting the house to Graham and you."

"His Grace is your cousin Bennet now, Louisa, and it was his, the whole family's pleasure," Lizzy assured her.

"We will go to Phillips House and overnight there, then leave for the cottage on the morrow early in the morning," Mrs. Caroline Phillips informed them.

"If you are not too tired to rise early sister," Franny interjected impertinently.

"*FRANNY!*" Caroline blushed as scarlet as Elizabeth had before. "Let us join my husband before he thinks that you three reprobates have kidnapped me."

The ladies descended and returned the bride to her very relieved groom who could not imagine what was taking his beloved wife so long. As she hugged her mother-in-law, Caroline was reminded of how much warmth, love, and acceptance she had received from Graham's parents, who she was now honoured to call mother and father. The newlyweds waved to the crowd of family that saw them off in front of the house as the open carriage bore them to Portman Square and the newly renamed Phillips House.

<center>~~~~~~~/~~~~~~~</center>

The day after the wedding was momentous for Lady Elizabeth Bennet. It was the first Tuesday she would walk in Hyde Park with only Biggs and Johns to escort her. It also happened to be the day that George Wickham initiated the gathering of intelligence using his vastly enlarged group of young scalawags. Close to sunrise, Elizabeth entered the park with her two guards trailing her. They kept at a distance where she was in view all the time and they could reach her if needed in seconds, but far back enough so that their charge had a feeling of independence.

At the wedding breakfast, upon hearing that Lady Elizabeth planned an early morning ramble in Hyde Park, Darcy had requested the honour of accompanying her. She had politely refused his company which had disheartened him until she elucidated her reasons for wanting a solitary stroll. Elizabeth had explained that she missed her rambles that she used to take with just one footman as her escort before the Wickham incident. He understood that it was not just his company that she did not want, she wanted no one else's either. He would have loved to spend as much time in her company as possible, but he understood her reasons for desiring some solitude.

When Lady Anne Darcy saw the change in the way that Lady Elizabeth looked at her son, she was as sure as she could be, that it was no longer a question of if, but when she admitted the truth of her feelings to herself. She could not help but notice when William asked Elizabeth if he could join her on her walk, that it was a look of regret that she demurred and explained her seasoning to him. On Friday they would all depart to Rosings to attend Anne's wedding to Mr. Ashby. Lady Anne intended to suggest to William that he offer to show Lizzy the natural areas of the park as she knew how much that lady enjoyed nature. She was sure that Elizabeth would be enamoured with the glade and its pond.

The urchins that followed the lady and her huge footmen had been instructed to stay a good distance away and to make sure that they changed who was doing the following often. Luckily for them it was a common sight to see children begging in Hyde Park, so they did not look out of place.

Lady Elizabeth felt very good about her perceived independence. She knew that it was not complete, but it was a lot more freedom than she had enjoyed on a ramble for a while. She took a two-mile circuit of the park where she was always visible to the trailing guards, except very briefly just before they exited the park back onto Grosvenor Square where the path crossed a bridge over a stream. She was visible on the incline, but then for less than a minute as she descended, and the two men reached the top of the incline to cross the bridge, she was out of sight. It did not perturb Biggs overly much as the instant that they started the incline of the bridge the top of the miss's head was visible and not many seconds later, all of her was seen.

On entering the breakfast parlour to break her fast, Lady Elizabeth thanked her father profusely as she had enjoyed her semi-private walk very much. She decided that she would walk on Tuesday and Thursday mornings, if the family schedule allowed it.

~~~~~~~/~~~~~~~

Two days after his sister's wedding, Mr. Charles Bingley was shown into the family sitting room at Bennet House where he promptly asked to speak to Mr. Phillips. At a nod from the Duke, Mr. Phillips and Bingley retired to the Dukes study. Without preamble, Bingley requested permission to request a courtship from Franny's father. Phillips wouldn't admit it to Bingley, but he was impressed that the young man had not been at his door begging him to relax his restrictions weeks ago. He was well pleased as it showed that Bingley was an honourable man. After his wife shared with him that Franny loved this man, he wanted to be sure her love was returned and now he had no doubts.

Bingley was given leave to declare himself after Phillips extracted a promise that his daughter's suitor would wait at least a month before proposing. With that single restriction, Bingley was told to wait where he was, and Phillips returned with his blushing daughter in tow.

"You have ten minutes, and the door will remain open a crack," Mr. Phillips stated, then left them with the door open just enough to satisfy the rules of propriety.

"Franny, will you..." Charles started to make his request, but she cut him off before he could complete his sentence.

"Yes, Charles. The answer is yes, no matter the question," she promised.

"...grant me a courtship?" he completed his question.

When he saw his disappointment reflected in her eyes, he explained that her father had received his word of honour to court her for a month complete before any proposal of marriage was made. A month Franny could live with. When Mr. Phillips returned, he bestowed his consent and the courting couple joined him and announced their courtship which was a surprise to no one.

~~~~~~~/~~~~~~~

At long last Wickham had finally received good news! In the intelligence provided by one of the boys that he believed was the break he had been waiting for. The virago took a walk in Hyde Park with only two guards not following too closely behind her. He had learned from a scullery maid working at Darcy House that the family would decamp by the end of the week for Kent for the sickly one's wedding. Wickham supposed that her fortune must be grand to tempt one into marriage with such as Anne de Bourgh. Frustratingly, the Bennets would be travelling to Rosings Park as well.

He had waited this long, another fortnight would not kill him, unless the chance passed the end of April. He was sure that this second deadline the *Spaniard* had given him was one with no flexibility. It was time to contact *Scarface*. Wickham had hoped that once Withers was with him that the two toughs would leave. He was only partially right. One would leave but the other stayed to keep watch at night while Withers slept to make sure that Wickham did not disappear again as he had in the past.

"What'yer want, Wickham?" Withers scowled as he had been pulled out a game of cards in which he was up.

"It is time for you to join us here, or should I tell your boss that you refused to do the duty that he ordered you to?" Wickham knew that although he did not fear many, *Scarface* feared the *Spaniard*.

"A'right, but if yer waistin' me time, yer be none to 'appy," Withers vowed with a malevolent voice.

Wickham shared the intelligence and the intimidating man agreed that it sounded like the best opportunity to kidnap the lady. He returned a few hours later with some of his clothing and 'tools of the trade', and he then sent one of the two men home. The two would rotate every few days, so Wickham had not seen the back of either man just yet.

~~~~~~~/~~~~~~~

Lady Elizabeth took her ramble on Thursday morning and followed the same path. If Biggs had thought about it more, he would have insisted that they vary their walk each time, both the timing of and the path they took. He had not noticed the boy he had tried to catch sniffing around for over a month now, nor had he seen anyone show marked attention to Bennet House or its inhabitants. Friday she, her brothers, as James was home for a break so he could attend Anne's wedding, Darcy, and the four girls took a ride along Rotten Row earlier than the fashionable hour, but then none of them cared about that.

Shortly after midday, a convoy of carriages with many outriders and footmen guards departed for Rosings Park.

Wearing a heavy disguise, George Wickham, accompanied by Withers, had one of the boys show them the path that the lady had taken on both occasions. For the circuit through the park, they saw no place that they could ambush the mountain sized footmen until almost at the very end. There was a good border of shrubbery either side of the path before the bridge. The men had the boy go and stand the same distance away from where the lady was, from her two trailing footmen, and told the lad to walk. They followed, keeping the same spacing between them. Once the ragamuffin crested the bridge, he *disappeared from sight!* It was only when they walked up the incline that they could see him once again.

After experimenting several times, they returned to Edward Street. "What do you think, Withers?" Wickham knew better than to call him *Scarface* to his face, the man had killed for less.

"I thinks it cood work. If we time tings just so, 'es, it will work!" Withers opined.

Now all they could do was to wait for the Bennets to return and see if she kept to a schedule or if she walked on random days. The thing most in their favour was that, so far, she had followed the same path for her walk. Silence would be essential. They would also have to cosh the footmen, and while one restrained them the other would have to take the woman. If they fired a shot, they would have seconds before they would be overwhelmed by footmen and residents from Grosvenor Square.

The more that they went over the plan, the more convinced Wickham was that it would work. It had to! That night he almost enjoyed being with Karen Younge in bed.

CHAPTER 21

Rosings Park had not hosted so many for a long, long time. Besides Lady Catherine and Anne's family which had grown considerably larger when Andrew and Richard had married their wives, the Ashby's and their family were also guests at the estate, though some guests were being hosted at the estate of Lord and Lady Metcalfe. Her ladyship and Lady Catherine had been friends from the time that they shared their first season. Rosings Park manor house, with some help from both of her sisters, and her daughter's input, was decorated with understated elegance. All of the gaudy and ostentatious baubles that had made the house cold and uninviting were gone. Ironically, what items sold for Miss de Bourgh by Gardiner and Associates had earned back an amount that was close to the original cost of the items, even after the commission was paid.

Lady Catherine could not have been happier. She was no longer the 'crazy aunt' that the family would tolerate for duty. The family enjoyed their visits to Kent, and the visits at Easter had become a time that the whole family looked forward to and stayed for a month complete.

The Marquess of Birchington was elated that Lady Amy Ashby was at Rosings. It was not that he was unaware that she would be at her brother's wedding, but it was the feeling that suffused his body every time he saw her. There was no doubt that Lord Tom Bennet had fallen in love with the intelligent and very comely Lady Amelia Ashby. They had seen each other a few times in town, he called on Ashbury House regularly, and the families had attended a good number of events in common. Like he had at Anne's engagement ball, Tom would dance the three sets with the lady, sending a very clear message to the Ton and to the lady herself that he wanted her as his own, the same as he did at any ball that they both attended.

After requesting a private audience with Lady Amy from her father, he received permission for said interview on condition that he request no more than a courtship. Anne de Bourgh told her cousin that he may use a parlour next to the drawing room. The Earl of Ashbury escorted his daughter to the parlour, allowing a reasonable time limit and admonishing them that the door would be left ajar.

"Amy Ashby, I have lost my heart to you," the Marquess began. "Never has any lady engendered tender feelings, never mind the depth of the love that I feel for you." Lord Tom paused when he noticed that there were big tears rolling down the lady's cheeks as he thought he had upset her until she smiled at him and indicating that he should continue. "While you are the most beautiful woman that I know, that alone is not what attracted me. I was drawn in by your humour, wit, and intelligence. You are companionate, and I have noticed that you treat all, no matter the station, with respect, and you are the keeper of my heart. When I view my future there is no version that I see where you are not standing alongside of me. Would you grant me the honour of allowing me to court you, Amy?" He held his breath as he waited for her answer.

"Thomas, Tom, you hold my heart as much as you say that I keep yours." Lord Tom let out the breath he had not realised he was holding after hearing the sweetest words imaginable. "I too love you, Tom. Not because you are a marquess, or for your wealth or connections. You are a good and honourable man with whom I know I can be myself. When I am with you, I never feel like I have to act less than I am so that you are not intimidated. You meet all of what I want and need in a husband. If you had been the King, I would have refused you had you not been able to accept me as I am. "Yes Tom, I want to be courted by you, and I pray that it will not be a long courtship. In fact, if I were to be honest, there is nothing a courtship will achieve that I do not already know," Lady Amy offered boldly.

"There was a condition imposed by your father, my love, and without his revoking that condition, even if you are of age, my honour will not allow me to gainsay your father," Tom said sadly. Lady Amy strode to the door with purpose and asked the footman stationed in the hall to request that her parents and the Duke and Duchess of Hertfordshire join them. The lady well knew what she was doing by asking for both of their parents. Having Tom's parents present would guarantee that her father would not be able to raise any spurious reasons against a betrothal.

Their parents entered the parlour and looked at one another questioningly and then to the couple. "I requested that you join us to help us solve a dilemma we are facing," Amy started cryptically.

Lord Ashbury had a sneaking suspicion what the 'dilemma' was, but played along. "How can we assist you Amy, Lord Birchington?" he asked, dreading her reply. He was about to lose his little girl and her mother would overrule any nonsensical objection he would try to raise. He was not ready to let her go yet, but then he checked himself as he heard how selfish his words sounded in his head.

"Well Papa, it is strange you should ask …" Amy was cut off by her beloved father.

"Let me save some time. The Marquess kept his word and only requested a courtship, and when you heard about my restriction…" Now it was his turn to be interrupted by his wife.

"Maxwell! What did you do?" Lady Gillian Ashby, Countess of Ashbury asked with no little asperity.

"As I was about to say when you interjected, Gillian my love," he looked apologetically at his wife and daughter as Lord Thomas and Lady Sarah looked on in amusement at the scene playing out in front of them. "I realise my restriction was of purely selfish reasoning trying to hold onto my girl for a while longer. There is no restriction; it shall be as you two decide."

Lord Birchington leaned toward the lady he loved and whispered, "Take everything I said earlier except substitute 'courtship' for 'marry me'."

"Yes, absolutely yes, Tom!" she announced before he could add anything more.

"As I witness my Amy's enthusiasm in answering your question, you have my consent and blessing. Welcome to the family, Tom. Never hurt her," the Earl warned as he shook his daughter's betrothed's hand.

Crying tears of joy for the happiness and love that she saw flowing between the newly engaged couple, Lady Gillian said, "And you have my blessing, my dear daughter and future son."

Lady Sarah hugged Amy. "Even though I have many daughters already," she teased, "I am very happy to welcome one more, especially one who I know will make my Tom so very happy."

The Duke hugged his son, and with a voice full of emotion he congratulated him and welcomed Amy to the family. A notable and powerful family had just become even more so. While power, wealth, and connections were never a motivating factor for any of them, all would be increased on both sides of the family. Lady Amy requested that they would not make an announcement until they returned to Town after the wedding at Rosings Park as she and Tom did not want to take focus away from the bride and groom.

The family was in anticipation of the arrival for both newly wedded Fitzwilliams on the morrow. Lord and Lady Matlock had not heard from their sons since they departed the wedding breakfast back in mid-January as they had been in town when the family had sojourned at Snowhaven. Men do not tend to write to their parents during their wedding trips. Both Jane and Marie had written letters to their new mother-in-law once they arrived at their respective estates and had written at least once more before the couples met at Snowhaven to begin the journey southward to Rosings Park. The plan was for both couples to return to Town with the family after the wedding and spend the rest of the season in London.

The Duchesses of Bedford and Hertfordshire were no less excited to see the new Fitzwilliam wives. Aside from the letters on their wedding trips, Lady Sarah had received two more from each from their estates, but she could not wait to hug them again. The two months since their wedding had been the longest that Sarah Bennet had ever been separated from any of her daughters, and Lady Rose Bennet missed them as much as Lady Sarah as they were her daughters of the heart, and she was no less looking forward to seeing the sons-in-law who had long been loved like sons by blood.

In London both couples would preside at Hilldale House on Portman Square. Richard and Lady Jane Fitzwilliam had not decided whether they would invest in a town home for themselves. The Bennet family alone owned eight homes in London between both Dukedoms, even after the one they gifted to Graham and Caroline Phillips. If they really felt the need for more privacy, they had only to ask and one of the homes not in use would have been put at their disposal expeditiously. The couples had arrived in Town the previous day and would leave for Kent early the next morning, so they were expected between noon and one in the afternoon on the morrow.

Darcy, Lady Elizabeth, Lord James, Miss Darcy, and Ladies Mary and Kitty took a walking tour of the park. Darcy, as the expert among them, first took them up to the little folly, a small replica of a Greek temple, which provided a panoramic view of the estate as the structure had been built on the crest of a hill. In front of them they could see the very well-ordered formal gardens with the manor house behind it. To one side was the wild woodland area that they would soon be exploring, and the Hunsford church's steeple could be seen above the trees at the end of a natural avenue that led to the parsonage.

After some time at the folly, they entered the wooded grove and Darcy guided them to the glade. The path that led to it would have been missed if one did not know it was there. They wound their way through vegetation and verdant trees until they arrived at the glade. It was a nice-sized clearing with a pool they were told was fed from an underground spring. At one end of the pond was a brook that carried the excess water until it joined a stream a few hundred yards away. There were benches and some nice-sized rocks to sit on to take in the beauty of nature on display.

Darcy told them how, as young boys, he, Richard, and Andrew would play in the glade for hours pretending to be searching for buried pirate treasure, and that in the heat of the summer they used to enjoy swimming in the pool. It was always cool, thanks to the water that bubbled up from the spring at the bottom.

Lady Elizabeth watched William as he was so at ease, fielded their questions, and answered one and all with patience and good humour, no matter how inane. This was definitely a man that she had started to admit that she was forming tender feelings for. The thought struck her as surprising. It was the first time that she admitted to herself that her feelings were deeper than friend or cousin and it excited her.

They walked toward the church before they made a turn back toward Rosings Park. As they were passing the parsonage, they could not help but see the man who was bowing and scraping to them as they passed. Before Mr. Collins was able to embarrass himself, his wife Miranda, a Benet as was, joined him near his beehives, and with a simple pressure on his arm was able to still him. Elizabeth knew the face, she looked so very much like her older sister Harriet.

"I know we have not been introduced, but if you are Miranda Benet then I feel like I know you from talking to your sister, Harriet Forster," Elizabeth stated with a questioning look.

"I was indeed Miranda Benet, though I am Mrs. Collins now that I am married," she said with a curtsy. "From letters that Harriet wrote, am I correct that you are Lady Elizabeth Bennet?"

"Yes, Mrs. Collins. I am afraid that I am guilty as charged. Will you introduce your husband to us, please?" Elizabeth asked. The lady obliged and then as she had been introduced, albeit by herself, Lady Elizabeth introduced the rest of her party. It seemed that the clergyman was about to start fawning over the highborn people, one of them a marquess, that he had been introduced to when his wife touched his arm again and his mouth closed with a clack and he remained quiet.

Miranda Collins invited them to tea, but they had to decline as they were expected back at Rosings for tea. They bid their goodbyes to the Collinses and turned back toward the manor house. During the walk back, they discussed how fortunate Mr. Collins was in his choice of wife for without her gentle guidance, they could imagine him being very servile and sycophantic on one hand while pompous on the other. When they were having tea at Rosings, they mentioned the encounter with the residents of the parsonage and Elizabeth shared their suspicions about Mr. Collins. Lady Catherine explained how he used to be before having the good fortune to be accepted by a strong and intelligent woman.

~~~~~~~/~~~~~~~

Anne de Bourgh was glowing with happiness on the day that she was joined forever to Mr. Ian Ashby. Not only had she married the love of her life, but her mother had blessed the union without any reservation. The previous night her mother and Aunt Anne had given her 'the talk', and thankfully had removed any lingering apprehension that the bride may have had.

Mr. Collins had done a credible job, and thanks to his wife effusions and fawning were almost non-existent during the ceremony. Anne signed her maiden name for the final time and the new Mr. and Mrs. Ian Ashby emerged from the vestry to warm congratulatory hugs and wishes from the family, both hers and his. The party mounted their carriages and preceded the newlyweds to Rosings for the wedding breakfast. Mrs. Anne Ashby felt warm all over as Lipton, the butler, announced the Honourable Mr. and Mrs. Ian Ashby to their assembled friends and family.

Darcy looked wistfully at Lady Elizabeth. Although he did not begrudge her brother Tom his happiness in being accepted by Lady Amy Ashby, he was envious. Not of them, but rather of the fact that he had not yet attained the bliss that they so obviously had gained. The engagement had not yet been announced; however, Elizabeth had shared the glad tidings with him. He could not but see her willingness to confide in him as a good sign. When his mother had approached him with the suggestion that Anne and her betrothed may enjoy Seaview Cottage, he had offered its use without delay and the couple had immediately accepted his offer.

At the wedding breakfast Lady Sarah Bennet was sitting with Ladies Elaine, Catherine, and Anne. "Your Anne is glowing with happiness, Catherine," the Duchess observed.

"A blind man would be able to see that, it is so obvious. I could not be happier for my Anne. There is no doubt in my mind that Ian will always make her happiness his priority." As she spoke a single tear slid down her cheek and her sister squeezed her hand and handed her a silk. "It is as they were formed for each other," she added.

"You are correct, Catherine. My namesake will have a very felicitous marriage," Lady Anne agreed.

"It is a good thing that my niece has followed the family tradition and made a love match," Lady Matlock said as she watched her niece talking to Lord and Lady Metcalf. "Are you packed and ready to depart to town with us this afternoon sister?"

"Yes, Elaine," Lady Catherine smiled sadly, "everything is packed. Did I inform you that I have retained Mrs. Jenkinson as my companion?"

"No, you had not mentioned that, Catherine," Lady Anne's smile brightened, impressed that her sister had made sure that Anne's former companion did not have to shift for herself. "That was an excellent idea."

"The lady served my Anne faithfully for many years, so I offered her a choice. She could take the retirement that Anne and Ian offered her, or she could be in my service and act as my companion."

"She is still relatively young, so I suppose that she did not feel ready to retire. Although she is paid as a companion, she too receives companionship with one she has known for many years," Lady Sarah stated then looked at her friends with an arched eyebrow just like her middle daughter was wont to arch when she was teasing. "I am bursting to tell you a secret, so long as you swear that you will keep my confidence until the official announcement."

"Do you mean to tell us the Lord Birchington has an understanding with Lady Amy, Anne's new sister?" Lady Catherine asked the very surprised Duchess.

"How..." Sarah Bennet did not complete her question.

"Just as anyone can see the happiness between my niece and her husband, it can be seen between your son and Amy," Lady Anne teased Lady Sarah.

"We understand and respect that no announcement was made before Anne's wedding," Lady Catherine added, "It speaks well for your son and new daughter that they did not want to draw attention from the bride and groom."

It was not long after that Anne Ashby retired to change into her travelling attire and once, she returned, she and her husband made a circuit in order to take their leave of their guests. The family members accompanied them outside to wish them a good wedding trip, and after a last hug and kiss from her mother Anne and her husband entered their carriage and were off on the five-hour journey to the cottage.

~~~~~~~/~~~~~~~

George Wickham was as sure as he could be that Lady Elizabeth Bennet took her rambles in Hyde Park on Tuesday and Thursday mornings and was followed by only the two footmen. He had been informed of the Bennets return to Town on Monday the three and twentieth day of March, and the next day, Tuesday, the harlot had taken her walk along the same circuit she had previously taken, the footmen the same distance back from her as she walked. He had instructed some of his spies to hide near the bridge and they had reported the same thing; that once the lady was descending the bridge, and before the footmen gained it, she was out of sight for but a moment.

On Wednesday she had ridden in the park with some of her family, the mouse, and the prig. He cared not a whit about the mouse's thirty thousand when he was about to demand one hundred thousand for the harridan. After she repeated her walk with no variations on Thursday, Wickham and Withers sat together and planned while Mrs. Younge made sure that they were not disturbed.

It would just be the two of them to cosh the footmen and take the girl with Mrs. Younge's support, as too many would draw attention. They could not make noise when they took the footmen down or the girl may bolt, and the spot was quite close to the exit from the park. Wickham and Withers would have to make a stealthy approach then hit the escorts with enough force to knock them out or kill them; they did not care which. Wickham would close in on their quarry while Withers secured the two guards. Karen Younge would wait in a hired carriage with ropes and a gag to secure the woman as they spirited her away.

"This will be our only chance," Wickham stated the obvious, leaving out that thanks to the *Spaniard's* deadline it was the *only* chance! "I have a plan."

"What this ere plan, Wickham?" *Scarface* demanded.

"We know that our window is when she crosses the bridge." His co-conspirator nodded. "The bushes on either side of the path are high and thick enough to hide us. We will wait for the oversized footmen to pass us, and as they walk onto the bridge, while they cannot see her or she them, we will sneak up behind them and cosh them."

"One of us will tie them up and the other will go get the girl.

We will have Karen waiting in the hack just outside the park; when we have the girl, we will gag her and take her to Álvarez's brothel to hold her until we receive the ransom." The two men repeated their plans so they would be sure of their roles when they made their attempt.

"Sounds like it could work, Wickham. Do not forget what 'ill 'appen to you if you try a double-cross," Withers finished with a warning.

"You will dispose of Mrs. Younge once we get to the brothel for a thousand from my share as we agreed?" Wickham asked quietly.

"Yeah, alls that needs takin' care o' will be done," Withers agreed, George had not guessed that Scarface could speak words with double meanings so it raised no alarms.

The last Tuesday of March, the lady took her now familiar walk. The plotting men decided that they would make sure that she again walked the first Thursday in April and if she did, they would put their plan into action on the following Tuesday, the seventh of April. As it happened, she did not walk on Thursday so the execution date for the plan was pushed until Thursday the ninth, so long as the lady took her walk the Tuesday prior.

As it so happened, the Thursday that Elizabeth Bennet missed her walk was the day that she joined Lady Anne to call on Caroline Phillips at her Portnoy Square home. The two had returned from their wedding trip the same day that the de Bourgh-Ashby wedding had been celebrated. The family had allowed the new Mrs. Phillips some time to settle into her new home after her return from the wedding trip before descending on her to visit.

Caroline exuded happiness as she welcomed both her friend and mentor, now her family in fact, into her home. She pointed out the additions she had made to the home to give it a woman's touch, and everything was tastefully done, nothing ostentatious or gaudy. Her husband was at work at Norman and James, now a fully licensed barrister. The ladies enjoyed their morning together and Lizzy informed her friend that her brother Tom was betrothed to Lady Amy Ashby. Caroline requested that Lady Anne again thank her son for the use of Seaview Cottage and, like others before her, stated that it was anything but a cottage. When she discussed the beach in the secluded inlet, she blushed profusely. Lady Anne knew what had caused the blush while Caroline's cousin, being a maiden, did not nor would she be expected to be.

On Tuesday, the seventh day of April, Lady Elizabeth Bennet took her ramble in Hyde Park just as she had on previous occasions. Once Wickham was apprised of the news, the plan was set for Thursday, two days hence. George Wickham was happier than he had been in a long time. He would soon repay the harridan for the pain from his flogging even as it was naught but a sometime dull ache that he hardly noticed. The scars would be a reminder of her calling out his deeds for the rest of his life, but he would get his revenge on Thursday or die trying, the last of that bravado he would never stand behind as he was a coward. Everything fit perfectly in his 'fool proof' plan. He ignored the fact that he had considered every ill-advised scheme of his to be a plan without fault. There was no room in his mind for self-doubt, especially on this day.

He went over his mental checklist, thinking about what he would do to the lady. He salivated as he thought about the success that he was certain was about to be his on that day. He had not told the others, but once they received the one hundred thousand pounds for her return, he would ruin her and break her before he made the drop off. The question was, would she be dead or alive when he returned her. She would never laugh at him, or for that matter never laugh again when he was through avenging himself on her.

Scarface sent a note to the *Spaniard* to let him know the day they had chosen to execute the plan, and that everything was in place to remove any impediments to their receiving the full ransom amount.

CHAPTER 22

Lady Elizabeth Bennet departed Bennet House for Hyde Park a little after sunrise that morning. She loved the feeling of freedom that she had when taking her ramble in the huge park. Biggs and Johns did a good job of giving her the impression that she was alone while always keeping a watchful eye on her person. As she left the house, she saw a young boy begging, so she removed a half crown from her reticule and placed it in his cap. The boy felt a twinge of guilt as he was spying on a lady who was so generous. He doffed his cap, giving the signal that the lady was on her way as he had been told to do. Harry saw the signal and ran to inform Wickham that the lady had commenced her constitutional.

As Elizabeth ambled along, she was thinking about a man, a specific man who was a cousin and had become so much more to her. She was finally ready to admit to herself that which so many in the family already knew...that she had tender feelings for Fitzwilliam Darcy. She was almost sorry that she had refused his entreaties to join her early morning walks. She acknowledged to herself that she enjoyed his company greatly, and that if she were honest, she had recognised that they were well matched. His being an honest and honourable man was not in question, and she already loved his family. Lady Anne had quickly become one of her favourite aunts, while she had for some time, looked on Georgiana Darcy as a younger sister.

There was little doubt in her mind that Darcy was interested in her far beyond being cousins. At Anne's engagement ball when she had signalled her agreement to the final set, Elizabeth had not missed the way the normally stoic man had displayed his joy. The dance had been a waltz, and Elizabeth felt naught but pleasure as he held her so intimately.

'*After what happened in Meryton, if you had told me that he would be the man I would start looking at as the one that I could walk through life with, I would have vehemently disagreed with you! So much has changed. I feel that William is a man who would do anything to protect me, as he would do for anyone that he loves,"* Lady Elizabeth Bennet stopped dead in her tracks. "*He loves me! Not as a cousin, but romantically. Do I love him? I am well on my way if not already there."* It would not be too much longer before her thoughts about Darcy's protective instincts would be proven correct.

~~~~~~~/~~~~~~~

After receiving the signal from Harry, Wickham and Withers hid themselves behind the tall bushes either side of the path just before it met the incline of the bridge as had been planned. Wickham was now sure that nothing could go wrong. Everything had been planned to perfection, they knew what to expect, and nothing would stop him receiving his due and taking his revenge on the virago.

One unplanned variable that would affect Wickham's 'perfect' plan was Darcy. In his town house, Darcy was readying himself. Like the boys who had been spying on the woman that he loved, he too was aware of her habit of walking during the early morning hours in the park two days a week. He had requested to join her on a few occasions, but she had demurred. He did not, however, miss that on their ride the day before she had seriously contemplated acquiescing before choosing her solitude for the morning walk. On this cool Thursday morning in April, Darcy had decided that he would meet her by 'chance' as she was returning from her excursion. He knew the approximate time he would see her approach the steps of Bennet House, so he was to start his 'unplanned' walk a quarter hour or so before he normally saw her exit the park.

She so far seemed to welcome his companionship during the times they had been in company together. Ever since the former Miss Caroline Bingley's engagement ball at Netherfield, she had seemed much more than just friendly. He remembered with pleasure that was the first time that he had danced with Lady Elizabeth, but certainly not the last. At the Netherfield Ball she had granted him two sets; he had danced with her a number of times since. At some balls, a single set, and others two sets, never once had she demurred when he requested a set. At the engagement ball for his cousin Anne and Mr. Ashby she had accepted his application to dance three sets with him. The memories made him feel very happy as he dreamed about holding her in the waltz soon again. Something had changed after the visit to Haven House, he was not sure what yet, and he did not want to presume too much, but something had definitely changed between them. They were now on much more than friendly terms, and as his mother had predicted to the lady, he had revelled in debates with her on histories and philosophies that they had read. Yes, they had debated both Plato and Socrates! As he had Carstens prepare him for his 'spontaneous' walk, his spirits felt a lot lighter than they had for since his father had passed, and he became prey to be hunted by the huntresses of the Ton.

~~~~~~~/~~~~~~~

Another thing that Wickham could not have known, and therefore could not have accounted for, was that Ladies Marie and Jane Fitzwilliam had planned to ride in Hyde Park with their husbands on that morning. They were staying at Hilldale House on Portman Square which meant that they would enter the park via a different entrance than the one where his 'paramour' watched and waited. Their plan was to ride along the Serpentine then head to Bennet House to join the Duke, Duchess, and the family to break their fasts.

An hour after the sunrise, the four were accompanied by a groom and two footmen as they entered the park for their ride. They were aware that it was a day that their sister would be taking one of her rambles and Lady Jane opined that they may meet up with Lizzy before they exited the park onto Grosvenor Square.

~~~~~~~/~~~~~~~

Lady Elizabeth Bennet was approaching the bridge toward the end of her walk. She felt invigorated, as she always did, when she had good exercise. She had taken much pleasure in reviewing her interactions with William, and she had owned that she did in fact have very tender feelings for her cousin. If she were completely honest with herself, she would say that she loved him. The revelation had made her feel warm and jittery inside. Biggs and Johns were where they always were, following at a distance so she could enjoy the little bit of solitude that it afforded her, but close enough in the case that they were needed. She could not repine that she only had the two with her. She was comforted to think that they were both armed as each man secreted two pistols on his person and both were excellent shots.

She did not see the two men hiding behind the bushes on either side of the path as she ascended the bridge. Both men tensed as the huge footmen drew level with them. They each held a cosh, shortened so they had been able to hide it on their persons, with a heavy rounded head. As the guards passed them and were about to follow their charge over the bridge, at the very spot as she was out of their sight for a very short time, the two criminals made a stealthy approach, at least what they thought was stealthy. Biggs and Johns sensed them and alerted by the crunch of the gravel behind them they moved slightly just before the cowardly men delivered their blows. Both footmen fell.

"*Go, Wickham,*" Withers said with a hiss, "get that there lady and get er' into the 'ired carriage. I be right behind you afte' I ties these two mountains up."

Wickham nodded and ran up and over the bridge while Withers, aka *Scarface*, approached Biggs first. *Scarface* was not aware that due to the slight movement of their heads just before they were struck, both men had received only glancing blows. They had been stunned, not incapacitated, and had rapidly recovered. Biggs had signalled Johns to keep still as each had retrieved one of his pistols.

Feeling very confident, *Scarface* bent down to start to secure Biggs with rope, and as he did the big man turned and jumped up with cat like reflexes. Rather than tying the man up as planned, he was staring down the barrel of a loaded and cocked pistol. It went from bad to worse when he felt the barrel of another pistol in his back. Biggs saw Johns had the situation in hand, so he made to sprint toward his charge.

At the same time, the supremely confident George Wickham very nonchalantly spoke behind the lady he hated, "Last time I was near you, you laughed at me. Let us see who will laugh today, *Lady* Elizabeth." He spat the "lady" appellation out as if it were a swear word.

When the lady turned, rather than Biggs and Johns, she saw George Wickham waiving an un-cocked pistol in her direction. As her courage always rose at any attempt to intimidate her, she decided that she must delay him as long as she could. "Do I know you? You do not look like the class of individual that I would associate with." Elizabeth spoke with disdain as she locked eyes with the overly confident man.

Wickham was taken aback; she should be afraid, not mocking him! Was she not afraid of him? Did she not know what he was going to do to her? "You caused me to be kicked out of the Derbyshire Militia, lose my money, and receive thirty lashes. And if that was not enough, you *laughed* at me!" Without realising it, he had just exposed to Lady Elizabeth his overly fragile ego.

Darcy entered the park in anticipation of seeing the lady he had fallen in love with. Mrs. Younge was looking away as he entered so did not see the man. Darcy thought that if God was beneficent, mayhap she would condescend to allow him to escort her home that day. He was snapped out of his reverie when she saw a sight that made his blood run cold. The blackguard and profligate seducer, George Wickham was holding a pistol on his Elizabeth. No one threatened one he loved no matter what! He sprinted toward the lady, who was more than a hundred yards ahead and just his side of the little bridge.

Wickham was incensed as he saw Darcy sprinting toward his quarry. "If you come any closer, Darcy, I will shoot you and then I will take this whore anyway!"

Darcy stopped just to the side of Lady Elizabeth and tried reason, "You are not a killer, George. Put down the pistol and we can talk."

"Not a killer? It was no *accident* that ended your father's life! He was going to cut me out of his will, so I made sure that he had a little 'accident'. *No* one cheats me out of my due and lives to tell!" Wickham yelled at him.

Darcy was incensed as the profligate wastrel boasted so callously about murdering his honoured father but knew he had to regulate himself, his beloved's life depended on it. Elizabeth, who knew that the blackguard's ego was fragile, taunted him further. "Come now, you are too stupid to plan something like that!" Then she did the thing that made him lose all reason, she threw her beautiful head back and laughed at him.

He was no longer looking at Darcy, nor did he hear the man that would soon reach him from behind. "You dare laugh at me again, you slut. Forget the ransom, **I will end you now**!" As he yelled the last, he cocked the pistol and aimed it at her heart.

Lady Elizabeth had displayed much courage, but she was now frozen in place as Wickham took aim at her. She had no doubt that he was about to shoot her and was saying her final prayers as she saw her life flash before her eyes. Everything happened at once! There were loud reports as two shots fired, Elizabeth was roughly pushed aside by Darcy as he dove in front of her to shield her from the bullet fired by the wastrel, and there was the thunder of horse's hooves as the Fitzwilliam brothers and one of their footmen came flying over the bridge at a full gallop. Wickham, his face an exclamation of disbelief, dropped like a stone and was dead before his worthless body hit the ground as Biggs had exercised his excellent marksman's skills as soon as he saw the man daring to threaten his Miss Lizzy.

Elizabeth, realising that she was unharmed other than some possible scrapes from falling when she was pushed out of the bullet's path, looked down and in horror saw Mr. Darcy with a red stain spreading from his left shoulder. The man that she had once hated and thought most prideful arrogant man, the same man she now loved, had just saved her life at the possible cost of his own. She knew that she must stem the flow of blood so she took out one of her silks and applied pressure to the source of the bleeding as hard as she was able to.

Richard and Andrew jumped from their mounts even before they had come to a halt. Immediately going into military mode, the former colonel took control. "Ride like the wind man; get everyone!" He ordered the footman that had ridden with them then examined his cousin as his sister kept pressure on his wound. "He lives still," he said with obvious relief.

Karen Younge realised something had gone very wrong as soon as she heard the shots. She entered the park and saw her George lying on the ground in a pool of his own blood, obviously dead. Her first instinct was to try and exact revenge on the murderers of her beloved George, but she was not that delusional. She could see that she had no hope of reaching either the prig or the Bennet whore. She backed out of the park, climbed into the waiting hired coach, and had it take her to Edward Street with all speed.

There was the sound of many running feet as footmen from Darcy, Bennet, and Matlock Houses poured into the park just missing the retreating Mrs. Younge. They were followed by the Duke, the Duchess, the Earl, and Lady Anne Darcy. The latter would have collapsed when she saw her son lying prostrate if not for the footman who kept her from falling. When the initial shock wore off, she resolved that she had to try to remain calm, which would be almost impossible as she looked at her son, her William, who was lying on the ground. She watched their Lizzy push down on his wound with no small amount of blood evident on his clothes, her hands, and the ground around him. A group of footmen carefully lifted Darcy, one of them taking over the duties of holding pressure on his wound from Lady Elizabeth.

Elizabeth, who had never fainted in her life, had almost swooned as soon as she had been relieved of her task to hold pressure on his wound. She was able to see that the bullet had struck him just below his left shoulder and prayed that it had not hit anything critical. Lady Anne followed the group carrying Darcy to his house, supported by a footman for the whole of the distance. Lady Sarah put her arm around her daughter, who was clearly in shock, and gently led her toward Bennet House with a cadre of footmen surrounding them, just in case. As soon as Biggs saw that the known perpetrators were either dead or secured, he joined the group as he did not want his charge to go anywhere that he was not with her.

Johns, who had a headache of epic proportions, roughly pulled the trussed-up Withers behind him while the Fitzwilliam's groom led the rest of the horses. The criminal was secured with the ropes he had intended to use on his victims. The footman that had followed Ladies Jane and Marie approached the bloody scene. After their husbands confirmed that Lizzy was safe, the twins headed to Bennet House to confirm with their own eyes that their sister was uninjured.

"What the devil happened here?" the Duke demanded. As he asked the question, the man who could elucidate them, Withers, was dragged by Johns toward the irate group of men. The men all turned toward the captive with murderous looks in their eyes.

"This ere was one them that be involved, your Grace," Johns reported as he pulled Withers forward roughly.

"What was this all about?" Lord Matlock demanded, but Withers did not answer.

"When I was in the army, I learnt a lot of very painful ways to extract information. Give me ten minutes, he will be singing like a Robin." Withers could not miss the malevolent look that Richard Fitzwilliam assessed him with. He had no doubt that it was not an empty threat, so he decided to try to save his own life, and that of his family.

"I will swing no matter, so why shoulds I elp you toffs?" he asked with as much bravado as he could muster.

"Because it will *be* the difference between life and death!" the Viscount told him as plainly as he could.

"If my family is transpot'd wif me, then I'lls tell what I knows." Withers held his breath. The men conferred and nodded, agreeing to meet his demand.

He told them how Wickham had presented the plan of kidnapping the lady to the *Spaniard* as a way to repay his debts. He added that Mrs. Younge had been an active and willing participant in the conspiracy. Withers also gave up just how long they had been planning and watching Lady Elizabeth. He reported the amount that was to be demanded, how much each party to the conspiracy was to receive, and how he was to let his boss know when they had the victim so he could come and take her to get the whole ransom, not just the amount he had been promised. Withers knew that his employer would dispatch Wickham and Mrs. Younge as soon as he confirmed for himself that the lady was secured in a house of ill repute, one of the *Spaniard's* 'businesses'.

The men quickly decided that they would have Withers send the missive that the *Spaniard* was expecting so that they could capture this member of the conspiracy. The Duke, with Johns dragging Withers, and his footmen returned to Bennet House. The rest of the men headed directly to Darcy House after the Earl asked one of his footmen to have the Countess escorted thither to join them. As soon as possible, they would send men to seek Mrs. Younge, although Richard opined that she would be long gone.

Before the footmen had carried the master back to Darcy House, the former colonel had told one of them to take his mount and ride with all speed to his former unit's base. He was to seek out a Mr. McGregor, a surgeon, and one who, after many battles on the continent, had vast experience with gunshot wounds like the one his cousin now suffered. The instruction was to use Colonel Fitzwilliam's name and to convey the request that the surgeon attend Darcy post haste. Another man had been dispatched on the Viscount's horse to summon the Darcy family's physician, a Mr. Tristan Bartholomew, and to come to the Darcy's home at all speed.

Lady Elizabeth Bennet, normally unflappable, sat between her Mama and brother Tom, sobbing uncontrollably. She was wracked with guilt, the man that she had been so hard on and now loved, had saved her life! But at what cost? His own? She was not sure that she could bear so high a cost for her own safety. Would God be so cruel to separate them after she finally realised that he was the only man for her?

"H-he j-j-umped in f-front of me!" she hiccupped between sobs. "After the w-way t-that I t-t-treated him, w-why would he s-save me?" As she asked the question, she knew the truth; William loved her and would do anything to protect those that he loved.

"Lizzy, look at me," Lady Sarah said gently as she wiped away the tears that were still streaming down her daughter's cheeks. As she held her Mama and brother's hands in a death grip, she looked at her mother, "We pray that he will be well, but he made a choice, and it was one that we will forever be in his debt for. We will pray to God and ask him to spare our cousin."

"As to why," the Marquess of Birchington opined, "he did it because he is as honourable a man as there ever was, and I suspect that he has tender feelings for one of my sisters and would do anything, including giving up his own life, to protect those he cares for." Lord Tom knew that he would do the same for his Amy, the woman who now owned all of his heart.

Lady Elizabeth looked at her brother as if he had sprouted two heads, At least she had ceased crying. "Do not look at me as if I belong in Bedlam Lizzy. Since you forgave him, have danced with him on numerous occasions, and he has been in our company, I think that you are the only one who has not acknowledged that he holds you in tender regard."

With a sheepish look, Elizabeth looked at her older sisters who had arrived, her other brother and the younger twins and finally at her mother, and she could not miss the looks of all that showed that they all had seen something that she had not admitted to herself until that very day.

"I can tell you this, Lizzy. He would not want you to choose him because of gratitude or a feeling of obligation, he is not that kind of man," said Lord James, who was in town for a short in term break before his graduation in a month.

"There will be time for these kinds of discussions and thoughts later. After I change, I, we, must go to Darcy House to see how he fares," Elizabeth stated with resolution; and no one was willing to stop her. "It is the least that we can do!" She was determined to be there for him, and she was resolved to do anything that she could to make sure that he survives. If he offered for her, she would accept him, but not due to gratitude. The feelings she had been ignoring and denying for far too long she had finally admitted to *before* he saved her life.

In a dank, windowless room in the basement where Withers was being held, he wrote the missive to his boss. Once the note was complete, Withers gave them the direction to the house of ill repute and the name of the boy that would be waiting for the note to take to the *Spaniard*. Withers would remain locked in the room with two of Biggs's men outside on guard, at all times, until his employer was in custody.

~~~~~~~/~~~~~~~

Lady Anne Darcy was beside herself with worry and grief. She knew that William would have done what he did even had he not been in love with Lady Elizabeth. His newfound revival of honour would not have allowed otherwise. The surgeon and the Darcy family physician were upstairs working on her son William. A tearful Georgiana was sitting with her and her sisters, Elaine, Countess of Matlock, and Lady Catherine de Bourgh. Lord Matlock and his sons were upstairs with William. She dreaded having to write the missive she may have to in order to inform her niece Anne Ashby if the worst came to pass while she was on her honeymoon at Seaview Cottage. She prayed to God with all her might that when she communicated with her niece it would be of an injury, not the alternative.

Killion knocked on her sitting room door and asked if she was home to the Bennet and Fitzwilliam ladies. She nodded and as the four ladies entered, she stood shakily. Lady Elizabeth went to the lady that she had come to think of like another aunt and stopped her from standing.

"There is no need to stand on ceremony, Aunt Anne! I felt like your niece before, but I dare say that what William did today will bond our families forever," Elizabeth said with as steady a voice as she could manage. Jane and Marie sat either side of their young cousin to comfort her while the Duchess joined her daughter on the settee where Lady Anne was sitting.

"Thank you, Elizabeth," Lady Anne wiped her eyes, "I hope that you are not trying to blame yourself." Seeing her young companion's head drop she said with a strong voice, "Lady Elizabeth Bennet, that dastard was determined to attack you, and neither did you have control over my son's decision to behave in the heroic way that he did."

"You are not the first to tell her that, Anne," the Duchess added, "but you know my Lizzy, stubborn to a fault," she teased her middle daughter to try to lighten the mood.

"Aunt Anne, Mama, my head knows what you say is true, but I still feel guilty. I pray that William recovers so at the very *least* I will be able to thank him." It was a sentiment that was felt by all the ladies.

Mr. McGregor, with Mr. Bartholomew assisting, had just completed Darcy's stitches after thoroughly irrigating the wound. Darcy had not regained consciousness, but both doctors stated that it was due to the loss of blood and the blow to his head as he fell. Both were sure that if Lady Elizabeth had not taken action to apply pressure to the wound, that he could have died from loss of blood where he had fallen. The surgeon informed the men that he believed that he had recovered all scraps of fabric that had been pushed into the wound as the bullet entered, but warned that infection of the wound was still a real and dangerous possibility. The army surgeon went on to explain to the men that although the bullet did not appear to have hit anything vital, it had been in an area rich with blood vessels, a major one included, which had been the cause of the heavy bleeding. Carstens had been given explicit instructions on how and when to change the dressing and clean the wound site. Fever was a great danger, but if there was none or he survived any fever, then Mr. McGregor believed that the chances were good that Darcy would make a recovery with no long-term effects.

The surgeon needed to return to his army unit, but Bartholomew would stay at Darcy House until it was decided that the master of the house was out of danger. The doctor remained in the master's chambers with Carstens while the three Fitzwilliam's escorted the surgeon out with many thanks on behalf of the family. Reggie Fitzwilliam led his sons into his sister's sitting room and none of the men were surprised to see the Bennet's, Anne's sisters, and their own wives comforting the two Darcy women. Georgie had her head resting on Jane's shoulder and was flanked by Elaine and Marie Fitzwilliam.

Lady Anne was still sitting with Lady Sarah and Elizabeth. As soon as the ladies saw the three men enter, there was a cacophony of voices demanding information, led by the strident tones of Lady Catherine's voice. Lord Matlock held up his hand and as the room went quiet, he sat on the settee between his sister and the Duchess. He gave them the same unvarnished news the surgeon had imparted to them. There was much relief expressed that if things went well, William Darcy would make a full recovery.

~~~~~~~/~~~~~~~

Karen Younge knew that she had to act fast. With Withers in captivity, it was only a matter of time before the Runners would be knocking on her door or possibly worse. That scary colonel, the cousin of the prig, may in fact be the one to come, and he would not care for the niceties. No, she definitely did not want to be in her boarding house when she was looked for. The hack dropped her off on the corner closest to her house and she made haste to get off the street. All of their plans had been spoiled again. Why would no one give them their due?

She had some funds she had managed to squirrel away which she had hidden over time. If she was honest with herself, she would have admitted that had her 'love' been aware of her hidden funds, they too would have been taken and lost at the tables and used on drink, leaving her with no means of escape. She would not allow herself to admit that George had never truly loved her; that his only interest was what he could get out of her, because that would hurt too much. While it was not a lot, it was enough to get out of London and establish herself somewhere where no one would know her under a new name. As she was packing, she chose Mrs. Georgiana Wick. It was as close as she could get without using her lover's surname in full, and Georgiana was a common enough name. She threw whatever clothing would fit into a valise with no care about how her clothes would look; all she knew was that time was not her friend and she needed to leave. She donned a blonde wig and stole others, some of the 'working' ladies that rented rooms from her had left behind. The foresight of packing extra wigs would come in handy later.

She slipped out the back, walked two streets over, and found a hack that conveyed her to the post. From there she took a stage to East Essex. Her eventual destination was Cornwall, but she intended to create as much misdirection as possible in case anyone tried to discover her whereabouts. From East Essex she would go to Gloucestershire, and then to Dorset. From there she would travel to her intended destination, the town of Fowey on Cornwall's coast. At each place she would change her appearance before starting the next leg. She was not willing to take any chance of discovery before she was ready to return to claim vengeance for herself and her George. The town was selected for a number of reasons: it was relatively large, it was a port town, and best of all, her brother Clay Younge, and his smugglers frequented the area. Thankfully none of the prig's family were aware of Clay's existence; or so she believed.

Yes, Clay would help her achieve her aims. He would do it for monetary gain, but she cared not why so long as he helped her. The added advantage was if she needed to escape by sea, with her brother's aide she would be able to. She would use the size of the population to remain anonymous while she made her plans to get the revenge that her poor deceased George had not attained in this lifetime. She would work in service, become a nameless, faceless servant. No one ever looked twice at a servant; as abhorrent as going into service again was to now Mrs. Georgiana Wick, but she would do it to gain greater aims.

They took the one she loved; she would take one that they loved. She ignored the fact that her lover had caused all of his own problems and she had no idea who it was that had actually killed her George. It had started with the Bennet woman, so she was as good as any for the slightly deranged woman to blame. She would succeed where her beloved had failed. Unfortunately for her, she overestimated her abilities, which was a failure she shared with her lover. In death George Wickham was remembered without his myriad of faults by 'Mrs. Wick,' so the more she thought about him, the more determined she became to succeed in his honour.

Mrs. Younge suffered from the same delusion that her late lover had; she blamed everyone that she could think of for her woes, except the one that was actually responsible: herself. She hoped that the *Spaniard* would help her avenge her George. She would write to him once she was safely away.

~~~~~~~/~~~~~~~

'Please God, I beseech You. Please do not take William from me now. I have finally admitted that I love him, today, the day that he

saved my life. He is the only one for me,' Lady Elizabeth prayed as tears again pooled. *'I pray to you, Lord God, in your son Jesus's name, please return William to me.'* After she sent her prayer heavenward, Elizabeth Bennet sat stock still. She had just admitted to God above that she had fallen in love with Fitzwilliam Darcy. She knew then that like he had done anything he could to protect her, that she would do the same for him.

~~*The end of part 1*~~

COMING SOON

February 2021: Part 2 Of The Duke's Daughter:

The book picks up from the ending of Part 1 and answers the questions that the ending of the first part leaves us with. Does Mrs. Younge make her escape and meet up with her brother? We find out what happens to ODC and the question of whether Lady Elizabeth realised too late that she loves Darcy is answered. We meet some new villains as our heroes deal with the vagaries of life.

March 2021: Part 3 Of The Duke's Daughter:

The third part is the conclusion of the series. Are the villains successful? How does the family move on from the death of a loved one? We see the younger ladies come to the fore and are shown how their lives develop. Do not worry that the main characters are forgotten, they are not and figure prominently in the final part of the story. As in life, there are ups and downs, but in the end love wins.

Later In 2021: The Discarded Daughter

Fanny Bennet is convinced that her second daughter will be the son that is needed to break the entail on Longbourn. When she bears another daughter, she is furious and takes all of her frustration out on her new baby. She refuses to feed her and wants her sent out to one of the tenants. Thomas Bennet will not hear of that, he hires a wet nurse as he instantly falls in love with his dark haired hazel eyed daughter.

As she gets older, the resentment and hate that Fanny feels intensifies exponentially as her husband showers her second daughter with love. Even at an early age, the babe shows intelligence far beyond anything the blond three-year Jane has. She starts to walk at nine months and to talk before her first birthday. Convinced that Elizabeth is the devil's spawn, Fanny secretly pays an unscrupulous man to make her eighteen-month-old daughter disappear and to end her life. When it is discovered that his daughter is missing Thomas Bennet is shattered while his demented wife is secretly beside herself with joy.

This book will be a series that follows our heroine through the trials and tribulations of life as she grows up as the Discarded Daughter.

BOOKS BY THIS AUTHOR

A Change Of Fortunes

What if, unlike canon, the Bennets had sons? Could it be, if both father and mother prayed to God and begged for a son that their prayers would be answered? If the prayers were granted how would the parents be different and what kind of life would the family have? What will the consequences of their decisions be?

In many Pride and Prejudice variations the Bennet parents are portrayed as borderline neglectful with Mr. Bennet caring only about making fun of others, reading and drinking his port while shutting himself away in his study. Mrs. Bennet is often shown as flighty, unintelligent and a character to make sport of. The Bennet parent's marriage is often shown as a mistake where there is no love; could there be love there that has been stifled due to circumstances?

In this book, some of those traits are present, but we see what a different set of circumstances and decisions do to the parents and the family as a whole. Most of the characters from canon are here along with some new characters to help broaden the story. The normal villains are present with one added who is not normally a villain per se and I trust that you, my dear reader, will like the way that they are all 'rewarded' in my story.

We find a much stronger and more resolute Bingley. Jane Bennet is serene, but not without a steely resolve. I feel that both need to be portrayed with more strength of character for the purposes of this book. Sit back, relax and enjoy and my hope is that you will be suitably entertained.

The Hypocrite

The Hypocrite is a low angst, sweet and clean tale about the relationship dynamics between Fitzwilliam Darcy and Elizabeth Bennet after his disastrous and insult laden proposal at Hunsford. How does our heroine react to his proposal and the behaviour that she has witnessed from Darcy up to that point in the story?

The traditional villains from Pride and Prejudice that we all love to hate make an appearance in my story BUT they are not the focus. Other than Miss Bingley, whose character provides the small amount of angst in this tale, they play a very small role and are dealt with quickly. If dear reader you are looking for an angst filled tale rife with dastardly attempts to disrupt ODC then I am sorry to say, you will not find that in my book.

This story is about the consequences of the decisions made by the characters portrayed within. Along with Darcy and Elizabeth, we examine the trajectory of the supporting character's lives around them. How are they affected by decisions taken by ODC coupled with the decisions that they make themselves? How do the decisions taken by members of the Bingley/Hurst family affect them and their lives?

The Bennets are assumed to be extremely wealthy for the purposes of my tale, the source of that wealth is explained during the telling of this story. The wealth, like so much in this story is a consequence of decisions made Thomas Bennet and Edward Gardiner.

If you like a sweet and clean, low angst story, then dear reader, sit back, pour yourself a glass of your favourite drink and read, because this book is for you.

Made in United States
Orlando, FL
26 January 2025

57860919R00183